MEN UNDRESSED

MEN UNDRESSED

Women Writers and the Male Sexual Experience

Edited by

Stacy Bierlein
Gina Frangello
Cris Mazza
Kat Meads

Foreword by Steve Almond

OTHER VOICES BOOKS
Chicago

OTHER VOICES BOOKS
an imprint of Dzanc Books
3629 N. Hoyne
Chicago, IL 60618
www.ovbooks.com
OVBooks@gmail.com

Cover photo: Margo Berdeshevsky
Book design: Steven Seighman

First Edition October 2011
ISBN-9781936873081

Printed in the United States of America

With special thanks to our associate editors:

Wendy Duren
Keala Francis
Tracy Miller Geary
Kathryn Kosmeja
Laura Taylor Kung
Allison C. Parker
Barbara Shoup
Iliana Regan
Rob Roberge
Leah Tallon

CONTENTS

MEN UNDRESSED

FOREWORD:
THE REASONS WE UNDRESS

———·———

Steve Almond

I once dated a woman who released from her body a miraculous volume of fluid during sex. We got together at her place, a tiny studio tucked behind a single-family home. We'd eat (sometimes), drink wine, and proceed to the single mattress on her floor. We were in our early twenties, ashamed of everything. The things we did were done in the dark. We didn't kiss much or gaze into each other's eyes. It was as if our bodies were having an awkward but necessary conversation.

Years later I wrote about this experience in a short story. I described the fluid emerging from her "as colorless and odorless as rain." That sounded poetic, and I wanted quite badly to be seen as the sort of writer who could write poetically about female ejaculation, because I figured this would get me laid. But I didn't get laid, and the fluid in question *did* have an odor. It smelled like the hammers of an old piano, musty and acrid.

The human body is a complete mystery to me.

And what did she look like in those moments of release? Her head was tipped up and away and her eyes were closed, and though at the time I took this as evidence of a debilitating ecstasy, it seems to me now that the greatest share of her feeling was shame.

I have no idea, really. I'm just The Guy. And The Guy is always trapped within his Guyness and its small questions of pleasure and power.

All you sensitivos out there can relax. I am *not* suggesting that Guys are incapable of more subtle lines of inquiry, only that we don't look to sex as an invitation to self-investigation. We view it (more often) as an expressway to gratification and acclaim and dominion. By way of evidence, I would ask the court's permission to introduce Exhibit A: The Totality of Human History.

As for our reigning paragons of femininity, they appear to have been devised in the adolescent male mind: depilated self-colonizers flashing their niblets at the paparazzi, housewives with faces cinched into ruin and egos aflame, models caressing phallic products, lipsticked demagogues who murder logic and call it Feminism. These are the women our daughters stare at day and night, bound in their cords of vanity. Forget the Enlightenment, we might as well be living in the Book of Isaiah.

Lost in this cesspool of misogyny are actual, you know, women. What does it feel like for a woman to undress in front of her lover, or touch herself, or suck a cock she doesn't want to suck, or to withhold from herself the orgasm she has been told all her life to want? These experiences remain mysteries of the age, largely untraceable in our literature, like the blemishes and hairs scrubbed from fashion magazines.

The Puritans prophesied a country overrun by anarchic sexual urges. For them, the only suitable cure to the crisis of desire was moral prohibition. The body as a source of disgust, its natural urges a road unto Gomorrah. The Puritanical code, with its panting devotion to carnal ignorance, has been invoked over the years as a banner of virtue—most often by male politicians cheating on their wives. But the sexual revolution of the 1960s wasn't a campaign to corrupt the spirit. It was an effort to liberate the body from shame and anxiety.

Over the past three decades, late-model capitalism has subverted that revolution. Sex has evolved into a marketing tool, a vital export, a kind of cultural climate. What was once a private communion of souls has become a public transaction with commercial implications. Where the Puritans failed, the pornographers have succeeded.

I suspect this is why so many people write so badly about sex. They have lost their sense of physical congress as a complex emotional, psychological, and moral event. And thus they run wild with the genital euphemisms. Their women heave and moan; their men engorge and erupt. It's all surface and no interior. They forget that sex is only interesting to the extent that it reveals character.

I was well into my thirties before I wrote my first sexually explicit story. I got tired of the whole Serious Young Writers shtick, the devising of clever plots and disguises. So I just told the truth about what mattered to me at that moment, which was fucking (then not fucking) this one woman. I showed the story to a friend of mine.

"Dude," he said. "I don't want to think about you doing this shit."

I put the story in a drawer for two years.

Reviews of my eventual first book ran along the same lines. I thought I was writing about the suffering of desire. But it turned out I was writing smut. One critic complained that she found the title story particularly obnoxious and implausible, because it featured a woman ejaculating.

A number of writers, nearly all of them male, have made their nut pushing back against the sexual taboos of their given era. Sade. Lawrence. Miller. Roth. To say they wrote about sex is accurate but unspecific. They wrote about the sexual conquest of women. They wrote from the male prerogative that spawns most of our literature. Their women were a collection of holes, sometimes granted shape and texture and scent, bits of saucy dialogue, ardent mutterings, degrading nicknames, but rarely fully imagined as human beings.

A lot of my stories, especially the early ones, fall into this category. But at a certain point, I lost interest in the male point of view. My dudes were too earnest, too eager to advertise their empathy, too *me*. So I started listening to my female friends. As a rule, they were foul-mouthed and fed up with their options. The questions they asked—before, after, and during sex—were far more interesting than the ones I asked. *Do I love this guy? Does this guy love me? Will I be able to relax enough to get there? If I let him come on my face, will he lose respect for me? Is it possible to lust after someone I find despicable? What does love mean anyway? Why am I still awake?*

I've been happiest, or proudest anyway, when I try to write about sex from a female perspective. It forces me to get outside of my Guyness, to yearn for an intimacy not bound to glandular release, to confront the impatient needs and insecurities of male vanity. It forces me to inhabit a body whose mechanisms of pleasure feel ornate and foreign and thrilling. More than once, in the midst of writing a scene, I've been tempted to turn down the lights, unplug the phone, and crank that vibrator to eleven.

I'm more interested in the feminine experience of sex, because it's one I'll never have. I have to imagine my way in. But it's also true that I'd simply much rather hear women talk about sex than men. They're more ruthless and tender. They don't get squeamish; they get specific.

I once wrote an entire story about a girl describing her first orgasm to another girl. They're sitting in a pizza parlor, and the guy making their pie is eavesdropping on them. He's not a letch.

He's just lonely, like the rest of us. At the end of the story, he brings them their pizza:

> And standing there, in the clattering yellow light, both of them aware of me, just at the edge of a nervousness that would force them to notice me, I was seized by a thick dread. The blonde's story was over. The one connection that existed between us had been cut, and I was destined, now, to fall away from them, into the cold grasp of my own life. Who was I but another boy with certain ideas about them?

It was a story about my desire to understand women, to be closer to them.

The stories in this collection reflect the same desire. They are written by women struggling to understand men, what sex feels like for them, how it functions in their lives.

We are sorely in need of that understanding.

As a demographic, Guys are still very much in charge of the planet, still killing things left and right and refusing to apologize. But as a group of potential blind dates, we're a mess. We've been told to ignore our fears and misgivings (or at least to disavow them), and yet we face a life of bewildering psychic dislocation. We've been instructed to rid ourselves of the violent impulses that once safeguarded us, to attune ourselves to the gender we once ruled without question, to master a world whose complexity we can barely conceive. Gone are the days of hunting and gathering, replaced by passive tabulation, cubicles, traffic, tranquilizing screens. On weekends, we stalk the grocery aisles for shrink-wrapped prey.

You want to see true modern humiliation? Head out to your nearest garage and watch us, me and the other poor slobs, consulting our mechanics, nodding our heads like we understand what the timing belt is and why it needs to be replaced for $700, sick with the hunch that we are being ripped off by men with oily hands.

Men feel more powerless and emasculated than ever before. This explains all the pornography and sports and violence. It's a classic shame spiral. Most of what we should know about ourselves we can't bear to acknowledge, including how women perceive us.

A number of critics will write about this collection in the spirit of "turnabout is fair play." That's what critics do: they look for an angle. And it's certainly true that men have been writing from female points of view for years. Anna Karenina, Emma Bovary, Lady Chatterley. It's a long list.

But I don't really care who the writer is. If the prose is any good, I've thrown in my lot with the characters. And the pressing issue isn't their gender (or race or class) but their internal lives. When I spoke earlier about the excitement of writing from outside my gender, I was speaking as a writer. As a reader, my basic attitude is: parts is parts.

We are all carried into sex by the same torrent of emotions: lust, hope, pride, fear, embarrassment, guilt. Men tend to lead with lust. Women use their hope as a hedge against guilt. But our sexuality is further complicated by our own peculiar histories, our mommies and daddies, our siblings, our early experiments in love and loss. These are what shape our fears and desires. They have nothing, or almost nothing, to do with our physiology.

So while it is true that the authors of these stories are women, and the protagonists are men, and that some of these men will be engaged in adult situations, the stories in question are larger than all that. Hope is slipping away from a troubled soul, mercy is granted to another. The Puritans of the literary world will say, *Aha! Look there! Dirty parts*. But we know the truth.

I get asked a lot why I write about sex so much. My basic answer is: because I care about it. I fantasize about it and fret about it and occasionally I experience it, alone or with my wife. This doesn't make me a freak. It makes me a human being. The real question is why everybody else writes about sex so little.

Back when I was teaching college students, I received hundreds of stories about death and violence and existential malaise. These were taken to be the topics of Great Literature. But they were so boring, most of them. I never felt implicated, or exposed. How my heart thrilled when one of my students showed the courage to write candidly about the one thing that most preoccupied all of us. How happy we all were to be talking (finally) about something we cared about.

I still think about that old lover from time to time. I offered my version of her to the world, with its predictable emphasis on her physiological quirk. But she was a lot more interesting than that. Her family lived in Mexico. They had a ranch down near Chihuahua City, I think, where she went some weekends. She swam like a dream and had a twin sister. She was an exile from a family that would not allow her to be who she needed to be. We had that in common at least.

I have an odd memory of her that I should mention. This was the time she called to ask me to give her a lift. I could see her across the parking lot, totally decked out. Then I saw her embracing a woman who appeared to be her exact replica in a white satin gown. I was picking her up from her twin sister's wedding, an event she had not told me about.

I honestly don't know if this ever happened, or if it's something I dreamed up that somehow migrated into my memory. But I do remember that her sister got married while we were involved. We didn't talk about the wedding, or whether she was happy for her sister. Maybe she wanted to invite me. Maybe she wanted to flaunt her resistance to the conventional path her sister had taken. Or maybe seeing her sister walk down the aisle had made her eager for some answering intimacy. I was only interested in reaching that exalted moment when her body tensed and loosened at once and she became real to me. I thought that was where the action was. It takes a long time to figure out that sex is never the point. It's what brings us to the act that matters, the reasons we undress and reach through the dark and hope.

We stopped seeing each other not long after her sister's wedding. It eventually dawned on me why we had come together in the first place, that we were lonely but self-hating, hungry for an entanglement with no hope of survival. I spent another twenty years in roughly the same state. I might have saved me a lot of heartache if that young woman had offered the world some more honest accounting of me, though of course I wouldn't have recognized it.

You'll recognize the Guys in these pages. Chances are you've been a few of them. Or been with a few of them. It made me sad to read of their escapades, but sad in a happy way, like I was finally getting a clear view of myself from a source that wasn't exactly objective, but brutally precise.

I kept returning to this one passage in particular, at the end of the story "In the First Place," by Vanessa Carlisle. It's about a guy thinking back on an unrequited affair with a younger woman:

> She did not allow me any romantic gestures outside of paying for dinner, but she kissed me on the beach in Venice once, because the beauty of the sunset took over. ... And although she seemed to always be disappointed, always protected, always ironic, at that time in my life I would call and call and call because I was forty-four years old and she was twenty-six, and it was unbelievable that I got to touch her at all.

I'm sure this struck me initially because I'm forty-four also, and because I wooed my wife on the beaches of Southern California. But the more I turned it over, the more it seemed a story about something larger than individual desire. It seems now, to me, to be a story about the desperate gratitude that lives beneath all our Guy posturing; the secret debt we carry toward all the women in our lives, for their ridiculous patience, their affection, for knowing us better than we know ourselves and forgiving us anyway.

A BLOW FOR THE PICARO?

———— • ————

Cris Mazza

In my high school American literature class, every author we read was a male. Exactly two of the male-written works featured female main characters: *The Scarlet Letter* and *The Crucible* (two adulteresses). When I was sixteen, I didn't question the absence of a female "authority" on female experience; I reflexively accepted that only male experience was important enough to make literature, and I wrote my earliest fictions with male characters from male points of view—possibly not the best reason to venture into creating the imagined experience of an "other."

Similarly naive in my own sexuality, my first literary ventures into sexual experience included a concealed copy of *The Playboy Advisor* (fake letters written by men) and then *Lady Chatterley's Lover*. Here was the female orgasm described on paper, where I could read it over and over and, hopefully, begin to understand it.

It did not occur to me to distrust Lady Chatterley's sexual expressions until I read *Fear of Flying*, the book that really, and finally, influenced what kind of *writer* I would become. It was Erica Jong who pointed out (to me) that the "definitive" literary exposé of the female orgasm had been written by a man.

> Until women started writing books there was only one side of the story. Throughout all of history, books were only written with sperm, not menstrual blood. Until I was twenty-one, I measured my orgasms against Lady Chatterley's and

wondered what was wrong with me. Did it ever occur to me
that Lady Chatterley was really a man?[1]

The history of sexuality in literature—even narrowed to Western
or American literature—is too vast and many-tentacled for this
introduction to synthesize, influenced (and/or repressed) by
too many factors, from Marxism and socialism to old New York
society. *The Columbia Literary History of the United States* offers
Kate Chopin and, possibly astoundingly to some, Edith Wharton
as trailblazers in the new (pre-Freud) tradition of women writers
exploring sexual consciousness. Because of the male-dominated
reading lists I continually encountered, I didn't discover until
later the simmering sexual desire in Edith Wharton's *Ethan Frome*
(told from a male perspective) and then her more searing *Summer*
(which Wharton dubbed "the hot Ethan"). But I can't, after
the fact, look upon these as my foundation, my tradition, my
predecessors. Not after I'd already had my own "awakening" from
Lady Chatterley's Lover and *Lolita*, subsequently been jerked *fully*
awake by *Fear of Flying*, followed by the disparate combination
of Anaïs Nin and *Looking for Mr. Goodbar*. No one can preplan
the "right" literary influence from the "proper" inspiration(s),
ensuring growth as a writer along a constructive, affirming path.
That would be boring. Thankfully, I stumbled onto this oddly
assorted group that liberated for me the still somewhat cloaked
world of female sexuality to literary exploration.

But still, Wharton's themes of burgeoning (and repressed)
sexuality, and Chopin's earlier, scandalous depiction of a woman
transformed sexually (even if it leads to her suicide), did not include
frankly dramatized scenes of sexual experiences. It's that thinner
slice of literary history—not just themes of sexual development
and consciousness, but the *use* of forthright descriptions of sex
in literary works—that, at this anthology's early idea-phase, I
intended to be the core literary territory of this project.

---

1. Erica Jong, *Fear of Flying* (New York: Holt, Reinhart and Winston, 1973).

Naturally, then, a concise summary of the history and development of that particular feature of fiction would be expected here, but I didn't know where to begin looking for it. By Googling variations of "sex in literature," I found close to nothing. "Sex" usually refers to gender issues and is almost always paired with class, Marxism, or religion. "Sexuality" works better, but likewise is often coupled with religion, and the listed results reference literature's use of the unspoken (or taboo) *idea* of sex, not frankly written sex scenes. What I should have been searching was "obscenity in literature," but I failed (at first) to do so—failed to even have the notion to do so—because I don't consider these types of scenes *obscene*. But that's what they were in the United States before 1959. In fact *Lady Chatterley's Lover*, published in Italy in 1929, had been banned in the U.S. until the 1957 Supreme Court case *Roth v. United States,* whose decision resulted in works with literary merit being exempt from obscenity rulings. "Citing *Roth,* the U.S. Court of Appeals in 1960 freed *Lady Chatterley's Lover*, and it became Grove [Press]'s first best seller. ... Over the course of the decade [Grove] would publish many of the key texts—including Henry Miller's *Tropic of Cancer* and William Burroughs's *Naked Lunch*—that would precipitate what [Grove's] lawyer Charles Rembar called the 'end of obscenity' for the printed word."[2]

Which is why I didn't consider using "obscenity" in my search for foundation. Finally "frank sex scenes" did produce lists of documents with familiar names in the summaries: Lawrence, Miller, Burroughs, Roth, Jong, and hoards of writers being compared to them. But if Miller, Burroughs, and a few years later Philip Roth opened the door for Erica Jong to follow them through, she discovered, once inside, that the party was for *them*, and she was like an uninvited cake-jumper.

---

2. Loren Glass, "Redeeming Value: Obscenity and Anglo-American Modernism," *Critical Inquiry 32*, no. 4. Rembar quoted in Edward de Grazia, *Girls Lean Back Everywhere: The Law of Obscenity and the Assault on Genius* (New York, 1992), p. 369.

And if self-invention was a largely male prerogative, talking dirty in print was even more so. Four years before *Fear of Flying* appeared, Philip Roth published *Portnoy's Complaint*, a book that foregrounded a man's candidly described sexual obsessions while aspiring to be more than mere pornography. Can a writer do this? Pack a book with sex and four-letter words and still get taken seriously as literature? Roth proved it could be done. If you were male. As Erica Jong found out when she wrote a novel four years later that tried to do just that—but from a woman's point of view—the same rules don't apply. Roth evoked titillation where Jong provoked outrage. (Critics Alfred Kazin and Paul Theroux, for example, both called the book hopelessly 'vulgar.') While Roth was celebrated for breaking the rules, Jong was castigated.[3]

The atmosphere for Jong and women writers who followed her improved from there; it had to. If Jong had opened a door, Kathy Acker, Mary Gaitskill, and others followed, and were not met with the surly welcome given Jong. As well, Jong's book did not suffer obscurity but enjoyed all the trappings of a successful blockbuster. But, at first, not for the most salient reasons: not for the influence it would have on American fiction (and the future of at least one nascent novelist). Despite rocketing to provocative prominence and her decades of durable fame, Jong and (her contemporary) Roth don't share the same kind of literary stature. Some would argue there are other factors involved in this, as there always are, but Roth's legacy hasn't been summed up and defined by a witticism from *Portnoy's Complaint*—he hasn't been referred to as "the masturbation novelist," while Jong seems forever consigned to literary history as "the creator of the *zipless fuck*."

Before writing *Fear of Flying* Jong began writing an earlier

3. Shelley Fisher Fishkin, "Erica Jong," *American Writers; A Collection of Literary Biographies*, Supplement V, Charles Scribner's Sons, 2000.

novel manuscript from a male perspective because she "didn't think anyone would be interested in a woman's point of view."[4] Familiar? That a New York City poet educated with the beats in the 1960s, and a Southern California fiction writer coming of age in the 1970s would carry this same involuntary assumption about what was interesting or important in literature should be of no surprise, since it seems Jong's influences, as well, were male. "Jong had read John Updike's *Couples*, Henry Miller's *Tropic of Cancer* and Philip Roth's *Portnoy's Complaint*, and wondered why women weren't writing about their emotional and sexual lives with the same candour."[5]

> I think that what I sought to do in [*Fear of Flying*] was to slice open a woman's head and show everything that was happening inside. To make a woman's mind and fantasies as naked as certain writers like John Updike and Phillip Roth had made a man's mind. And that had not been done. Yes, there were many wonderful books about women that were written. Many of them inspired me. But what Roth and Updike had done for the male psyche had really not been done for the female.[6]

Interestingly, Jong *could* have had a female inspiration, and it would have been the same Edith Wharton whose exploration of (mostly repressed) female sexuality was itself "repressed," both within literary techniques of dramatic urgency, language and narrative tension, and in plots where sexuality was stifled by surface trappings of furnishings, fashion, and the social order. But Wharton had produced an unpublished fragment of a story that was the true predecessor of the "awakening" in women's fiction. In 1974, a year after *Fear of Flying* was released, a scholar named Cynthia Griffin Wolff discovered the fragment while researching for her book, *A Feast of Words: The Triumph of Edith Wharton*.

---

4. Sharon Krum, "Flying High," *The Guardian*, 17 July 2003.

5. Sharon Krum, "Flying High," *The Guardian*, 17 July 2003.

6. Bill Moyers, "Bill Moyers Interviews Erica Jong," *Now*, http://www.pbs.org/now/transcript/transcript_jong.html, 27 June 2003

But she hardly heard him, for the old swooning sweetness was creeping over her. As his hand stole higher she felt the secret bud of her body swelling, yearning, quivering hotly to burst into bloom. Ah, here was his subtle forefinger pressing it, forcing its tight petals softly apart, and laying on their sensitive edges a circular touch so soft and yet so fiery that already lightnings of heat shot from that palpitating centre all over her surrendered body, to the tips of her fingers, and the ends of her loosened hair.[7]

We can only speculate, if this fragment had become a published story in its time, would the reaction to frank sexuality in women's work have moderated so much by 1973 that *Fear of Flying* would have been just another novel, now forgotten? And by 1996 would frank sexuality in literature by women not have offended the senses of the Congressional Subcommittee on Oversight and Investigations which, under the leadership of Representative Peter Hoekstra (R., Michigan), condemned independent publisher FC2 for the last anthologies I helped to edit, *Chick-Lit; Postfeminist Fiction* and *Chick-Lit 2 (No Chick Vics)*[8]? And then in the twenty-first century, would the issue of frank sexuality in women's literature create no blip at all on the critical radar, as it apparently did (again) for Jong's 2003 book, *Sappho's Leap*?

Jong says feminists can only pack up and go home when women can write erotica and our culture will consider it literary, not dirty. And that hasn't happened yet. "I was amazed when *Sappho's Leap* came out and I am still getting bullshit about writing about sex."[9]

---

7. Edith Wharton, "The Beatrice Palmato Fragment," first published in Cynthia Griffin Wolff, *A Feast of Words: The Triumph of Edith Wharton* (Oxford: Oxford University Press, 1977) and R. W .B. Lewis, *Edith Wharton: A Biography* (New York: Harper & Row, 1975).

8. Cris Mazza and Jeffrey DeShell, eds., *Chick-Lit: Postfeminist Fiction* (Normal, Ill.: FC2, 1995). Cris Mazza, Jeffrey DeShell and Elisabeth Sheffield, eds., *Chick-Lit 2 (No Chick Vics)* (Normal, Ill.: FC2, 1996). [Not to be confused with recent banal romances marketed under the same tag.]

9. Sharon Krum, "Flying High," *The Guardian*, 17 July 2003.

Jong said "it hasn't happened yet" in 2003, and yet Acker, Gaitskill, A. M. Homes, and a host of others had been publishing since long before that. Perhaps this means that Jong was never allowed to shed her status as "dirty," even though she blazed the trail for other women to claim this territory as well as literary repute, as shown in this (not quite unqualified) praise of Gaitskill's *Bad Behavior*.

> All of the stories have something to do with what used to be called sexual perversion, mostly sadomasochistic fun and games. These things, along with the usual ingestion of chemical substances and the run-of-the-mill, end-of-century despair, are matter-of-fact, mundane, unmemorable, neither shocking nor titillating. Remember the late stories of John O'Hara? How well he used the shock of sexual perversity as the central revelation? Here we go a step further. It is never revelation, just another quality in the cumulative discovery of character.[10]

Back to the 1970s, long before I would publish my first book: Lisa Alther was writing a book she "thought would never be published—so I could say whatever I wanted."[11] Alther unwittingly caught the wave created by Jong's 1973 *Fear of Flying*, when *Kinflicks* came out in 1975.

> *Kinflicks*, in fact, is soaring in the slip stream of *Fear of Flying*, Erica Jong's bestselling hymn to the body electric. The novel proves again—if any doubters still remain— that women can write about physical functions just as frankly and, when the genes move them, as raunchily as men. It strikes a blow for the picara by putting a heroine through the same paces that once animated a Tom Jones or a Holden Caulfield. And it suggests that life seen from what was once called the distaff side suspiciously resembles

---

10. George Garrett, "Fun and Games for Sadomasochists," *The New York Times Book Review,* 21 August 1988.

11. Katherine Hikel, "Alther Writes It Hot and Steamy," *Vermont Woman*, February 2005.

the genitalia-centered existence that male novelists have so long monopolized.[12]

Though the severe sexist hostility had worn down even as soon as three years after *Fear of Flying*, and critical responses have not been as starkly misogynistic since, there still might have been a tacit discrepancy in the literary establishment: that male writers had written about women's private and sexual lives, even from the female point of view, with impunity, but when women writers imagine the male sexual experience, would they be scrutinized for "authenticity" and "fairness"?

In subsequent novels Alther included frank sexuality from a male point of view, and it's interesting to compare that basic shift in perspective with another male writer who wrote women's sexuality from a female point of view, John O'Hara:

Alther wrote in the early 1980s from a 1950s teenage male POV, rendering what the male character thinks about women's sexual needs: "She couldn't seem to get enough. She acted like a man that way, and he didn't like it. She mounted him and moved up and down on him. ... [He] was flooded with contempt." And, "He smiled, thinking about making love that morning ... he'd woke up with a big hard-on, had just rolled over and put it to her. ... At night and on weekends you had to go into all that do-you-really-really-love-me junk that sometimes made jerking off seem preferable." And, "The fun was getting them to go along even though they didn't really want to."[13]

John O'Hara wrote in the early 1960s from a 1940s middle-aged female POV, revealing how the female character views her sex life: "All the things that excited him she did eagerly, to bring him to such excitement that he would not notice the lack of tenderness." And, "they made love precisely, bringing each other

---

12. Paul Gray, "Blue Genes," *Time Magazine*, 22 May 1976.
13. Lisa Alther, *Original Sins* (New York: Knopf, 1981).

to their recognizable signs of advanced preliminaries, to the ultimate closeness, and to simultaneous climax."[14]

I wonder which is more likely: that someone reading Alther's manuscript would deem her fabricated male attitude to be feminist ball-busting, or that someone reading O'Hara's manuscript might speculate how the author made the hilarious assumption that compulsory traditional marital intercourse always resulted in simultaneous orgasm or that an uninterested wife would still "eagerly" excite her husband? Likely, if any women readers or critics scoffed at O'Hara's macho presumption, they did it behind their hands; I doubt it would have come to him in either a review or an editor's rejection letter. My research has not been able to answer my hypothesis. And it seems equally difficult to discover the *pre*-publication editorial response to women writing sex in the male psyche in the 1970s or even 1980s.

By 1990, the tone of the literary landscape had shifted enough for *Publisher's Weekly* to say of A. M. Homes, with the publication of her first novel, *Jack*, that she "perfectly captures the feelings, actions and even the speech cadences of a typical adolescent American male." The brutal criticisms and censures Homes received in subsequent years, mostly for her novel *The End of Alice*, narrated by a male child rapist, were more concerned with the violent pedophilia, and not that the echo of Humbert Humbert had been written by a woman. And in 2006, the tables completed their turning when one woman critic found Homes's latest journey in a male perspective unconvincing.

> A. M. Homes's dreadful new novel, *This Book Will Save Your Life*, reads like a cartoon illustration for a seminar on men and middle age ...[15]

14. John O'Hara, *Elizabeth Appleton* (New York: Random House, 1963).
15. Michiko Kakutani, *The New York Times Book Review*, 14 April 2006.

For me it is, of course, my own experience of which I can speak with most authority:

Besides various short stories, my first lengthy foray into the sexual life of a male point of view character came in a novel, *Girl Beside Him* (2001, FC2). The man I chose to live vicariously through was cloaked with masculine trappings I'd never experienced in my own acquaintances: a sharp-shooting champion, helicopter pilot, wildlife biologist. He was also sexually repressed, badly scarred by adolescent experiences witnessing his sister kill herself after years of sexual abuse at the hands of her *mother*, and was a 40+-year-old virgin before a movie made this condition into a comedy sketch. Above all, or as a consequence, he was neurotically apprehensive that he was a sex-killer-waiting-to-happen, and thus viewed any sexual arousal as a danger sign. The book was received much as I intended it: a dark psychological journey into mental torment and violent outlets. My research included books on sexual serial killers, on general male sexuality. Reviewers and critics did not comment on the close third-person perspective of a male character written by a female author. But before the manuscript was placed, editors *did* respond to this aspect of the book—male editors. Most memorable was the comment: "Men don't think about their erections like this," (i.e. as a danger sign). This was before the wave of erectile-dysfunction drug advertising on television and in the backs of sports and hunting magazines (which might have prompted me to respond: men think about their erections with every metaphor possible!). At the time, however, my case was merely practical: *maybe most men don't—and obviously you don't—but is it inconceivable that one troubled man could think this way? That's why there's a book about him, instead of about all the normal men who don't think this way.* I'd long known that *I* didn't think about my body in exactly the way Isadora Wing (*Fear of Flying*), Theresa Dunn (*Looking for Mr. Goodbar*), or Anna Wulf (*The Golden Notebook*) did. And yet I was still able to feel my gender—human—connectedness with them. Books are written about *particular* characters, not the composite of "normality" in case studies, so the determining factor shouldn't be that "most people don't think this way" but that it's plausible that one *could*, and isn't it interesting when one *does*? And what can we learn about ourselves when we imagine life this way?

That question might have been the true inception (conception?) of this project. Before I ever saw a submission or searched my bookshelves for published stories in this vein, the reasons I wanted to gather this type of story had as much to do with another way of learning about women's views of sexuality as they did exploring this reaction to my gall at trying on a man's sex life. Wouldn't it be true that the ways women *imagine* how a man views, thinks about, remembers or approaches sex, say something about the view we might have of ourselves?

But, as well, prior to putting my ideas and editorial tastes together with the three other smart, talented women writers who have helped me edit this book, this project was always wedded to the more idealized concept that literature is more than the illustration, expression, and crying out of one's own identity and experience; the bigger picture is the willingness to envisage, audition, investigate, and comprehend someone else's.

The name of our publisher is significant. Sometime in the 1990s the word "voice" began to be applied liberally to literature, as in New Voices, Overlooked Voices, and Giving Voice to the Underrepresented. Thus literature began to be viewed as a venue by which an author spoke for herself, her culture, her background, her family, her class, her race, her gender. The notion of adopting someone else's voice, telling someone else's story, imagining someone *else's* life became almost viewed as taboo. It was exploitive; it was appropriating; it was colonizing.

This, paired with the emergence of memoirs, has seemed to move fiction away from being an "I want to understand others" medium to a more self-invested "I want you to understand *me*." While it's been beneficial for women's and unrepresented groups' experiences to bloom in literature, I'd like to assert that literature's power goes beyond a forum where unrepresented groups can be heard. Literature should allow us to imagine people who are unlike ourselves—to slip into their lives, their minds, their perspectives, not for the sake of parodying alleged deficiencies, but to discover both our innate similarities and our enigmatic differences, and thereby appreciate them more.

CLAIMING THE PENIS:
A CELEBRATION OF NARRATIVE
CROSS-DRESSING

From the pre-Modernist era forward, there has been a collective-if-sporadic movement among women writers and artists to "take back" their own bodies and sexualities from the male domain through creative work. Consider Georgia O'Keefe's vaginal paintings. *Écriture Féminine*. Innovative novels by Jean Rhys and Kathy Acker. Eve Ensler's *The Vagina Monologues*. Cindy Sherman's "Sex Pictures." By exploring and depicting female sexuality in art and literature, more and more women have found their voices and presented their own truths.

This represents progress, but it is only half the battle. The most stunning artistic works mix things up, treat the familiar in unfamiliar ways, and defy expectations. Like our male counterparts, women artists and writers must imagine their way in and boldly distinguish the other.

As Cris Mazza points out in her introductory essay, the publication of works by female writers exploring male sexuality—and from the male viewpoint—is a relatively recent literary development. But it is happening. From A. M. Homes's groundbreaking short story, "A Real Doll," to Mary Gaitskill's subversive collection, *Bad Behavior*; from Francine Prose's critically acclaimed *Blue Angel* to the writers whose works are collected in *Men Undressed;* women have moved beyond merely trying to define their own sexual experiences. The writers we most admire have broken out of the sexual box and made rapturous, questioning, or mutinous leaps into narrative cross-dressing. Their fictions insightfully, confrontationally, and yes, *feelingly*, present the male sexual experience.

On these pages, men succumb to temptation, but also create it. In Lydia Yuknavitch's "In the Garden of Earthly Delights," Bosch believes his pain "multiplies and deforms into ecstasy like hours on a clock, endlessly repeating, until there is no telling night from day, pleasure from torture, a single room from the cavities of the body." Diane Williams's narrator in "To Die" has the most basic needs. He wants sex and more sex, and believes his money and beauty guarantee it. In Jennifer Egan's "The Gold Cure," Benny is faced with losing his sex drive. While he finds the world a more peaceful place without "the half hard-on that had been his constant companion since the age of thirteen," he's not convinced he can live in that world. He considers his assistant, Sasha, realizing his glances at her breasts become "the litmus test he will use to gauge his improvement."

Men crave sex in the wake of disaster. In Elizabeth Benedict's *The Practice of Deceit*, an earthquake becomes a sexual prelude: "She cradled me and suckled me and held me in the most exquisite embrace of my life." In the days after 9/11, a house under suspicion in Searle's "And a Dead American" does not have bombs in the basement after all, but a fantasy-inspiring girl named One. Joe imagines her "soft girl lips do a blow job," then finds himself jerking off again, harder than ever before. Christine Lee Zilka's stunning "Erasure" investigates war's contamination of sex. "He wanted to fuck the panic out of his head ... to erase his memories and replace them with a pleasure that Yong could only describe as heat and light and flight and rushing warm water."

Sex itself becomes dangerous—or, in contrast, a continuous mystery of interlocking parts. In Suzanne Hudson's *In the Dark of the Moon*, seventeen-year-old Royce knows he has entered the danger zone with his attraction to twelve-year-old Elizabeth Lacey. His mind draws an image of a "liquored-up Elizabeth with her braids down, lying on top of him, loose hair hanging down across her face and into his." In Kristin Thiel's "Patient," Pete and Coryl should have a normal, fulfilling sex life. Coryl's vagina isn't cooperating, and a series of doctors and therapists offer little help. Yet, with the aid of a vibrator, Pete watches her "laughing this maniacal, ecstatic laugh."

Men unite with past lovers; an unending dance of questions without answers. In Sherri Joseph's "The Winter Beach," Kent reunites with Paul, hoping the past will fail to interfere. But Paul's kiss is "an assault, a bashing of lips on teeth." In Rachel Resnick's gothic "Evening at the Cryo-Crystal Circus Hotel," Chip tries to be faithful to Zoe, but finds it difficult to resist Go-Go. "I almost just shoved a hand up her skirt right there at the table, lost for a second in memories of the red rosebud I knew was stitched deep in her inner thigh."

Of course, some reunions are condemned to emptiness. In Susan Minot's *Rapture*, we meet filmmakers Benjamin and Kay, somehow in bed together in the middle of the afternoon. "He especially liked seeing her down there after this long time [. . .] He'd learned that, for them, there was no right thing to say." Allison Amend's Garvey attends the darkest of homecomings in "And Then There Was Claire." While Claire's funeral holds some disorienting surprises, Garvey's balance is skewed first by the realization that she's "the first of us to die. The first of my lovers I'll outlive."

Aging lovers in Jonis Agee's "Private Lives" seem to have lost something they cannot re-create. "When Frederick held Albert's cock in his hand, it felt foreign now, not an instrument of love, just an instrument." Nava Renek's "Mating in Captivity" is a portrait of a marriage that should have ended long ago—and may have, if not for the comforting distraction of Internet porn. "Fuck foreplay when you can just hit 'Favorites' and scroll to your choice of the day," Gary muses.

In stories by A. M. Homes and Tawni O'Dell, sex becomes powerful enough to kill shame—if only for a moment. In "The

Whiz Kids" by A. M. Homes, a gay teenager seems to understand that his classmate-lover is a sociopath, but performs analingus on him anyway. In O'Dell's *Back Roads*, Harley knows that Callie is just another thing that is wrong with him, yet for an instant she has the power to make the world right. "She took me in her mouth, and at that instant I believed in God again."

Sex is lawless, a possible catalyst for anarchy. Wanda Coleman's "In Rita's Lair," introduces a once "spirited beauty" now "a hellion" whose men know she becomes violent at the slightest dissatisfaction. But crazed and powerful Rita is not the only character playing havoc with men's fates. Ex-con Junior in Vicki Hendricks's "Boozanne, Lemme Be," knows that the antics of his thief girlfriend may send him back to jail, but he can't remember what he used to do without her. Richard, the owner of a sex-trafficking business in Aimee Parkison's "Cradled," might be one of the most repulsive men who ever entered an orgy room, but not to his assistant Leonard. "Pretending to watch naked women dance, I see only Richard. Richard's enormous cock is so long and so hard that it chooses women for him."

Sex works against reason. In Susan Solomon's "Chicks with Two First Names," Vince worries that most men are such fuck-ups, "ruining it for the rest of us guys who are actually nice." Of course, Vicky Diane will never believe that nice guys have monster stashes of porn. In the darkly comic "Family Bed," Cris Mazza's Dale strives to put the "party" in birthing party. When it becomes clear no one is going to serve booze, let alone a bowl of nuts, he resorts to sex with "the fatty." Dale starts "pulling her shirt over her head and at the same time [trying] to get her legs farther apart by spreading his own knees," admitting, "It wasn't easy."

In many stories sex overwhelms, becomes a humbling or equalizing force. Errol wants a break from his girlfriend, Audrey, in Alicia Erian's "Camp Whitehorse." Errol passes Audrey off to Marcus, a timid-with-girls (or so he thinks) Marine just back from Iraq. Marcus wants to hit Audrey, and then he does. "On the ass. [. . .] He thought she would kick him out, but she didn't. She uncurled herself and began to suck his dick. Finally, he got a little hard." Likewise, sex satisfies any number of cravings. An anorexic turns out to be more than one sex addict bargains for in Su Avasthi's "Greedy, Greedy." He feels her "frenzied mouth move over to his arm, licking, then gnawing, seeking to satiate herself." She leans forward, bites down hard on his bicep. "What the hell," he cries. In Aimee Bender's "Motherfucker," a starlet is no match for the fucker of mothers. "'You throw your emotions on other people in the room,' he explained, 'and see what they do then.'"

The observations of lovers are unrelenting. In Gina Frangello's "Blood," Michael remembers that Kendra's lipstick "had been the exact same color as her blood. Really it was so uncanny that at first he thought she must have planned it that way, had somehow managed to take in a sample when buying her makeup and matched the shades directly."

Sex becomes a most divine mode of communication. The narrator in Rosebud Ben-Oni's "Nude Studies of an Affair" says, "I thought I could fuck it into you, the details of my life." In Vanessa Carlisle's "In the First Place," a lonely bartender recalls a sex therapist's hands touching his back "with palms so urgent I would feel them burning my skin throughout the next day."

In Kim Addonizio's "The Gift," the penis becomes a fairy tale. In a story that becomes emblematic of our goals for this anthology, a woman's mind must conform itself to her new male body. At first she resists, but then: "already, as I look at myself, the horror begins to fade [. . .] I walk confidently, feeling my penis bulge against the zipper of my jeans [. . .] it will accompany me everywhere." Inevitably, passion takes over.

Certainly there are no limits to the risks a character might take when carried by the momentum of his sexual hunger; no limits to the risks a writer might take when recognizing the power of her own curiosity. We hope that you will be as inspired as we have been by these authors and their stories; by the wisdom and fervor they bring to this collection. We believe that together these works champion fiction's divine right to go anywhere, do anything, and be anyone.

Stacy Bierlein, Gina Frangello, and Kat Meads
May 2011

THE GOLD CURE

————————•————————

Jennifer Egan

The shame memories began early that day for Bennie, during the morning meeting, while he listened to one of his senior executives make a case for pulling the plug on Stop/Go, a sister band Bennie had signed to a three-record deal a couple of years back. Then, Stop/Go had seemed like an excellent bet; the sisters were young and adorable, their sound was gritty and simple and catchy ("Cyndi Lauper meets Chrissie Hynde" had been Bennie's line early on), with a big gulping bass and some fun percussion— he recalled a cowbell. Plus they'd written decent songs; hell, they'd sold twelve thousand CDs off the stage before Bennie ever heard them play. A little time to develop potential singles, some clever marketing, and a decent video could put them over the top.

But the sisters were pushing thirty, his executive producer, Collette, informed Bennie now, and no longer credible as recent high school grads, especially since one of them had a nine-year-old daughter. Their band members were in law school. They'd fired two producers, and a third had quit. Still no album.

"Who's managing them?" Bennie asked.

"Their father. I've got their new rough mix," Collette said. "The vocals are buried under seven layers of guitar."

It was then that the memory overcame Bennie (had the word "sisters" brought it on?): himself, squatting behind a nunnery in Westchester at sunrise after a night of partying—twenty years ago was it? More? Hearing waves of pure, ringing, spooky-sweet sound waft into the paling sky: cloistered nuns who saw no one but one another, who'd taken vows of silence, singing the Mass. Wet grass under his knees, its iridescence pulsing against his exhausted eyeballs. Even now, Bennie could hear the unearthly sweetness of those nuns' voices echoing deep in his ears.

He'd set up a meeting with their Mother Superior—the only nun you could talk to—brought along a couple of girls from the office for camouflage, and waited in a kind of anteroom until the Mother Superior appeared behind a square opening in the wall like a window without glass. She wore all white, a cloth tightly encircling her face. Bennie remembered her laughing a lot, rosy cheeks lifting into swags, maybe from joy at the thought of bringing God into millions of homes, maybe at the novelty of an A and R guy in purple corduroy making his pitch. The deal was done in a matter of minutes.

He'd approached the cutout square to say good-bye (here Bennie thrashed in his conference room chair, anticipating the moment it was all leading up to). The Mother Superior leaned forward slightly, tilting her head in a way that must have triggered something in Bennie, because he lurched across the sill and kissed her on the mouth: velvety skin-fuzz, an intimate, baby powder smell in the half second before the nun cried out and jerked away. Then pulling back, grinning through his dread, seeing her appalled, injured face.

"Bennie?" Collette was standing in front of a console, holding the Stop/Go CD. Everyone seemed to be waiting. "You want to hear this?"

But Bennie was caught in a loop from twenty years ago: lunging over the sill toward the Mother Superior like some haywire figure on a clock, again. Again. Again.

"No," he groaned. He turned his sweating face into the rivery breeze that gusted through the windows of the old Tribeca coffee factory where Sow's Ear Records had moved six years ago and now occupied two floors. He'd never recorded the nuns. By the time he'd returned from the convent, a message had been waiting.

"I don't," he told Collette. "I don't want to hear the mix." He felt shaken, soiled. Bennie dropped artists all the time, sometimes three in a week, but now his own shame tinged the Stop/Go sisters' failure, as if he were to blame. And that feeling was followed by a restless, opposing need to recall what had first excited him about the sisters—to feel that excitement again. "Why don't I visit them?" he said suddenly.

Collette looked startled, then suspicious, then worried, a succession that would have amused Bennie if he hadn't been so rattled. "Really?" she asked.

"Sure. I'll do it today, after I see my kid."

Bennie's assistant, Sasha, brought him coffee: cream and two sugars. He shimmied a tiny red enameled box from his pocket, popped the tricky latch, pinched a few gold flakes between his trembling fingers, and released them into his cup. He'd begun this regimen two months ago, after reading in a book on Aztec medicine that gold and coffee together were believed to ensure sexual potency. Bennie's goal was more basic than potency: sex *drive*, his own having mysteriously expired. He wasn't sure quite when or quite why this had happened: The divorce from Stephanie? The battle over Christopher? Having recently turned forty-four? The tender, circular burns on his left forearm, sustained at "The Party," a recent debacle engineered by none other than Stephanie's former boss, who was now doing jail time?

The gold landed on the coffee's milky surface and spun wildly. Bennie was mesmerized by this spinning, which he took as evidence of the explosive gold-coffee chemistry. A frenzy of activity that had mostly led him in circles: wasn't that a fairly accurate description of lust? At times Bennie didn't even mind its disappearance; it was sort of a relief not to be constantly wanting to fuck someone. The world was unquestionably a more peaceful place without the half hardon that had been his constant companion since the age of thirteen, but did Bennie want to live in such a world? He sipped his gold-inflected coffee and glanced at Sasha's breasts, which had become the litmus test he used to gauge his improvement. He'd lusted after her for most of the years she'd worked for him, first as an intern, then a receptionist, finally his assistant (where she'd remained, oddly reluctant to become an executive in her own right)—and she'd somehow managed to elude that lust without ever saying no, or hurting Bennie's feelings, or pissing him off. And now: Sasha's breasts in a thin yellow sweater, and Bennie felt nothing. Not a shiver of harmless excitement. Could he even get it up if he wanted to?

Driving to pick up his son, Bennie alternated between the Sleepers and the Dead Kennedys, San Francisco bands he'd grown up with. He listened for muddiness, the sense of actual musicians playing actual instruments in an actual room. Nowadays that quality (if it existed at all) was usually an effect of analogue signaling rather than bona fide tape—everything was an effect in the bloodless constructions Bennie and his peers were churning out. He worked tirelessly, feverishly, to get things right, stay on top, make songs that people would love and buy and download as ring tones (and steal, of course)—above all, to satisfy the multinational crude-oil extractors he'd sold his label to five years ago. But Bennie knew that what he was bringing into the world was shit. Too clear, too clean. The problem was precision, perfection; the problem was digitization, which sucked the life out of everything that got smeared through its microscopic mesh. Film, photography, music: dead. An *aesthetic holocaust*! Bennie knew better than to say this stuff aloud.

But the deep thrill of these old songs lay, for Bennie, in the rapturous surges of sixteen-year-old-ness they induced; Bennie and his high school gang—Scotty and Alice, Jocelyn and Rhea—none of whom he'd seen in decades (except for a disturbing encounter with Scotty in his office years ago), yet still half believed he'd find waiting in line outside the Mabuhay Gardens (long defunct), in San Francisco, green-haired and safetypinned, if he happened to show up there one Saturday night.

And then, as Jello Biafra was thrashing his way through "Too Drunk to Fuck," Bennie's mind drifted to an awards ceremony a few years ago where he'd tried to introduce a jazz pianist as "incomparable" and ended up calling her "incompetent" before an audience of twenty-five hundred. He should never have tried for "incomparable"—wasn't his word, too fancy; it stuck in his mouth every time he'd practiced his speech for Stephanie. But it suited the pianist, who had miles of shiny gold hair and had also (she'd let slip) graduated from Harvard. Bennie had cherished a rash dream of getting her into bed, feeling that hair sliding over his shoulders and chest.

He idled now in front of Christopher's school, waiting for the memory spasm to pass. Driving in, he'd glimpsed his son crossing the athletic field with his friends. Chris had been skipping a little—actually skipping—tossing a ball in the air, but by the time he slumped into Bennie's yellow Porsche, any inkling of lightness was gone. Why? Did Chris somehow know about the botched awards ceremony? Bennie told himself this was nuts, yet was moved by an urge to confess the malapropism to his fourth grader. The Will to Divulge, Dr. Beet called this impulse, and had exhorted Bennie to write down the things he wanted to confide, rather than burden his son with them. Bennie did this now, scribbling *incompetent* on the back of a parking ticket he'd received the day before. Then, recalling the earlier humiliation, he added to the list *kissing Mother Superior.*

"So, boss," he said. "Whatcha feel like doing?"

"Don't know."

"Any particular wishes?"

"Not really."

Bennie looked helplessly out the window. A couple of months ago, Chris had asked if they could skip their weekly appointment with Dr. Beet and spend the afternoon "doing whatever" instead. They hadn't gone back, a decision that Bennie now regretted; "doing whatever" had led to desultory afternoons, often cut short by Chris's announcement that he had homework.

"How about some coffee?" Bennie suggested.

A spark of smile. "Can I get a Frappuccino?"

"Don't tell your mother."

Stephanie didn't approve of Chris drinking coffee— reasonable, given that the kid was nine—but Bennie couldn't resist the exquisite connection that came of defying his ex-wife in unison. Betrayal Bonding, Dr. Beet called this, and like the Will to Divulge, it was on the list of no-no's.

They got their coffees and returned to the Porsche to drink them. Chris sucked greedily at his Frappuccino. Bennie took out his red enameled box, pinched a few gold flakes, and slipped them under the plastic lid of his cup.

"What's that?" Chris asked.

Bennie started. The gold was becoming so routine that he'd stopped being clandestine about it. "Medicine," he said, after a moment.

"For what?"

"Some symptoms I've been having." Or not having, he added mentally.

"What symptoms?"

Was this the Frappuccino kicking in? Chris had shifted out of his slump and now sat upright, regarding Bennie with his wide, dark, frankly beautiful eyes. "Headaches," Bennie said.

"Can I see it?" Chris asked. "The medicine? In that red thing?"

Bennie handed over the tiny box. Within a couple of seconds, the kid had figured out the tricky latch and popped it open. "Whoa, Dad," he said. "What is this stuff?"

"I told you."

"It looks like gold. Flakes of gold."

"It has a flaky consistency."

"Can I taste one?"

"Son. You don't—"

"Just one?"

Bennie sighed. "One."

The boy carefully removed a gold flake and placed it on his tongue. "What does it taste like?" Bennie couldn't help asking. He'd only consumed the gold in his coffee, where it had no discernible flavor.

"Like metal," Chris said. "It's awesome. Can I have another one?"

Bennie started the car. Was there something obviously sham about the medicine story? Clearly the kid wasn't buying it. "One more," he said. "And that's it."

His son took a fat pinch of gold flakes and put them on his tongue. Bennie tried not to think of the money. The truth was, he'd spent eight thousand dollars on gold in the past two months. A coke habit would have cost him less.

Chris sucked on the gold and closed his eyes. "Dad," he said. "It's, like, waking me up from the inside."

"Interesting," Bennie mused. "That's exactly what it's supposed to do."

"Is it working?"

"Sounds like it is."

"But on you," Chris said.

Bennie was fairly certain his son had asked him more questions in the past ten minutes than in the prior year and a half since he and Stephanie had split. Could this be a side effect of the gold: curiosity?

"I've still got the headaches," he said.

He was driving aimlessly among the Crandale mansions ("doing whatever" involved a lot of aimless driving), every one of which seemed to have four or five blond children in Ralph Lauren playing out front. Seeing these kids, it was clearer than ever to Bennie that he hadn't had a chance of lasting in this place, swarthy and unkempt-looking as he was even when freshly showered and

THE GOLD CURE | 45

shaved. Stephanie, meanwhile, had ascended to the club's number one doubles team.

"Chris," Bennie said. "There's a musical group I need to visit—a pair of young sisters. Well, youngish sisters. I was planning to go later on, but if you're interested, we could—"

"Sure."

"Really?"

"Yeah."

Did "sure" and "yeah" mean that Chris was giving in to please Bennie, as Dr. Beet had noted he often did? Or had the gold-incited curiosity extended to a new interest in Bennie's work? Chris had grown up around rock groups, of course, but he was part of the postpiracy generation, for whom things like "copyright" and "creative ownership" didn't exist. Bennie didn't *blame* Chris, of course; the dismantlers who had murdered the music business were a generation beyond his son, adults now. Still, he'd heeded Dr. Beet's advice to stop hectoring (Beet's word) Chris about the industry's decline and focus instead on enjoying music they both liked—Pearl Jam, for example, which Bennie blasted all the way to Mount Vernon.

The Stop/Go sisters still lived with their parents in a sprawling, run-down house under bushy suburban trees. Bennie had been here two or three years ago when he'd first discovered them, before he'd entrusted the sisters to the first in a series of executives who had failed to accomplish a blessed thing. As he and Chris left the car, the memory of his last visit provoked a convulsion of anger in Bennie that made heat roll up toward his head—why the fuck hadn't anything happened in all this time?

He found Sasha waiting at the door; she'd caught the train at Grand Central after Bennie called and had somehow beaten him here.

"Hiya Crisco," Sasha said, mussing his son's hair. She had known Chris all his life; she'd run out to Duane Reade to buy him pacifiers and diapers. Bennie glanced at her breasts; nothing. Or nothing sexual—he did feel a swell of gratitude and appreciation for his assistant, as opposed to the murderous rage he felt toward the rest of his staff.

There was a pause. Yellow light scissored through the leaves. Bennie lifted his gaze from Sasha's breasts to her face. She had high cheekbones and narrow green eyes, wavy hair that ranged from reddish to purplish, depending on the month. Today it was red. She was smiling at Chris, but Bennie detected worry somewhere in the smile. He rarely thought of Sasha as an independent person, and beyond a vague awareness of boyfriends coming and going (vague first out of respect for her privacy, lately out of indifference), he knew few specifics of her life. But seeing her outside this family home, Bennie experienced a flare of curiosity: Sasha had still been at NYU when he'd first met her at a Conduits gig at the Pyramid Club; that put her in her thirties now. Why hadn't she married? Did she want kids? She seemed suddenly older, or was it just that Bennie seldom looked directly at her face?

"What," she said, feeling his stare.

"Nothing."

"You okay?"

"Better than okay," Bennie said, and gave the door a sharp knock.

The sisters looked fantastic—if not right out of high school, then at least right out of college, especially if they'd taken a year or two off or maybe transferred a couple of times. They wore their dark hair pulled back from their faces, and their eyes were glittering, and they had a whole fucking book full of new material—*look at this*! Bennie's fury at his team intensified, but it was pleasurable, motivating fury. The sisters' nervous excitement jittered up the house; they knew his visit was their last, best hope. Chandra was the older one, Louisa the younger. Louisa's daughter, Olivia, had been riding a trike in the driveway on Bennie's last visit, but now she wore skintight jeans and a jeweled tiara that seemed to be a fashion choice, not a costume. Bennie felt Chris snap to attention when Olivia entered the room, as if a charmed snake had risen from its basket inside him.

They went single file down a narrow flight of stairs to the sisters' basement recording studio. Their father had built it for them years ago. It was tiny, with orange shag covering the floor, ceiling, and walls. Bennie took the only seat, noting with approval a cowbell by the keyboard.

"Coffee?" Sasha asked him. Chandra led her upstairs to make it. Louisa sat at the keyboard teasing out melodies. Olivia took up a set of bongo drums and began loosely accompanying her mother. She handed Chris a tambourine, and to Bennie's astonishment, his son settled in beating the thing in perfect time. Nice, he thought. Very nice. The day had swerved unexpectedly into good. The almostteenage daughter wasn't a problem, he decided; she could join the group as a younger sister or a cousin, strengthen the tween angle. Maybe Chris could be part of it, too, although he and Olivia would have to switch instruments. A boy on a tambourine . . .

Sasha brought his coffee, and Bennie took out his red enameled box and dropped in a pinch of flakes. As he sipped, a sensation of pleasure filled his whole torso the way a snowfall fills up a sky. Jesus, he felt good. He'd been delegating too much. Hearing the music get *made*, that was the thing: people and instruments and beatenlooking equipment aligning abruptly into a single structure of sound, flexible and alive. The sisters were at the keyboard arranging their music, and Bennie experienced a bump of anticipation; something was going to happen here. He knew it. Felt it pricking his arms and chest.

"You've got Pro Tools on there, right?" he asked, indicating the laptop on a table amid the instruments. "Is everything miked? Can we lay down some tracks right now?"

The sisters nodded and checked the laptop; they were ready to record. "Vocals, too?" Chandra asked.

"Absolutely," Bennie said. "Let's do it all at once. Let's blow the roof off your fucking house."

Sasha was standing to Bennie's right. So many bodies had heated up the little room, lifting off her skin a perfume she'd been wearing for years—or was it a lotion?—that smelled like apricots; not just the sweet part but that slight bitterness around the pit. And as Bennie breathed in Sasha's lotion smell, his prick roused itself suddenly like an old hound getting a swift kick. He almost jumped out of his seat in startled amazement, but he kept his cool. Don't push things, just let it happen. Don't scare it away.

Then the sisters began to sing. Oh, the raw, almostthreadbare sound of their voices mixed with the clash of instruments—these sensations met with a faculty deeper in Bennie than judgment or even pleasure; they communed directly with his body, whose shivering, bursting reply made him dizzy. And here was his first erection in months—prompted by Sasha, who had been too near Bennie all these years for him to really *see* her, like in those nineteenthcentury novels he'd read in secret because only girls were supposed to like them. He seized the cowbell and stick and began whacking at it with zealous blows. He felt the music in his mouth, his ears, his ribs—or was that his own pulse? He was on fire!

And from this zenith of lusty, devouring joy, he recalled opening an email he'd been inadvertently copied on between two colleagues and finding himself referred to as a "hairball." God, what a feeling of liquid shame had pooled in Bennie when he'd read that word. He hadn't been sure what it meant: That he was hairy? (True.) Unclean? (False!) Or was it literal, as in: he clogged people's throats and made them gag, the way Stephanie's cat, Sylph, occasionally vomited hair onto the carpet? Bennie had gone for a haircut that very day and seriously considered having his back and upper arms waxed, until Stephanie talked him out of it, running her cool hands over his shoulders that night in bed, telling him she loved him hairy—that the last thing the world needed was another waxed guy.

Music. Bennie was listening to music. The sisters were screaming, the tiny room imploding from their sound, and Bennie tried to find again the deep contentment he'd felt just a minute ago. But "hairball" had unsettled him. The room felt uncomfortably small. Bennie set down his cowbell and slipped the parking ticket from his pocket. He scribbled *hairball* in hopes of exorcising the memory. He took a slow inhale and rested his eyes on Chris, who was flailing the tambourine trying to match the sisters' erratic tempo, and right away it happened again: taking his son for a haircut a couple of years ago, having his longtime barber, Stu, put down his scissors and pull Bennie aside. "There's a problem with your son's hair," he'd said.

"A problem!"

Stu walked Bennie over to Chris in the chair and parted his hair to reveal some tan little creatures the size of poppy seeds moving around on his scalp. Bennie felt himself grow faint. "Lice," the barber whispered. "They get it at school."

"But he goes to private school!" Bennie had blurted. "In Crandale, New York!"

Chris's eyes had gone wide with fear: "What is it, Daddy?" Other people were staring, and Bennie had felt responsible, with his own riotous head of hair, to the point where he sprayed OFF! in his armpits every morning to this day, and kept an extra can at the office—crazy! He knew it! Getting their coats while everyone watched, Bennie with a burning face; god, it hurt him to think of this now—hurt him physically, as if the memory were raking over him and leaving gashes. He hid his face in his hands. He wanted to cover his ears, block out the cacophony of Stop/Go, but he concentrated on Sasha, just to his right, her sweet-bitter smell, and found himself remembering a girl he'd chased at a party when he first came to New York and was selling vinyl on the Lower East Side a hundred years ago, some delicious blonde—Abby, was it? In the course of keeping tabs on Abby, Bennie had done several lines of coke and been stricken with a severe instantaneous need to empty his bowels. He'd been relieving himself on the can in what must have been (although Bennie's brain ached to recall this) a miasma of annihilating stink, when the unlockable bathroom door had jumped open, and there was Abby, staring down at him. There'd been a horrible, bottomless instant when their eyes met; then she'd shut the door.

Bennie had left the party with someone else—there was always someone else—and their night of fun, which he felt comfortable presuming, had erased the confrontation with Abby. But now it was back—oh, it was back, bringing waves of shame so immense they seemed to engulf whole parts of Bennie's life and drag them away: achievements, successes, moments of pride, all of it razed to the point where there was nothing—he was nothing—a guy on a john looking up at the nauseated face of a woman he'd wanted to impress.

Bennie leaped from his stool, squashing the cowbell under one foot. Sweat stung his eyes. His hair engaged palpably with the ceiling shag.

"You okay?" Sasha asked, alarmed.

"I'm sorry," Bennie panted, mopping his brow. "I'm sorry. I'm sorry. I'm sorry."

Back upstairs, he stood outside the front door, pulling fresh air into his lungs. The Stop/Go sisters and daughter clustered around him, apologizing for the airlessness of the recording studio, their father's ongoing failure to vent it properly, reminding one another in spirited tones of the many times they themselves had grown faint, trying to work there.

"We can hum the tunes," they said, and they did, in harmony, Olivia too, all of them standing not far from Bennie's face, desperation quivering their smiles. A gray cat made a figure eight around Bennie's shins, nudging him rapturously with its bony head. It was a relief to get back in the car.

He was driving Sasha to the city, but he had to get Chris home first. His son hunched in the backseat, facing the open window. It seemed to Bennie that his lark of an idea for the afternoon had gone awry. He fended off the longing to look at Sasha's breasts, waiting to calm down, regain his equilibrium before putting himself to the test. Finally, at a red light, he glanced slowly, casually in her direction, not even focusing at first, then peering intently. Nothing. He was clobbered by loss so severe that it took physical effort not to howl. He'd had it, *he'd had it!* But where had it gone?

"Dad, green light," Chris said.

Driving again, Bennie forced himself to ask his son, "So, boss. What did you think?"

The kid didn't answer. Maybe he was pretending not to hear, or maybe the wind was too loud in his face. Bennie glanced at Sasha. "What about you?"

"Oh," she said, "they're awful."

Bennie blinked, stung. He felt a gust of anger at Sasha that passed a few seconds later, leaving odd relief. Of course. They were awful. That was the problem.

"Unlistenable," Sasha went on. "No wonder you were having a heart attack."

"I don't get it," Bennie said.

"What?"

"Two years ago they sounded . . . different."

Sasha gave him a quizzical look. "It wasn't two years," she said. "It was five."

"Why so sure?"

"Because last time, I came to their house after a meeting at Windows on the World."

It took Bennie a minute to comprehend this. "Oh," he finally said. "How close to—"

"Four days."

"Wow. I never knew that." He waited out a respectful pause, then continued, "Still, two years, five years—"

Sasha turned and stared at him. She looked angry. "Who am I talking to?" she asked. "You're Bennie Salazar! This is the music business. 'Five years is five *hundred years*'—your words."

Bennie didn't answer. They were approaching his former house, as he thought of it. He couldn't say "old house," but he also couldn't say "house" anymore, although he'd certainly paid for it. His former house was withdrawn from the street on a grassy slope, a gleaming white Colonial that had filled him with awe every time he'd taken a key from his pocket to open the front door. Bennie stopped at the curb and killed the engine. He couldn't bring himself to drive up the driveway.

Chris was leaning forward from the backseat, his head between Bennie and Sasha. Bennie wasn't sure how long he'd been there. "I think you need some of your medicine, Dad," he said.

"Good idea," Bennie said. He began tapping his pockets, but the little red box was nowhere to be found.

"Here, I've got it," Sasha said. "You dropped it coming out of the recording room."

She was doing that more and more, finding things he'd misplaced—sometimes before Bennie even knew they were missing. It added to the almost trancelike dependence he felt on her. "Thanks, Sash," he said.

He opened the box. God the flakes were shiny. Gold didn't tarnish, that was the thing. The flakes would look the same in five years as they did right now.

"Should I put some on my tongue, like you did?" he asked his son.

"Yeah. But I get some, too."

"Sasha, you want to try a little medicine?" Bennie asked.

"Um, okay," she said. "What's it supposed to do?"

"Solve your problems," Bennie said. "I mean, headaches. Not that you have any."

"Never," Sasha said, with that same wary smile.

They each took a pinch of gold flakes and placed them on

their tongues. Bennie tried not to calculate the dollar value of what was inside their mouths. He concentrated on the taste: Was it metallic, or was that just his expectation? Coffee, or was that what was left in his mouth? He tongued the gold in a tight knot and sucked the juice from within it; sour, he thought. Bitter. Sweet? Each one seemed true for a second, but in the end Bennie had an impression of something mineral, like stone. Even earth. And then the lump melted away.

"I should go, Dad," Chris said. Bennie let him out of the car and hugged him hard. As always, Chris went still in his embrace, but whether he was savoring it or enduring it Bennie could never tell.

He drew back and looked at his son. The baby he and Stephanie had nuzzled and kissed—now this painful, mysterious presence. Bennie was tempted to say, *Don't tell your mother about the medicine*, craving an instant of connection with Chris before he went inside. But he hesitated, employing a mental calculation Dr. Beet had taught him: Did he really think the kid would tell Stephanie about the gold? No. And that was his alert: Betrayal Bonding. Bennie said nothing.

He got back in the car, but didn't turn the key. He was watching Chris scale the undulating lawn toward his former house. The grass was fluorescently bright. His son seemed to buckle under his enormous backpack. What the hell was in it? Bennie had seen professional photographers carry less. As Chris neared the house he blurred a little, or maybe it was Bennie's eyes watering. He found it excruciating, watching his son's long journey to the front door. He worried Sasha would speak—say something like *He's a great kid*, or *That was fun*—something that would require Bennie to turn and look at her. But Sasha knew better; she knew everything. She sat with Bennie in silence, watching Chris climb the fat, bright grass to the front door, then open it without turning and go inside.

They didn't speak again until they'd passed from the Henry Hudson Parkway onto the West Side Highway, heading into Lower Manhattan. Bennie played some early Who, the Stooges, bands he'd listened to before he was even old enough to go to a concert. Then he got into Flipper, the Mutants, Eye Protection— seventies Bay Area groups he and his gang had slam-danced to at the Mabuhay Gardens when they weren't practicing with their own unlistenable band, the Flaming Dildos. He sensed Sasha paying attention and toyed with the idea that he was confessing to her his disillusionment—his *hatred* for the industry he'd given his life to. He began weighing each musical choice, drawing out his argument through the songs themselves—Patti Smith's ragged poetry (but why did she quit?), the jock hardcore of Black Flag and the Circle Jerks giving way to alternative, that great compromise, down, down, down to the singles he'd just today been petitioning radio stations to add, husks of music, lifeless and cold as the squares of office neon cutting the blue twilight.

"It's incredible," Sasha said, "how there's just nothing there."

Astounded, Bennie turned to her. Was it possible that she'd followed his musical rant to its grim conclusion? Sasha was looking downtown, and he followed her eyes to the empty space where the Twin Towers had been. "There should be *something*, you know?" she said, not looking at Bennie. "Like an echo. Or an outline."

Bennie sighed. "They'll put something up," he said. "When they're finally done squabbling."

"I know." But she kept looking south, as if it were a problem her mind couldn't solve. Bennie was relieved she hadn't understood. He remembered his mentor, Lou Kline, telling him in the nineties that rock and roll had peaked at Monterey Pop. They'd been in Lou's house in LA with its waterfalls, the pretty girls Lou always had, his car collection out front, and Bennie had looked into his idol's famous face and thought, *You're finished*. Nostalgia was the end—everyone knew that. Lou had died three months ago, after being paralyzed from a stroke.

At a stoplight, Bennie remembered his list. He took out the parking ticket and finished it off.

"What do you keep scribbling on that ticket?" Sasha asked. Bennie handed it to her, his reluctance to have the list seen by human eyes overwhelming him a half second late. To his horror, she began reading it aloud:

"Kissing Mother Superior, incompetent, hairball, poppy seeds, on the can."

Bennie listened in agony, as if the words themselves might provoke a catastrophe. But they were neutralized the instant Sasha spoke them in her scratchy voice.

"Not bad," she said. "They're titles, right?"

"Sure," Bennie said. "Can you read them one more time?" She did, and now they sounded like titles to him, too. He felt peaceful, cleansed.

"'Kissing Mother Superior' is my favorite," Sasha said. "We've gotta find a way to use that one."

They'd pulled up outside her building on Forsyth. The street felt desolate and underlit. Bennie wished she could live in a better place. Sasha gathered up her ubiquitous black bag, a shapeless wishing well from which she'd managed to wrest whatever file or number or slip of paper he'd needed for the past twelve years. Bennie seized her thin white hand. "Listen," he said. "Listen, Sasha."

She looked up. Bennie felt no lust at all—he wasn't even hard. What he felt for Sasha was love, a safety and closeness like what he'd had with Stephanie before he'd let her down so many times that she couldn't stop being mad. "I'm crazy for you, Sasha," he said. "Crazy."

"Come on, Bennie," Sasha chided lightly. "None of that."

He held her hand between both of his. Sasha's fingers were trembly and cold. Her other hand was on the door.

"Wait," Bennie said. "Please."

She turned to him, somber now. "There's no way, Bennie," she said. "We need each other."

They looked at one another in the failing light. The delicate bones of Sasha's face were lightly freckled—it was a girl's face, but she'd stopped being a girl when he wasn't watching.

Sasha leaned over and kissed Bennie's cheek: a chaste kiss, a kiss between brother and sister, mother and son, but Bennie felt the softness of her skin, the warm movement of her breath. Then she was out of the car. She waved to him through the window and said something he didn't catch. Bennie lunged across the empty seat, his face near the glass, staring fixedly as she said it again. Still, he missed it. As he struggled to open the door, Sasha said it once more, mouthing the words extra slowly:

"See. You. Tomorrow."

FROM *THE PRACTICE OF DECEIT*

Elizabeth Benedict

In the middle of our wild mushroom raviolis that first night, the earth moved, as it does every so often in California, and something shifted between us.

Before that moment, which lasted fifteen seconds, we were eating our appetizers by an open French door on a Santa Monica street as pristine and unreal as a movie set. The air was warm, dry and smelled of grilled garlic. Colleen had told me about the art galleries she had visited that afternoon and was now telling me about the book she had just finished writing with a journalist she knew in Boston. On one channel of my brain I was trying not to look at her breasts and wondering whether she would let me put my lips to them when we returned to the hotel. I hoped she wasn't still mourning the loss of her husband, wasn't carrying a torch for him. She hadn't said a word about him all through dinner. On another channel, I noted her work habits, her organizational skills, her industry: divorce, new baby, new town, new law practice, she collects art, and she finds time to write a book? File this away in case our fling has legs: She will not have time to cling to me. She gets a gold star for that.

"My book is more of a handbook, Eric, for women dealing with divorce," she was saying, "to guide them through the challenges, like the husband who hides money in offshore accounts or transfers deeds to business properties when those should be—"

At that moment, the table began to shudder, the plates on it, the silverware, wine glasses and forks fell all over the room, pinging and shattering as they hit the tile floor. Three or four people ran for the open doors and banged into others who were trembling in place. Colleen and I gaped at each another, hands flung out to keep our dishes from sliding. We shook in our seats, or was it the seats shaking? Paintings quivered and fell from nails on the walls. None of us screamed—because we were holding our breath. It was over in a matter of seconds. Fifteen, maybe twenty? You could hear loud sighs, choruses of "Jesus," and "Omigod," and "Are you all right?" Everyone, not just the waiters, began to pick things up from the floor, a gesture of common cause, solidarity. Salt shakers, bread baskets, slippery plates that had held olive oil for dipping, piles of broken wine glasses. All at once, cell phones began to ring, a cacophony of electronic bleats and tones that must have been playing all over town.

"Zoe," Colleen said and drew her hand to her face. "I don't have a cell with me. Do you think the phones are out? There must be a pay phone somewhere. What if the hotel—"

"Where you staying?" said the woman at the next table. In an instant, we were a community in crisis, reaching out to our neighbors, California style.

"The Mondrian."

"That's a fortress. Anything built since 'ninety-four is solid. Don't worry. This was nothing. Ninety-four was a cyclone. That was Tarzan lifting up your bed and hurling it across the room with you in it."

Colleen turned to me, eyes wide with apprehension. I countered it with calm, though I was shaken myself, not with fear but memories. Frantic calls for days to reach my father after the quake in '94. His apartment was a mile from the epicenter. My mother asked me how he had fared, when her mind was still intact. Even my sister, who went for years without speaking to him, panicked at the thought that the earth had swallowed him up whole. It hadn't, but his building cracked in two and he had to move. Now, years later, he was dead.

"We'll be fine," I said to Colleen.

As we walked to my car across Ocean Avenue, with its Rockettes-like lineup of towering coconut palms, I took her hand. On another night, after another dinner, it would have been a romantic gesture, a touch of foreplay, an invitation. But that night it was purely tender. We were survivors. I squeezed her hand and she squeezed mine back. At the car, I folded her into a hug, and she drew her arms around my back. She was a sturdy package with a strong back and breasts that ballooned against my chest. I was certain this would be a sweet night.

The quake, which turned out to be a 3.7—no serious injuries; minor damage to stoplight timers and chandeliers—had flung us together, cracked our prim social inhibitions and our carapaces of immortality. The earth rumbles and we're swapping stories with the woman at the next table. Our forks skitter to the floor and suddenly the notion of our being lovers—even for the night— is not such a hard sell. The quake shook things up and tilted us closer together. It gave us an urgent, well-defined but still traditional role to act out: she, the mother, was afraid for her child and I, the hunter, the warrior, could protect and comfort her. The wound of her husband leaving her was distant, but our mutual quake was fresh, an injury we sustained together. And my having seized the lead in taking care of her, made it easier for her to console me, later that night, in my peculiar, my peculiarly detached mourning.

She came to my room after she checked on her family, but there was more talking than there might have been on an ordinary night. She seemed more tentative than she had during dinner, before the quake, which, I'm sorry to say, only made me want her more urgently. "Isn't the view amazing?" she said, moving toward the vast wall of windows. "We see the same thing from our room."

"It's better in the dark." I flipped off the overhead and joined her at the edge of the curtains, drew an arm around her shoulder and felt her move into my embrace. When she did, I held her for a moment and then reached with one hand for her bottom, her clothed bottom. I wanted just to touch it, to feel it in my palm, but she turned schoolmarm on me and abruptly moved my hand to her waist.

"Let's just look at the view." She maneuvered us to the window, the glittering valley of lights. It is something to behold, the vast Los Angeles basin, black backdrop with a golden yellow glow of lights, some of the strokes of light so thick they seem painted by de Kooning with an electric crayon and others as faint as gold dust. It was mesmerizing, an entirely different sight from the upright Manhattan skyline, which is sharply etched, obdurately vertical. The valley oozes yellow light as far as the eye can see.

"It's something, isn't it?" she said. "Five million people."

We stood facing the window chastely, her arm around my waist and mine around her shoulder.

"And at least that many cars," I said. This was becoming a parody of a seduction; I was not used to women who were so uptight. Especially those who had issued lunch and dinner invitations.

"It's such a long way from the East Coast," she said. "Do you ever think about living out here?"

"Fleetingly. The way I think about owning a sports car. It would be fun, until I got tired of it. What about you?"

"It's daunting to think about starting over again."

"Your husband—" When I said that I could feel her flinch and turn to me. "He didn't want to reconcile? A lot of men have flings but when push comes to shove, they're not willing to abandon their families. Especially when there are young children."

For a long moment she was silent. "I learned late in the game that I hadn't married one of those men." She said this matter-of-factly, not harshly, not bitterly, and I was struck by the lack of bitterness. "But even if he were more agreeable, he's in Boston and we're in Westchester now."

"Did you say you'd grown up in Boston?"

"I think I did." Her arm tightened around my waist and I could feel her turn into me, giving up her reserve. She tipped her face to me, inviting a kiss. "South Boston."

"You don't have an accent." I complied, kissing her lightly.

"Good. That was my plan. My husband gave me elocution lessons. I was very determined student."

"Talk for me the way you used to."

"You don't want to hear that." She drew her arms tighter around my torso and pressed her hands all the way down my back to my buttocks, doing to me what I had tried earlier to do to her: a serious invitation, a sure way to halt my questions. I was compliant. My cock complied. The rest of me was not far behind. I walked her backward, in little steps, to the foot of the bed.

"I suppose I should take off my stockings." She reached down to the hem of her skirt and hiked it up, plucking at something.

"Don't tell me you're wearing real stockings."

"But I am."

"A garter belt, too?"

"How else would I hold them up?"

For a moment, I couldn't speak. This accessory was as surprising as the earthquake, as startling as seeing her breast-feed her child by the pool. Why had she been so nervous before if she had this up her sleeve—or down her leg?

"I hear men like this sort of thing," she murmured.

"I can't imagine who told you."

"Word gets around."

Bing. Bing. Bing.

When we were half undressed, when our shirts were off and her breasts were bare, and one of them was cradled in my hand, I did what I always do, what I like to do, as much as I like any part of this—endeavor? There must be a better word on the formal side, short of "intercourse." The sex act. The sexual endeavor. Neither sounds like fun. Making love? Why does that sound archaic to me? I picture Maurice Chevalier in a crooning black-and-white seduction, the Eiffel Tower just over his left shoulder; or myself as an eleven-year-old boy, finding in my parents' one bookcase, *A Modern Marriage Manual*, and this sentence I have never forgotten: "While it may take a new wife some time to adjust to the demands of making love, she may eventually come to feel great pleasure in the act." The language problem comes up when I talk to my patients, and it can be tricky. Often I use the expressions they use, though I try to steer them away from the most vulgar, unless there is context for it that needs reaffirmation.

What I did that night: I lowered my head and put my mouth around Colleen's engorged nipple.

Had I never done this?

Of course I hadn't. None of my nubile Brandys or fourteen-carat Tiffanys could offer such a nipple, such a feast. It was a taste I'd never be able to remember having tasted. It was bittersweet. It was slightly sour. Thicker than what comes in a carton. It was delicious.

She cradled me and suckled me and held me in the most exquisite embrace of my life. It would have been enough had she said nothing, but soon she was whispering as she fed me: "Poor lamb, I can see how sad you are even though you're trying not to be, because your daddy died." With her nipple between my lips and her child's milk filling my mouth, I did something that astonished me: I choked when she said the word "daddy." I had called him nothing except his first name or "fuck face" or "asshole" since I was fourteen. Now I coughed and had to pull away from her tit, and, as I sat up to keep milk from pouring into my nasal passages, she kept whispering to me, "Poor lamb, poor Pooh, poor dear," and she didn't let go of me, she was so utterly tender just then.

All of this happening at once, in a matter of fifteen or twenty seconds—it was like the earthquake that way—made me shed some of my armor. Shed some of my tears. She couldn't have been sweeter. She coaxed me back down to the pillow with her, and this time she held out her breast to my mouth and whispered, "Here, this is for you."

This was chemistry; this was physiology. This was Mother Nature, Father Time, and Reason #7 that I fell in love with her.

AND A DEAD AMERICAN

———————————

Elizabeth Searle

"And a dead American," Rasha said to my mother.

Mom's smiley face froze over the wood bowl she held out. That bowl full of homemade popcorn balls and unpopular raisin packets, lame candy alternatives I'd warned her might get our house toilet-papered. But even I—only playing a cynical guy back then, before you appeared—felt a jolt in my gut. Because Mom and I faced, on our brightly lit doorstep, on Halloween of 2001, two Terrorist Trick-or-Treaters.

"Goodness," Mom had exclaimed in stagey surprise when she swung open our door. Then her shoulders stiffened in real surprise. It was late; her reddish hair was springing free from its ponytail. "What are you two supposed to be?"

A tremor in her usual sing-song made me slip behind Mom. I was Man of the House with Dad away on the plane trip Mom had begged him to cancel. To look older than fourteen, I sealed shut my mouth over my braces-hidden-by-plastic-vampire-teeth. But my lips quivered.

From behind Mom, I took them in: two coolly staring teenage dudes.

Rakeen (but I didn't know his name then) stood tallest, his head covered in a white cloth ghutra. Only his manly black eyes showed, unblinking. His shoulders stuck out like a wire hanger, holding up his draped white robe. In one brown fist, he gripped a metal dog-leash chain.

The leash was clipped to the collar of the Toys"R"Us U.S. Marines uniform that his companion, boy-sized Rasha, wore, its camouflage print splattered with what looked like real dried blood. More fake blood streaks dripped from Rasha's long-lashed eyes, the red extra bright against his white face-paint.

Rakeen gave Rasha's leash a rough tug. On cue, Rasha stretched his mouth—his teeth were crooked—into a death grimace.

"I can't even guess—" Mom managed, less shaky, determined to see us all through this awkward moment. Behind the trick-or-treaters, in the chill Halloween night, the familiar orange-lit brick houses glowed in neat stairstep order up Riverview Road. Distant kid voices piped in neighboring streets. "What," she prodded gamely, "*are* you two supposed to be?"

Rakeen stepped forward, everything silent except for the rumble of traffic on Mystic.

"A terrorist," Rakeen pronounced, his *r*'s softened in Arabic style. Another tug of the chain leash.

Then boy-voiced Rasha chimed in from his bloodied Marine uniform. "And a dead American."

Like I said, I didn't know their names then. I knew them as the "Middle Eastern" (Mom would say) or "A-rab Fucker" (my new secret bro, TJ, would say) boys on Mystic. They ran wild around what had been That Rundown House on the River and had become, to TJ and me, our neighborhood's Terrorist Cell.

The house where slashing black must-be-Arab graffiti appeared and disappeared on the garage door, where United Air boxes littered the curb from post-midnight deliveries spotted by Riverview Road insomniacs like my dad.

Not to mention what-all TJ and I had spotted close up from our bikes on our separate, intersecting patrols. We didn't know you yet at Halloween. But you knew me. Or at least you'd seen me, glimpsed me, from the window of your basement room.

Me: Josiah Simon, with my freckled boy face, my newly stretched-out body. One of the American boys biking back and forth in front of your house.

No, I mean: in front of the house where you were held.

"And a dead American," Rasha pronounced perfectly, punch line to his and Rakeen's Terrorist Trick or Treat routine. Then he swallowed hard, no Adam's apple showing in his throat. The taller, calmer Rakeen cracked a close-lipped grin, planting a firm hand on the younger boy's shoulder.

Mom's shoulders stood up under her sweater. Was she going to smack these kids? But my mom never smacked; she faced both of them, still holding her wood bowl of healthy treats.

Get the hell outta here, I wanted to say, loud and clear.

Behind Mom, I drew a big breath and almost swallowed my fangs. Mom, too, drew an audible breath. I pleaded her with brainwaves not to resort to her Teacher Voice. Too loud, too clear. Rakeen flicked his glance at me, maybe recognizing me from my bike, sizing me up. My lips buckled over my toy teeth.

And Rakeen looked right back to my mother like I was just an overgrown boy, my mouth overfull of candy. Mom was standing taller, teacher height.

Keep quiet Mom, I thought, inching up beside her.

"Do you think that's funny?" Mom asked Rakeen and Rasha, deadpan.

"No," Rasha answered, his boy-voice factual. Under his bloodstained head bandage, his big-eyed stare fixed on dumbstruck me. He tensed up like he expected a fight. From me?

Rakeen shook his ghutraed head. "We are not joking, Missus. You think we are joking?"

Mom drew another breath but didn't speak. Rakeen crammed his long-fingered hands into Mom's bowl. He scooped out three popcorn balls, leaving the raisin packets. Rasha reached in next and tilted the bowl Mom held rigidly, dumping the Sun-Maids into his pumpkin-printed bag.

Firmly, Rakeen tugged Rasha's chain. Then they both turned heel, in light-footed unison. They ran off into the night, up Riverview Road hill. Rakeen's ghutra flew out behind him; Rasha's chain clinked. They were not laughing.

Mom stepped back fast, bumping me, slamming and bolt-locking our door. She let the bowl drop to our polished wood floor. A hollow, rolling clunk. "Good god, who *were* they?" And Mom grabbed me in a hard hug that I found myself returning. Clinging to her slender warmth, surprised by how small Mom felt in my arms.

"Dose kids from dat house," I mumbled through my toy teeth into Mom's frizzy falling-down ponytail.

She pulled back from our sudden hug; she met my widened green eyes with hers. Her face looked so pale all her freckles stood out. I yanked out my unmoored vampire teeth: a string of saliva like when I used to pull out my retainer. Mom, being my mom, didn't flinch.

I swallowed as hard as the younger boy had done.

"From that weird house on the river," I told Mom, like how-could-she-be-so-dense. "The house Dad and everyone calls a Terrorist Cell—"

"Your father, yes; we have to call him. That house by the river; of course. I'm sure it's nothing really, just some ghastly prank, but . . ." Mom turned in a trance. She stepped past our crowded bookshelves, into our kitchen with its smell of roasted salted pumpkin seeds, slightly burned.

In the dim living room, between the open shades of the window facing the street, our grinning jack-o'-lantern's flame wavered. Mom dialed. Dad was in Denver. Though he liked to jokingly sing, *Ah found my thrill on Riverview Hill*, Dad made so many consulting trips, I wondered sometimes if he found his real thrills elsewhere.

He worried aloud that I'd become a Mama's Boy, left alone with Mom so much. But he kept up his travels, kept shelling out tuition for Fairwell School even though he didn't approve, grumbling sometimes that Fairwell was a hippie-dippie bubble, shielding me from real life.

This real enough for you? I found myself thinking. Here Dad had gone and missed a rare shockwave in our quiet brick house, leaving me Man of the House. My man-sized arms and legs felt electrified. Mom's urgent voice murmured to distant Dad. But what had I *done*, facing the Terrorist Trick-or-Treaters, besides almost swallow my Dracula teeth?

I paced the living room, peering out the candlelit window. Mom was repeating into the phone Dad's instructions about calling the police but not leaving our name. I was sending brainwaves to TJ to bike out tomorrow. To meet me in the bushes by the Terrorist Cell.

TJ and I had both started biking by your house on the hushed afternoon of September 11.

My mom broke into my rainbow-painted eighth grade classroom at Fairwell School at 10:00 AM that day, her hair wild and her voice fake-calm. She whisked me home, where Dad himself waited. Dad, in daylight: his face as he hugged me as sobered as Mom's. We sat around the TV, Dad muttering about the Palestinians and scratching his curly beard.

All that long morning, Mom softly admonished Dad for his angry comments. Dad, drunk not from beer but from nonstop TV (usually it was on only for the single hour I was allowed). All of us drunk, that day, from the planes flying over and over into the buildings that seemed—the weirdest part to me—not to explode but to disintegrate. Zap. Gone.

Mom kept smoothing my own wild hair like I was her little boy again.

"Yeah," I egged on my madder-and-madder dad, when he mumbled something about nukes. "They can't do this to *us*."

Mom and Dad nodded distractedly, glued to some update. I

slipped into the day, the sunny silent sky. No planes flying. Only one neighbor, Mr. Spivac, out sheepishly mowing his lawn.

"Couldn't watch anymore," he called to me on my bike.

I whizzed down Riverview Road hill to usually busy Mystic Ave. *They* can't do this to *us*, I chanted to myself as I rode up and down near-empty Mystic, pumping hard with the thrill of un-Fairwell thoughts. Not that it was clear who *they* were. Not that I had anything clear in mind as I biked back and forth before the Rundown House on the River.

A once-luxurious ranch house on Mystic Avenue, facing Mystic River. Your overgrown yard was deserted like every other yard that day. Where was the maybe-Middle-Eastern family? The boys? I pedaled way faster than my norm, imagining my home in flames: Dad off on a trip and me rescuing Mom; then me attacking back, machine-gunning those scary-brave skateboarding boys who'd made me afraid to bike near this house, till this day.

And who was that zooming toward me?

"Whoa," I called out, startled. I almost rammed the only other biker on Mystic. His bike wobbled, but TJ stayed tall in its seat. His T-shirt proclaimed across his broad chest, IT MUST SUCK TO BE YOU. I straightened in my DRUMLIN FARMS AUDUBON SOCIETY tee, squaring my narrower shoulders. I shut my lips over my braces, bike to bike with a blank-faced acne-scarred Arlington High dude. We gave soldierly nods. Then we pedaled off equally fast, both of us thinking (I wouldn't find out till later) the same things. Yet it was me you noticed, maybe, from your belowground window.

You: the girl in the basement. You: the girl named One.

At Fairwell, the rest of September, our teachers got teary-eyed talking about different gods and different cultures and Not Hating. Gentle Mr. Hamal, our Saudi-born computer tutor, visited each class, telling us in a voice almost too soft to hear about Real Muslims.

What about the freaking unreal ones? I thought. Not that I was any expert on religion. Me: son of a so-called lapsed-Catholic Irish Mom and a Just-Hanukkah Jewish Dad.

Me: all-American everything-and-nothing kind of guy.

After school, almost every day, I kept up my patrols on the sidewalk in front of your house. Don't bike down to Mystic, the mothers of Riverview Road used to warn us kids. But at fourteen, I was old enough to brave the Mystic Avenue traffic and troll by the fancy houses on the river. Fancy, anyhow, compared to ours.

From your bare basement room—that room I will never stop seeing inside my head—those middle-class houses of Riverview Road must have looked pretty good. Like you thought I looked, at first. A nice boy, everyone always said, despite my shaggy hair. What Mom called my Jewish-Irish hair. When I sketched cartoons of me and my six fellow eighth graders—gentle cartoons, since we'd been taught never to make fun of each other—I always drew myself hidden by a Scooby Doo mop-top. *A lurker*, Dad told me oddly. *Like me.*

All September, into October, I'd park my bike behind your house's hydrangeas. One early October day, through the hydrangea branches, your garage door rose. Your yard filled with three women in head shawls who draped damp patterned clothes on the yard's bushes to dry. Following the women came the hyper, black-haired boys.

The women retreated inside in serene single file. The boys swooped up and down the driveway as I'd often seen them do from a distance, pre-9/11.

Hairpin-spinning onto Mystic on battered bikes and suicidal skateboards.

Me, I fled. I veered around the soaring, spinning boys. I pedaled all the way up Riverview Road hill to its peak. Panting, I gazed out toward the distant, ghostly buildings of Boston. I imagined I was somehow guarding those buildings, sitting tall in my bike seat, the way I did with TJ beside me.

"Joe," I told TJ, instead of Josiah, the late-October day we exchanged names.

That was the day Arabic graffiti had appeared, sloppily painted, on your house's garage door. Slashed there by the bold skateboarding boys? Or by sneaky neighborhood white boys like us? TJ and I had both stopped our bikes behind the ragged hydrangeas to contemplate the unreadable message.

Then TJ gave me a mumbled account of the "fucking A-rab boys" behavior at Arlington High. How they hung together and rarely spoke, except to claim that their father (the old guy we'd glimpsed being loaded in Symmes Medical Center vans in a wheelchair) was a Saudi prince.

I volunteered in a low voice that my dad called this house Arlington's own Terrorist Cell. TJ replied that his dad called it way worse. Then TJ spat hard into the bushes. His face looked soldierly behind his mask of acne. I didn't dare spit, too, scared I'd do it wrong. Was this tough, football-fit Arlington High guy somehow joining forces with me?

Me: Josiah Simon, who'd never even been allowed to play Guns.

Me: a Fairwell School boy from a small, cozy class of eighth graders, as familiar to each other as brothers and sisters. Me: a boy who before 9/11 used to "find my thrill" biking by Arlington High to steal glimpses of the unfamiliar giggling girls and daunting jocks crowding the playground there, jostling each other. Fights brewing?

I'd never learned to fight at Fairwell. I'd learned *not* to fight. Something I hoped TJ never found out.

"See ya, Joe," TJ muttered as he biked off. The two of us connected by our shared sense that your house needed watching.

Day after Halloween, after school, I biked down to Mystic and waited behind the blossomless hydrangeas for TJ. I was bursting to tell him about Halloween night, how it practically proved our suspicions about the house.

When I heard the *whoosh* of his mountain bike tires, I fought my big, braces-revealing smile. The bushes rustled; TJ halted beside me, breathing hard, slipping off his black helmet.

"Whassup, Joe," he mumbled into the branches.

"Lots is up," I told TJ, breathing his sweat even in the chill November air, he rode his bike so hard. Like he'd been as eager to see me as I was to see him.

Before I could say why, the Terrorist Cell garage door whined and opened. The Arabic lettering folded neatly up and away.

The women came out in their usual head shawls. The most bosomy one dragged at her sides two single-bed mattresses. These she dumped in the knee-high grass. The women stood around the mattresses, wielding brooms.

"Whoa-ho," TJ muttered, like they might attack us. He snorted.

The women beat the mattresses. I shifted, feeling a hard-on stiffen inside my zipped jeans, against my bike seat. Not that the women were sexy in their shapeless robes; not that I had any control over my hard-ons. I tried to snort like TJ, but it came out a cough. I watched the women gripping those brooms with their strong-looking hands. My hard-on felt like a broom handle. Finally they finished, my hard-on beginning to deflate as mysteriously as it had arisen. God; would I ever be able to control it, use it like a real man? The women trooped inside. The garage door stayed half open, with half the gracefully slashed Arabic lettering on display.

I leaned toward TJ. "Know what those A-rab boys dressed up as last night?"

"Huh? You seen 'em, last night?" TJ stopped picking at his zit.

I gave a chin-jerk nod. TJ's blond eyebrows rose when I described in a whisper the boys in their ghutra, their blood-stained bandage attire.

"'And a dead American,'" TJ repeated in hoarse, whispered disgust. Then he spat extra hard into the bushes. The dried leaves shivered. "What they want us to be." TJ shook his impressively spiked head. "Dead and all . . ."

He jerked his head toward the other side of Mystic, toward the upwardly climbing rows of homes on Riverview. TJ lived in the more crowded East Arlington.

"Dead to the world," I echoed, like we were the only ones who weren't.

"We'll all be dead for real, 'less someone does something." TJ abruptly turned toward the half open garage. He motioned me to follow. "C'mon."

Before I could think (overthink, Dad says), TJ and I were ducking our heads. We crept around the bushes, the only barrier to your yard.

"C'mon," TJ commanded again over his bigger-than-my shoulder, like I was going to be the one to wimp out. We scurried down the driveway. It was TJ who hesitated, standing in his hydrangea hunch beside the garage.

So I went first. I bent double, ducked under the door. The floor was white concrete, stained with oil like any garage. I scrambled to my feet, panting, alone in the vast, dim, two-car-with-no-car garage. Was TJ coming at all? I wondered in a mix of pride and panic.

I went first, I imagined somehow saying to my dad. Though I couldn't tell him—or could I? Wasn't this the sort of thing he'd been waiting to hear from me? Some exploit, some adventure, some proof I was no Mama's Boy?

I stepped blindly forward, blinking in the dimness. As my eyes adjusted, I saw (mentally I took notes like a real spy) piled boxes labeled INSULIN. Metal devices that looked medical. And the infamous plastic U.S. AIR DELIVERY bins piled in one corner, neatly.

A door leading inside stood ajar, a gleaming tile floor visible. A kitchen? I inched back toward the garage door, not sure if I was going to duck out and flee or drag TJ in with me.

"Dude, dude—somethin's happening out here," he stage-whispered through the low garage door opening. "They're on the fucking *roof!*"

"*Fuck!*" I whispered back. On the roof? Like snipers with rifles?

I dropped to my knees on the cold, oil-sticky concrete. I peered under the garage door in time to see boys swoop down from above. Rough thumps and gasps and laughter. Their sneakered feet bounced on the freshly beaten mattresses. So they'd jumped down from the single-story roof? To catch us?

"Hey, yo: Pig! You offa here, *Pig*—" One boy's breathless voice rose, sounding startled. Gracelessly, TJ scrambled into view. He booked up the driveway, lunging toward the bushes, his bike. Ditching me. The boys bounced off the mattresses, racing after TJ.

"Pig, Pig! You OFFA here—"

Outta here, did they mean? How in hell would *I* get Outta Here? I bent lower, still kneeling, when your light hand touched my shoulder.

I jerked upright, wobbling on my knees.

"No hurt, no hurt," you begged me, holding up small womanly hands. You wouldn't hurt me, or I shouldn't hurt you?

Standing on my knees, I met your stare, that's how short you were.

Girl-sized, but with breasts poking out under your blank T-shirt. Maybe you were fourteen like me? Your round face slashed by bright watchful eyes. Your bangs cut at a jagged angle. Your mouth half open, showing big teeth like mine. Lips peachy pale, soft looking.

Kinda cute, I thought through my fear. Not Arab but Asian—but why?

You jerked out a thin arm, tattooed with a blurry dragonfly. You shoved a folded note into my hand. Head bowed so your angled bangs hid one eye, you whispered one word.

Please?

Then a commanding woman's voice called from the kitchen, "One? One?"

You spun around, your ponytail bouncing. I wanted to grab that shiny ponytail, pull you back, look at you some more. But you slipped across the garage, shut the door behind you. You left me sealed in doubled dark.

Too dark to read your note, except to see that it was sloppily block-printed in English.

Outside the garage, the boys were jabbering in English, too; like ordinary boys, high after the thrill of chasing off TJ.

"A-gain! Gonna go a-gain," a soft-voiced boy called. And, sounding like any boy anywhere: "Race you—"

Their sneakered feet thumped across the driveway; my heart thudded. Then they were veering as one and thundering on around the house. To climb some ladder or drainpipe up to the roof again, jump again?

I stuffed your note in my jeans pocket. I wriggled under the door into an empty yard, empty mattresses knocked askew. Awaiting those boys diving like paratroopers from above.

I ran. I charged through the high dry grass, fought hydrangea branches for my handlebars. Letting my helmet swing from those bars, I mounted the bike. I could've veered right toward Arlington Center, East Arlington, where TJ might have been waiting along the way for me.

Instead I veered left, toward the Whole Foods Market a mile up Mystic and its parking lot where I could read your note all alone. Where TJ couldn't see that note, or my shaking hands.

MY NAME LE TI ONE.

I AM VIETNAM OF BIRTH.

MY FAMILY OF HIGH ESTEEM BUT FALL INTO NEED.

MY VISA TAKEN BY PRINCE.

I AM OF WORK TO PRINCE FAMILY

BUT NOT OF PAY.

PAY IS NOTHING HERE I FALL INTO NEED
ALL KINDNESS MUCH I PAY BACK—
LE TI ONE

I did not tell Mom or Dad or the FBI or even TJ.

Because it was me you had given the note to. I would somehow find out what you needed, then I'd figure out what I should do for you. I pedaled back home from the Whole Foods lot, tall in my bike seat. Holding in my jeans pocket the first secret of my life.

A real secret, not some superhero cartoon I'd sketch then crumple. Mockingbird Man with his feathered arms or Otter Man, slinky and impervious to cold. What Mom called me: her Otter Boy swimming the chill offseason waters of Walden Pond with her.

Why as I biked was I thinking of Walden Pond, of the Popsicle hard-ons I got under Walden Pond waters sometimes, swimming with Mom and watching distant girls onshore and wondering how I'd ever find a girl who was, well, mine.

I parked the bike in our single-car garage, as dark in that November dusk as yours. And I double-checked for your folded note in my pocket.

I wore the same jeans the next day to Fairwell, carrying your note against my butt. But I didn't touch the note till we were filing out for the day, down the central rainbow-painted corridor. I shuffled behind Alison Jester (Alison Jet-Star in my R-rated cartoons). She smoothed back her already-smooth butterscotchy hair. For once, I ignored her like she always ignored me. I thought of your shiny back hair. I fingered your note. Would you somehow become my (I'd read that in Vietnam first names came last) *One*.

"Comin' over?" Joo Lee asked me, barely making it a question.

We stepped out together into the noon sun. Wednesdays were short days at Fairwell, one truly cool thing about our funky little school. Wednesday afternoons were for Teacher

Enrichment. Usually, I'd bike over to Joo's to Game-Boy the afternoon away.

"Naw, I gotta—see someone."

"Who?" Joo straightened his sliding-down glasses. Too-thick glasses he'd have been teased for at most schools. Joo folded his skinny but strong arms. He always beat me at thumb-wrestling. Joo'd had his own crush on Alison; Joo Lee was the only one I'd shown my Alison Jet-Star cartoons to. He'd have been the logical person for me to tell.

"Later, bro," I told him instead in my new TJ mumble.

Then I left Joo behind, climbing in my Mom's waiting humming Volvo.

TJ in Arlington High wouldn't be off on a Wednesday afternoon. He wouldn't be there to act tough, then leave me stranded in a terrorist garage. Wouldn't be there to horn in on you.

I booked my bike down Riverview Road, too fast, heading straight onto Mystic. I whizzed across a break in the traffic like the supercool superhero I felt I was fast becoming. Then I was careening toward boys on skateboards.

"Yo, Pig, where you GO-ing?" one hollered. I steered away from him.

A horn blared; an SUV barely missed clipping my bike. And I glimpsed—through the open garage door, holding an armful of cloths—you.

You: watching me like you longed to leap on board my bike and wrap your slim legs around me and escape. You: your black hair undone, blowing around your tensed shoulders. Had anyone besides Mom ever watched me so intently?

I veered toward the mouth of your driveway, straight toward the skateboarder boy hurling himself into my path. We crashed midair.

"Holy shit!" I called as I tipped off my bike, hit gritty sidewalk. The boy flung backward into the bushes. But he sprang back up as if made of rubber. Scrawny, younger than Rasha. He bounced on his heels, gaping down at me. I lay beside my fallen bike, its wheel still spinning.

"Rakeen, Rakeen—" the kid called. Like he'd bagged some prey they'd all been after. But he didn't know what to do with it, me.

Boys thudded up the driveway. I sat abruptly and snuffled and feared I'd burst into tears, my elbow throbbing. I swiped at my nose as the bigger boys hustled around the bushes.

And I saw, on my palm, blood. Shit: my nose was bleeding. I raised my hapless face to theirs: four boys, Rakeen from Halloween the oldest. He stepped closest, standing over me. His lean, strong-boned face stood out, the most sober.

I heaved myself to my feet. Despite his manly gaze, Rakeen was slightly shorter than me. Blood trickled from my nose. I brushed past Rakeen, stumbled like a wounded bull down their driveway. Heading, instinctively, toward you.

You'd dropped a pile of elaborately patterned cloths. All but one. You stepped toward me holding out that crumpled gold and red cloth.

"You her, you her," you cried, scolding the boys following behind me. *You hurt*, I thought you were saying as you stopped before me.

You gripped my elbow, your girl-sized hand strong.

You hurt him. Or maybe, addressed to me: *You are hurt.*

Either way, you sounded pissed, appalled at everyone's bad manners. Maybe, young though you seemed, you were sitter or nanny to these wild boys. The boys, anyhow, had shut up. They followed us in abashed silence.

You led bleeding me straight into the wide-open garage. You seated me on a splintery wood crate marked TANGERINES. It creaked, plywood popping.

"I'b OK," I managed through my blood-choked nose.

"Shh, shh," you soothed like a professional—what? What were they not paying you to be? You shook back your jaggedly cut bangs. You sat beside me so your thin thigh pressed mine. No girl my age had ever sat so close to me.

"Let-me," you told me matter-of-fact, one word.

Then you squeezed my nose hard. You bent me forward so the cloth muffled my mouth. So those boys could sneak up behind me?

Dead American, dead American. Would they chop off my head the way terrorists were threatening on TV to chop off some U.S. hostage's head?

I bolted upright, bumping your arm. I locked gazes with you. Through your cool bangs, you were studying me hard, making me hold my breath. No girl had ever looked at me that way, like I was somehow—but how?—hugely important, just then. Your breath was held, too.

The boys backed up, maybe ready to shut the garage, hold me hostage. I had to wrench my head around, force my eyes off you.

"Don't touch that door," I blurted. "My mom'll call the police, the FBI!"

At FBI you stood, clutching the bloody cloth, looking purely afraid. Staring at me frozen-faced, like I could either wreck you or save you.

The younger boy piped up: "Our father, he is a Saudi Prince! Your FBI, you cannot touch him! He, he—"

Rakeen shot this eager-eyed kid a look: Shut up.

Get out, I told myself, though I wanted to stay there with you.

Turning unsteadily, I stumbled toward the still-open garage door. Rakeen muttered as I passed, "Let the Piggy go cry to his mommy. . ."

I swiped the thickening blood from my nose, angry at my own teary eyes. I hesitated in the garage doorway. You, One, were the one to follow, on light feet. You halted in the doorway, too, as if you didn't dare step farther.

Rakeen was admonishing the younger boy in harsh-sounding Arabic.

"Help," you barely breathed to me. You shot an anxious glance toward Rakeen, who still scolded his brother.

"No moany," you added under your breath. *Moany?*

"I'll help you," I dared whisper, just as Rakeen stopped talking.

"Sank—" You reached out with your deft, cold-fingered hands. Your head bowed, your bangs hiding both eyes. Your breath held again—like mine? Just for a second, you clasped my hand. Man, One. What that did to me: your touch.

"Hey! Leave her alone, Pig Boy—" Rakeen shouted over the hammering of my heart. "You get away from him, One."

Rakeen strode toward us, his bony shoulders tensed and his head high as if he were, in fact, the son of a prince. "What are you doing to her?"

Rakeen's narrowed gaze moved from your to my dumbstruck face. I backed out of the garage. My lips slack, my braces showing.

"What is he asking you, One? To get dirty for his dirty dollars?"

You turned with brisk dignity. You shook your head firmly at Rakeen. A babysitter shake. Then, your face hidden again by those cool jagged bangs, you scurried around him. You marched past his watching brothers, into their house.

I spun round. I hurtled up the driveway, amazed not to be chased. Maybe Rakeen was scared of me, too? Of what I might know? I fumbled in the bushes for my bike. I did know you'd meant not *moany* but money. No money.

I was the one who moaned, in your basement room. The secret of your house turned out not to be hidden bombs, but hidden you.

My bike seat rubbed my crotch as I pedaled faster than ever across Mystic, snuffling blood. *Get dirty for his dirty dollars?* Rakeen had asked so strangely. Like you were—god, what *were* you? Why were you so scared?

Back up Riverview Road, I pedaled to my empty house. To my bedroom where I jerked off, then reread your note. I couldn't stop myself. First I'd kiss you gently, so your big teeth and my braces wouldn't bump. Then I'd let your slim strong hands do a hand job on me; your soft girl lips do a blow job. And I was jerking off again. Harder than I'd ever done before.

That weekend, I almost told Dad. He was home for a change; we were playing self-conscious football catch on our cool, darkening lawn. As we tossed the ball, Dad asked me what I'd been up to. I found myself saying I'd been thinking about those Halloween kids, the Terrorist Trick-or-Treaters.

"You worried about them?" Dad tossed me the ball too lightly. "You scared they really are terrorists, son?"

Dad's "son" came out stagey. I shrugged, annoyed. I tossed the football back extra hard while Dad was smoothing his beard. Dad scrambled to catch it. Then he hesitated. Concern or suspicion lit his distracted, dark eyes. "*Are* you scared of them, those people in that house?"

Dad hurled the ball. When it smacked my palm, I pictured your breast filling my cupped hand, fitting like it was meant to be.

"Nope," I lied as I threw the ball back.

I stole the money for you—*filched*, I told myself—from Maid Pro. The Maid Pros (as Mom liked to say, instead of calling them what they were, the maids) cleaned our house every week: Wednesday afternoons, when I was usually at Joo's. Mom always left the Maids a thirty-buck tip. I'd thought of stealing it before, when I spent my birthday checks too fast on art supplies, when I begged Dad to reconsider about the allowance he said I had to *earn*.

Wednesday afternoon, one week after my nosebleed, I told my spacey mom I was off to Joo's. She was heading out to an art teacher paper-making workshop. I stalled, the last to leave. Shakily, I slipped the Maid Pro envelope in my denim jacket pocket. Then I pedaled away into the sunlit cold.

I'd avoided biking past your house in the week since my nosebleed. I didn't want to cross paths with TJ. I didn't want

TJ asking me what happened in your garage, didn't want cooler, older TJ taking over my story.

The story of how I'd (this part was still fuzzy) rescue you.

I had filled my sketchpads with dramatic black-and-white images of me carrying you out of that house, the two of us whizzing off on my bike. At the same time, with the thinking part of my brain, I was convincing myself I first needed to talk to you, really talk. Get your whole story, all the facts. Then I really would find you help. And you'd be grateful, for life.

MUCH, you had promised in print. ALL KINDNESS MUCH I PAY BACK.

Feeling watched by every shaded window in the house, I stepped toward your closed garage. Then I heard a faint rapping: your fist on the garage door window. Your hand pointing me around the back of the house.

I ducked, pushing apart dry knee-high grass. An American GI in 'Nam, trudging through a rice field after the Vietnamese girl he will—what? Rescue, I reminded my tensed-up self.

The grass behind the house looked even taller and deader than the grass in front. A door opened; I stumbled down two overgrown concrete steps. You held open that lowest-level door. I stepped inside like you were my doorman, squinting in sudden fluorescent brightness. A rec room?

Or, anyway, a carpeted basement half filled with a ping-pong table and carelessly stacked skateboards, boy bikes. From the floor above, I heard the sound of televised explosions. Shit. Not those boys, skipping school?

"Are you, are we—alone?"

You shook your head hard at my dopey question. "No-no," you told me. "All-time. They watch. Old man at doctor. But boys…" She rolled her eyes toward the ceiling. More muffled explosions and screams and sirens.

A Terrorist Cell. So I reminded myself as, daringly, I pulled shut the door to the outside. I faced you in the harsh rec room light. You wore a faded sweatshirt—but clean, ironed-looking. Your breasts showing beneath.

You pushed back your shiny bangs. Pink acne dotted your forehead. Your round face looked coarser skinned than in my fantasies. Your angled bangs fell back into place, over one eye. Your other eye and your hair shone brighter than ever; your mouth looked ready to smile.

You nodded at a shut door behind the ping-pong table. A secret storage room? Where they kept their anthrax and bombs?

"See see—" You stepped over to that door, opening it.

"W-what? See what?" I edged around the ping-pong table, reminding myself I was here to hear your story, find out your facts. "This—is where you live?"

You nodded. We stood together at the doorway to a small paneled room, a mattress (one of the battered, jumped-upon mattresses) on the floor. Clean sheets flung back at the foot of the mattress. Tacked to the wall above it: a piece of raw silk printed with a purplish-black dragonfly. Clothes folded in a cardboard box under the room's smeary basement window.

"My mother. Before die, Saigon hospital. She find me—Jiluwi family." You stepped into the room first. "She not know—they not—pay."

You looked at me like: You see my room. What're you gonna do about it? I stepped in the doorway. I fumbled in my jacket pocket, tugged out the Maid Pro money. You snatched the bills from me, fingered them. Then you looked up at me through your bangs, disappointment in your all black, seen-it-all eyes.

"Sank," you murmured, but I felt it was your heart that had sunk.

"S-sorry, maybe you wanted—I know you want—more?" I took one step into your unlit room. Standing in its center, so slumped, you looked small.

"*More*?" You seized on that word like it was the only one you understood. And you tossed the Maid Pro money into the box that held the folded clothes. You stepped right up to me so we stood toe to toe. You shook back your bangs and nodded. "Yes-yes. You give more, if, if—*you* want more?"

"No, no, I mean yes," I stammered, stiffening up all over, including in my jeans. Wishing TJ was here with me. No: wishing I were TJ, the kind of cool guy a girl might want. But I swallowed, pressing my lips in a manly line over my braces—was it possible you wanted me? Me, not just *more moany*.

I want *moany*, I thought. I blurted: "I don't have more. Not with me. First I want to, um, know more. About you, I mean. Are you, like, a h-hostage? Should I, like, call someone for you? Call, um—the F-B-I?"

"No, no—" you blurted back, echoing me. More scared than me, I sensed as you brushed by me. And you shut your room door.

God, were we locked in? You flicked on the light like you didn't want me getting any (too late on that) ideas. You shook your head at me, sternly. "No-no F-B-I! No-no, lis-ten: what you want? Want more, got more?"

I shook my head, in over my head. "No, no. It's OK, look, I won't call the FBI, OK? I don't even know *how* to call the FBI, OK?" I stepped up to you. With the door shut, I felt the chill of your little room. Without thinking, I took hold of your arms, slim but hard-muscled under your sweatshirt.

You didn't pull back. You just lowered your eyes behind your bangs.

"You help? You—pay?" You asked in a straightforward whisper.

"Yeah, I—I promise I'll help you," I told you, quiet too, holding your arms tighter to keep my hands from shaking. "But no, I'm not, like, giving you—pay. See? Not pay. Just, if you want, um—" I don't know what made me say it, the words just popped out. "Play. We can, like—play."

Play? God, had I really said that, standing in this bedroom, holding this girl's—this woman's—arms? You kept your eyes low. I knew you could see or sense, at my zipped crotch, my hard-on.

You gave a brief uncertain laugh like a cough.

"Play?" you repeated, like you hadn't heard that word in a long time. "If you want?" you repeated, too. But I'd meant to be asking you.

"*You* want?" I asked, my voice even more uncertain than yours. My grip on you stayed firm, like I knew what I was doing. "How—how old are you?"

"Eighteen." You answered so fast it might've been a lie.

Might've been something you'd been trained to say. Maybe (the thought flashed fast) you'd been one of those teenage prostitutes in Vietnam, on CNN?

So I should let go of you. I sniffled, my nose slightly runny in the basement chill. I thought of leaning down and kissing you, but I hesitated, tasting the metal of my braces.

"I—" you began again. You drew a breath like you were going to tell me what I'd supposedly come for: the story of you. But you stopped yourself, too.

"I sank you," you repeated instead in an odd, stiff voice, bowing your head. You slid downward, out of my grasp. You knelt before me, just like in my drawings. You faced my stirred-up crotch. Man, my cock jumped at that. So stiff so fast. You didn't look up. "Sank you, you help. You want—we play?"

Your hands: so steady you must've done this before. You were no dumb virgin like me. Maybe you *were* eighteen. Maybe you *did* want to play, like me? Did you—could you—like me?

My head on its own jerked a nod.

Your quick hands: unzipping my jeans. God, was this real? I held myself still, frozen. Should I help you, stop you? I couldn't hear anything but my heavy breaths. Effortful breaths; I couldn't think of anything but breathing. I was so hard as your fingers freed me that I moaned.

Moany; you wanted only *moany*. You were desperate for *moany*. So I was telling myself in my head. But my head was just nodding and nodding.

"Yeah," I mumbled. Then I gasped as you roughly tugged my jeans down around my knees. So I was bound at the knees; so I couldn't leave this room.

Tock, tock, tock.

You bent forward. Your bangs brushed my balls. Your tongue flicked against my penis. Against *me*. Lights flashed on inside me; I squeezed shut my eyes. I sucked in my breath to moan again. But *tock tock* stopped me.

A freaking ping-pong ball? *Tock tock.* Those boys, down from upstairs? Boys playing ping-pong right outside your door? You must hear it, too, I thought in blurred panic as I blinked my eyes open. Stop, I started to say.

But I looked down to see your bowed head go lower, closer.

Your cushy-lipped, smooth-tongued mouth surrounded me. *Me, me.* All engulfed in moist pressure; all of me funneled into the hardness you sucked. "*God*," I moaned, clenching my teeth.

You sucked me harder. The *tocks* had stopped; everything stopped. Pleasure and pressure gripped me, my fullness about to burst.

The door cracked open, hard. And your mouth opened, releasing me. Strings of warmed spit. I jolted as you pulled away; I cried out in protest and staggered sideways. Blinking and reeling, still so hard.

Rakeen Jiluwi stood in the doorway. He was waving a ping-pong paddle in one hand and something small and shiny in the other. "What has he done to you?" he demanded. He pointed, sweeping his paddle toward me.

I bumped your mattress, falling. I landed on my bare ass on the mattress. And I grabbed handfuls of your sheet to cover me, my poking-out penis. Dumb American about to be killed.

"Pig!" Rakeen turned his fury on me. He stepped to the edge of the mattress still wielding the ping-pong paddle. He whacked the side of my face.

Smack against my flesh: a blow that popped my eyes out. So I barely saw, stinging, what else he held. Waving it in his other hand: a mini cell-phone camera. "I took a *picture*, Pig. I caught a *picture* of you and her and, and—"

Caught, I was thinking in smack-faced fear. Rakeen was stuffing the shiny cell in his jeans pocket. Fast; everything just then happening fast. Behind Rakeen in the doorway, the smallest brother hovered.

"Rasha, go get Rasha," Rakeen turned to holler at the boy. Before he turned back, I pulled myself to my feet, fumbling. I yanked my pants up over my half-swollen hard-on. You still knelt on the floor, regarding Rakeen and me with blank-faced shock or calm. Were you and Rakeen working together?

"She's *ours*, but *we* never *defile* her, Pig," Rakeen told me, waving that paddle at my stinging face. "Muslim never touch the not-Muslim girl. I will tell your mommy. I will *show* your mommy you are such a dirty greedy pig—"

My face burned, but I blurted out: "What about *her*?" I pointed to you, your blank face suddenly tense, on alert. "What—what's she *doing* here? Don't you know it's illegal to, to—to *hold* her here?"

A flicker of something uncertain showed in Rakeen's stare. He blurted out his next words, sounding tense and defensive. "I am aware, yes, of your *laws*; I tell my mother, yes, about these laws . . ." Rakeen shot a pointed glance at One, like that last admission was for her. But Rakeen re-faced me, talking on like he couldn't stop. "You think we do not know, my brothers and me, that you piggies call the police on Halloween? We knew the police would call our mother, warn her like we try to warn her how much trouble you pigs could make us—"

Here he stopped himself, shot another glance at intently listening One. She looked like her brain was racing, like mine. So Rakeen knew it was illegal to hold her here; he'd wanted his mother to be scared by police calls. Wanted her to let One go, maybe?

I drew my breath to somehow ask, but Rakeen raised his paddle again at me. "This all—it is not of your business! You *outta* here—"

I bulled past him, past you. I lunged into the doorway and charged across the rec room. Rasha came rushing down the basement's carpeted steps. In one sidelong glance, I recognized his skinny body and round, long-lashed eyes. He looked scared. I seized the doorknob. I thrust open the door and ran into the cold sun, the tall dead grass, all still there.

God, god, I thought as I ran, breathless, through grass and up the driveway. Someone shouted behind me. I mounted my bike in one leap, my pants still half zipped. I pedaled faster than ever before.

The bike seat rubbed my crotch through my jeans. I gripped my handlebars, hearing in my mind Mom's voice: the question she used to call to me when I came out of the bathroom, till I told her I was too old for her to ask.

All clean? she'd sing-song to her boy. *Are you all clean?*

This time, I did tell. It was me, see.

I can't really tell you that, except in my head. But I tell it in my head all the time. See, I was scared. I'd never been so scared, never been hit hard like Rakeen hit me with the damn paddle. Who knew what else he would do? I'd never, really, been scared at all before.

Home from your house, shaking, I took a long shower, my penis raw and pink. Despite the steamy heat, I couldn't stop shaking, questions raining down on me with hard hot water.

Had Rakeen really taken a clear photo of us? Would he somehow show that photo to my mom, tell Mom what I had done? And what *had* I done, exactly? What would Mom say? That I'd taken advantage of a poor desperate girl who might be—for weeks I'd known she might be—in real trouble.

Or maybe it was Rakeen who'd be in trouble, his family. He'd admitted it, I reminded myself as I cranked off the faucet. He knew what his family was doing was illegal. He was scared I'd get them in trouble before he got me. So much trouble, maybe, they'd be arrested; they wouldn't be able to get to me? And One—maybe One would go free? Because of me?

Wrapped in my towel, my mom making supper downstairs, I did it. I called on my own cell phone, not the FBI, but the Arlington Police. I told them I couldn't give my name. But I did give them yours. I told them your visa was supposedly being held by the Saudi family in the house by the river.

You've got to see, One. I was thinking (standing there in my bedroom, on my cell phone, shaking with my towel sliding down) you might die. You might die or disappear or become a teen prostitute for real and it might be my fault. So, see, I was just doing what I'd been taught to do all my life, by my mom.

If you're ever separated from me, ever in trouble, find a policeman.

A girl, yes, I told the sympathetic-sounding lady on the phone, between the shrieky beeps that meant this call was taped. A girl is being—*held* inside that house. I swear. A girl named (I even spelled it before I hung up) Le Ti One.

Wednesday evening, Thursday morning, my heart exploded each time the phone rang. I rushed to grab it before Mom. Each time it was my long-distance dad.

Asking, "How's it going, kiddo?"

I'm not a kiddo, I wanted to answer. But what was I, now?

My heart exploded again—thudding my throat so hard I couldn't believe Mom couldn't hear—as she drove me home from school on Thursday. An Arlington Police car was parked in front of your house. The garage door was shut all the way, the graffiti at last painted over. Painted last night? Or had it been gone yesterday (it felt like ages before) and I hadn't noticed?

"Hmm," Mom murmured, flipping her left turn signal for Riverview Road. "Looks like the police are finally looking into that—strange house."

I jerked one nod. *The jig is up*, I thought, as Mom's Volvo climbed Riverview. In the passenger side rearview, I eyed the cop car on Mystic.

God, what had I done calling the cops when you wanted me to call no one? What would Rakeen and those boys tell the cops? That I'd "defiled" this girl (what was it Rakeen had shouted?), this girl his family thought they owned?

She's ours but we never defile her.

In my room that long frozen afternoon, as the year's first snowflakes spiraled outside my window, as I braced myself for an Arlington police officer's hammering knock, I tore into tiny pieces all the cartoon sketches I'd made of you, Jet-Black Jet-Star. You with your inky hair hiding one eye and both breasts; you chained up, pleading with your all-black eyes for help.

The next frosty morning, the *Arlington Advocate* arrived at our doorstep. Only this day I was up at dawn awaiting its arrival. I was expecting maybe an item in the police blotter, usually filled only with high school vandalism and the occasional "domestic incident." But there you were, One, on page one, below the fold. A photo of the house, not of you.

VIETNAMESE GIRL HELD AS SLAVE IN RIVERFRONT HOME

Two columns summed up the story. Acting on an anonymous tip (my pulse thickened at that singular "tip," like there'd only been one, mine) police had "visited" the Mystic River address and questioned several female residents. Later, after securing a search warrant, they returned to find the fully furnished home deserted—except for a teenage girl identifying herself as Vietnamese who was hiding in a basement room. She claimed that the family who had held her as an unpaid domestic had left on an "extended trip."

The young woman further claimed that the Jiluwi family had extricated her from Vietnam a year before and had then "confiscated" her visa and enlisted her unpaid services as a servant. Police were seeking information on the family, consisting of four sons, numerous female relatives, and an ailing patriarch alleged to be a distant relative of the Saudi royal family.

The Vietnamese girl was now, the article curtly concluded, being "held by U.S. immigration officials." The Jiluwi family "appears to have fled the state."

Weeks later, feeling I was fleeing, I sat strapped into our Volvo's backseat for our drive to Grandma's for Thanksgiving. As Dad swung onto Route 2 toward Concord, I piped up hoarsely from the backseat, like a kid: "Hey Dad, what's it mean to be 'held by immigration officials'? Like that, that girl in the paper—"

"Oh that house," Mom chimed in. "Those awful boys, on Halloween . . ."

Dad nodded vigorously, rallying his best Holiday Dad manner.

"Yes, well—that girl. If she really was here illegally, she may very well be sent back to Vietnam. Which she probably doesn't want, to say the least. See, son, sometimes immigrants want so badly not to be sent back to their own countries, they put up with any sort of treatment just to stay here."

I swallowed, remembering how scared you'd been of me calling the FBI. "And you think that old guy in the wheelchair really is a prince?"

Dad at the wheel shrugged. We were gliding along snow-cleared Route 2. "Sure. As I understand it, there are hundreds of so-called princes connected to that Saudi family. Half the country claims to be royalty. They're born with servants. Working for next to nothing, for life. It's a—"

"A different culture," Mom put in beside him, sleepy-sounding.

"And the sons of bitches miss it," Dad finished boldly, taking on his harder-edged, talk-radio tone. "The princely life they led back there . . . it gives them all this goddamned—this inborn sense of entitlement."

"We've got servants, too," I ventured after a driving pause.

Wakened by my claim, Mom cut in, "What, you mean the Maid Pros? But sweetie, we pay—and tip them very well for the work they do."

"Not lately," I muttered, thinking of the thirty dollars I'd stolen.

"What was that?" Mom turned her mussed ginger-haired head, her pale eyes flashing concern and maybe something more. "You OK, Josiah? Did that story in the paper upset you? Because of what happened to us with those boys at Halloween? Believe me, I was upset, too. That's why I did call the police, the very next day. But of course we had no way of knowing there was a, a—"

"A slave in our town," I finished for her, flatly.

"Oh, sweetie," Mom told me with a sigh, turning back to the cleared country road ahead. "Don't worry yourself over it. We tried. We did what we could."

I biked to your abandoned house one early-December day.

I mean: to the house where you were held. Now you were being held elsewhere, by Immigration Officials.

I could have held you, I thought on the sidewalk, hugging myself in my denim jacket, its cloth too thin for December weather. I could have hugged you instead of just letting you kneel in front of me. Like you, for those charged-up minutes in your basement room, were mine.

At home in my own room on my PC, I kept Googling your story. It hadn't made it beyond the *Boston Herald*, and there were no photos of you.

But there might be, I thought, as I hugged myself hard against the cold. A photo of you and me out there somewhere. A photo in Rakeen's cell-phone camera. A photo that might pop up on my computer screen or my Mom's screen, someday.

Shivering in the hard-edged December chill, I half wished such a photo *would* materialize. Maybe only that would jolt me from the guilty, sad daze I'd fallen into since reading your story in the *Arlington Advocate*.

Or maybe, I told myself as I scanned the still-shaded windows of your house, maybe you were better off away from Rakeen's family. Even though they probably did not—like I did—"defile" you. A curtain seemed to flicker in one window. Was it 4:00 PM yet? I was due for my Paper Boy training. I wanted to start my own route, to earn for starters thirty bucks to replenish the Maid Pro tip I'd stolen. I could at least do that.

I bent over and lifted my prone bike. I mounted it with a fresh, familiar pang of guilt: not for the Maid Pro money, which I could repay, but for you. What I'd done with—to—you.

We did what we could, Mom had told me to comfort me.

Yes, I thought, as I pedaled off toward my training in Arlington Center. Yes, Mom chose the right words, but they were right in a way that did the opposite of comfort me. Right in the way that you, in your mattress room, understood when I stood over you. I pictured you kneeling, your head bowed.

I did what I could.

EVENING AT THE CRYO-CRYSTAL CIRCUS HOTEL

Rachel Resnick

F uck me with a leather-clad fist, I was one focused dude. After seven days, seven nights, and forty-nine twilights, I wrote FINIS, printed *Blood Wedding Redux*, and slapped the binder shut. I, Chip, raging sex addict, fuck-up and canyon stud, had managed to play shut-in for one whole week. The entire time I channeled Lorca by way of Kubrick in a cinematic lovefest. Brought that project to the twentieth dimension. I couldn't wait to see my fiancée, Zoe, the whip-smart femme fatale P.I. with the vice-grip pussy.

Only—what do you know? The night I wrapped the screenplay, Zoe was busy, searching for clues for that damn case of hers in a stack of files on the epileptic catamite Dakota, the lying stripper. On her own deadline. "I'm sorry, Chipolaki. You go celebrate. *Opa!* You deserve it."

Yes, I did. Didn't I. Opa ropa dopa. Dakota Stinkota. I'm sick of Dakota. I hoped Dakota's fake tits exploded.

Zoe didn't understand how big a deal this was because— well, 'cuz I hadn't exactly told her. I couldn't expect her to drop everything. But I was still kinduv sore. Hadn't even shagged in a week. A week! I know, I know. Chip the baby. His majesty the infant. Shaking his pink baby fists at the world. Whatever. It was an eternity.

Buzzed from finishing the script, ready for a real drink or two, or a few, restless and a tad irritated, a touch horny, I drove Lightning into Santa Monica before sunset and hit the posh Cryo-Crystal Circus Hotel right on the beachfront.

This would make it all right.

Neo-mod architecture, prolly by the same guy who did the landmark Randy's Donut with some help from Gaudi, the Cryo-Crystal or Triple C as it was known, was novelty itself. A giant refrigerator, seven stories high, built from sleek burnished steel. There was even a simulated fridge-glow bleeding diffuse light from the building seams. Visible at night. But somehow it all worked. Maybe it was the proximity to the world-famous pier, the way the pier's carnival lights glanced off the fridge's polished sides, mixed with the moonlight and building glow. Maybe it was the perfect geometry of the architecture. The calculus of home appliances writ large.

The place came to life at night. I wanted to be there before. Ready. Braced for the magic. Let someone else do the conjuring tonight. I was spent.

From the beach entrance to the hotel, when dark fell, light-reflected waves stippled the gleaming steel façade and gave the illusion the Triple C was a ship. A luxury liner. About to drift from its sandy moorings. Kind of like the fabricated islands the Extropians dreamed of, where they would thaw when the time came, reanimate, and throw wild future-tastic rebirth parties. Extropians ran the joint. Rumor was they were backed by some secret celebrity or celebrities. The Extros were all about moving upward, onward, forward, starward, skyward—no negative thoughts allowed! Their philosophy was eerily shot through with Nietzschean zing, but most people ignored that. Cryonics was their bag. Freeze your head, then defrost when ready. Like a take 'n' bake pizza. Attach a fresh young body. And party!

All this combined to make the Triple C wildly wacky. Super-popular. And pricey. But unlike the Shanghai, which was off-limits to mere mortals for the most part, this place was yours for the freezing—if you had the dough.

Just what I needed. I cracked open the Log at a stoplight, scribbled quickly. *At the Triple C. Goals: Keep the faith. Stay true to love. Luxuriate in the flush of nailing a deadline before it vanishes. Freeze this moment of fiery creation. Melt in the moment.* I stuffed the Log back in my jeans. Tore through the green light.

Parked Lightning in a free parking lot only locals know about and walked into the hotel with my old swagger. Twitched my pecs. Winked at a few hotties out on the town, leggy in their cheap but sexy Steve Madden shoes and saucy sundresses. Vacant, hungry eyes met mine. Lips were licked, smacked. Stray hair tucked suggestively behind responsive ears. I smiled but didn't stray from the path, the image of Zoe blazing in the brain, upper and lower. I was a new man, about to be the next hot thing in Hollywood. That would solve a whole lot of problems, from career to cash flow. *Blood Wedding* would happen. *Had to.* Keep the focus. Stay true.

Up the carpeted steps, past flickering fireplaces, early eve clusters of schmoozers, awkward blind dates, superficial hustles, Persian party animals. Past the frozen heads. Past the cryo-waitresses with their silver uniforms and neck tattoos—dotted lines with the words CUT HERE and an inked pair of mini scissors. Straight for the window seats so I could watch the sunset and the lights prick up on the pier Ferris wheel, and contemplate my imminent change of fortune. I was in such a rush I didn't even hear my name called out, until a hand clutched my pant leg and yelled, "Chip!"

Then this same voice spiraled back down in volume to the sultriest whisper this side of the Chee-Zee celluloid, one I knew all too well. "Why don't you come join us?"

Go-Go. Go-Go clad all in leopard. Leopard halter—no bra—leopard skirt hugging her hips so tight it looked painted on and maybe was: I flashed on that hot chick in the film *Creamaster*, Aimee Mullins, the one with the fake legs below the knees, costumed up like a cheetah, bare-chested, painted in cheetah fur, wearing her spring-sprong metal legs with hoofs on the tips—manimal allure. What Go-Go had going for her but sans the sexy amputee thing. Go-Go's animal was all instinct, and all woman. Clutchable, fleshy, full and ripe—those creamy, flesh-lush thighs stretching out under the skirt, barely parted, same as her lips, in whispery wet invitation. I almost just shoved a hand up her skirt right there at the table, lost for a second in memories of the red rosebud I knew was stitched deep in her inner thigh, when I heard Zoe's voice in my head, quiet and sad. *S'agapo. I love you.*

Saved by the bell. Fidelity vow intact. At least for that moment.

Clearly the sex addiction wasn't tamed. The beast just had been lurking in the basement, jaws lathered with foam. Starving. Waiting patiently for a chance to rush the door. To wake. Now the chains rattled. The beast was roused. The whole basement shook with its roar.

"Siddown and join us, amigo." A familiar voice. One that echoed, sawed, sent shivers. Cuban-flavored. Everything was in slow motion. Viscous in the twilight of the low-lit hotel bar. I swung my head with difficulty away from Go-Go's lushness and saw a dashing old Latino guy sitting right next to Go-Go. Where'd he come from?

A thickly rolled Romeo y Julieta clenched between his lips. Stinking of Old Havana. Fat old Latino guy. Barrel-chested with long legs. Crisp white guayabera shirt. Rolls of dough spilling over his natty dark trousers. Porky jowls, thick head of hair still. Salt and pepper. A checkered cap pulled jauntily over his ancient skull. Wrinkles wreathing a sardonic, fleshy grin. Something about him was familiar. Maybe he was a musician. Or a friend of her lately deceased moneybags hubby. I was thinking Buena Vista Social Club.

I stuck my hand out. "Chip. Pleased to meet you, sir."

The Cuban guy ignored my hand, puffed more smoke. This time directly in my face. I glanced at Go-Go, like, what'd I do wrong? She was trying to look stricken, but giggles were bursting out all over her pretty painted face. "It's Red!" she burst out. "Isn't it amazing? That's Buster Ortale for you."

Buster Ortale. The Oscar-winning special effects wizard. I heard about celebrities getting disguised by him just for a night on the town. Especially if they had a need for lower profile than usual. Like Red.

Go-Go leaned over and gave Red a wet smooch on his Cubanized lips.

"Pretty good, huh? Even gotcha with the accent," Red aka Fat Cuban Fuck said, grinning mischievously. "Fooled ya! Sucker."

"One born every minute," I said with some irritation. I didn't like looking stupid. Plus, I guess I was surprised to see Go-Go and Red together. I hadn't seen the two of them in the same space since that fateful decadent night that set this whole summer chapter into motion. When I first took up with Go-Go again, and saw Red after the ten year dis. I was even more surprised to feel something like—was it jealousy? A pricked ego? But I was in love! Zeta Orion Epsilon. Zoroaster Oracle Eggplant. Zee Oh Ee. The only one for me.

"So you nailed the grand ole opus?" Red asked, eyes gleaming. "The heat is on. We gotta move. You hear the news today?"

Go-Go clapped her hands. A silvery I.D. bracelet flashed in the glowy light. "Tell us you've finished!"

"Indeed I have," I said, chest puffing, head growing, mastodon in my pocket thawing and swelling. I was a regular dirigible. Air-bloated and inflatable. Afloat.

"Well ain't that swell. Sit, sit," said Red, patting the seat next to Go-Go, so we would flank her.

"Don't mind if I do," said I, and sat. Let the games begin.

We three in the Ultra-Deluxe-Extra-Extro booth, set up privately from the club/bar scene but able to see all. The three of us sunk into iridescent softness, surrounded by silver cushions. Our own frozen head—a middle-aged man with buzz-cut salt-and-pepper hair, blue eyes, and a worried brow—cased in thickly ice-frosted glass against a personalized diorama with painted backdrop of a private jet, fake plastic palms framing the head; the whole display gently tracklit and set into the wall behind the booth, overlooking our revelry.

The chatter flowed easily. The vibe cozy, sociable, intimate, teasing. It was like we all three had been best buds for years. We talked sports, exploding coyotes, disappearing tribes, butt implants, asshole bleaching, psychic hotline addictions, the merits of ear candles, and other sundry topics. One frozen drink led to another. And another. Time passed pleasantly. Glasses clinked, swirled. Drained.

"Bring on the extropiates!" Red said into the booth vid-phone. Our waifish waitress in the silver baby-doll uniform, sporting an elegant swan neck and shaved head, the better to show off her personal tat, a purple-inked zipper, appeared seconds later. She set down three large glasses filled with clear liquid; multicolored glow cubes floating on the chrome table.

"On the house and extra dosed," she said, batting her blue frosted lids, nodding toward Go-Go. "Since you're one of us now."

The waitress jutted out her hand. Up and forward. Go-Go met hers. They entwined fingers. Then they both swooped their arms together, hands clasped, up, up and away, skyward, pumped them high and said "Yo!" in the ritual Extropian greeting.

"One of us, one of us," Go-Go whispered excitedly, extending her wrist so we could see the glittering cryo-bracelet. The one the parameds would see when they came to get her should something happen. Something fatal. And would know, and call the Cryomeds. Who would come instead, lop off her head, freeze it, and save the glory of Go-Go for the Future Par-tay. Paintings, interpretations by various fine artists of the Future Parties, grace all the interior walls. Near us a raucous one in day-glo acrylic by none other than Ringo. The Extropian movement was growing.

"You're so L.A.," Red said.

"Yeah, and you're so Jersey," she flung back. "You're a thug."

"Only someone from here would go for cryo," Red said. Turned to me. "Don't you agree? Chip's not from here either, Go." Sounded scarily close to Zo. I did a double take. Red was staring at me. I breathed deep. "Would you freeze your head?"

"I'd freeze my family jewels! Now that's the real ice. Fuck diamonds. Fuck heads."

Everyone laughed. Whatever it was, was iced over for now.

We raised our glasses of extropiates. To *Blood Wedding*!

"To getting sick-rich and sick-sex!"

"To the three of us!" we all cried out and drained our drinks. Instantly, with snake venom speed, the hotel bar scene, the bubbling surging crowd, turned on, tuned in, and dropped outside inn. Melting sparks skirts, glow sticks, flashing body blinx a blur of candy colors. *Opa!* Happy happy!

"Let's gear up!" said Go-Go, rifling through the goodies in the complimentary inflatable bowl. She handed me a strand of tiny lights.

I pushed them away. "I'm no X-mas tree."

"They're lobe strobes, silly." She clicked on the power, threaded the lights through my baby dreads. Giggled.

"And you, my Cuban mystery man, how 'bout this?" She handed him the belly light, grinning evilly. "For your Communist paunch."

Red smiled thinly, clicked the light on, and stuck the blue disc on his forehead.

"And this, babycakes, is for you," said Red mock-gallantly. Offering Go-Go the Glowing Bloody Mouth.

"How totally random!" she said with delight, clicking on the mouth and popping it into hers. The effect was grotesquely charming. The punchy red light beaming cheery gore in the center of her face.

"I want to be white trash when I grow up," she said. "Dolly Parton. My hero."

"What, slinging quotations are we? Our sexy airhead gone scholar thanks to drugs?"

Go-Go ducked her head shyly, cutting her eyes at me. I glanced up, looked above her, and thought I saw the frozen head—barely visible behind thick frost—pucker its blue lips. These extropiates rocked. My tundra Popsicle strained to stand at attention. Liquid mercury slithered through my rousable veins. With each drink, Go-Go seemed to inch closer, until—how did that happen?—she was on my lap, and Red was sitting in her chair. I didn't know whose leg was touching whose.

"More frozen daiquiris!" I called out, and frosty carafes magically appeared, lofted by slender pale arms in the dim light, reaching out to provide with generous flutters.

The weight of Go-Go on my lap. The Ferris wheel creaking around with its blurry spine of lights. The crowd pulsing. Red praising the play. Me, sinking into a hazy stupor. At one point, Go-Go reaching down for my hands, placing them on her soft, pliant breasts.

"Remember when you saw these bare the first time?" She pressed them closer. "You said you had a spiritual experience." She giggled, and Red smiled enigmatically. But I did not. Something snapped, maybe the extropiates turned. Maybe the trip went bad. All I know is I heard Zoe's voice in my head—Skílos! Dog!—even though all I wanted to do was take Go-Go right there, the bitch. I snatched my hands away from Go-Go's dreamy tits. The beast growled. The mighty iceberg in my jeans creaked, groaned, shifted.

"I thought you said Red was only good for one go-round," I snarled. Lashing out. Leopard tipsy, hostile. Covering. "But here you are again. You and him. Together at last."

In answer, Red poured another round of drinks. And Go-Go purred and slurred, "Relax, darling, relaxxxxxx," while she settled her leopard-clad plush derrière in deeper to my lap, adjusting herself so her buttocks deftly straddled a raging caveman torch. I was in deep shit. I could snipe all I wanted. The truth glared.

"I don't give a fuck anyway!" I said, merrily giving up decorum, forgetting my normal discretion. "I have a secret."

Red's eyes sharpened. Go-Go didn't seem to notice. She was groping around my jeans with her new glow gloves.

"What're you talking about?" Red leaned in closer, studied my face. I jostled Go-Go, squeezed her waist.

I shook my head, cheerfully slinging nopes left and right. "No can tell, Red. Mum's the word. Zip the lip. Semper Fi."

Red slammed down his glass. His saggy jowly Fat Cuban Fuck face hardened. But he didn't say anything else. Go-Go jumped into the void, spoke rapidly. Lucid. "I've got us something special in my room. All of us."

"You rented a room?" Forgetting in my daze this new Go-Go had millions.

"I've got a suite, silly," she cooed. "What do you think? After the party, there's the afterparty. Don't you know. How many do we have, Red?"

Red slugged the rest of his glass down.

Go-Go splayed her fingers on the table, pushed back into me. "One highclass whore, two highclass whores, three highclass whores, at least one barely legal, one gigolo, two, one luscious transvestite, a handful of eager-to-please Extropians—aw hell, we've got a lineup!"

Go-Go sensed me pulling away. Her tone turned more wheedling. More urgent. Naked in its need. Ugly.

"Honey, Chip, you want an amputee? You want a juggsy? Some midget twat? Whatever, we'll get you whatever you desire, long as we can all get our circus groove on tonight. Won't you come up? We're going to have a real party."

During this speech, each word pelted me like the needles from a cold shower, sobering me instantly. Zoe. Stay true. Remember the secret vow of faithfulness. You already did the big work. You wrote the script. And it's golden. Semper fidelis. Chip, Shit-for-brains. I shook Go-Go from my lap and stood up.

"Red, Go-Go, this has been real. But I've got to go. I can't keep up with you two. This script took the stuffing outta me." And before either Go-Go or Red could say a word, I threw down a wad of bills and ran like hell to get out of that hotel. Fast as I could. Long legs loping, threading past the thick pulsating glowing crowd, ignoring gasps, curses, kisses and even slaps when I knocked into people. I didn't stop sprinting until I hit the street, where I took a huge gulp of air, then took off sprinting toward the lot. Not until I jumped in to Lightning, gunned the engine, and crested onto the Pacific Coast Highway did I begin to feel the panic subside.

FROM *RAPTURE*

Susan Minot

He lay back like the ambushed dead, arms flung down at his sides, legs splayed out and feet sticking up, naked. He lay in the familiar bed against the familiar pillows he'd not seen in over a year. Eyes closed, face slack, he might indeed have been dead save for the figure also naked embracing his lower body and swiveling her head in a sensual way.

He opened his eyes, barely, and looked down at her. He looked with cool, lowered lids at her mouth pressed around him. As he watched he felt the pleasant sensation, but it was not making it up to his head. The good feeling remained relegated to what was going on down there. It stopped in the vicinity of his hips. He did like it, though. Who wouldn't? He especially liked seeing her down there after this long time.

He had no idea what had gotten her there.

He certainly wasn't going to ask her about it. There was no way he was going to wade into those dangerous waters and try to find out why she'd changed her mind or what she was thinking or why she'd let him back in or even *if* she'd changed her mind. He didn't want to jinx it, their being in bed together. Besides, he didn't really want to know. If he'd learned only a few things in their long association—and he considered over three years to be pretty long—one of them was that when Kay did tell him what was going on in her mind, the report was usually not very good.

I honestly think you don't have any conception of what love is. She had a knack for being blunt in a way he didn't particularly want to deal with at the moment. He preferred this side of her, her solicitous side, which he was getting the benefit of right now.

And even if he did want to know, he no longer trusted himself to ask her in the right way or have the right response ready for what she might say. He'd learned that, for them, there was no right thing to say. Plus, he didn't want to risk the subject of Vanessa coming up. He couldn't face that. Whenever Vanessa's name came up, it always ended badly. Of course, it worked the other way around, when Vanessa brought up the subject of Kay Bailey. If Kay Bailey came up things were likely to take a turn for the worse. He might be dense about some things, but he'd learned that.

But wait, now that he thought about it, and being in this position allowed his mind sort of to drift and wander, Kay had already brought up the subject of Vanessa—earlier while she was making them lunch. She had her back to him, standing at the counter. She did not pause from slicing tomatoes in long, patient strokes when she half turned her face back to him. "How's Ms. Crane?" she said. A little alarm alerted him to check her face and he saw no clenched jaw, which he interpreted as an encouraging sign and so told her that he and Vanessa were still talking, which was true, and that Vanessa had not *ruled out* the possibility that they get back together, which was somewhat stretching the truth. It was, instead, a reflection of what he hoped the truth might be, despite the fact that Vanessa had told him *in no uncertain terms*—that was the phrase she used—that it was finally and absolutely over and she could not imagine them ever repairing the damage he'd done. Except that she did happen to be saying this sitting on the edge of the bed where they'd just spent the night together. So all was not lost. She was still seeing him. He didn't bother getting into these specifics with Kay. He wanted to be honest, but no one wants complete honesty if it's going to rip open your heart.

Kay had simply nodded, uncharacteristically not reacting, and put the lopsided bread in the toaster. She was in one of her calm frames of mind. At one point while they were eating she looked at him in a pointed way and smiled, beaming.

"What are you smiling at?" he said, a little frightened.

"It's good to see you," she said. She looked genuinely happy. He did not understand women.

Like a draft in the room, he could still feel how bad things had gotten and didn't expect to see her beaming at him this way. He certainly hadn't expected ever to be back in here either, in her small bedroom with the tall window and the afternoon light going along the long yellow curtain. He looked up at the ceiling. It told him nothing. But he kept his gaze there. If he was going to make sense of this it would be easier if he didn't look at her or at what she was doing to him. Instead, he thought, he should just bask in the sensation and, if he was lucky, it would take over his mind.

God, he was lovely. God, he was sweet. God. God. God. This had to be the sweetest thing she'd ever felt, nothing had ever been sweeter. It was overwhelming, the feeling that this was pretty much the only thing that mattered, this being with him, this sweetness, this . . . communing . . . this . . . there was no good word for it.

Her fingers encircled the base of his penis and she ran her parted lips up and down him, introducing her tongue like a third lip. Her other hand traveled over his stomach, exploring. It stopped. It moved over his hips. Her palm rested lightly on his skin, as if she were testing the heat over an electric burner. The palm descended, flat. It was a wonderful feeling: skin. Her brushing back and forth was hypnotic and lulled her. With her head bowed she glanced to the side with blurred lazy vision and saw his arm lying there on the sheet. The veins were raised over the back of his hand. She liked seeing his hand there, the manliness of it, and liked the fact that it was his hand and certain, and love for his hand spread through her. It seemed so large for how narrow the forearm was. She closed her eyes and brushed over him, not hurrying. His hand was certain while he had always been uncertain. But this, she thought, this.

But he couldn't empty his mind. He hadn't seen her in so long. He'd finally gotten used to not seeing her. When last had he? Once eight months ago. Probably not two or three times in the six months before that. Her refusal to see him had been part of the continual attempt to enforce *something*. Not that she wasn't right to, not that he didn't deserve to be barred, and not that it wasn't the best thing for her and, truth be told, for him. He had himself told her she was better off without him. He himself had admitted he was a sorry bastard and that she ought to have run away in the opposite direction the moment she saw him. He was the first person to own up to that. Not that he actually thought she'd believe him. It's easy not to believe the bad things about a person when you first meet, particularly if you're kissing that person. But he had warned her. He couldn't be accused of trying to put one over on her, or of pretending to be something he wasn't. He'd let enough people down recently not to be maintaining certain illusions about himself.

Still, he wasn't going to take the blame for everything. Not everything was his fault. Some things a person can't help. Was it a person's fault if he fell in love with someone else? Could he have stopped that? He couldn't've helped it. How does a person help falling in love?

Or, if you were going to take first things first, how does a person help falling *out* of love? That was the problem before anything. He'd fallen out of love with Vanessa. He still *loved* her, he'd always *love* her, but he wasn't *in love* anymore. He'd just lost it. So was it not understandable if a person found it difficult to face the excruciating fact that the person he'd fallen out of love with happened to be his fiancée?

Well, he did face it. He hung in there. And, given his reasoning, he didn't think it so outlandish to believe that if he just stuck with her anyway she hopefully wouldn't notice that he, the guy who used to plead with her to marry him, to the point that it became a running joke, no longer felt the same lovestruck urgency. After all, they had been together for eleven years, which made the lack of urgency not surprising, but also in a way kind of worse.

So anyway you do your best. You continue with the plan to get married—fortunately no date has been set—figuring she'll never notice the difference and will be spared the hurt. And it might haunt you a little, but you figure deep down that this is what was bound to happen over time anyway and that one can't stay in love like that forever. So you are pretty resolved with the situation when into your preproduction office of the movie you've been trying to make for the last eight years, which is finally, actually, coming together, walks a production designer named Kay Bailey who has a way of frowning at you and looking down when you speak as if she's hearing something extra in your voice. And slowly but surely is revealed to you your miserable situation in all its miserable perspective.

The bedspread was sloughing off the end of the bed, the white sheets were flat as paper. This was not what she'd pictured when she asked him over for lunch today. It really wasn't. She may have changed her shirt a couple of times dressing this morning and put on lipstick, then wiped it off. It was Benjamin, after all. But she was not planning on winding up in bed.

She was well aware there'd been other times in the past when she'd met him ostensibly as a friend and it had been known to evolve that some admission like, *I think about you still*, or the more direct, *I still want you*, would cause a sort of toppling of their reserve and before she knew it she'd find herself blurrily pushing him away at the same time that she was kissing him.

When she finally managed to separate she would be half buttoned and unbuckled and the internal army that she'd had at attention to face him would have collapsed into a dreamy, entwined heap. And, she had to admit, there'd been times when things had evolved a little further. She wasn't perfect. But there definitely were plenty of times when she *had* remained polite and restrained, when they didn't talk about matters of the heart or, to be honest, about anything important to either of them. That's how it'd been recently, for over a year now. Or more, if she thought about it. It always helped to resist him if she were sexually in thrall with someone else. Then the troops would stay at attention, no problem.

But now, at this stage of things, she'd thought as she set out their lunch plates on the Indian bedspread which covered her plywood table, enough time had passed that she could feel safe whether there was another man or not. (At the moment, there was not.) Isn't that what everyone said? That after enough time had passed you wouldn't be affected anymore?

What did they know? Look at her now. With him. Time hadn't protected her at all. Fact is, time had thrown her in the opposite direction. Look where it threw her: back in bed with the guy. And with fewer qualms about being with him than she'd ever had. Apparently time eroded misgivings, too. No one had mentioned that. No one mentioned how time saturated relations between people with more meaning, not less. None of this undressing would have happened without the passage of time. It wasn't exactly adding up as she'd figured.

Small tentative blips of danger appeared on her radar screen, but they were easy to ignore. The little alarms of the mind are less likely to be detected when the body is taken over by pleasure.

The first time he met her he was struck by something right away. She was leaning in the doorway of his office, a head with a fur-fronted hat like the Russians wear, talking to his assistant. He hardly saw her, a figure out of the corner of his eye, but that was enough. His chest felt a thump. When she walked in, he looked away. Not that she was so amazing-looking or anything, but there was something promising about her. His body felt it before he even knew what it was. Somehow his body knew she was going to change things.

She was wearing a blue Chinese jacket with all these ties on it, and when she sat down at the table she undid some of them but didn't take off the coat. She sat and listened to him like a youth recruit listening to her revolutionary assignment. She even knew something about Central American politics. He gave her the usual spiel about the script, which of course she had read or she wouldn't have been there applying for the job, but he had to rely on automatic because he was feeling strangely backed into himself. He felt as if most of what he was saying was ridiculous, but it didn't really bother him, because he was also feeling strangely vibrant. She stayed very still listening to him, frowning, businesslike, which was in contrast to the flaps on her hat, which were flipped up kookily and trembled slightly when she moved. She kept her mouth pursed in concentration. Every now and then a twitch escaped from her mouth, as if it wanted to say something but was restraining. He told her about his struggles to get the movie made and cracked some usual jokes. He made her laugh. That was one thing he knew how to do, make a girl laugh. Her laugh had relief and surprise in it. It had a lot of girl in it. He wanted to keep making her laugh.

She asked him, "What was the first thing that made you want to make this movie?" Her brow was furrowed. Her mouth twitched as if suppressing a smile. It was a normal, regular question, but it seemed as if no one had ever asked him it before, or, at least, not with the interest she had, and he felt as if she'd just inserted one of those microscopic needles into his spine and was making an exploratory tap down into the deepest recesses of his psyche.

It was weird. He liked it.

The sun had moved into the room so it was brighter. He preferred rooms dark. He looked down at Kay, as if to remind himself where he was, and thought there was a time he would have been dying for this. It was hard not to think of the months he'd dreamed about being in bed with her doing what she was doing now. He touched her hair, affectionately, limply. Things had simply never lined up for them; that was the truth of it.

MOTHERFUCKER

———— • ————

Aimee Bender

"I fuck mothers," he said to anyone who asked him. "And I do it well," he added.

He was also reasonable; he didn't fuck married mothers, only available ones who wanted to date and who'd lined up an appropriate babysitter for the child who'd made them a mother in the first place.

He wined, dined, danced, romanced—martinis and kisses on the neck, bloody steak and Pinot Noir—the word *beautiful* said sincerely with a casual lean-back into a booth. He asked pointed, particular questions. By midnight had most of them in bed, clothes off in a flash, the speed of a woman undressing changing rapidly over time, faster and faster, and he was a very good lover, attentive and confident, a giver and a taker, and the mothers lined up to see him, their babysitters growing rich, twenties stuffed in those tight teenage pockets.

He never liked any of them for longer than one or two times. Or, he liked them but not enough to keep calling. I love all women, he told himself. He liked to try on hats in stores.

One afternoon, he was at a fancy Bel Air party on a damp lawn talking to some damp-and-fancy people. They stood in groups of three and four, stirring lemonades laced with vodka, that liquid shark swimming amongst the yellow feathers of their drinks. The motherfucker wandered over the lawn to the starlet, famous for her latest few films, standing with the red straw hat and matching red dress, the one watching her four-year-old play on the lawn chairs, the one whose husband had left her for a man, or so said the newspapers. Everyone else was afraid to talk to her.

She had shiny hair under her red hat and was drinking nothing, hands still at her sides.

The motherfucker told her he liked her hat. She said thank you. He asked about her son; she said: he's four. The kid rolled in the grass, collecting stains on his clothes like lashings from a green whip.

"I think you're a good actress," the man said. "Why do you always pick such sad characters to play?"

"Me?" she said. "Sad characters?" And she flashed him her teeth, the long white ones that had been photographed a million times by now, each tooth a gleaming door into the mysteries of her mouth.

The motherfucker said yes. "You," he said.

He stood with the starlet for a while and told her he was a graduate student at the school for emotional ventriloquists. She raised one carefully shaped eyebrow. "No," he said, "it's true." She laughed. "No," he said, "it's true. You throw your emotions on other people in the room," he explained, "and see what they do then."

"So what do they do?" she asked, keeping that perfect eyebrow halfway up her forehead.

"It depends," he sighed. "Sometimes they lob them right back at you.

"Turns out life," he said to her, "is a whole lot like tennis."

They walked to the gazebo. The party was ending, and the sun was going down, and the grass had turned a softer shade of green. He knew he needed to do something to make her remember him so he just stood there with her on the gazebo, watching her son, and put his hand on her famous shining hair, just for a second, lifted it off her back and let it down again. She jumped.

"Oh!" she said; "Oh," he said, "your hair was stuck."

Then he didn't touch her again, not for weeks.

He got her phone number from the host. Motherfuckers have their ways. It took only one lie and he left with those ten numbers, one dash, and two parentheses tucked with care inside his shirt pocket.

At home, he put in a call to crazy Heddie from Butte. He asked her a half-hour of penetrating questions and then tried to have phone sex but found he couldn't really muster up the gusto. His mind was elsewhere. The next day, he called up the starlet and asked her to dinner.

She laughed. She sounded even prettier on the phone. "Aren't you afraid of me?" she asked. "After all, I am a movie star." He said no, he wasn't afraid of her, he thought of her as an interesting, attractive woman who happened to have a very public job. She said that was sure a new way to put it. They set a date to meet at an Italian bistro on Vermont, and there she signed twelve autographs and he asked about how what she did as an actress and what he did as an emotional ventriloquist were similar, but she said they were in a restaurant and it was too distracting so they should talk about something light while they were there. "Maybe *you're* afraid of *me*," he said. She looked closer, eyes green and piercing. "Maybe I am," she said, and the rest of the dinner was quiet. The waiter asked for an autograph on a napkin, and by the time they left, it was already hung up by the host's podium with a red thumbtack, next to some signed black-and-white photographs of other stars, many of whom by now were regular people or else dead.

The motherfucker recognized one of the mothers he'd fucked at a table to the right and waved while exiting, but the mother didn't acknowledge him because she was jealous and also starlets made her nervous.

The starlet found the motherfucker trustworthy so she invited him back to her new house in the dark curves of the Hollywood hills, the wood floors brown and shining, the pillows sentimental, the magazines unread. They sat and had a good talk on her thousands-of-dollars couch. He mentioned his train trip, and she said her father had been a conductor for years. They discussed depots. At the door he did not kiss or hug her but just said he'd had a terrific time, and she closed the door behind him, pensive. She paced a little and then watched some TV. She saw herself on the news.

The motherfucker went home and rented one of her latest movies and watched it closely, and even though it was a comedy, he looked at the smile on her face and decided she was possibly the saddest person he had ever met or pursued.

He didn't touch her even when they went to lunch and she cried about her empty house. About how she had known all along with her husband but never would say it was true to herself. He didn't touch her even when she raised limpid movie eyes up to him and gave him the look that meant Kiss Me to film fans from all over the world. He let all his other mothers call and call but he didn't pick up or call back. He invited the starlet to the ballet and during Act Two, he picked up her hand, and while the stage was full of people as flowers and birds, trying with all available muscles to be lighter than air, their hands learned each other, fingers over fingers, palm on back, palm on palm, edge to wrist, watchbands clinking because both of them liked to know what time it was at all times.

He dropped her off, said he couldn't come in. She was disappointed. She dreamt he was making love to her in a hamper.

Heddie from Butte called. Heddie's father was mad at her about something that had happened four Christmases ago, and Heddie was upset. The motherfucker talked to her for a while but he couldn't concentrate and said he had to go write his graduate school paper on the relationship between sadness, mime, and ping-pong. "Why, I didn't know you were in school," said Heddie. "I wish you would talk more about yourself." The motherfucker pretended he had call-waiting. His good-bye was rude.

He asked the starlet to dinner again. She was pleased. "He treats me," she told her friend, the other hot new starlet, "like a regular person." "Why on earth," said her friend the other starlet, "would you want that? What's the point," said the other starlet, "of being a starlet in the first place?" Our starlet put her hand on her cheek. Her blush was the color of a coral reef, but smooth. "I think it has to do with getting emotions thrown on you," she said.

This dinner they shared a bottle of wine and no one stopped to get an autograph. (She was wearing a hat.) She said he could come back to her house again, maybe they could have some tea. They played the hand game under the table, and this time the volume was twice as high. His whole body was taut for her. "George is asleep," she said, meaning her son. They drove back and she paid the babysitter, a huge tip to get her out as soon as possible, and she went to the kitchen to put the kettle on, and the moment of the first kiss was prolonged, longer, prolonged; she offered tea, she offered wine, she went to the bathroom and he pictured her in there, looking down at the toilet paper which was not yellow but clear with other liquid, and she returned, sat next to him on the couch, picked up a magazine, stood, sat, stood, sat, and he thought: it has been a while since this woman has been with a man who wants to be with women. And so he just sat there first and thought of women, thought of what he loved about women, thought of the slopes and the jewelry, the lines and the circles, breasts of all sizes, emotion, opening, contraction.

He watched her. She put her head on her own shoulder—coy, twitchy.

"I think about you," he said.

"What do you think about?" she asked. She ran through the movie scenes in her head. They all were very pretty options. He said, "I think about how nervous you are."

Her face fell. "What?"

"No," he said, flustered, "it's great that you're nervous." His expression, for once, was open and earnest. She kept her eyes on him and laughed once then, the laugh that stole the hearts of a million moviegoers, that fed the wallets of a fat handful of studio executives, and he said: "Wait."

"What?" she said.

He took a step away and looked at her. She made a wry little joke about directors. Then put her face nearer, ready to kiss him, to prove herself unnervous—how bold, how witty—but he didn't move forward. "Hang on," he said.

She grew bolder, interrupted, said "Hey. Let's go outside. There are bushes out there." The motherfucker paused and smiled, said no. She twisted and said "Come with me, let's go to the bathroom counter." She'd had movie sex scenes on the bathroom counter and in the bushes, both. Audiences had liked those a lot. He shook his head, no. "Let's do it on a cliff under a tree!" she sang, and he said no. "I want to make love to you in a bed," is what he said.

This made her feel completely out of control.

He stepped closer. For some reason, his hands were shaking. Using his finger as a pointer, he drew an invisible line around her. He said: "Listen. Look. Desire is a house. Desire needs closed space. Desire runs out of doors or windows, or slats or pinpricks; it can't fit under the sky, too large. Close the doors. Close the windows. As soon as you laugh from nerves or make a joke or say something just to say something or get all involved with the bushes, then you blow open a window in your house of desire and it can't heat up as well. Cold draft comes in."

"It's not a very big house, is it?" she said.

"Don't smile," he said. She pulled in her lips.

"Don't smile," he said. "It's not supposed to be big at all. It should be the closest it can to being your actual size."

She could feel it brimming on her lips, that superstar smile, the bow-shape, the teeth long and solid tombstones. She knew just what she looked like.

"Don't," the motherfucker said, harder.

And the smile, like a wave at the beach, receded. And when she didn't smile, when the windows stayed shut, the glass bending out to the night but not breaking, the glass curved from the press of release but not breaking, then the tension went somewhere else, something buckled inside her and made the longing bigger, tripled it, heavied it, made it so big the whole house grew thick and murky. This was not something she knew well, this feeling; she was used to seeing her desire like an angora sweater discarded on the other side of the room.

And she felt like she needed him, then. In the same basic way she needed other things, like water.

She was up again refilling her cup of tea and he followed her in and as she was pouring it he took the teapot out of her hand and balanced it right on top of the teacup and while she was looking at that, her hands shaking now, he took her fingers and leaned in and kissed her. Took her face in his palms, then suddenly the faces were too close for anything else to be happening and the kiss was soft and so sweet and in the next room the kid shifted and his dream switched to one about lightning and a boy who stuck his hand in the electrical socket and what happened next.

"What do you want?" asked the motherfucker, getting ready to motherfuck, and he stepped into her house and her hands were all over his face, his neck, his bones, his hair.

"Stop asking questions," she said to him, kissing him again. "That breaks open your windows, doesn't it?" And the motherfucker felt he could crush her, because she happened to be right, and he shut up and his house grew smaller, smaller than he was used to, and she didn't smile or run to the bushes, so hers grew smaller, smaller than it had ever been, and then smaller, and then smaller, until she fit inside, gloved, a house of desire the exact size and shape of her. She thought she might wheeze away but then his hands touched skin, and her throat cleared and lifted.

The next morning, a dry clear day, the starlet made the motherfucker banana pancakes. Her son wandered in in pajamas and got some pancakes, too. The motherfucker took a shower in her gourmet shower and used shampoo made from the placenta of sea urchin. He came out as fresh and clean as an underwater urchin infant. She was a yield sign, all sinews and mush, and he sat down and she whispered: "That was a wonderful night," and he said: "It was," and he meant it and he meant it too much and he said: "I think I have to go now."

She called him a motherfucker, but in a teasing way.

He said: "It's true, though."

He didn't call her that day. He didn't call her the next day. She realized she did not have his phone number, could not tell him that she had to go on location to shoot the movie about people with problems but would miss him. During her movie the director asked her to smile but she said no. "This movie," she said, "I am going to stay in my house."

On the screen, she was so luminous in her seriousness, she made the whole cinema fill with tension, so much so that every cinemagoer went home charged up like an electrical storm, fingers in sockets, so much so that she got nominated for seven awards. The motherfucker, who never called again, watched her win from the quiet of his small bedroom. She was wearing a dress the color of the sky before it rains and had become, suddenly, beautiful. She had been something else before, but now she was something else from that. She thanked her parents most of all, her father the train conductor, her mother who rode the trains back and forth across the country to be with him. The motherfucker held his own body close. His apartment was very plain. "This is the house of your desire," he whispered to himself, looking at the small walls around him, and when he closed his eyes, the torrent of longing waiting inside was so thick he thought he might drown in it.

CAMP WHITEHORSE

———————•———————

Alicia Erian

Errol took a hiatus from his girlfriend, Louise, thinking that he might want to be with Audrey instead. Then it turned out that he didn't want to be with Audrey, he wanted Louise again, except that Audrey was clinging to him. Errol had an idea to pass Audrey off to his friend Marcus, a Marine who had just come back from Iraq. Marcus had killed a kid on accident. He was taking antidepressants for it and seeing a therapist, but neither was really helping. Errol thought that maybe Audrey could help Marcus. Mostly, though, he was hoping to get her to stop clinging.

By way of introduction, Errol showed Marcus a video of Audrey masturbating with her vibrator. She'd made the video for her ex-boyfriend, who was also a Marine, and when she came, she said his name: *Hutch*. Errol didn't know much about the guy, except that Audrey had come to Connecticut to try to forget him. She said that he was always vanishing, and that it was time for her to move on.

When she first gave Errol the tape, Audrey instructed him to watch it with the sound down. He said fine, then left the sound up. It turned out that hearing Audrey say another man's name when she came was the least of Errol's worries. What really got him was Audrey herself. The way she writhed and moaned and whimpered and cooed. The confidence with which she held her pussy open. He'd never really known the woman on the tape, but she was the one he wanted.

He had, however, caught a glimpse of her when they'd first met. She'd come into his western wear store to order a pair of boots, and had treated him with indifference. She was slightly taller than Errol, which contributed to the effect. He started chasing her immediately. He was still with Louise, but he didn't really think about that. This was something separate. He wanted to know if he could get Audrey to like him.

It turned out that he could. At first, this was gratifying. Audrey was pretty and smart. She taught video production at the local college. Anyone would've wanted her. Then Errol told her about Louise, and everything changed. Audrey grew anxious. Even with the hiatus, she couldn't seem to relax. She panicked constantly that Errol wouldn't pick her. He tried to tell her that it was a self-fulfilling prophecy, but that only made her panic even more. And her panic sent her into action. His dick was sore from the constant blow jobs. He was getting fat from the cookies she was always bringing over.

Then she gave him the video. For a while, it made things better. He would watch it, and he would see who she was supposed to be, and he would want very much to fuck her. Then, afterward, she would ask hopefully if he was going to pick her, and things would go back to the way they really were.

Finally, he put the video away. He was beginning to hate himself. He had ruined her, and the tape was the evidence, and he couldn't stand to look at it anymore. Meanwhile, he'd started to miss Louise. Maybe she was a little distant and cold, but here was someone he could never ruin. Here was someone who would never let him get that close.

Errol let Marcus keep the video overnight, then called the next day to see what he thought. Marcus said that he'd enjoyed it, and agreed to a meeting. Errol had Marcus come to his store, then he invited Audrey on the pretense of showing her some new boots. When she arrived, he introduced her to Marcus, saying that Marcus had just happened to drop by. She seemed irritated by this, like she had thought it was just going to be her and Errol. Then Marcus started talking about being a Marine, and that calmed her down. She said that her ex-boyfriend had been stationed in Nasiriya. She said that apparently she attracted Marines like flies. Marcus laughed. He asked her if that was such a bad thing, and she said that maybe it wasn't. Errol excused himself then to go and get the boots. He hoped that this was actual flirting, and not just Audrey trying to get to him through his friends.

A couple of days later, Errol called her. He made small talk, then told her that his friend Marcus had really liked her and was bugging him for her phone number. Immediately, she started to cry. "You're passing me off to your friend?" she yelled. "You're passing me off to your friend?"

Errol was taken aback. He hadn't expected Audrey to notice, and now he realized that this had been stupid. He said, "He just came back from Iraq."

"You're pimping me out?" Audrey wailed.

Errol thought that pimping was a strong word. "No," he said. "Of course not."

Audrey kept crying.

"Maybe I made a mistake here," Errol said.

"I guess so," Audrey sniveled.

"I'm sorry," he said.

"I demand to know your feelings for me," she said.

Errol thought for a moment, then told her the truth: that the hiatus was over, that he was getting back together with Louise.

Audrey hung up on him. He sat there for a while, holding the phone, then called Marcus and gave him her number.

At first, Marcus reported, Audrey was furious. She said that she'd never given Errol permission to hand out her number, and that Marcus had no right to be using it. Marcus told her that he understood, but that he'd like to check back with her one more time, just in case she changed her mind. When he called again in a week, she'd softened a little. She said that even if she was interested in seeing him, she couldn't, because she'd promised Hutch that she would never fuck another Marine. "Who said I wanted to fuck you?" Marcus asked, which she had apparently found funny. By the third week, she'd decided that Hutch had no right to tell her who to fuck since he was probably fucking god knew who as she spoke, and so she agreed to a date.

Marcus told Errol that he'd taken her to dinner and a movie, then tried to have sex with her afterward, but couldn't because of the antidepressants. Audrey took it personally, like she thought he didn't find her attractive. She started crying and curled up into a ball. Marcus didn't know what to do. He wanted to hit her for not knowing what a real problem was, and then he did. On the ass. He couldn't believe he'd done it. He thought she would kick him out, but she didn't. She uncurled herself and began to suck his dick. Finally, he got a little hard.

Errol didn't know what to say to this. He and Marcus were sitting in a bar, drinking.

"Was she like that with you?" Marcus asked.

"Like what?" Errol said.

"You know," Marcus said. "Submissive."

"Yes," Errol said.

"And you didn't like that?"

"I did like it," Errol admitted.

"But you passed on it."

"I passed on it, but I liked it."

Marcus said, "It's making me feel a little bit better."

"About what?" Errol asked.

Marcus shrugged. "Everything."

"Don't hit her," Errol said.

"She likes it," Marcus said.

"Just don't," Errol told him.

Errol was having a hard time readjusting to Louise. She was depressed a lot and always talking about her painful childhood. Errol appreciated how this kept her distracted, but at the same time, he missed having a woman pine for him. He tried calling Audrey a couple of times to see if he could get a dose of it, but she wouldn't answer.

He still had the video she'd given him, so he watched that instead. Lately, though, he'd begun to turn the sound down. He was starting to get a little jealous of Hutch.

Now that Louise was coming over again, she stumbled across the video. "What the hell is this?" she asked Errol one night. He had just come home from the store.

He looked at the tape in her hand. Errol had never told Louise about Audrey. When he'd suggested that they take a hiatus, his reasoning had been that he was overwhelmed. "Overwhelmed by what?" Louise had asked him, and he'd said just overwhelmed.

"Who is this woman?" she demanded now, shaking the tape. "Who's Hutch?"

Errol took his cowboy hat off and hung it on the post at the end of the banister. He tried to explain to Louise about the video. When he was finished, she said, "You're watching a tape of a woman masturbating for another man?"

"Yes," Errol admitted.

Louise sat down on the couch. She was still holding the tape. Errol was desperate to get it back from her, but he knew that now wasn't the time. He knew that any sudden movements could result in its breakage.

"I don't know what to say to this," Louise told him.

Errol tried to be quiet and leave her to her rage.

"Is this why you wanted a hiatus?" she asked.

He nodded then said, "But I don't want it anymore. I pick you."

"Gee," Louise said. "Thanks."

Errol didn't say anything.

"Is this the kind of thing you like in a woman?"

"No," Errol said, even though it was.

"Because I can't make you any videos. That's just not me."

"I wouldn't want you to," Errol lied.

Louise started to cry then. She said that the last thing she needed was some woman making her feel insufficient in the bedroom. Errol sat down beside her. He gently took the tape out of her hands, set it to one side, and explained about how sufficient he found her. He accidentally used the word sufficient, and that made her cry even harder. She got her coat and went home.

Errol hoped that Louise would leave him because of the tape. He hoped that she would make some kind of final decision, since he felt unable to. The next day, though, she called to say that she was staying. She said that she was hardly going to be threatened by someone who hadn't even managed to steal her boyfriend. She added, however, that he had better get rid of that fucking tape.

Errol knew that Audrey wouldn't pick up if he called, so he drove over to her place. When she answered the door, he saw that she had a black eye. "Jesus," he said.

"What?" she said.

"Your eye."

"Oh," she said, touching it.

"Did Marcus do that?" he asked.

She nodded.

"I don't want you to see him anymore," Errol said, hoping to sound like Hutch.

"Are you going to see me?" she asked.

He paused for a moment, then said, "No."

"Why not?"

"Because I'm seeing Louise," he said.

"Why?"

He was starting to get agitated. "Because," he said, "she's my girlfriend. You know that."

Audrey didn't say anything.

"Here's your tape back," he said.

"You don't want it?" she asked, hurt.

"It's not that," he said.

"How come you don't want it?"

"I do want it," he said. "It's just not a good idea."

She took the tape.

Errol didn't know what to do then. He thought he should probably call the police about her eye. He took out his cell phone.

"What are you doing?" Audrey asked.

"I don't know," he said, putting the phone away.

"I can't believe you passed me off to your friend," she said.

"It was wrong," he agreed, and then he left.

Errol went over to Marcus's house to tell him to stop hitting Audrey. "Why?" Marcus said. "She likes it."

"What are you talking about?" Errol said, even though he kind of knew. Still, he thought that there was a difference between letting someone suck your dick endlessly, and hitting them.

"Look," Marcus said, "this is mutual consent. I'm not hurting anyone who doesn't want to get hurt."

"How's she supposed to teach her classes if she has a black eye?"

"It's spring break," Marcus said.

Errol didn't know what to say to this.

"Lighten up," Marcus told him, and he closed the door.

Errol knew that Hutch was short for Hutchinson, and that night, he called every Hutchinson in Manhattan until he found the right one. "Who is this?" Hutch asked.

Errol said that he was a friend of Audrey's, and that Audrey was having a problem. "What problem?" Hutch said.

"Some guy is roughing her up."

"She likes that."

"Yeah, but it's too much," Errol said. "He gave her a black eye."

"Can't you take care of it?" Hutch asked. "What kind of man are you?"

"I don't think I can take care of it," Errol said.

"Well," Hutch said, "that's her business."

"He's a Marine," Errol said.

"What?" Hutch said.

"The guy who's roughing her up."

Hutch was quiet for a moment. Then he said, "I told her not to do that. I don't care if she fucks you, or anyone else. But I told her not to fuck another Marine."

"I don't think she's actually fucking him," Errol said.

"Why not?"

"He's on antidepressants. They mess up his sex life."

"He's beating her without even fucking her?"

"I think so," Errol said.

"That's fucked up," Hutch said.

"He killed a kid in Iraq," Errol said. "On accident."

"Oh Jesus," Hutch said.

"He's got problems," Errol said.

"How do I find this guy?" Hutch said, and Errol told him.

A couple of days later, a man roughly Errol's height came into the store. What Errol noticed about him was that he was very broad. There was his head, then the extension of his shoulders out from his neck. To Errol, they seemed never-ending.

The man was wearing sunglasses, and he took them off, exchanging them for a pair of regular glasses. They looked like the kind you would find in a magazine. The latest style.

Once the man could see, he said, "Are you Errol?"

Errol said yes, and the man came behind the counter and hit him in the face. Errol fell back against the wall a little.

"You fucking set her up with that guy," Hutch said. "You left that part out, asshole."

Errol took a moment to right himself, then said, "Yes. I did."

There was one other customer in the store, a man, and he asked then if he should call the police. "No," Errol said. "It's all right."

The man walked out, and Errol felt relieved. He was pretty sure he was bleeding, and he didn't think that was good for business.

Hutch paced the store a little before returning to the sales counter. This time he stayed on the right side of it. "Have you seen her face?" he said. "She looks terrible."

"Yes," Errol said.

"How's she supposed to teach like that?"

"I don't know," Errol said.

"You're the one responsible, do you understand? You passed her off to your friend. She's not a whore to be passed off to your friend."

"I didn't mean it that way," Errol said.

"She thinks you did," Hutch said. "She thinks that's exactly how you meant it."

Errol didn't say anything.

"Jesus Christ," Hutch said, and he started walking around the store again.

Errol couldn't tell if Hutch's pacing was a way for him to calm down, or a way for him to get more excited. In general, he didn't seem that excited. Even when he had hit Errol, he'd seemed vaguely fatigued.

Now he stopped in front of a hat rack. He reached over and took down a beige Stetson. "This would look good on her," he said.

Errol nodded.

Hutch put the hat on, dipping it down a little in front so that it cast a shadow across his eyes. "She could maybe teach wearing this."

"Yes," Errol agreed.

Hutch took the hat off. He examined the inside of it. "Would this fit her?"

"What size is it?" Errol asked.

"Seven and a half."

"She's a seven and an eighth," Errol said. "Let me see if I have any more in back." He went in the back room and found the hat, then brought out the box. "Here you go," he told Hutch.

Hutch came up to the counter. He took out his wallet and gave Errol a credit card.

"It's on the house," Errol said.

"Nope," Hutch said flatly. "We don't want anything from you."

Errol paused then took Hutch's credit card. He rang up the hat for him, then tied string around the big box, so that he'd have an easy time carrying it out of the store. He took awhile doing this because he didn't want Hutch to go. He wished that he could spend the rest of the afternoon with him. He wished he had something that Hutch wanted.

Later, Marcus called Errol to tell him that Hutch had come to see him, and that it had been helpful. He said, "That guy was at Whitehorse. The fucking detention center. He didn't kill anyone, but he did stuff on purpose. I only did stuff on accident."

"Did he hit you?" Errol asked, and Marcus said, "Why would he do that?"

Errol had a split lip. When Louise asked him where he'd gotten it, he told her the truth, and she cried. She said that he'd been the real man in all of this. That hitting wasn't the answer.

Privately, Errol disagreed. He liked his split lip. He liked the way it implied that he had hit someone, too, instead of just standing there. When it healed, he grew miserable again. He waited for Audrey to come back into his store, but she never did.

THE WINTER BEACH

Sheri Joseph

It was a compulsion: at every mile marker they passed on the drive to Florida, he flicked his wedding band with a thumbnail. He kept his eyes on the road. Paul's voice was a soft continuous monologue from the passenger seat, remarking on the landscape, laughing, luring him by slow degrees into *remember* and *we've always* and *us* and *our*, and by the time they reached the Gulf-side condo where they would spend the weekend, the sound of that voice had curled up to purr in Kent's ear, louder than the waves eight floors below their rooms. He felt it as a vibration from within his own body rather than without, now that Paul had gone out on the balcony to look down at the beach.

Standing in the dim interior of someone else's vacation home—a living room with glass-topped tables and pastel furniture and framed square prints of seashells on the walls—he gave the ring a twist. Outside, Paul's blond head was crowned in a brilliance of late-day sun, his hands braced on the wrought-iron rail, and the same chill wind that carried through the open doorway the faint shouts of children and gulls ruffled the shirt along Paul's shoulders and flattened it to the lean contours of his torso. He was twenty-one. In three years, it seemed he had changed little; same downy stem of a neck and stuck-out ears flushed deep pink along the rims. If an inch taller now, broader in the shoulder, his body was still cut as much for Peter Pan as for Hamlet, the role he claimed to have played in a college production the year before. But he was not the pliable thing that had lived in Kent's imagination over the missing time, and it was good to have a minute to adjust to the reality of him—Paul, there, in his willful and difficult flesh.

Probably he was waiting to be coaxed back inside. One foot was hooked behind the other, his face canted toward the beach where there were only a few off-season tourists like themselves— couples strolling the winter sand, a family or two on blankets. Children, yearning for a chance to swim, dashed to test the surf with their toes again, and again, though it was January and they must have known the water would never be warm enough.

Kent tuned to the inner vibration that made his empty hands at his sides quiver. It sounded like *wrong, wrong, wrong*, timed to Paul's steps as he returned inside. To be here was to be already out of control. But he had a plan, insubstantial and fine as a wire. To indulge. To remain detached.

"You're married," Paul said. They were kissing, fumbling with buttons.

"I know that."

"Why?"

"Because I am. Don't talk about it." The contentious breath rose in Paul's chest, and Kent pressed a thumb under his collarbone. "What do you care about that? I'm here."

Paul considered, eyes level. "I don't care about that," he said, and his next kiss was an assault, a bashing of lips on teeth.

He said it again when they were naked and cooling in a damp knot of sheets. Outside, the gulls quarreled in muted shrieks and the gulf shushed them, over and over. Paul raised himself on an elbow and said, "You're married"—as if the marriage and not his presence in this bed were the character flaw Kent should examine.

"And if I weren't, would you be interested in me now at all?"

Paul huffed. "What's that supposed to mean?"

"Nothing. Nothing. I don't want to fight," Kent said, though he couldn't help asking it, couldn't help wanting, partly, to know the answer. At one time, little had been so worthy of Paul's disdain as a played-out trick.

Paul settled back reluctantly against him, the high-strung mood still palpable in the taut muscles of his back. But here was an instrument Kent hadn't forgotten how to play, in long, slow strokes, smoothing the static from his skin until he eased and relented.

"Do you have any idea how much I've missed you?" Kent was glad to say it, though it needed to be revised. There wasn't room in the weekend to admit too much of the personal. "Missed this," he said.

Paul breathed under his hands. "When you're with her, do you think about me?"

There were three answers to that: no if he had any sense, yes to make Paul happy, and the truth. But the last two were the same—he couldn't revise memory to make it otherwise—and the second, from this place, was all he could find the strength to care about. So with a word, he opened the first door on his marriage.

It was not about Maggie. Maggie's near-black eyes lit with humor, cherub cheeks, brows so aggressive and dark against her flour-white skin that "pretty" didn't fit. Just short enough to qualify for "cute," she claimed, but he found her beautiful in her strangeness. She was thirty; he was thirty-one. Together they were called a cute couple—he mainly for his eyes, a sleepier brown than hers, and his head of dark shaggy hair. He liked his mass beside hers, enough of him to fold her in—Maggie in pilled flannel pajamas like a child's, dreaming of legal briefs and the betterment of mankind.

Maggie in gray winter light at the kitchen window, wearing one of his sweaters, moth-bitten sleeves that flapped loose off her hands. "It's snowing, look," she said. Her face was serene, framed in wispy, every-which-way hair, and tinged pink at the tip of her nose. When he held her from behind, the top of her head nestled his chin. Arms crossed around her, he breathed in her scalp, watched the wind drive across the side yard a fine, dusty snow that began to catch and gather along the edges of green blades. The first snow of their marriage, and who knew if it would be a blizzard, unseen in the history of Atlanta, falling to bury the creaky house they had shared for little more than a year. What if the roof didn't hold? What if the furnace broke? He should have considered these things earlier.

"It won't stick," she said. And he believed her. For one, she was a Mennonite, consulted daily with God. But more, she was the sort of person who was instantly trustworthy about things she couldn't possibly know, like future weather.

It was at that moment he decided. Because he loved her, and not the reverse. Because he needed to keep them safe in this house, forever, or in the better house they would one day build. "I have to go away this weekend," he said. Knowing this part at least was the truth offered him no solace. He closed his eyes, cheek to her hair. "I have a web-design conference. Down in Florida."

A small lie, to normalize the bigger truth. He liked to think that in this way he was open with her, always, if through a veil; that on some level she understood what he needed her to. The torment he'd passed through, the regret and longing that still plagued him—these things.

"That should be fun," she said. "Sun, sand, eighty-five degrees."

"I doubt it."

He'd told her before, in fact, everything that mattered about his last long-term relationship, though he'd said it was with a girl named Kristin: a girl who had been too young for him, nearly a decade younger; intensely passionate but also selfish, mercurial, incapable of fidelity; a tornado of a girl indifferent to the damage she caused, because Maggie would not have understood a boy. She would have worried it meant he was gay, which was not quite the case. She'd imagine enormous, serial trouble that in reality was more local and left of center. So Kristin was a truth with a different name.

He wanted to do the same about this weekend, to somehow bare his soul within the lie of it. To say something like, "There are things around us—we two together—that aren't us, that are bigger than us in some ways but also separate, that don't hurt us. They don't touch us." And Maggie, who knew more than he wished she did about the messiness of the world, who lived most of her life with it and apart from him, would have been quick to understand and agree.

He almost said, with fullest possible disclosure, "It's unfinished business, and I can't tell you about it. It's something I have to do, and then I'll come home." He hated himself for lacking that courage.

But it had nothing to do with her at all, or their marriage. It was Paul. It was that, no matter where his life had arrived, some ghostly piece of him haunted this small room of the past, though memory troubled him less and less frequently as time went on. But still, it might have been one of these fevered, half-conscious waking dreams that, at 7:00 PM on a Sunday, on the fifth floor of a university library, brought them quite suddenly face to face. Paul, at the opposite end of a row of shelves, both of them frozen in recognition. Seeing him there brought back in a rush every other instance over the past three years when he had imagined catching sight of him in just this way, in a hundred other public places. But Paul had said New York, Los Angeles, Paris, said it would be a city bigger than this one, and far. Atlanta was barely an hour's drive from where he'd started. Kent had simply never expected to see him again, except in the mind's tricks, those random, blind-side memorials.

And now. It seemed a private trouble had followed him from the last life into this, like bad credit, too sordid to bother his wife with. He had to go away for a few days, tend to something necessary. He wasn't sure what. But necessary.

Red royal shrimp. Or royal red shrimp. It was one of the two, no question, and they could not sit down to eat until they had found this delicacy—Paul marched them out of one, two, three restaurants that professed to have no idea what he was talking about. Later, past ten o'clock, they were in bed with a pizza: mushrooms and anchovies, one of the rare things they had ever managed to agree on.

"I can't believe those idiots." Paul's mouth was full as he spoke, tomato sauce dotting his chin. "This area is, like, famous for red royal shrimp. People used to think they were trash in the nets until someone figured out how to cook them. You flash-boil them, like lobster. Dip them in butter, god it's good. We've always had red royal shrimp here, every single time."

Kent grimaced faintly at the *we*, which did not include him. "How many times have you been here?"

Paul rolled his eyes and conceded. "Twice." Shirtless, he ate sprawled on his side, lifting the long wedge of pizza to dangle over his mouth. Kent had removed only his shoes, ate cross-legged with a spray of napkins over his knee.

"With him, I guess. What's-his-name."

"Bernard. He's not as awful as you think."

During the six-hour drive, Paul had spoken enough of his present life to reveal that Bernard, the owner of the condo, was well into his fifties and Paul's college professor before he had moved Paul into a spare bedroom and began paying his way. As Paul explained it, Bernard was not a horny old man but simply a philanthropic soul with more money than he could use, a lonely, kind-hearted man who chose from time to time to sponsor a bright and talented member of the younger generation as the lad worked to achieve his full potential. "Potential in *what*?" Kent had to ask, since Paul was on his third major somewhere in his senior year and seemed to waffle between his "acting" and his "writing," and—Kent would bet on it—spent more time in bars than engaged in either one.

But, he reminded himself, Paul's life was his own business. Remain uninvolved. All talk was small talk, mere conversation.

"And he knows you're down here this weekend. With me."

"Like I said, he's a decent guy. Generous. I don't exactly parade guys in front of him, but he's aware I'm not a monk."

"No, you're not."

Paul smiled, dropped a languid arm over Kent's thigh and rubbed denim with a knuckle. "How would you know? You don't know me at all anymore."

Kent considered that—Paul chewing dinner on the bed's disarray, his careless eyes cast toward the wall, the lamplight in the heavy gold of his lashes—and wondered again what he was doing here. *Call Maggie*, he reminded himself. He checked his watch, careful not to move his wrist in doing so because Paul had quick eyes, hair-trigger moods. It was ten fifteen. He needed to be dialing within the next forty-five minutes.

Paul sat up and wiped his greasy hands on the sheets, a smirk of apology lodged in the corner of his mouth before Kent could voice an objection. "Relax, will you? We'll change rooms." He lolled his head along one shoulder to meet Kent's eyes. "Let's fuck in every room."

Words, voice, eyes, mouth—Kent never knew which one kicked the breath out of him, tilted him forward. Paul's power had always been this way, planetary, disquieting, inexplicable, effortless, while past his shoulder a thousand men waited like shades. But they were illusion. Kent knew this much. No matter how real they were somewhere, how real in Kent's mind, Paul had no thought of them. He didn't hear them whisper from dreams, past or future. If ten minutes after they parted ways on Sunday night Paul might be with someone else, that was not yet. Here, now, he was Kent's alone, eyes fixed on him, blue and absolute.

For a second, Kent made an effort to hold in mind what he needed to remember, and then abandoned the effort. Such ecstatic relief, to not think. He licked the tomato sauce from Paul's chin, and more from the pale, hairless hollow of his stomach, and they were out of their clothes, and the pizza box was on the floor, and it was eleven thirty and too late to call.

Paul recited the things other men had bought him. "I was with this guy for a week," he said, fingering one of three bracelets, a complex chain of interlocking silver. "He was from India. His name was *impossible* to say."

Kent was surprised that none of the three was from the professor. "He bought me the leather jacket," Paul offered. "He likes to buy me clothes." They lay under the sheet, speaking softly as if they might wake someone. The room was dark except for the flickery gray-white light of the TV, the sound too low to hear. Beyond the heavy drapes, the sky would be pinking the water with first light any minute.

"You should buy me things," Paul teased.

"I don't have any money."

"No. You have a wife."

Kent closed his eyes briefly, until the words were gone. It was only the two of them alone in the bed. He touched the inside edge of Paul's middle finger that curled on the sheet between them, thinking how much he might have given on a bad night to have just this much of him.

"I don't love any of them," Paul said. "But you love her, don't you?"

"Stop."

"Sorry." He brooded, the skin of his forehead twitching.

It was a quandary for Kent, whether to enjoy this new helping of power. He was used to Paul having all of it, lording it over him. He didn't want to consider the likelihood that he had his marriage to thank for the pleasure. And then, what Paul ever showed was mostly shell, like those spiraled sea creatures polished to a dazzle and coiled to a point, testament in itself to what a raw and tender thing lay beneath. Any visible twinge of his distress was rare enough to make Kent flinch, to weaken him before he could enjoy it.

He nudged two fingers between three of Paul's, took the lightest hold, knuckle to knuckle. Their hands were back to back, as if to avoid too much connection, but the result seemed more intimate than holding hands. A week before, when Paul had suggested this trip, Kent had told himself it would be a fling, a balm for longing, a one-time indulgence in the peaceful life of his marriage. But here, now, he couldn't seem to imagine the end of it. His plan was so wire-thin there was almost nothing out here in the middle to see or hold on to.

"Don't sleep," Paul said. Kent had let his eyes close, and the next time, Paul was astride his chest, thumbs jammed into his eyebrows. *"Don't sleep."*

The weight of him forced a chuckle from Kent's lungs. "Ever?"

"Not until I say."

They were making new rules, it seemed, so Kent took the opening to goose him in his hyper-ticklish ribs. Paul sprang clear but didn't flag the play, only set his jaw and came back for more until he was shrieking off the edge of the mattress.

He returned with treasure. "Look, this was under the bed." He rolled out a tube of lipstick, a cheap, stale red, gave Kent a narrow look. "Did you bring a girl?"

"That looks like it's been down there a while."

"One of Bernard's old fag hag theater buddies must have left it." Paul leapt up from the bed, flicked on the lamp beside the vanity mirror. He proceeded to smear the lipstick over his mouth.

Kent rose and stood over his shoulder, watching in the mirror as Paul drew the full circle, open-mouthed, a single bold stroke. Greasy swaths reached far past his lips into the faint blond glisten of stubble. He puckered and pouted in the mirror, bared his lower teeth like a model mugging for the camera. Standing naked in the lamplight with his red mouth and fierce gaze, he looked less like a woman than a savage.

Kent was repulsed, and awed. He felt dizzy. "Look at you," was all he could say. Laughing, Paul turned and kissed him with deliberate roughness. Back in the mirror, his mouth was a faded mess, half printed away, but the red on Kent barely showed, as if somehow the color had vanished between them. He leaned in and kissed Paul's neck, his ear, half hoping that Paul would paint him to match.

Undistracted, Paul glared into the mirror. He drew his mouth in fresh red. He shoved his bald chest forward and traced one nipple, filled it in. The lipstick wore down to a nub under the force he used. Around the other nipple he made a bull's-eye ring, a thick glob breaking off at the end of the circle. Kent took the tube from his hand, and Paul stood passively, with half a smile, while Kent drew a garish heart around the second circle.

Paul's turn. He smoothed a hand over the canvas of Kent's chest. "Too hairy," Kent said, but Paul drew anyway a line down the center, lightly; there was little left to waste. He set the spent tube on the dresser and leaned into Kent's arms. In the mirror, his body was an immaculate white curve, his face against Kent's shoulder stunned, used, whorish.

"Paul, god," Kent whispered, "angel," and turned him, propelled him backward to the bed. Another condom from the bedside box, and Paul took up fistfuls of the bedcovers, throat arched out, but his eyes were distant, almost disengaged, a faint smile playing in his painted lips as Kent moaned into each thrust like a lost soul, a wounded animal.

"I'm about to head out," he said to Maggie, 9:30 AM. "Yeah, I slept in a little, but I don't really have a session until ten that I can't miss."

Maggie had been at work for an hour, was on her third cup of coffee, and it was Saturday. "I thought this was your weekend to sleep," he said, though he'd never worry about waking her at this hour and hadn't tried her at home first.

"I've got to go down to the jail again," she said, sounding perky. "One more talk with Jamal and then I give up."

"Mags, you gave up on him last week."

"See, I need you around to remind me of these things."

"You're crazy, you know that."

"I'm persistent."

He'd stopped a year ago saying *relax*. It wasn't in her nature. But it bothered him immensely, the idea of sweaty, grunting criminals pushing her around—even if they were seated and chained—forcing her to work harder than she needed to. "You want me to come back there and smack him a little?"

"Oh, that's what I need. 'Don't mind my husband, officer, he's just here to rough up my clients who fail to contribute to their own defense.'"

He chuckled, receiver to his face, that little curve of space like a room they seemed to share, somewhere in the air between Florida and her cluttered, cheery Atlanta public defender's office. She would be in casual clothes today, something artfully mismatched from a vintage store, a boyish girl-woman without makeup. On the bulletin board beside her would be photos of her with her arms around the released murderers in whom she found so much pain and beauty; a blown-up line from Eleanor Roosevelt ("You must do the thing you think you cannot do"); a card he had given her after a tough case had gone sour, of a 1950s-style comic-strip woman with a wind-up key in her back, saying, "I love my job! I love my job!"

He turned, and Paul was standing in the doorway, squinting against the living room's white sunlight. The room with Maggie dissolved. "I've got to go," he said, deadpan. "I'll call you later."

Paul was back in bed, the tight mound of him lumping the covers. Kent crawled back to the place where he had awakened, apart.

Covers rustled. "Was that her?"

"Yes."

More rustling. "What'd she say?"

Kent closed his eyes, sheet to his chin. "Not much," he mumbled. "Go back to sleep."

"What'd you tell her?"

"That I was fine, on my way out the door." He opened his eyes to the dormant wooden blades of the ceiling fan, an arm behind his neck, hearing Maggie's low voice speak through her morning again, intimate and without suspicion.

"To the conference?" Paul snickered, dragging a fingertip along Kent's bicep. He wanted so badly, Kent knew, for this to be a joke between them, but Kent couldn't indulge him. He rolled away, face to the pillow.

A few hours later, Kent awoke more rested, heard the shower running. He got up and cracked the drapes on a day that had turned gray, thick with clouds, the surf mounting and restless. Far out, there was a white sail, and he couldn't help checking the weather for her sake, gauging the distance to the bay. He guessed the boat a thirty-footer. If it were some novice hotshot who thought open water took no particular skill, he'd be in trouble pretty quick.

He turned to face the ravages of the room. For one clear moment, he saw himself standing there, bare-ass naked in the middle of the stupidest thing he had ever done to his life, and he was ready to pack. There was nothing rational in being here and nothing good about it for anyone involved—not even for Paul, who had breezed out of his life after two on-and-off years of being repressed and thwarted and misunderstood in every way Kent could think of to do it. Not that his efforts had ever left a dent.

He tried to locate a reason Paul would accept for leaving now. And then, how he might explain to Maggie his early return. Hand on the bathroom door, he ran the possibilities, while inside, the hiss and slap of the water reflected the shape of the body moving under it. He opened the door to a roomful of steam, slid back the shower curtain, stepped inside.

"What are we doing?" he asked, with something desperate in his voice. "Why are we here?" Paul smiled and went to his knees, which was and always had been, for better or worse, his best and most eloquent answer to everything.

The sun came out in fits, minutes, between a soot-bellied cover of clouds. The storm seemed to be holding off. They had an almost private expanse of white sand stretching out from either side of their blanket and back to where the dunes began, golden with sea oats. Behind the dunes rose their tall building, pink stucco tiered with multiple balconies. Another like it was visible at the farthest point before the next cove. Between were low bungalows, blue, tan, white, set on pillars against the tide. To the west, a pair of middle-aged men and their wives fished with rigged poles set into the sand. A group of college kids started a volleyball game. Periodically, others passed along the water, winter-tanned in twos and threes: old brown people, couples, buff joggers warmed enough to bare arms and legs to the chill breeze.

They were barefoot in jeans, long-sleeved flannel over T-shirts. Paul lay on his back, cloud-gazing through orange-tinted, silver-rimmed sunglasses, knees bent, arms outstretched and hands upturned as if he were staked out for some primitive torture but planning to enjoy it. Kent sat in the opposite corner, facing the water. They had brought a cooler full of cheap beer in cans and had killed the first six hardly moving from their spots.

"I get bored with my classes," Paul said to the sky. "All of them. They're too easy. I want to do something different, but I don't know what."

"You're writing plays, you said."

"A few." His nose wrinkled. "I don't know if they're any good. Bernard calls them 'Christ-haunted erotic journeys.' How do you like that?"

"Am I in them?" Already he wanted to withdraw the question. It wasn't even exactly what he wanted to know, though he was curious about his own role in whatever had been produced, or would be. He'd always suspected Paul of harboring the sort of untried brilliance that might suddenly burst forth into real art—though the medium remained, like Paul's concentration, loose. He was too much of a sensualist, too young to bother yet with lasting expression.

Paul crooked an arm under his head, looked up at Kent over the tops of his shades. "Maybe. Do you want to be?"

Kent cracked a new beer and looked out to the water's horizon. At every new topic, it seemed, he reached one of these walls, as if their conversation were forced to turn through a maze no bigger than their blanket. It was painful to know that to a stranger, to anyone else at all, he would mention that his wife ran a soup kitchen, that she was writing grants to fund halfway houses for her paroled prisoners, that she volunteered in a store founded on the mission of fair trade with third-world countries. Try volunteer work, he might have suggested, the solution to boredom if nothing else. And yet, to Paul, he could not even raise the subject. Paul's questions—*do you want to be?*—tapped seductively from the other side of one of those same walls, and Kent could do nothing but smile wanly and look away.

"I didn't think you would," Paul said. "Well, Bernard's all hot about producing one of them next fall, but I don't know. I might try to get away from the theater, do something different. I get tired of all the faggots, you know?" Kent laughed, incredulous. Paul laughed, too. "I mean, for real. Like, Bernard—he's an old queer from a mile off, and everyone else I know lately is so fucking gay I want to puke." He upended his beer can over his mouth, and Kent sensed something not quite sincere in this, Paul fishing in an idle way for a reaction.

"Are you being serious or what?" Kent handed him another beer from the cooler, opened, and Paul sucked the foamy top from the can.

"I've started hanging out at a frat house," he said after a minute. "How's that for serious?"

"What?"

"Don't think I can pass? You don't think I can funnel beer and scratch my balls and talk about snatch with the best of them?"

"What the hell are you talking about? And no, I don't think you can pass."

"I am an actor, you know. You've just never seen me act."

"Lately," Kent said, but considered Paul: reclined on his elbows, chin tipped toward the sky, supremely at ease in his body, even masculine. His voice seemed to have lost the stagy punctuation that used to flare when he was nervous or defensive. Now it was so smooth and soft that, over the gulf, Kent had to strain for the sound.

"You do seem a little different," Kent said.

"I would, I guess. To you. You seem different to me."

"How's that?"

Paul crossed his ankles, bare foot not quite brushing Kent's knee, and studied him with the angelic gaze that hadn't changed a bit. Kent had long ago ceased thinking of angels as sweet—those lofty, perfect creatures who had no patience with human weakness and no time for pity.

"Colder," Paul decided, mild but exacting. "More distant. Guarded. More afraid. If that's possible."

He slurped his beer and went on lightly. "These frat guys I've been hanging with—I really like them. They're kinda dumb, as you'd expect, but I don't care. Isn't that funny? I crave the company of straight guys. That's my curse, I guess. Comes from growing up in the sticks in Greene County with nothing but rednecks to lust after for miles. And, well, I don't have you anymore."

"Paul." Kent shook his head, knowing in advance the futility of warnings. "God, be careful."

Paul waved him off. "I'm fine."

"These guys think you're straight?"

"More than that." He grinned conspiratorially. "They might give me a bid. But what's the difference? A frat house is just one big cover for straight guys who want to jerk each other off in secret and call it brotherhood—am I wrong? They're gonna love me."

Kent bit his tongue—*remain uninvolved*. But it was hard when he knew this was Paul's real life, more than wordplay. Even at two or three removes, Kent fought the urge to take a fist to everything that waited to harm him.

"You scare the shit out of me," he muttered, and watched the waves build and roll flat. Meanwhile the rational voice not yet banished entirely from his head listed again, gentle reminder, the many reasons they had broken up.

Paul smiled fondly at his fear. "Promise you'll never change. By the way, if you moved two inches closer to me, who exactly out here do you think would even notice?"

Kent met his eyes, settled into a long gaze without moving any closer. There were so many things to leave unsaid, and the crucial one, he knew, was love, or anything that sounded like it. The wind blew over them, stinging their faces with a light spray of sand. Already their hair was gritty with it. Though they would shower twice, it seemed certain a few grains would stick to their scalps, stow away in their crotches, follow them home.

At dinner, no red royal shrimp, but Paul was too looped to care, and they ordered martinis and a bottle of wine and an assortment of unidentifiable seafood, fried. Later, back at the condo, Paul mixed more martinis, and then they were out on the beach in the chill of the night, clutching plastic cups full of gin.

"I just want to know if she's pretty!" he shouted, his voice ragged in the windy dark. All decorum on this topic had worn away over dinner, when he'd squeezed out of Kent—what could it hurt?—her profession (lawyer), and where they had met (in a music store), and the color of her hair and eyes (deep brown, both), and now Maggie was with them. They had no more walls to keep her out and no memory of the walls.

"Is she like your mother? You can tell me *that*. The dark hair and eyes. It's a mother thing, right? Do you look like brother and sister together?" Paul walked apart, staggering a bit along the water's edge, and in the weak light from the buildings his head was thrown back, his arms out away from his body as if he might spin a circle. "I bet they do," he said, a private chuckling aside to the sky.

"Paul." Kent's voice, and its hundredth calling of the name that night, didn't carry far against the wind. "Can we please drop it?"

"No." Paul circled back. "Stop telling me to shut up. Who says you get to say what we talk about. I'm just taking an interest in your life, which I'd say is being polite. So tell me."

"Tell you what?"

"If she's pretty."

"Paul—"

"Long hair or short. That's all!"

Kent gasped out a breath. "Short. Okay? Please stop." He palmed the back of Paul's head with his free hand and tried to steer him into a facing position. "You're drunk."

"So what?" Closer, Paul's voice softened almost to a whisper, but there was a strained note that ran through it like a whine. From somewhere out of their prior years came a brief, disturbing body-memory, but it was Kent begging, as drunk as Paul was now, saying *please, one night, just stay . . .*

"Do you really think I would hurt you?" Paul said. "What are you afraid of?"

"Everything."

Paul stepped back, stung. "Afraid of me? You think I'd hurt you."

"No, no. That's not what I meant."

Paul walked away with slow, wandering steps, and Kent followed, aware that he needed to rein Paul in, calm him, and that he was too drunk himself to be very effective. Off to their right, they passed the volleyball players, now trying to build a fire back toward the windbreak of the dunes.

"Valentine's Day is coming up," Paul called back, his voice light. "Don't worry, I won't expect anything. I already got mine, didn't I?" He laughed. "But you, sir, you got a lot to make up for at home. That's flowers *and* a box of chocolates for her, I'm betting. Dinner, movie . . . anything else? Will you fuck her? Or do you two call it something different? Or does she even *do* it—"

Kent grabbed his arm hard and jerked him around. "Enough."

Paul let out a teary gasp, hid his face behind a hand. "I'm sorry," he mumbled. "That was . . . I didn't mean that. I'll shut up now, I promise. But god, Kent, just talk to me. I'm not the enemy. I won't hurt you."

"I know you won't." Paul slumped against him, and Kent held him with one arm. "But my marriage, that's . . . it's separate from us."

Paul sighed, and his voice was calmer. "So there's an us?"

"Let's just enjoy the weekend."

Paul smiled a little. He took Kent's arm and led him along, ignoring Kent's suggestion, yet again, that they go inside. "Come on, it's a nice night. It's the beach. Gotta enjoy it while you're here."

The tide was in, and the waves forced them into softer, looser sand, until Paul gave up trying to walk through it and sat, dragging Kent down. Side by side, they faced the water. The sand was dry but so cool it felt damp beneath them.

"Are you glad you came?" Paul asked quietly, his arms around his knees.

"Glad? No. But if I hadn't come, I'd be at home miserable. Worse, probably."

Paul shook his head, watching the water. "Why did you get married?"

"Because I did. It's my life now. Stop asking."

"It doesn't make sense."

"Well, guess what. Your life has never made a bit of sense to me. So here we are."

They sat in silence for several minutes, the waves folding up onto the shore closer and closer to their feet. One more night. Paul slid over and took hold of Kent's collar. "If you're gonna torture yourself later anyway, better get your money's worth."

Kent almost laughed, that Paul had said aloud the hopelessly cynical thing he had been thinking—except that he kept pretending he could keep the two things separate: have only pleasure now, save all the pain for later. Paul was already digging for the buttons of his jeans, and Kent caught him back by the arms. "No way. Time to go back inside, for real."

"Come on. Don't pretend you can hold back now."

Kent kept a bracing grip on him, and Paul's voice climbed sharply in response, louder and louder. "Two weeks ago you were fucking me in a public toilet, for Chrissake! In the fucking *library*, ten minutes after you laid eyes on me!"

"Calm down. Let's just go inside. It's cold—"

"It's not *cold*." Paul jerked out of his grip and stood. "You're such a baby."

Kent pulled himself out of the sand. Paul stood a little ways off, facing the water where the night was transforming itself into splendor. "Look at that, will you?" Paul said. "Wow." The moon, nearly full, was engaged in a fitful struggle with the fast clouds, covered and clear and covered again, and then it tore loose, illuminating an operatic swell of water and moving sky.

"Better idea." Paul smiled over his shoulder, shrugged out of his jacket. "I'm going swimming."

"The fuck you are."

Paul laughed, and his humor vanished. His voice fell low with seductive urgency. "Come with me."

Kent stood staring. It was three simple words like these that had once led him into another night, blacker than this, the night he first met Paul, and was dating girls, and Paul was seventeen years old. Five years later, and here he was, still stumbling through that same unending night on the trail of Paul's voice.

Paul whipped off his flannel shirt and T-shirt, kicked off his shoes. "Live your life, Kent. Let someone else do the worrying for once." He opened his jeans, grinning. Kent turned about-face and walked away, long strides away from Paul and back to the condo, not looking back.

But with each struggling step through the loose sand, another part of him moved back to Paul, a ghost that was not afraid, that shed its clothes and slipped with him into the Gulf water as if it were any summer night, as if there were no stingrays beneath the black surface or jellyfish or sharks, or sharp stones or rusted curls of metal, and most of all no wicked undertow to drag them together into the water's belly, beyond the farthest hope of return. He went with Paul, and together they dove deep and sprang back to the surface like seals, laughing in the cold, rolling chaos of water for no reason except that they were alive and it felt good.

In the condo, alone, Kent buzzed with a dim anger. Maybe Paul would drown and he'd be rid of him. But if he died, the cops would have to be called and Kent's life would be over that way. At least he felt himself sickening of the surfeit. By Monday, it would all be behind him.

Soon Paul was scratching at the door in his underwear, soaked, shivering out of his skin. "Jesus fuck, Paul. You want to kill yourself? You want to drown or just die of pneumonia?" Kent hauled him inside, wrapped him in a blanket where he convulsed, blue-lipped, trying but unable to speak.

He hadn't intended to remember tenderness, but here it was again. He drew Paul a hot bath. Sitting beside the tub while Paul relaxed by degrees and the shaking stopped, Kent felt mute with unwanted relief to have him back unharmed, and next caught himself half admiring what had once infuriated him: that foolish daredevil bravery with which Paul flung himself at the world, at any whim. He watched the bathwater slip and bead over the unbroken integrity of Paul's skin and tried to bring back his anger, as if he could choose what to feel.

"My bones are still frozen," Paul said with a sleepy grin, face resting on the tub's edge. "I don't think they'll ever get warm."

Kent frowned his disapproval. "Was it worth it?"

"It was amazing." His eyes were brim full of the irony that said Kent couldn't fool him or pretend they were strangers. "What kind of question is that?"

Kent shook every grain of sand from his clothes before he packed them, bagged the ones in plastic he needed to wash, though he could tell Maggie he'd spent a free hour on the beach. As they tossed their things into the car, he inspected the floor mats and the bottom of the trunk for sand, for anything amiss, thinking about how, as they neared the Atlanta skyline, the sun would be setting behind them and Maggie would be unlocking the doors of the stone church on Baxter for the Mennonite congregation's small evening gathering. When he turned the key on their empty house, her alto voice would be joining the other singers', a cappella, beautiful as a single flower in a field but inseparable from the harmonious union of sound.

They were ready to leave, heading toward the door, but Paul stopped. He stood unmoving in the living room.

"What?"

"I'm not ready." He went and sat on the sofa. Kent stood in the door for a minute, before going to sit beside him.

"I don't want to go back yet." He said it like something reasonable, looking at his knees.

"Paul."

"You're already back there, aren't you? You're thinking about her. You're thinking about getting there, and what she'll cook you for dinner and what you'll . . . talk about or whatever." He gave Kent a level look. "Let's stay. Just another hour."

"We can't."

"You choose her over me," he said, simply, flatly, but emotion flared in his face. "You can't choose her. That's fucked."

Kent rolled his eyes. "Can we have this discussion in the car?" Before Paul could snap back, explode, Kent took hold of his shoulder. "Paul, you and me, we were lousy as a couple, you know that. We broke up because we don't work." He restrained himself from saying *you left me, remember?* Easier to think of it as the mutual thing it should have been in anyone's rational world. "We make each other nuts. We've got nothing together."

"It's not nothing."

"Fine. We have great sex."

That would end it, Kent knew, because Paul would be unable to think of anything that mattered more. He wouldn't see the lie at the back of it, wouldn't admit he even cared to hear there was more between them, still, than sex. If they stayed another hour, Kent might be deluged in all there was, overwhelmed, lost.

And if they left now, he told himself, it would fall away behind them, eventually, like the water and sand, turn peaceful and remote like memory.

Paul mocked him. "You have something more with her, I suppose?"

"Yes."

Their faces were inches apart, eyes locked, Paul breathing through his flared nose, but any fight was beneath his effort if he saw Kent would win. "Fuck it," he said. "Let's go.

In two months, he would be twenty-two years old. Kent followed him out the door, wishing he didn't know just as certainly that Paul would stiffen against touch, would tip his forehead to the passenger window and gaze in a listless, soulful way at the passing palmettos and cows, punishing him with silence until Alabama and he couldn't bear it anymore and would simply begin speaking again as if nothing had ever been wrong.

GREEDY, GREEDY

———————•———————

Su Avasthi

The sex addict met the anorexic at a bookstore that kept its cookbook section next to the erotica. Sometimes he prowled the aisles of the erotica section, looking for women who grew short of breath as they read certain passages. Today, the aisles were empty, but the sex addict noticed a girl standing nearby staring at a magazine. He instantly saw the gleam of desire shining in her eye. He circled twice.

Stepping up close behind her, he peered down over her bony shoulder to see what caused her to look so rapt and pearl-eyed. It was a glossy photo of a Thanksgiving feast. A table was artfully littered with fiery autumn leaves and in the center, a gleaming, magnificent bird.

— That looks delicious, he said, his voice turning silky.

The anorexic looked up at him with her large, somber eyes, then turned back to the page. Together, they stared at the turkey, the assortment of flaky casseroles and chive-flecked potatoes, the glazed breads, the bowl of glistening cranberries.

— Delicious, she breathed, in a reverential whisper.

The sex addict took this as a sign of encouragement.

— Especially this, he said. The hair on his arm lightly brushed against hers as he traced his index finger over a drumstick. It was trussed up with a paper crown and shone with fat. The sight of his finger there focused the girl's attention on the richness of the meat. She trembled slightly.

— So delicious, she breathed.

The sex addict felt his blood start to pound and he felt the familiar sensation of ants racing along his spine. His eyes glazed over. He moved his hand farther down the page of the magazine, his hand an inch from the girl's sunken abdomen. He stroked a gleaming round of bread. He dropped his finger down farther and lightly touched the tiny crock of cranberries.

She licked her lips. He saw the muscles in her neck grow taut under her thin sweater. He took a step closer to her, resisted the urge to press himself against the back of her too-big jeans. She smelled like fallen fruit, left to spoil and burn in the sun. He swallowed hard. She shut her eyes.

— Let's go eat, baby girl, he whispered into her lank hair.

At that, she slammed the magazine together, trapping his hand between the pages. For an instant, their hands were locked in spontaneous prayer. She pulled her hands away, let the magazine drop.

— I'm not hungry, she declared.

She spun around and left.

The anorexic raced down the stairs of the bookstore. She moved quickly, frightened that he might follow her. He was sure to follow her. She ducked behind one of the aisles, positioning herself against a wall of biographies because it offered her a view of both the staircase and the exit. She waited for him to come downstairs.

She couldn't remember what his face had looked like. She could only remember his hands, so she fervently studied hands of the men nearby. He'd had large hands, dignified and square. A gold ring on his fourth finger. She remembered a bright blue shirt, and a silver cufflink. She surveyed the room. One man's hands were too pale, and another man's hands were too spindly. Too clumsy, too hairy, too delicate, too dark.

Then she saw a man in a dark suit descend the stairs. She saw the blue shirt. He held a cell phone in one manicured hand, a briefcase in the other. She tried to fold herself into a smaller space. She realized that he was not scanning the room for her. He was talking to someone on the phone. He looked angry, purposeful. He held the phone against his graying temples, and she saw his index finger stroke the black nub of the antenna as he strode briskly out the door. She followed him.

The raw desire that he'd seen on the skinny girl's face had agitated the sex addict to such a degree that he loosened his tie on the crowded street. He placed one call to his secretary and told her that he'd be out for the rest of the afternoon. He placed another call to a woman he visited from time to time.

— I'll be there in ten minutes, he said into the phone.

There were other women that he might prefer right now, but they were fussier and difficult. This woman was reliable. She accommodated his moods without making any demands of her own. She didn't require expensive dinners or calls to the florist. He didn't need to think about foreplay or small talk. That was the only thing he liked about her. He didn't like the spray of red pimples on her back or the cat-smell all over her apartment. A whiff of litter box reminded him of tawdry afternoons at her place, her thighs pressed against the filthy cushions of her couch, skirt over head, panties twisted down over her ankles. The thought repulsed him and made him walk faster down the street.

He passed a grocery store, and an idea flickered briefly. Maybe he should grab a can of cranberry jelly. He smiled. That could be kinky. He was so fired up that he had to will himself to slow down and go inside. He summoned the self-control by reminding himself that a quickie on the floor wouldn't suffice. He'd want the cranberries for a second act.

The girl at the cash register was a dark-haired teenager who cracked her gum. The buttons of her shirt pulled tight against her upturned breasts, spunky and full of attitude. He smiled as he pulled out his wallet.

— For my baby girl, he said. My wife asked me to stop and pick some up, because my baby loves the stuff. She can't get enough.

— Adorable, the cashier said blandly, flicking away a strand of hair with a long, multi-colored fingernail. A gold earring dangled against the tender, dusky skin of her neck.

— Oh, she's a doll. Just like you. He winked, and the cash register girl raised her eyebrow at him and smirked.

The anorexic kept her distance, ready to duck into a storefront or hide behind a pole, in case he happened to look behind him. But the man strode forward at a fast pace. *This is crazy,* she told herself. *Turn around! Go back to the library! Right now!!* She had a term paper due Friday and a midterm next week. Then she remembered his finger, gliding down the drumstick, all that crispy skin and delicious juice. *Delicious, delicious.* The image of the rich meat flooded her thoughts. She could almost smell it. She could almost taste it. She swooned on the street, bumping into a hefty man wearing a red baseball cap. He reached out to make sure that she didn't lose her balance.

— Whoa, you OK there?

She jerked, alarmed at his touch, then kept hurrying down through the crowds. *So good, so pure,* she thought. *Close to the edge, sharp as knife.*

Ahead, she spotted the man going into a grocery store. She stopped cold in the middle of the sidewalk. She couldn't go in there. No way. Her knees trembled. *This is too much, too much, too much, I don't know if I can stand it.* She approached the glass doors, and they parted before her. Her skin began to prickle. Then she was inside, standing at ground zero. Rows of sardines and Miracle Whip and fusilli. Miles of Pop Tarts. *So much, so much.*

Her head began to spin and she nearly raced out. But then she caught sight of the man's blue shirt and she kept her eyes fixed on him. She imagined that there was a rope between them, one that would keep her from straying, from falling into a food-filled crevice.

The man was smiling at the cash register girl. The anorexic moved closer to see what he was buying, and when she did, she had to steady herself by gripping the side of a magazine rack.

A single can of cranberries.

She gasped, staring at it. She couldn't believe it. Did he know that she was following him? Was he toying with her?

All at once, he was gone, striding out of the store, the can dangling in a plastic bag. She darted out behind him. He moved quickly down the crowded avenue for some blocks, then abruptly turned onto a quiet, tree-lined street. She saw him climb the steps of a brownstone, ring a bell, then tap the door impatiently. She heard the door buzz, and then he was gone.

The anorexic sat down on the stoop and tried to catch her breath and waited. She thought about calzones and banana splits with gooey chocolate syrup. She thought about bowls of fondue. Her gaze fell upon some dusty blades of grass trying to grow between the cracks of the cement, stunted and overlooked. It was a far cry from the grassy lawns that she remembered playing in when she was a child. Those were lush and thick and speckled sometimes with delicate sprays of yellow dandelions and their downy seeds. She felt that there was an immense chasm between then and now, an ever-widening gulf that was sweeping her away from places that were simple and green, places to which she could never really return.

She told herself to think about cranberries. She imagined the man in a white room, seated at a table. He was twisting a can opener in his dignified hands, slowly and methodically prying open the lid. She imagined him sliding the quivering red cylinder onto a china plate. What would he do next? Would he slice it into neat and perfect rounds? Would he tease it into a luscious, trembling pulp? Would he hold a shivering spoonful to his lips?

Cranberries had exactly 110 calories per serving. No fat, but lots of sugar. Too much sugar. She loved sugar, the way its sweetness exploded on her tongue. A little sugar was okay. She allowed herself three Life Savers each day, sucking each one slowly, slowly, making it last for forty-five minutes.

But cranberries! She couldn't remember how good they must taste. *Too much, too much.* She closed her eyes, resting her cheek on her knees. The bones of her kneecaps dug into her face, and that felt reassuring. She waited.

The sex addict heard the lock slide shut behind him, and stood at the top of the stairwell. It was all so familiar, the odor of cat litter and sex on his skin, the tiny window that gave him a view of the darkening orange sky, the bone-deep exhaustion. He dreaded this moment, when the clouds cleared for a while and when the distance that it took to travel from these encounters to his home, to his shower, seemed unimaginably far. Never again, he told himself; and that, too, felt familiar. He paused to light a cigarette—even though he wanted to quit—before going outside. He inhaled deeply and stepped out of the building.

There was someone on the stoop, a girl hunched over, poking a twig at a small tuft of grass. He could see the structure of her rib cage and the knobs of her spine through her thin lilac sweater. He recognized her lifeless hair. He thought, *No it can't be.* He went down the stairs and put his hand on the back of her neck. She looked up at him, her eyes large and startled and hungry. Her face looked different than it had in the bookstore, pained and sunken, still desirous.

— I . . . I . . . , she began. Then she stopped and took a deep breath and said, Why did you buy the cranberries?

— Shhh, baby girl, he said, putting a finger to his lips. A scrawny little mutt, he thought. Just a scrawny, abandoned little mutt. He reached for her hand. She took it, gingerly at first. Then she clutched it tight.

— Would you like to come home with me? he asked.

The girl nodded, utterly relieved, and he helped her to stand. She seemed so frail that he suddenly felt incapable of getting both himself and the girl back to his apartment. Instead of walking the twelve blocks to his home, he hailed a cab.

His apartment reminded the anorexic of a supermodel's body. It was sleek and perfect, with no sign of excess. It was unsullied by stacks of books or drooping houseplants or framed snapshots. She ran her finger over an armoire that was all ash wood with sharp angles and clean lines.

— No one's here, he told her. These days, it's just me and the maid who comes by a couple times a week. He waited for her to respond. She was silent.

— Aside from my wife, she's the only other woman . . . , he began, then faltered. What I mean is that I don't normally bring women here.

She didn't respond. She felt itchy and hot. She thought that he expected her to say something clever.

— Where's your kitchen? she blurted out. He looked at her strangely, so she wandered into the dining room. A gleaming mahogany table stood in the center, flanked by metal chairs. In the center was a silver bowl, filled with four perfect green apples. She inhaled deeply, savoring a faint whiff of their crisp, sweet-tart aroma.

He followed her, pointing the way to the kitchen. It was sleek and filled with stainless steel. A supermodel, she marveled. She wanted to open the refrigerator and rummage around. She wanted some privacy. She realized that he had followed her and was watching her. Suddenly, he reminded her of her first therapist, the way that he seemed stern and patient at the same time. She never knew what he wanted her to say.

— Aren't you worried to hear that I have a wife? the sex addict asked. I mean, what if she came home and found you here? He took a step toward her and stroked her cheek with the back of his hand. She brushed it away.

— She doesn't like it when I bring home strays, he said.

— Oh yeah. I bet you're nice like that, she said, sarcastically.

He snorted. Well, my wife had a problem with it. She left me. I haven't seen my daughter for five months.

The anorexic studied him carefully for a moment. He leaned forward and ran his index finger down her nose, then let it come to rest on her mouth. She parted her lips slightly and began to nibble lightly on his finger. He tasted like rich, roasted chicken. Delicious. She bit down harder, and he drew his hand back.

— You're a mutt, he told her. A poor, pathetic stray that I dragged home off the street.

— How come? Her tone was sulky.

— It wasn't to fuck you.

— Oh no?

He rolled his eyes.

— I mean it, he said. I didn't bring you here for that.

She looked at him, suddenly alarmed.

— Why not? Am I too fat? she cried, the panic causing her voice to quaver.

— Jesus, he muttered, running a hand through his hair. He took a deep breath. Listen, I'll be right back. Chase your tail or something. And don't steal anything while I'm gone.

He walked back to the other room, and she heard the front door click shut. Now was her chance. Finally, she was alone in the kitchen. The anorexic yanked open the refrigerator door. It was empty, just bottles of champagne, a moldy lime, and a jar of mustard. She opened the freezer and saw nothing but two bottles of vodka and a small bag of coffee beans.

Her breath became a little ragged. He had to have some food in here. She spun around and opened a stainless steel cupboard. Inside, plain white china was neatly stacked up in rows along the shelf. She opened another one and found nothing but stemware, bowls, and several pin-striped coffee mugs. Her heart started to pound.

The sex addict needed to get away from her for a moment. He needed to think clearly. He could hear the girl poking around his kitchen, scavenging. He left the main apartment and ran up the stairs. On the top floor of his brownstone, there was a photographer's darkroom that the sex addict and his wife had intended to renovate at some point. They'd talked about turning it into something, and until then, they decided that he'd use it for storage. Ellen never went up there anyway, and after a while, he installed a high quality lock. Now, he fumbled with the key and flicked on the red photographer's light. The room was cramped and disordered. Piles of porn magazines sat on a torn leather chair and sex books were stacked near the futon. In the corner sat an ancient VCR with dozens of tapes crammed nearby. Bottles of lotion and massage oil were everywhere, and on the walls there were Scotch-taped photos of women with large nipples, all tangled bodies, open lips. It looked especially lurid under the red bulb.

He sat on the futon and buried his head in his hands. He despised this room, despised its existence. Ellen had never discovered it. She only knew about a few hookers, and that was enough for her. What was he doing with this girl? Why had he brought her to his home? Suppose Ellen happened to return now, after all these months, and find her here. How could he explain that she was nothing more than a stray mutt he'd found on the street? Could he explain to her that something—maybe her jutting collarbones or maybe the weariness in her huge eyes—had moved him? That he didn't know how to stop himself?

With the girl, the impulse hadn't been about sex. Not the real impulse. When she squeezed his hand, it reminded him of the day, some years ago, when he'd lost and found his daughter. She was barely three then. She'd dropped his hand at a neighborhood street fair and toddled off. A short time later, he'd found her sitting on a crate near the Italian-ice vendor. There was enough time, however, for him and Ellen both to get frantic. Her face had gone masklike and terrorized as they searched for their baby during those miserable moments. And then he'd caught sight of her pink sandal and seen her chubby calf swinging back and forth.

She'd beamed up at him from the crate where she sat, and offered him a lick of sweet ice. Then she'd hopped off the crate and grabbed his hand and held it tight, like a vise. That's the way the world is, he thought. It's always waiting to humble you. His daughter had taught him that, but she'd taught him something else, too. That sometimes things could turn out better than one might expect. That's why he'd brought the girl here. But now what was he supposed to do with her? Especially since another part of his mind had already started to wonder whether her scrawny legs possessed hidden strength, and whether they were capable of gripping him tight, like a vise.

She'd started to ransack his kitchen in earnest, desperate to find something, anything, edible. But there was nothing. No peanut butter, no stale crackers, no stray jar of oregano. She began to panic. Who lived like this? What kind of kitchen was this? Her own kitchen—not her dorm room here in New York, but the one at her mother's house—was always in a state of busy chaos. Here, there were no cow-spotted oven mitts or bulletin boards crammed with recipes, workout schedules, or take-out menus.

Her heart started to trip within her chest, and she wondered if this was some kind of joke? Some bizarre trick? She had to get out of there. She remembered the apples and went back into the dining room. There they were, four of them. Ripe, crisp, fragrant, ready for the taking. She began to breathe easier.

She started doing the math. One apple, 60 calories; four apples, 240 calories. *Too much, too much.* But 60 was reasonable. That was within the limits. One apple might be okay. Especially if she skipped the Life Savers. She would peel the apple slowly, then slice it into sections, then slice each section into paper-thin slivers. She would stay at the gym an extra fifteen minutes tomorrow morning.

She reached in the bowl and seized one perfect apple. It felt surprising to the touch, springier than she remembered. It smelled incredible, heady; its texture seemed strange and pliable. She brought it to her mouth, tried to take a bite, and let out a shriek. The apple dropped from her hand to the wood floor. It bounced once and rolled under the table. She stared. It was plastic.

She was sobbing softly in the dining room when the sex addict came back downstairs. She saw him in the doorway and tried to pull herself together, but couldn't. He knelt down beside her.

— Shh, shh, baby girl, he said. What's wrong? He wrapped his arms around her, and they spent a few quiet seconds together. He stroked her hair, and she started to calm down. His hands began to roam down her back. He slipped his hand underneath her sweater and started to caress her bare skin. She tensed, but didn't pull away.

He pulled her up so that they were both standing. He kissed her, and he smelled like roast chicken. Kissing him made her instantly ravenous, and she moved her mouth to his neck, delighting in the salty, spicy, meaty scent. He took her hand and led her up the stairs.

A red light flicked on, and she could see that the room was a mess. The man sat down on a leather chair and pulled her on top of him. She inhaled roast chicken and began to nibble again at the skin on his neck.

— Oh yes, he groaned. She started to claw at his tie and felt him fumbling with the collar. She tugged at it, and a button exploded and went flying across the room. Impatiently, she buried her nose near his throat again, tasting, licking, nibbling. He worked off his shirt, and she could feel his hands moving around under her sweater. She sat up to pull it off, and then looked down at him. In red light, his chest looked like the luscious chicken in the magazine. He'd worked off his pants. *Delicious, delicious,* she thought, as her teeth sank into his shoulder. God, she was starving. Her frenzied mouth moved over to his arm, licking, then gnawing, seeking to satiate herself.

— Hey, baby, calm down, she heard him say. She bit down on his shoulder again and felt him jerk away. Suddenly, his whole body sprang out of the chair, and she was knocked to the ground. She climbed on top of him again and bit down on his lower lip.

— Goddamn, she heard him yell. In the red light, she saw him back away, holding his hand to his bleeding lip. She leaned forward and bit down hard on his bicep. He jerked away.

— What the hell, he cried, blood pooling on his lip. She crawled toward him and tried to bite him again, but he pushed her away.

— Christ! I'm bleeding, he said, pressing his finger to his lip.

She came forward again and licked her lips. She was lost, half-remembering the picture of Thanksgiving dinner and the way that the brown juices had shimmered, the way that he smelled like meat. She lunged for him again, this time sinking her teeth deep into his forearm. She tasted the salty skin. She heard him yelp, then he shoved her back hard and she spun onto the futon. He scrambled to the door and slammed it shut. She heard it lock. Then, as she lay under the red bulb, she heard his footsteps echo down the stairs.

The sex addict examined the damage she'd done as he stood by his bathroom sink, cleaning his wounds with cotton balls. Slight purplish marks had formed around his neck, and there was blood on his lip, and she'd managed to draw a little blood from the bite on his forearm. He doused a cotton ball in alcohol and touched it to the broken skin, wincing a bit at the sting.

Now what? He couldn't call the cops. If they found a hysterical girl up there, Ellen would find out. And now how was he going to get rid of her, this stray who'd turned nasty? An idea started to form. He checked his watch. It wasn't too late. There was a drugstore a few blocks away, and he decided to walk over to see if they had what he needed.

The anorexic cried out for help a few times, halfheartedly. She was dizzy from the tussle. Then she fell onto the futon and began to sob. She cried and ranted and cursed and cried some more. Then she blinked and began to focus on the room. There were pictures of fat, naked women taped to the walls. She looked around and saw porn magazines all over the floor. The women on the covers looked fat, too. She remembered how she'd attacked him, and felt ashamed. She wanted to crawl out of there, to disappear so that she would never have to face him again. She tried the door again. Then she splashed some cold water on her face at a sink behind the VCR, sat on the edge of the futon and tried to think. She decided that he wasn't dangerous, wasn't going to hurt her. He was freaky, though, especially with the porn and the red light. It reminded her of an all-you-can-eat buffet. It was a lot better than his kitchen. She felt clear-headed here, not crazy. She felt safe. She remembered the feel of his hands on her back. The way he called her baby girl. She realized that she hadn't eaten anything all day. Not a Life Saver, not an apple. Nothing at all. Yes, she felt safe in here. She picked up a *Hustler* and started to leaf through it. As she did, she let her mind drift again to food.

The sex addict left the store, bag in hand, and walked back toward his brownstone. It was chilly outside, and the streets were less crowded now. He noticed that the moon was hanging low in the sky, silver and huge. He traced its curve with his index finger, and it seemed almost within his reach. He wondered briefly if locking her in the room was a crime. She was a wild one, all right. He wondered how she would react to his purchase. Would she slap his face? Spit on him? Could she call the police? He pictured her, waiting for him, bathed in the red light. He started to picture her wearing the thing he'd just bought. He began to walk faster. When he reached his apartment, he bolted up the stairs, rapped on the door.

— Hello? she called out.

— Are you sufficiently calm?

— I'm so sorry, she said.

— Promise you'll be good, baby girl. He heard her giggle, embarrassed.

— I promise.

He unlocked the door and saw her sitting cross-legged on the futon. She had put her sweater back on, and had looked at him with her huge, eager eyes, and her expression made him want to throw her down and unzip his pants. He took a deep breath and held up the plastic bag. She gasped.

— What is that? Is that food? Did you bring food up here? she asked, panicked.

He sat down beside her and stroked her hair.

— Shh, don't worry. It's not food. It's something else. Something special. Want to see?

She nodded. He opened the bag and pulled out some sort of black, webbed mesh contraption. She looked baffled. He held it up to her mouth to demonstrate.

— A muzzle, he explained.

Her breathing grew shallow. She pulled off her sweater and nodded impatiently, and he fastened it awkwardly across her mouth. It fit badly, of course, because her head was shaped differently than that of a dog.

Once she was sure that the muzzle would stay in place, the anorexic felt as though she would explode. This was, without question, the most thrilling thing that had ever happened to her. His hands were everywhere, doing wonderful, nasty things to her. His meaty, roasted smell intoxicated her. She pictured the Thanksgiving banquet again. She pressed herself against him, trying to inhale him, trying to bite him, and thought *so close, so close.* The sex addict groaned, and she did, too. She tried and tried again to bite him, to bite into his neck, to taste his flesh. She threw her head back, and the scent of him made her thrash wildly. He smelled like butter, like grease, and she wanted *wanted* wanted to sink her teeth into him, to suck the glistening skin off his bones. *So close so close so close. Right on the edge.* She clenched her legs around him tight. Her mouth opened and closed as she tried to gnaw at him. She was crazed with delight. She thought: *So this is it. I finally know.* And she felt the high. *So good, so pure, so clean.* She heard herself sobbing. If only he would rip off her skin, destroy her body.

A few hours later, he stood under his shower, trying to wash off the day. Images of her flashed through his mind. With that muzzle strapped across her mouth, she looked so slutty, so incredible writhing around. She'd gone so wild, feistier and filthier than he had dared to hope. She'd held nothing back. She'd objected to nothing. He was disgusted. He had to stop.

He'd had a hard time getting rid of the girl. She hadn't wanted to leave, said she felt safe there. He'd urged her to go home, take a shower, and she had started to cry again.

— This city's so huge, so lonely, she'd said, pleading as they stood on his stoop. When she told him that she thought she was falling in love with him, he snorted and told her to forget it.

— I know where you live, she'd told him.

He noticed that the moon was now high and distant in the sky.

— Don't come back here, he'd said, and hoped he'd sounded threatening enough to scare her away. I mean it. Never.

But it was hopeless, wasn't it? One day soon, perhaps even tomorrow, he'd find her waiting for him on the stoop. He'd lead her up to the room and strap the muzzle across her mouth. Maybe he would stop by a grocery store and buy another can of cranberries, or perhaps, he thought with a sigh, a couple of those glossy food magazines, too.

AND THEN THERE WAS CLAIRE

Allison Amend

Funerals ought to have invitations was Garvey's first thought. Embossed ones: Dr. and Mrs. Herman Stoltz request the honor of your presence at the funeral of their daughter, Claire. 1:30 PM Steinberg Memorial Chapel, Washington, D.C. But instead, of course, there was a phone call—a calm, pretentious phone call from Buddy, that old son of a bitch, all Hello, how are you? How's Cleveland working out for you? Are Midwestern chicks really that ugly, and do you fuck them anyway? And oh, by the way, Claire's dead. Yeah, Primatene Mist, same as killed that model. You know. Some congenital heart defect thing reacted weirdly to the inhaler. Boom, her ticker just stopped. They found her on the floor of her apartment, that one on the Circle. Life is short and all that. Listen, the funeral's the day after tomorrow, if you want to come.

He looked around his office, somewhat stunned. His desk was neat, with just enough studied clutter to look as though he frequently used it. His name was painted on the glass door, like the set of a 1970s TV detective show. Andrew Garvey Masterson—his full name, not Garvey, what he'd been called since the first day of first grade, or Gravy, or Groovy.

So Claire was dead. He could hear the whirring machines below, the presses stamping messages onto cards. RSVP Josh Weinstein Bar Mitzvah; Mr. and Mrs. Kenneth R. Churchman request the honor of your presence at the wedding of their daughter Julie to

Connor McGuell; and the birthday, condolence, thank you, and business cards that were the backbone of their operation. Presses printing what should have been a news bulletin: Claire is dead.

A phone call—that's how things happened now. Now he would start dreading phone calls the way his parents did. Now his heart would start beating harder every time the phone rang. Garvey picked up the pen and wrote down Claire's name tracing it so that it was in boldface. What font would that be? Garvey probably should have known, but he left the day-to-day business, the actual printing, to his cousin, concerned himself with making sure everyone reported to whom they should, and that everyone knew his/her job. Not so different from the government job he'd held in D.C.—a lot of futile paper-pushing, a lot of lunches; vapid, encouraging words, posturing, and perky ass-kissing. When he'd arrived in wide-eyed innocence in Washington, he'd asked the secretary what exactly his boss *did* for a living. "He delegates," she answered, her eyes remaining on the computer screen where she was transcribing dictation. "He's excellent at it."

And now Garvey was in Cleveland and had a dead ex-lover. She's the first one, he thought; the first of us to die. The first of my lovers I'll outlive. How dramatic. He'd imagined a time when firsts would be less frequent, even nonexistent—a time after the first apartment, the first investment portfolio, the first wedding, the first custom suit—but they continued, and would, he now knew, until his death; his first (and only) death. Aside from the usual car accidents and suicides of distant acquaintances, he'd been left relatively untouched by death: his uncle Nick from cancer, a grandfather who'd kicked the bucket, but one he barely knew who left the entire family business to cousin Tate.

And then, back then, there was Claire. There was D.C. And now there simply wasn't anymore, not Claire. D.C. was still there, of course, but so distant as to be nonexistent. Do places exist if you're not there? And was it that strange, really, that Claire no longer existed when she hadn't anyway, not really, for two years?

Not since he'd left that fictional place called D.C. for Cleveland, another planet?

He should go and say good-bye to Claire, good-bye to D.C. He buzzed Laurie, who buzzed him back. It gave him great satisfaction to have a secretary of his own at age thirty-two, to buzz her and give her instructions like, "Book a flight to D.C. tomorrow," and she'd comply and wonder why. Why D.C.? Why suddenly now? And he owed her no explanation.

Garvey could see through the glass walls overlooking the factory floor that Tate was not in his office. He was down there in the trenches, so to speak, fiddling with something while the maintenance guys stood watching. Tate was wearing another loud, passé sport coat, no tie, and Doc Martens. Garvey banged, but there was no way Tate could hear him with the racket on the floor, and Garvey straightened his tie in the weak reflection in the glass before heading down the large metal stairs to the factory floor.

"Tate," he screamed. The din was deafening. "Tate." He tapped his cousin on the shoulder. Tate turned around suddenly, hands cocked in a karate pose.

"Hai-YAH!" he said, giving Garvey a fake chop.

"Tate, listen, I'm going to D.C. for a couple of days, OK?"

"You're going to the sea?" This was one of Tate's stupid games, pretending to mishear because of the noise. He turned his head, leaning his ear toward Garvey, and smiled goofily.

"No, D.C. Washington."

"Watch the sun, great."

"No, it's my old . . . girlfriend, Claire." Garvey tried to infuse his words with solemnity. He found no humor in Tate's juvenile stand-up routine, but at least Tate was consistent in his sophomoric responses. He respected Tate's stability, his predictability. He knew there would never be a moment of self-doubt in Tate's life, no crying into his beer, no might-have-beens.

And he didn't fail Garvey now: "What about her?"

"She's dead."

Tate nodded. He paused. The hair he combed over his bald spot toward the front of his forehead fell a little. He pushed it back absently. "Sure am sorry. Hey listen, the cylinder's broken again."

"Bummer," Garvey said, delegating. "I'll be back Friday."

"No rush, partner. I'll hold down the fort." Tate turned back to the press.

Garvey bought a paper and draped it over his knees as the plane took off for Dulles. Claire Stoltz. He could summon her face only vaguely now, the eyes a little too close together, the small button nose. Her memory provoked only that terrible feeling of loss from two years ago when he stepped onto the plane for Cleveland and she waved good-bye to him from the gate, her right hand in her pocket fingering, he knew, one of those cigarillos she liked to smoke, waiting for the plane to take off so she could step out of the airport into the unclean capital air and light it up. Little Claire, waving fervently, guilelessly, and that heavy nauseous feeling that he never took for grief or emotion but rather dismissed as indigestion, or nervousness. They'd eaten ribs at one of those places on the way to the airport where they tie plastic bibs around your neck. They'd eaten three whole slabs, tearing into the flesh (Claire, too, stuffing the food into god-knows-where on her five-foot frame), messy with the grease and sauce, eyes stinging from the spicy barbecue and laughing so loud that other tables turned to stare. They forked coleslaw at each other, retreated into the plastic bib armor, and stuffed whole unbuttered rolls in their mouths, wiped their faces with the backs of their hands, washed it all down with large Cokes, refilled. He asked for the check and paid it with his newly acquired company credit card.

Now, on the plane from Cleveland, the stewardess came by and asked Garvey what he wanted to drink.

"Gin and tonic—no, just tonic," he said, remembering the hour.

("How can you drink tonic, plain like that?" Claire had asked. "It's like that stuff they put on sore muscles, what—Ben Gay. It smells like a boxing locker room."

"You, Queen-of-Logic-and-Cigars, asking me how I can stand a smell?"

"They're *cigarillos*, thank you very much," she said and sparked one up right there in his Dupont Circle apartment. The cockroaches never returned.)

He sipped the tonic slowly, not sure what he was supposed to be feeling. Cleveland was good for that, for numbness: its industrial skyline, its small pond status. He was named most eligible bachelor by *Cleveland Weekend* magazine the month after he moved there. Welcome to Cleveland. Low rents, decent sports bars, lonely women—it was as though Cleveland stretched out the red carpet for him. If he wasn't happy he was, well, comfortable, which was the word his father always used to describe his living. Comfortable living: central heating, dry cleaning delivery, premium movie channels. Comfortable, but not permanent, not forever. The future was, of course, unknowable, but it was never supposed to include Claire Stoltz. Now it couldn't include Claire Stoltz.

D.C. *looked* unchanged during the slow, traffic-snarled ride from the airport to the hotel. It was hotter here, and humid, making him sweat. He could have stayed with Buddy or someone, but he had decided that a hotel was the way to go; he could afford it, and he wanted the vacant luxury of air-conditioning, a clean bath and a minibar, a basement workout center and a small shoe-shine kit. But of course D.C. had changed. Cities change faster than hemlines; stores are built, restaurants go under, streets are torn up, renamed. If he stayed longer it would be like visiting a foreign town—he'd make wrong turns and feel the continual disappointment of unfamiliarity.

Garvey watched out the window as the car wound through the busy city streets. Washington looked so different from Cleveland with its rows of endless museums, green parks, Victorian buildings. The monuments and the Mall lit up at night in a perpetual Christmas for tourists. D.C. was always "on," always showy. And it was true that at any given time, heads of state were deciding the fate of nations, major drug deals were going down, intrepid reporters were uncovering corruption. And the streets were swept clean, whitewashed almost, by street sweepers who were armed only with brooms in the fight against filth, who wore wires and sold stories to the *Enquirer*. You had to be on your guard in D.C. It could catch you unaware and sweep you away into the Potomac. Garvey felt that old tension coming back, the clenching of the jaw and of the gut. He never felt that in Cleveland. Cleveland had no aesthetic pretensions, no premeditated urban planning. It just was.

After he checked into the hotel, Garvey traveled to Claire's parents' house in Virginia in a taxi with torn vinyl seats and Islamic prayer beads hanging from the rearview mirror. He asked the driver to wait for him in the Stoltzes' long driveway while he ran up and rang the doorbell. He could hear the ancient dog barking inside. A black woman in a modified maid's uniform answered the door.

"Hello," Garvey said. "I'm Garvey Masterson. Are the Stoltzes at home?"

"No," the woman said. She stared at him. "They've lost a child."

"I know," Garvey said. *They've lost a child*, as though they'd simply misplaced her. *Now where did I put that Claire?* "I'm an old friend. I came here once, for dinner. Do you remember me?"

"I haven't been working here long," the woman said, and Garvey realized with embarrassment that she didn't look familiar at all. He wasn't sure what he had come to the house for, but there was something satisfying about the rows of neat begonias outside the front door, the tidy chaos of the flagstone walk and the pale symmetrical columns holding up the second-floor porch. He noticed a small dandelion growing among the begonias and thought immediately of Claire's sunflower dress: a huge, gaudy, yellow housedress she wore all summer. He wondered if she was really as small as he remembered. She was shrinking in his memory, dwarfed by the dress and by the amount of time that had passed.

"Right, sorry," Garvey said. "I'm sorry to have disturbed you." He turned and walked toward the waiting taxi.

"It's all right. Would you like to leave a note?" the woman called after him.

Garvey stopped and looked at her. She was young, probably not much older than he was, but fat with neglect, or maybe indulgence. He thought about leaving a note, but what could it say? "No. I'll see them tomorrow at the service."

Garvey got back into the taxi and gave the address of Steinberg's funeral home. Parked outside the austere building was a Lincoln Town Car with Virginia plates. Garvey paid the cabbie and walked toward the entrance. He pushed the door in and smelled the thick scent of air-freshener and shag carpeting masking a deeper, more pervasive odor. What was he doing here? He wanted to see her one last time, see if his memory of her size was correct. The casket would be closed at the funeral.

He could hear voices down the hall—a woman's, distraught, and an older man's. He walked toward them and was unsurprised to see Claire's parents. Mrs. Stoltz was crying into a handkerchief.

"Hello, young man," said the doctor, something Claire had told Garvey he always said to people whose names he couldn't remember. It was how he had addressed Garvey when he came to dinner that once.

Mrs. Stoltz looked up. "Oh, Gravy, I'm so glad you're here." She rushed toward him and fell into him, waiting to be embraced. Garvey obliged stiffly. He didn't correct her use of his old nickname. Mrs. Stoltz was small like Claire. She barely came up to his chest. The sharp corner of her purse, wedged between them, pressed against his leg. He felt awkward and intrusive. Mrs. Stoltz squeezed Garvey's arms with a strength that surprised him.

Then, just as suddenly, she stepped back. "I wondered if anyone called you. I was going to do it myself, but I just couldn't bring myself to. Do you want anything?" she asked, reverting to hostess mode though she was in a funeral parlor and not in her own home.

"No, thank you, Mrs. Stoltz. I just wanted to pay my condolences."

"Thank you, darling. You know, I always thought, the way Claire talked about you, that you'd be the one—"

"Dolly," Dr. Stoltz cautioned.

"This is Gravy," Mrs. Stoltz gestured to Garvey. They had always called him that. "You remember him."

"Of course I do." Dr. Stoltz put his arm around his wife's shoulder. She disintegrated into sobs. "I'm sorry," he apologized. "It was so sudden, so unexpected."

"Hmmm," Garvey made a sympathetic sound.

There was a long pause. "Do you know where Claire might have left her high school diploma?" Dr. Stoltz asked suddenly. "We've been looking for it everywhere."

It was a bizarre question for which Garvey had no answer. He looked around the hallway, which offered no help. Funeral homes were always so tacky, he thought; the carpet was red plush, as was the wallpaper. There was a cheap oil painting, a solemn plains landscape, on the wall above a cherry wood table with fake lilies in a vase. "Umm, no, sir, I really don't know where she would have put it. She didn't really have places for things . . ." Garvey trailed off, remembering an afternoon spent looking for his keys, tearing apart her chaotic, crowded apartment where she insisted nothing could be misplaced because nothing *had* a place. She sat on her bed smoking, watching him and laughing. Garvey wondered why he had ever wanted to see her corpse in the first place, what peace he'd imagined the sight of her dead body would bring him.

"Oh." Dr. Stoltz's brow furrowed. If he'd been crying, his face didn't show it. "I think I'll take Dolly home now." He looked down at his wife, shuddering into her square of cloth.

"Of course," Garvey said. "I'm so sorry to keep you. I'm sorry. Claire was . . . ," he started. Claire was unknowable, un-articulatable. "I'll see you at the service tomorrow."

Mrs. Stoltz was buried in her husband's shoulder; he had his arm around her. Garvey stepped back to let them pass and watched them, crippled by the difference in their height, hobble to the front door.

When he couldn't reach him at home Garvey thought he could probably find Buddy at their "local." It was Wednesday, and Buddy usually went out Wednesdays, or used to anyway. Garvey left the name of his hotel on Buddy's answering machine. The room was growing oppressive, small, and sterile. Garvey thought he should probably go out for a good piece of fish, since he was in D.C., and he walked to a restaurant he knew near the hotel, which, to his relief, was still there, though they'd changed the menu substantially. He brought along the paper from the plane.

Garvey really didn't like to eat alone, but he didn't feel like calling any of the old gang. He would see them tonight, or tomorrow at the funeral. He ordered Chilean sea bass and tried to read the paper, which was a little unwieldy for a dinner table. He thought he could sense pity in the waitress's officiousness.

Afterward, he walked to the pub though it was hot still, even at night, a two-mile stroll that made it late enough to possibly find some people he knew. The bar was almost empty, the large television sets playing soundless sports events, including a strange feed from Asia broadcasting an Indian version of what looked like that old schoolyard game, Smear the Queer. Garvey looked around. He didn't know any of the people in the booths or at the bar. He didn't like to be alone at bars; often he went out of his way to pick friends up in his car just so he wouldn't arrive first.

He sat down at the bar, and he and the bartender nodded at each other in vague recognition.

"Yes?" the bartender asked.

"A gin and tonic," Garvey said. He had thrown away the newspaper on the way over and now he was sorry. He watched Indian Smear the Queer while the bartender poured his drink. There was some sort of safe zone the player could take refuge in, and a no-man's-land where it was fair game to pin him to the ground until the fat referee blew his whistle. The bartender placed Garvey's drink on a napkin in front of him with a lemon wedge.

"Four fifty," he said.

"Do you still see Buddy Nothern and those guys in here ever?" Garvey asked.

"Tall blond guy? Kind of loud?"

"That's him," Garvey said.

"Sure. Sometimes." The bartender took his white cloth to the other end of the bar. Garvey sipped the drink and swiveled around to watch some people play pool. Two couples, on a double date it looked like. The men typical D.C. liberals, early thirties, government guys probably. The girls were thin, with long blond hair that draped down their backs and swung when they laughed. They'd been drinking awhile and were giggling, playing sloppy, interminable pool, accepting flirtatious instruction from their dates: "No, now line it up like this, and softly, but firmly, you know how I like it . . ."

Claire used to sit on the pool table while they were playing. He'd pick her up and move her like patio furniture when she got in the way, and she'd continue her monologue, moving through the air in mid-sentence as though it were normal to levitate while conversing.

Garvey watched NASCAR races for a while on the TV above the couples, and when his watch said midnight he left the bar and caught a cab to his hotel.

Garvey was a little early for the service, but most of the mourners had already arrived. Claire's relatives he could discern from their Eastern European hips and outmoded clothes—exactly the bumpkins Claire had painted them as. The Stoltz parents stood toward the front near the coffin. A large, youngish, well-tailored group was standing over on the right side of the large room. Garvey moved their way.

He shook hands with Peter and Josh and pecked Julianne on the cheek. Georgia had been crying; she had mascara tracks down her cheeks.

"Groovy, man, nice to see you." Buddy was in front of him suddenly, a little happy for the occasion. "So bad it had to be for this."

"Yeah," Garvey agreed, accepting the handshake and the shoulder pat that went with it. "How are you?"

"Good, really good. Hey listen, where were you last night? I tried your hotel a hundred times. We were all going to go out."

"I turned off the phone," Garvey said. "I was really tired."

"Well, after the service there's this reception thing in Virginia and then we can catch up. I want you to meet—here, honey." He tried to get the attention of the wiry brunette behind him. "Rhina, meet Garvey."

"Nice to meet you," they both said simultaneously. She was pretty, with green eyes and a long nose. She had on a short dress that just barely won the fight between risqué and appropriate.

"I've heard a lot about you," Rhina said. "From Buddy."

"Oh," Garvey said. He didn't really want to be making small talk. He wanted to be sitting, looking at the coffin, listening to those Jewish dirges. He wished, suddenly and violently, that he and Claire had been engaged when she died so that he could sit up in front with her parents and hand Mrs. Stoltz fresh Kleenexes, maybe shed a few tears himself, at least put his head in his hands, grieve publicly.

The lights dimmed, and they all took seats. From where he was seated on the aisle, Garvey could see the Stoltzes, rocking in time to the litanies. He understood little of the service. The rabbi gave the eulogy, and it was short, talked about the mysteries of God's ways, and proved, through the citation of various Old Testament passages, that the test of death was for the living, not the dead. When Garvey looked over once, he saw that Rhina and Buddy were holding hands and Buddy had tears in his eyes. Buddy had never dated anyone as pretty as Rhina, and he didn't usually like brunettes. Garvey tried to concentrate on the service, tried to drum up tears in his own eyes, but they seemed to all be located somewhere under his rib cage, attached to his sternum maybe, in a sac he couldn't dislodge.

There was a lot of standing and sitting and standing again and then suddenly it was over and everyone was filing past the Stoltzes telling them how sorry they were, and Garvey took his place in line. When he got to Dr. Stoltz, the older man looked at him blankly. "Thank you for your sympathies, young man." Mrs. Stoltz was sitting down, her eyes covered by the handkerchief.

Buddy and Rhina drove Garvey to the cemetery for another short service and the lowering of the coffin. It had started to rain, and Buddy offered Garvey a part of the newspaper to put over his head for protection. They all took turns shoveling dirt in the grave. Garvey took a large bladeful of dirt and followed it with his eyes all the way down until he saw it land like hard rain on the coffin's surface. He gave the shovel to Josh behind him, and he and Buddy and Rhina made their way to the Stoltzes' house in Virginia.

He was surveying the dining room table laden with food, and contemplating what to eat when a tall, dark-haired woman stepped up beside him. She skewered a mini hot dog.

"Jews serving hot dogs at *Shivah*," she sighed. She looked at Garvey. "Of course, I guess they could be kosher hot dogs." She narrowed her eyelids, gave him a look that Garvey could only describe as lascivious.

"Are you a *Lansman?*" the woman asked. She spoke softly and with her mouth full of hot dog he could barely understand her.

"A linesman? What?"

She held up one finger as a time-out and swallowed patiently. "A member of the tribe. Are you Jewish?"

"Does it matter?" Garvey was taken aback.

"Well," she considered. "Yes, I would say it does." She was whispering; he couldn't hear her above the din, so he leaned in close, as though he were the one making the pass, an admirable ploy on her part.

"No. I'm not a linesman. I don't even play football." Seeing the joke fall flat he added quickly, "No. I'm not Jewish." Christ, he was sounding more like Tate every day.

"What are you then?"

"Like, what religion? I don't know."

"What do you mean you don't know?" she asked sharply.

This was getting weird. Garvey speared a cold cut with a green sword toothpick and put it in his mouth to discover it was a small pickle surrounded by roast beef. He didn't like pickles, but felt obliged to swallow it. The sodium rush made him gulp down his gin and tonic and hang on to an ice cube to suck. Any port in a storm, he thought, then wondered if the port in the metaphor was the ice or the girl.

"I mean, I don't know. I wasn't raised anything. Episcopalian, maybe." He picked a religion at random.

"Episcopalian? Christ!" She threw back her head to laugh at the private joke that was Episcopalianism, but Garvey didn't get it. The room seemed to stop for a moment to listen to her laughter, a guttural rushing sound, like an avalanche.

He studied her now that she was at a distance. She had a pageboy haircut, wide brown eyes, and a loose-fitting suit that exaggerated her shoulders. The pants hung on her hips.

"So what are you?" he asked.

"Oh, I'm Zoroastrian." She set her glass of white wine on the table in order to place some melon balls on a napkin. The living room seemed to Garvey remarkably like a cocktail party all of a sudden. The woman busied herself with her food. Garvey thought she'd moved on, that he'd failed the religion litmus. He went to refill his glass at the self-service bar, tonging more ice in the cup.

"Are you from Cleveland?" She appeared suddenly, holding out her glass for him to refill.

"Yes," he said. "How did you—"

"You're Gravy Masterson."

"Garvey," he corrected, extending his hand.

"Diane Cristals."

"Nice to meet you," he said automatically.

"I was Claire's lover, when you were in D.C."

If his life were a movie, this would be the place where he'd spit gin and tonic all over the room. Except his glass was still empty. "Impossible," he stammered.

"Not really," Diane said. "What did she tell you she was doing for a living?"

"Playing accompanying piano for a ballet studio."

"Not a total lie. I do live in a studio." She paused. "That would make me the piano." Diane popped a melon ball into her mouth.

"I don't believe you," Garvey said, although it made perfect sense when he thought about it. It was something he could have expected from Claire: the unexpected.

"No? She had this strange thing about her breasts." Diane turned her back to the bar and looked around the room as though searching for someone in particular. Her finger traced the rim of her wine glass. "She loved the left one, but if you touched the right one she'd have conniption fits." Diane's voice was louder, now that the conversation had gotten more intimate. Garvey could hear her clearly for the first time.

He remembered the first time he and Claire had sex. They had been friends, pals, and he wasn't particularly attracted to her, or in any event, not more attracted to her than to any other female of his acquaintance in his early twenties. The encounter had all the awkwardness of two virgins. Bizarrely, they had discussed it first, rationally and soberly, and the more clinically they addressed the subject the harder his dick got. She insisted they drink before they disrobed, and they each did three shots of tequila before even touching the other. When they kissed she was completely passive, her tongue resting against his rather than moving.

Then Claire made him sit and watch her disrobe, swaying in front of him, just out of his reach. She had such a serious expression on her face that Garvey laughed, which made her smile, too. She continued to giggle as she took off her shirt. He looked at Claire, naked above him, her small breasts ending in nubs like a new eraser on a pencil. Then she backed up to continue to take her clothes off. It seemed like such a parody to him, at that moment, of what sexy was, like she was aping something she'd seen on television. In fact, the image brought to mind a child playing dress up, and his dick shrunk so that when she burrowed into his pants he had to close his eyes to get hard again, and then was barely solid enough to enter her.

She positioned herself above him. She was so small that she winced as she put the head inside her. For a second it seemed as though her weight was not going to be enough to penetrate the muscles, and then she lowered herself carefully as though getting into a hot tub. The tip of his dick reached her cervix; her pelvic walls pushed in on him. It was supposed to be good like this, he knew, supposed to get him more excited, make him come faster, but instead he felt as though he were being strangled, like there wasn't enough room for him to move. He let her move up and down; when he tried to sit up she grimaced. After a few minutes she smiled at Garvey, and they both agreed it was over. The best part of the evening was eating pizza in bed, not caring that the sauce dripped onto the sheets, using the blankets as napkins.

Though it hadn't been a particularly pleasurable experience, Garvey used the episode to masturbate still; it was the only scene guaranteed to get him off with a minimum amount of effort, in indirect proportion to the lack of orgasm at the time.

Here at the party the memory surfaced, and then some perverse instinct inserted Diane in Claire's place. Oddly, this image was erotic; he felt his dick pound.

"The sex was terrible," Diane continued. "In case you were feeling jealous, don't. The worst I ever had."

"She was date-raped in college," Garvey said softly.

"I know. That explains the frigidity, I suppose, but not the breast thing. What do you think?"

"I think I don't want to be talking to you about this here," Garvey said. He shifted his weight, feeling very uncomfortable.

"You still don't believe me, do you?" she asked. "I can tell you don't. Let's see. She liked to sit on your back and smoke cigars while you did push-ups. She said it turned you on. Maybe it's a guy thing," Diane continued. "I have to admit I don't really get it."

"It's complicated," Garvey said. It had turned him on, the feeling of power and strength. He couldn't believe Claire had told anyone. He felt betrayed, and stared into his sympathetically watery drink with self-pity. He sloshed it around twice and downed the meager liquid left in the bottom.

There was a moment of silence. "Time for a refill," Garvey said.

"Here, take my card," Diane said. She handed him a small business card that had her home address, an apartment not far from his old one in D.C. There was no profession listed. He put it in his jacket pocket and poured some Tanqueray into his glass, watching the ice cubes crack with excitement. He didn't like straight gin; he thought he could taste the filtering process. When he looked up from his potion, Diane had disappeared.

It was the kind of relationship Garvey had never thought existed. One he'd never read about, one he'd never talked about with the guys or seen on TV. One that Buddy wouldn't ever understand. It wasn't that Garvey *liked* Claire that much—that wasn't the right word—or that he *disliked* her at all, but once they met there was never any question that time spent would be time spent with her. Comfortable, like his maternal grandparents who were so close they spoke in a patois that only they could understand.

There were aspects of a mother/child connection in their relationship, though neither Garvey nor Claire was the clear offspring of the other. It was just that natural, that imperceptible, that mundane. The small weight of her lying on his back as he did his push-ups; her cigarillo, asthma be damned, sending smoke rings up to the ceiling like distress signals. Garvey moving up and down with the strength of his arms, the colossal power he contained.

And their two successful lovemaking sessions, after they'd tried everything for months—talking and electronic aids and doctor visits (physical and mental), alcohol and pornography— and it had been repeatedly disastrous. Even Garvey couldn't come, and he didn't tell Buddy because he was afraid he knew what it meant; something about a place he didn't want to go unless Claire came with him. She was so little in bed, so easily reduced to tears, uncharacteristic (impossible even) when she was clothed.

And then one Saturday afternoon she clipped the cigarillo and tapped Garvey on the shoulder midway through the push-up routine. He rolled over and she laughed at his hard dick. She kissed him furiously, her tongue stabbing at his, her arms shoving her shorts off, then grabbing at his. He rolled her over and put his finger inside her and she was wet, she was almost never that wet. Then he couldn't wait. She would have had to scream in pain to make him wait one more second; he thrust inside her. This time the muscles squeezed him, enveloped him, and he understood, finally, what men said about tight women. It felt like his dick was being hugged, like she was pulling his orgasm out. He massaged her clit, since he knew he wouldn't last very long, and it was just, well, the only way Garvey could describe it was right. It just was right.

Now it was ruined by Diane's revelation. If it had happened with Garvey, then it must have happened with Diane, too, he reasoned. How many times? It killed him to think that Diane might have reached Claire in a way he was unable to.

Not that he wasn't seeing other women, too. There was Heidi, and Jennifer and Lana from work, and Micha, and a couple of dates with Celeste, which was weird because that was his mother's name and it was a rare enough name that he associated it only with her. But it was the mid-nineties, and after sex no one actually wanted to *sleep* together—the actual physical sleeping being too intimate—and Garvey itched to call Claire when it was over, like a post-coital cigarette, and tell her nothing about it, not a word, but just let her ramble on to him about the guests on the late-night round table discussion she was watching or her theories of meditation and redemption, her voice as elemental as breathing or bread or water.

What was he to her? He couldn't know, didn't want to, couldn't even articulate her place in *his* life, suspected (arrogantly, he knew) that it couldn't be categorized, had never before been experienced in the however-many-thousand years of human history. He didn't bother to search for the words, to perform the existential honing in on accurate classification. It would have boiled down to something existential and banal.

And in Garvey's life things were changing. Senator Jordan was indicted for embezzling campaign funds, and the Republican congress vetoed the president's welfare bill. And then Garvey's grandfather died, and the phone call came from cousin Tate, encountered for the first time in twenty years at the funeral in a shiny black tuxedo jacket and faded black Dockers (*again*, no tie), asking would he like to join the family business. And change, Garvey realized, was the only thing life was sure to bring you, *fuck* death and taxes. And the firsts would continue, always the firsts. You could never get too comfortable in a life with firsts. And so he thought about moving to Cleveland.

They all went back to the local in reminiscence of the good times. A different bartender was working, a new one, but Buddy knew him and laughed loudly with the man about something or other. The bar seemed brighter than it had the night before, and he found the source: an enormous lit plastic advertisement in the shape of a bottle of Zima, a drink no one in the place would have been caught dead with a couple of years ago. He ordered a gin and tonic—no, wait, two. He'd just get two now and save himself another trip to the bar. It was getting to be a few too many, but Garvey wasn't sure he cared. He was getting that pleasantly buzzed feeling for the first time since he'd left Cleveland, and it was a welcome one.

Buddy and Garvey retreated to a tall table for two. Garvey sat on the stool; Buddy remained standing and poured himself a glass of beer from a pitcher.

"How are you, man?" Buddy asked. "I'm terrible about the phone thing, and it's not like I'm coming to Ohio to visit you."

"Don't worry about it," Garvey said. "But it's really not so bad."

"I can't believe we're here after a funeral."

"Me either." They took long sips of their drinks.

"What a way to meet up again," Buddy said.

"Yeah," Garvey said. He hoped that Buddy wouldn't try to pat him on the back or offer some sort of greeting-card consolation. But Buddy didn't try.

"We didn't see a lot of her after you left. A little bit, but you know . . . Hey, are you still around this weekend?"

"I'm leaving tomorrow," Garvey said, a little unkindly.

"Oh, well, next time then maybe." Buddy didn't reveal what he'd wanted to do. He took another long sip, finishing the beer, and then poured himself another glass and held it up to clink with Garvey, who downed his first drink and picked up the second.

"To old friends," Buddy said.

They watched the basketball game on the TV. Buddy finished his glass and poured another. He had gotten significantly older in the two years since Garvey had seen him: more jowly, the extra skin looser around his face, the hair thinner at the crown, and Garvey wondered what changes the years had worked on his own face.

"Can I tell you something, Groove?" Buddy asked suddenly, his eyes wide open. He wore a confessional look that Garvey dreaded. "Yeah . . ." Garvey froze. What other revelations did this day have in store?

Buddy took a deep breath. "I'm going to marry Rhina."

Garvey felt a wave of relief followed by the sharp jab of envy. "You, Mr. Good-Morning-Sweetheart-Last-Night-Was-Great-What's-Your-Name-Again, getting married?"

"Happens to the best of us." He looked over where Rhina and the others were laughing at a joke near the pool table. He winked and Rhina tossed her hair, blowing him a kiss.

"Wow, that's—that's just great, man. Who knew?" Garvey stood up and gave Buddy an awkward hug. "Hey, I should buy you a drink."

"I'm doing OK for right now." Buddy pointed at the quarter-full pitcher. "You get the next one."

Garvey recovered enough to say, "You are aware I have a moral obligation to tell embarrassing stories at the wedding?"

"I fucking hope so," Buddy said. "Why do you think I did those things? Just for fun?"

Garvey fingered Diane's business card in his suit jacket pocket. There was an awkward silence. An image flickered into Garvey's mind of Diane and Claire together in bed: Diane's dark head on Claire's chest, her hand resting on Claire's hipbone. The hand snuck over the mound, burrowed into Claire's sparse pubic hair. Diane's thumb rubbed while her index finger thrust in and out and Claire started to writhe—

"What's wrong, Groove?" Buddy asked. "You look like shit."

"I'm just a little freaked. I thought you were going to say something else is all."

"What?"

"No, forget it, it's stupid."

"Nah, what? Tell me."

"I just—I thought you were going to tell me you slept with Claire or something."

"Me?" Buddy asked. "Sleep with Claire? Come on, dude, you are not that deluded."

"It's not that ridiculous. She wasn't ugly or anything."

"Nah, she was cute, but I mean, it was all about dry ice, man."

"What?" Garvey wasn't following the coded slang.

"Cold fish. Terrible lay. She had it written all over her. I don't mean to be vulgar, but all that year you had that tight look around your eyes, like it wasn't working out so good between you."

"A tight look?" Garvey asked.

"Worried, whipped, like I'd never seen you before. I was glad you were moving to Cleveland, getting out of here."

Garvey just stared at Buddy. He never thought Buddy noticed anything, least of all subtleties in Garvey's physiognomy.

"Don't look so surprised. I'm not a total meathead. Cheers, bro!" Buddy raised his glass, and though Garvey's was almost empty, and it was bad luck to clink with water, the glasses touched, making a low sound like a quiet gong.

"Come on, let's join the gang. Enough of this bonding shit." Buddy poured another glass of beer, draining the pitcher. Garvey stood up and felt a little dizzy from all the alcohol. He took his hand out of his pocket and left Diane's card on the table before following Buddy to the bar.

One other memory: Claire was lying in bed with that flu that was going around, her face flushed by a fever, her breathing labored. She coughed weakly, more for show or out of habit than because of any physical need.

Garvey set the tray of chicken soup down on the bed next to her. She looked even smaller when she was sick, as though he was looking at her through the wrong end of binoculars. The tray must have been a gift from her mother. Its design—flowers pressed beneath glass—clashed with the art deco dishes Claire used.

"Here, try to eat something, honey," Garvey said. He lifted her up under the arms, like he would a child, and fluffed a couple of pillows behind her back ineffectually.

Claire reached for the spoon. Her arms were heavy, to let Garvey know she was going to eat just to humor him.

"No, let me," Garvey said and took the spoon from her hand. He dipped it into the soup, searching for a small piece of chicken floating near the top. He balanced it carefully, concentrating on keeping it level. He had heard that if you hummed while carrying liquids they wouldn't spill, so he hummed now, a low purring.

Claire looked at him. Her eyes were glassy, her face blotchy with sheet creases down the cheeks like surgical scars. Garvey was suddenly scared, terrified even, and his heart beat quickly. He continued to hum, louder now, around the growing lump in his throat. Claire opened her mouth and Garvey placed the spoon lightly on her tongue, waited for her to close her lips around it, felt the slight pressure of her tongue, the rim of the spoon touching the ridged roof of her mouth.

He removed the spoon and Claire swallowed, smiling weakly. "Good girl," he said, and reached down for another ladleful when Claire began to cough for real. The fit got worse, and she leaned forward to ease the racket in her rib cage. The entire bed shook as she coughed. And then she gagged and vomited on the tray, just bile, mostly, and the bite of chicken.

"It's OK," Garvey said. "Do you want the nebulizer?"

Claire shook her head and the coughing stopped. Garvey went into the bathroom and wet a washcloth in the sink. As he let the cold water run over his wrists, he looked at himself in the mirror. He didn't look much better than Claire: hair uncombed, pale and haggard with those black bags under his eyes that he was more accustomed to seeing on his father's face. What was he doing here?

He returned to the bedroom where Claire was settled, her chest still moving with the enormous effort of drawing breath. He wiped her mouth, then turned the cloth over and placed it on her forehead. "There, isn't that better?" She leaned back and closed her eyes; she sighed.

"Why are you being so nice to me?" Claire asked softly.

"Because I love you." He said it quickly, matter-of-factly, with the ineffable, unarguable "because it's there" logic of Everest climbers. It came from a place Garvey didn't recognize, and he was almost as surprised as Claire at the words.

She shook her head three times slowly. Then she rolled over onto her side, away from Garvey. Then he knew that there was no feeling better for Claire. Life held no low hope of comfort, of solace, of palliative de-sensitivity, just a series of unpredictable firsts. An awful moment passed when Garvey realized what his earlier fear had meant—that he wasn't afraid so much that he would lose her, but rather that she would lose him. That this much was inevitable.

Garvey could go now. He could clean up the flowered tray and turn off the stove and walk the half mile to his own apartment. He could call Tate and say, "Yes, cousin, yes," and make plane reservations, hire movers, a realtor. It could be so easy, comfortable. He could do what Claire probably wanted him to do. He could just walk away.

NUDE STUDIES OF AN AFFAIR

Rosebud Ben-Oni

I. Up in Smoke

Aitana, Aitana Inigo née Saramago, the prick of your short, spiked hair grazing my chin, how in my sleep I could trace the borders of your two-toned skin, the eternal sunburn of your limbs, face and chest, just where your heavy breasts begin, one bigger than the other and their color almost transparent, the indigo pathways of your veins, the three tiny, red moles near the nipples, my tongue becomes the porno-poet's, perhaps to demean you but also to please you, in tracing the fine down of your sternum leading to the pallor and curve of your stomach, its perfection not worth dwelling on—perfection is for men like your husband—and most of the time I'd flip you, and rest my head against your bluish-white ass with even whiter stretch marks that you'd curse and cup in your hands until I gathered and held them hostage in my own as I fell into you, without warning or the tenderness with which I speak to you, hurting you so you'd want more and want it to stop at the same time, the evening falling into night, the air muggy and cold mixing with our sweat and soaking us so you hurt less, as the pathetic light of the moon intruded from windows we intentionally left open, and sometimes you'd turn your head to look at me but I'd close my eyes, hoping you'd prefer this to the indifference you face all other times, but also wishing I could fuck you without this hostility and suddenness, wishing I could take you out one evening and stroll down Franklin Street with my arm around you, but then I hear you come and at last can let myself go, build and fall completely into you, but also farther away from you, and yes, Aitana, yes, it was always worth the risk.

And even as your husband is calling Tanya, Love—as he always calls you—even as he opens the last bottle of chilled Madeira that he brought from your island homeland off Portugal, in his immaculate polo and chinos protected by a spotless apron, I want to make you feel alive and dirty and unprotected.

We watch him drain his glass in one graceful swallow before he descends back to the charcoal pit and disappears in a dark veil of smoke that crawls up your long, white sundress, so it seems to float around you, and you quietly grab me by the balls, so I'll understand just how much shit we are in. Before I can think of reacting, he calls to you, Tanya, Love, and asks for a hand, so it is over but it also has just begun, Aitana, as smokes blows up to the deck where I take a seat, where only hours ago you pinned me on all fours and undid my zipper with your teeth, right out in the open, only now the smoke has swallowed both of you up and I am left on the deck, hearing only a stern, dry-as-a-bone sound without discernible words, yet he is not a man who speaks in a murmur, he is precise and careful, he is letting me know that no one should mess with a man who wears his Stetson and cowboy boots at the State Legislature, a man capable of cross-examining Vioxx victims and clearing the homeless from the streets without saying where they'll end up and marrying a foreign call girl three days after divorcing his wife.

II. Alone on the Pier

The first time I asked more from you, you slapped me in the face and pushed me down until my cheeks chafed between your skirt-hugging thighs, and in the back of my throat I tasted the bitter, pungent sweat soaking the rough cotton.

And I talked into your thighs, Aitana, still seeking answers, and you leaned down and slapped the back of my head, but I continued to talk and seek, my tongue alone pushing past the thin lining of the lacy underwear your husband gave you instead of a honeymoon, because my hands were bringing you down on the long, narrow pier that ran along the manmade, unsuitable-for-swimming lake, which smelled sulfurous, though it was frequently drained. Smelling like the space behind your knee, which I sucked when I started to move up on you.

It had been only two weeks since your husband welcomed me into his house, that beautiful tomb with its high ceilings and burgundy leather and mahogany woodworks that reflected the light with dull effect, which also felt uninhabited no matter how many people came to fill the large rooms. It had been only two weeks that we'd spent together dodging the drafts seeping through the large windows that never shut completely. It had been two weeks since I was left alone with you, and you'd pointedly asked me to take off my shoes as if I were uncouth, as if I'd steal the silver. As if you belonged in that house.

You were resistant to English lessons and would answer the door without saying hello, turn your back and I'd simply have to follow, stare at the back of your head, down the long, dark neck, the sloping shoulders wider than your small waist and hips. Of the four languages I spoke fluently, Portuguese was not among them, and that was why Mr. Desmond hired me—he didn't want any "cheating." It was English all the way, and I'd leave each night a few hours later, frustrated with you, wanting more.

You never tried very hard at first, answering my questions about the olive groves and coastal resorts of Portugal in a haughty, impatient tone, and taking long drags on a cigarette, sometimes blowing the smoke right into my face: in Madeira, life was "slow," your father's farm was "ill," your mother "mean" and "holy." An older brother São João who'd moved to Barcelona was "active" and a "night female." Since most of my students were young Asian mathematic geniuses, you, Aitana, sadly became the highlight of my week. I put my whole heart into putting together the pieces of your life, a life of events that you described "out-of-order." Nothing special. You chose the foreign words without much thought, though pain and frustration were evident in the furrowing of your brow, and still I demanded more, until one evening you ran out of that beautiful tomb and stood on the pier and turned to watch me follow.

After you slapped me, after you forced me to go down on you while trying to remain standing as if you were a queen abusing a servant, after I brought you down by finding that your vulnerability lay behind your knee, I moved up on you and you struggled like a fish resistant to his inevitable fate, and I spoke in the crudest English possible that you—before your husband found you—would know quite well, that I was going to fuck the life out of you, that I was sick of your shit, that I knew who you really were, *entertainer* my ass, you're a whore, I growled as I pushed down your sleeveless dress just so your breasts popped out and put a finger in your soaking cunt. As I bit into them, I proposed that you must be a pretty good fuck to have bagged a man like your husband, and with each insult you'd slap me, making me harder, and I'd add another finger until I nearly had my entire hand in, up to the knuckles, and you were moaning like crazy, getting wetter and wetter, until I undid my zipper, leaving my rough flannel on to scratch your chest, and entered you and came almost immediately.

I expected you to laugh at me, but you didn't. You didn't even push me off. We lay there for a moment, until you stretched out your neck as if it had a cramp and suddenly I felt tender toward you, because there had to be *something* between us, to take such a risk, to cross a man like your husband, and you began speaking slowly, sometimes in Portuguese and sometimes in simple English, repeating the same thing again and again until I softened inside you and fell out, until I understood that you'd left the *campo* you'd lived in all your life after being promised a desk job that really meant "dance girl," where you met your husband who had just separated from his first wife.

I was still lying on top of you, Aitana, just getting hard again when you claimed that their divorce had been "strange" and "calm"; he and the ex remained friends and talked a little too often for you, and maybe I should've lost my hard-on when I realized you were in love with him, but it came on even stronger and I cut you off with a deep kiss, entering you out under the open sky, our only protection was the large red maples filtering the first moments of moonlight and last light of day, a diffusion of pastel colors swathing us in the ensuing darkness and mosquitoes that settled over us.

III. Risk and Doubt

I tried to make it mean something more. I tried to make love to you, not just fuck. But it wasn't just sex—we fucked. And I thought I could fuck it into you, the details of my life. Make you care that I spent my life studying religions without actually believing in anything. That I was powerless to believe in anything but my own doubt. That I suspected truth was hidden in incongruities and therefore had to be hunted down or dug up—that, like fucking you, it was supposed to be exhausting and draining if it were real. None of this bullshit with flowers and courting and promises— who the fuck *knows* the future?—so perhaps your husband was the smartest of all men. He saw what he liked and got it and made no apologies. But while you belong to him, he does not belong to you. Not the house, the lake, the pier, nor I, belong to you.

I don't want a wife, Aitana, or a relationship that shrivels and pales, grows narrow-shouldered, becomes featureless. I don't want perfunctory kisses followed by quick laughter overtaking our lips, holding each other so awkwardly we make strangers in public nervous. I don't want pats on the shoulder, or having to introduce each other to friends by apologizing for things the other *might* and *certainly* would say. I don't want to explain having a PhD and refusing to teach and play the pity politics and egos of the academic field for being a mere translator of languages all dead—Latin, Ancient Greek, Ottoman Turkish—languages that somehow lead me to you and the pinkest, longest clit I've ever seen, the hood itself large enough to suck and hold between my teeth, and once I came just by going down on you as if I were fifteen again and couldn't stay longer inside my girlfriend than a minute, which convinced me I loved her, too, for even then I was scavenging through the scraps of time and slapping together truths from little bits of dead reality.

We have no future.

For you, Aitana, that seemed at first a relief.

For me . . .

Skeptics are those who remain children forever.

IV. What Lies Ahead

Both of you are slowly walking up on the deck with a huge plate of steaks. He still looks immaculate and unwrinkled as he takes a seat and gestures for me to have more wine. My glass is still full. You sit down next to him, across from me, and watch me carefully, with the same look on your face when trying to describe the last time his ex-wife had dropped by to "catch up" with him. Then you drain your own glass and wink at me. A very slow wink that doesn't quite fit with what is going on. You pour yourself another, and I see that beneath the lovely, weightless white floating around you, lies the familiar weariness in your eyes, as your husband wipes his ruddy face of a cherub with the back of his arm. He wants to speak, to confront me, to demand how I thought we'd get away with it. You clear your throat, but not to intervene.

"After we eat," he says, as I feel your cool foot on mine under the table, "you're going to show me exactly what you were doing."

I do not move my foot away.

You blink your eyes, like someone awakened from a well-deserved sleep.

"I might watch. I might to do more," he goes on.

I feel your foot pressing down on mine.

"But don't get any funny ideas about me. 'Cause I'll be the one calling the shots." He smiles and begins to carve up the steaks. "Just like your Ancient Greeks."

TO DIE

———— • ————

Diane Williams

I undressed myself. I wanted sex—I wanted sex—I wanted sex—I wanted sex.

I climbed into bed with my wife.

She wanted sex with me. She always wants sex with me.

When I discharged myself this time into her, I felt myself banging as high up into her as I have ever gotten myself up into her.

I had just done the same with another woman who always wants sex with me, too.

There is another woman that I do the same with.

There is another woman.

There is another woman. There are five women who always want sex with me. They are always ready. It does not matter when or what or where, but they are ready.

I have a great deal of money, which I have earned. I have physical beauty for a man. I have intelligence. I have work to do, which I love to do, but women are what I prefer to anything: to lie down with them, the turning to touch the woman and knowing I will be received for sex as soon as I wish to be welcome.

I have been at it like this, this way, for years. It does not matter when I will die. I have had everything I have ever wanted.

I should die now. There should be a killing at my house.

There should be so much more for me, which I am not able to conceive.

MATING IN CAPTIVITY

Nava Renek

Gary splashed cold water on his face and brushed his teeth, hoping to rid his mouth of the pungent taste and smell of another woman's cunt. Only an hour or two before, wasted from swigging down a number of margaritas, he'd found himself in a strange and overly warm railroad apartment, twisted around the very long and scrawny frame of a female of indeterminate age, although when he'd first met her earlier that evening, he thought he caught a sense of a certain unkempt beauty that he'd always found alluring in the past.

Once safely in her apartment, the stranger had gone at him as if she were a cavewoman starving for a piece of meat—his meat—sucking and biting on parts of his body he sometimes felt he preferred to touch himself rather than give over to a hungry beast who knew nothing about him, but he gave in anyway, for in that certain moment, that single blip of time, being touched, fawned over by another human being, brought an extra layer of comfort, like throwing a down quilt over his body on a cold night.

He thought he wouldn't come, or at least couldn't come with his crotch so drenched in her saliva, but then he flipped her around into that inevitable "69" position and found that having her upside down on top of him, a generic female, neither definitively his wife nor a stranger, helped, and he set his tongue and lips to teasing her clit, while he thought about Roxanne77 on

Cream Goddess, the Internet website that never failed to get him hard just by logging on.

Fuck foreplay when you can just hit "Favorites" and scroll to your choice of the day, he mused. But now he was in the hot wet rainforest, the vaginal bush for real, skin on skin, lips on labia, fantasizing about Roxanne77 whose page he'd visited earlier that day.

The woman sprawled above him started moaning to his practiced, darting tongue and efficient sucking of lips while simultaneously taking his prick deep into her mouth, following the shaft as she pulled him in and out, as if sucking on a Sugar Daddy. He wanted to let himself go—come like a hydrant in her mouth, spend the requisite few minutes in what some called "post-coital bliss," then ease himself out of the bed, dress, and slip through the door, back to Cora who was no doubt asleep in their one-bedroom apartment or engrossed in one of her novels about thwarted yuppie love that made him sick to see her read. After all, she'd been an English major at NYU and could have talked about the classics. Now, she'd given up real literature for easy reading, trendy novels about man-hunting in Manhattan. When had Cora become such a cliché of a dissatisfied wife?

He and the pickup woman had gotten into a rhythm, thrusting and bobbing in unison until he knew there'd be an inevitable finale, and it would be grand, and they'd both come and he'd be able to leave thinking of himself as a sexual conqueror, not a depraved pervert only able to shoot his wad after paging down on an Internet porn site while his wife slept only a few feet away, or was at her desk at Young and Rubicam hashing out ads for erectile dysfunction or nasal sprays.

The chick was making strange moaning noises, sounds Cora never made even in her lustiest days, but noises he'd noticed women who hunted for sex made once they'd caught their prey and were finally getting laid. For a moment, he wished he could shut her up, put his hand over her mouth and quiet her down, but he quickly realized that it would cause fewer problems if he just made her come, came himself, and got the hell out of there.

It happened abruptly, like a volcanic reaction, full of lava and magma, smoke and detritus, natives running scared into the jungle as the once dormant mountaintop unleashed stones and ash. Later, she held him in her grasp, her arms flopped over his chest, her sharp little nose sidled up against his rib cage, breathing heavily as if asleep. Cautiously, he moved over to one side, hoping to be able to release himself from her vise grip, but she groaned and stirred.

"Gotta go," he joked, knowing he wasn't being funny. "Lots to do, people to see, money to make."

"It's fucking 1:57 in the morning," she complained, but he was adamant. He would never spend the entire night with anyone but his wife.

"Will I . . ." The woman let the words trail off, smart enough to already know the answer.

No, he wanted to shout at her. She would never see him again, unless by accident they both found themselves in the same bar where she might glance at him twice, trying to remember where she knew him from, and he'd look away, certain that he'd picked her up once without bothering to put in the effort to recall where or when.

The walk down Bowery was quiet, the avenue strangely deserted, even for that location and time of night. Brightly lit apartment buildings made of steel and glass had cropped up where vacant lots used to be. The East Village was experiencing another transformation, first from immigrant slum to hip artist hangout, now from trendy bohemian quarter to expensive lofts and condos that only wealthy businesspeople and Europeans could pay for. Well, he'd let them have it. No one he knew could afford to live in that neighborhood anyway.

On his way home, he made and withdrew several deals with himself. First, if Cora was awake by the time he got home, he'd

offer to mix her a drink—Absolut and tonic was her favorite—
bring it into the bedroom and sit down at the edge of the bed
hoping to have some sort of conversation with her. Maybe they
could talk about the office, what smart-ass thing her friend Rachel
had said to one of the clients, or who was about to quit or get
married or have a baby. He'd try really hard to be interested in
her updates, knowing, as they'd talked about in couple's therapy,
that what seemed to be truly trivial and uninteresting to him were
events that made up his wife's everyday life.

If she wasn't awake, he imagined taking off his clothes and
climbing into bed next to her, slowly running his hand down the
side of her body: from shoulders to waist, over hips, and thighs.
Even at forty-two, Cora's body was still beautiful: petite—no
taller than five-foot-two—but well proportioned with strong
legs, shoulders, a slim neck, and two buttercup breasts. He still
might have enough juice in him to have another go at it, and
she, being his wife, would make it even more of a turn on . . .
or would she? He hadn't made love to Cora in months and was
beginning to wonder if it was he, more than she, who was now
incapable of reaching out and making the first move. So he set
up a final wager. It was an all-or-nothing offer, and the odds were
against him. If he didn't have sex with Cora that night or the
next morning, he would leave her. He didn't want to live the rest
of his life in a sexless marriage, and he was sick of going to bars,
picking up the endless supply of available chicks, fucking them,
then pretending everything was fine when he got home.

Grabbing the F train at Second Avenue, he changed to the J at
Delancy, a station with its soot-stained ceilings, darkened lights,
and oversized rats scurrying across the electric rails that always
reminded him of hell. He was grateful that five years ago Cora
had persuaded him to move across the river to a Williamsburg
neighborhood where nearby tree-lined streets and brownstones
provided a solace from the ruins of the Lower East Side.

At home, his apartment smelled sweet and soapy. Recently, she'd bought a number of tubes and bottles with names of herbs and spices that infused the varieties of lotions and creams inside them. He thought he picked up a whiff of cinnamon and cloves as he looked down at his wife, half naked but asleep, and lifted the quilt from the bottom of the bed to bring it up over her body. If he was going to follow the rules he set up for himself, he'd have to make love to her while she was groggy, still in a dream state.

When they were first lovers and couldn't keep their hands off each other, they used to make love like that all the time. He'd wake up first and lie next to her, as if her protector, waiting for her to stir. Sometimes it would take hours before she made motions of moving into consciousness, and there he'd be, leaning over her, kissing her eyelids, her mouth, behind her ears, knowing that whatever he did, she'd be in the mood to receive him. There would be no pushing away, as there was now, no sighing and making lame excuses.

Curling himself around her, he noted with pleasure that for some reason she seemed to have forgotten to put on her raggedy nightgown. He moved his hands to cup her breasts, then down the slope of her rib cage to the waistband of her panties, feeling her buttocks wedged tight against his groin, hoping that he could hear that barely audible little moan she used to emit even before he touched her erogenous zones. But now, even in sleep, she seemed to stiffen and pull away.

"Cor, Cora," he mumbled into her ear as he glanced at the night table where he saw a half-empty bottle of vodka and a drained glass, which seemed to explain her inability to properly undress for bed and that her sleep was a deep one from which nothing would wake her.

Discouraged, he turned toward the wall wondering if he could keep the deal. Could he actually leave her for drinking too much and passing out, after what he'd just done? There'd been no provisos for alcohol use, although they were both drunk or got high nearly every night.

The next morning, he was awakened by the sounds of retching coming from behind the bathroom door. If he hadn't been so familiar with the noise, he'd have thought his wife was having a bad case of the hiccups or was sneezing in some demure way. But he knew from their many years together, she was in there vomiting—vomiting up last night's meal of cheese and crackers and vodka and tonics. Like a used car he might have bought with bad brakes, she'd come to him with bulimia, and he'd known that when he married her. The craziest part of it was that, back then, he actually believed he could cure her.

"Rachel signed up for one of those Internet dating services," Cora called from the bathroom, seeming to be in a sunny mood. She'd just taken a shower and was brushing her teeth.

He groaned from the bed where he lay curled in a fetal position, staring through the blinds at a cold but sunny day. His fingers near his nose, he could still smell the strange woman's scent on his fingertips and wished his wife would hurry up with her ablutions so he could throw his hands under the faucet to wash the odor away.

"Why the fuck does she want to do something like that?" he called back. "She should just walk into a bar, pick up a guy, and get laid. All it'll cost her is the price of a few drinks."

Cora finally came into the bedroom, a towel wrapped around her slim body, and dug into the top drawer for panties. Which ones would she choose? He disliked the white cotton bikini briefs like the ones she had on the night before. Why did women insist on wearing them, as if they were still innocent little schoolgirls. Fuck it, he'd bought her several pairs of black lace panties from Victoria's Secret (the website wasn't so hot after all), but did she ever wear them? No! She kept them stashed at the bottom of the drawer as if waiting for the perfect moment to put them on, but now he was beginning to realize there'd probably never be a perfect moment—at least not with him.

As predicted, she took out a pair of cotton underwear, black this time but cotton nonetheless, and pulled them up over her hips. There were still her breasts to gaze at and dream of fondling, but they no longer seemed to call to him. Just to be sure, he swept his hand over his cock and gave it a quick tug under the guise of adjusting himself, but only got a slight response.

"It's not that easy," Cora complained, fully engaged in zipping up her wool A-line skirt over a pair of gray stockings and giving her curls a little encouragement with her fingertips. "Do you know what's out there? Nothing but rejects and retards. At our age, everyone is either hunkered down at home with a bunch of kids or insane."

"Or hunkered down at home insane," Gary joked, hoping she'd think he was being funny. She used to think he was funny and would laugh at practically anything he said, but now her face seemed to twist into an annoyed grimace whenever he opened his mouth, as if each one of his words caused her physical pain.

"Those websites get millions of hits a day. That's how people date. Julia, at the office, met her husband on Cupid.com. There's nothing wrong with it. If you go to a bar, you just end up with an alcoholic asshole."

"I'm going to make coffee," Gary mumbled, stumbling stiff-kneed toward the kitchen, hoping he didn't fit that bill. By the time he turned around again, his wife was fully dressed and looking exactly like her mother who was twenty-two years her senior. Each time Cora went to work, she looked a little older, dressed in her cold conservative clothes, a touch of lipstick to give her increasingly pale lips color, and concealer to hide the lines cropping up at the corners of her eyes. On her feet were heels he didn't think a normal biped should wear. Why had she become such an unknowable person? Was it because she had to go into that sterile office every day, while he could slouch around the apartment reading prospective movie scripts and never having to change out of his boxers?

"It's a good thing we have each other," she said, sidling over to give him a peck on the cheek. "I wouldn't want to be out there dating."

"No coffee today?" he asked, realizing she was saying good-bye and he was about to lose any chance of having an intimate connection with her.

"I'm sick of that coffee," she sighed. "Yesterday, when I walked past Rocco's, I saw this huge line of people coming out of the door and for the first time in all these years, I wondered what the hell was inside that would make them wait on line for so long? So I decided to blow off my first meeting and see what it was all about. When I got to the front, I ordered a latte like everyone else, and you know, it was delicious—so much richer than the shit we drink. Fuck making coffee every morning. Do something different for once. Go to Rocco's."

"So now you're pitching Rocco's Coffee Bar?" Gary laughed and continued with a voice-over imitation: "Are you a tattooed freelancer with nipple rings and more time on your hands than you know what to do with? Are you a stay-at-home mom with triplets who needs to get out of the house or else you'll blow your brains out? Are you a struggling singer/songwriter who has no money but gets up early to walk your two rescued mutts? Then go to Rocco's!"

"Are you a fucking asshole who thinks he's smarter than everyone else and has nothing better to do all day than read stupid movie scripts and jerk off to Internet porn?" Cora mimicked, then stopped short, wrapped a light blue scarf around her neck and prepared to leave.

"What's wrong?" she laughed nervously, looking up at Gary, who was leaning against the counter feeling as if he were about to cry. "Can't you take a joke?"

At that moment, Gary thought he actually felt the passage of time. He was just there with nowhere else to go, nothing to do—just be with his wife, who, at that second, seemed to know everything he was up to and was waiting for his response.

"Where were you last night?" she continued accusingly. "I thought you were going to come home early."

"You know where I was," Gary hedged, turning around to feed beans into the grinder and hide the fact that he felt as if he were ready to explode. When he pressed down on the top of the gadget, an awful noise was emitted replicating the way he felt inside. "I had that meeting, then a few drinks. If you're asking if I was with another woman, I wasn't," he lied, but Cora only looked at him with measured disgust, as if she'd just opened a package of rotten meat. "Besides, what am I supposed to do, live the rest of my life without sex? Without love? Hell. You won't even touch me."

"Look at yourself," she commanded. "You're not the person I married. Your hair's too long, you never shave, your pants are ripped, your stomach's so big you look like you're six months pregnant. You're going to have to do a little better than that if you want me to want you."

"Women want me all the time," he shot back, suddenly wishing she would just hurry out the door and get to work so he could have a little peace and quiet. It wasn't the first time he'd heard these complaints.

"You're a fucking fool. No wonder I'm not interested in you," she continued.

"With all your problems, maybe you could never be interested in anyone."

"Problems," she scoffed. "At least I get up and go to work every day. I get a paycheck at the end of the week."

"I get a paycheck, too. I just make money a little differently than you, and that takes skill. If I didn't have the talent, no production company would hire me. At least I've managed my life and my life doesn't manage me."

"The degree of denial that you're in is truly amazing," Cora snapped, edging toward the hallway.

"If you don't like it, leave," Gary stammered as she slammed the door behind her.

Another wonderful morning in paradise, he thought as he pivoted from refrigerator to Mr. Coffee Maker. He'd fix himself an extra large mug, sit down and check his e-mail, then see how Roxanne77 was getting along. Afterward, he'd shower, dress, and read some of the submissions to GreenLite Productions. Fuck it, maybe he'd go out to Rocco's and hang out with the tattooed, freelancing, dog walking set. At least his work kept his mind alive. Maybe marriage was never meant to be a lifetime proposition—five or six years at the most, then out while the going was still good.

So he made another deal with himself. He'd try again with Cora, prepare her a nice meal when she came home that evening. She never cooked for herself and claimed to hate eating, but usually she'd sit down and enjoy whatever he made. Perhaps he would marinate two salmon steaks in a ginger and lemon sauce and serve it over brown rice with a crème brûlée dessert. They could share a bottle of red wine and talk about fixing their marriage— but he'd tried that before, and all he was sure of was that the next morning, the meal ended up regurgitated in the toilet.

Roxanne77 was on screen, and he clicked on the photo of her sitting legs spread open toward him in a wide V. V for victory. V for variety. V for verisimilitude.

BOOZANNE, LEMME BE

Vicki Hendricks

I never needed "stuff," so it was easy to live—till Boozanne come along. Most stuff is just to impress women, and I didn't need them either—till Boozanne. I had a cute face, I heard—like a puppy dog—but being four foot ten, I was too short for normal chicks, too tall for a dwarf. I didn't try to fit in. I could afford a hand job now and then. Did me fine. Keep it simple was my motto. When Danny De Vito retired, maybe I'd head out to Hollywood, but for a young guy like myself, the deal I had going was almost as good—till Boozanne messed me up.

Ma had always told me, if you're gonna steal a VW, might as well steal a Cadillac. Well, Ma had that wrong. A VW would've been the right size for me. But when I got outta prison for stealing the Caddy, I gave up car theft altogether. My home was gone. Ma had passed on, bless her soul—Pop had never been around. Being broke and alone, I hitched down to Florida, remembering how warm it was that winter when Ma and me took a vacation, my best memory as a kid. I met Weasel in Miami, and he's the one told me about this gig. It fit me perfect, even better than a VW.

What you do is find a big old wood house, with two foot of crawling space underneath, and cut a hole in the floor under the bed. Easy, if you measure. Beds are never moved. Weasel burgled his way around the islands, so by the time each hole got discovered, he was long gone. With my carpenter experience, and considering I needed a home more than anything, I went him one better by saving the piece of floor, so I could latch it back in place underneath. No mortgage, no taxes, and free food as long as you're not greedy. Nobody would notice, even if they ran a dust mop over the hardwood, a thing that—I'm telling you—most people never do.

My home with the Lamberts, Bob and Melodie, was walking-distance from the beach, came with *Sports Illustrated* and *Gourmet* subscriptions, cable, big-screen TV, and a cat. They had those wood Bahama shutters that hang down and cover the windows, so nobody could see in, and a carport instead of a garage, so I always knew if either car was home. Thick foliage out to the sidewalk made it easy to sneak around back and go under, though I did most of my crawling in and out in the dark. I had plastic runners and a rug remnant from Goodwill under there, my clothes sealed up in black garbage bags to keep out the bugs, a flashlight, toss pillow, and a *Playboy* to pass the waiting time. I never needed toiletries, like toothpaste, shampoo, or deodorant, 'cause the Lamberts were well supplied. Didn't shave, or I would've got my own razor. It was like living in a full-service motel, except I had to clean up after myself. I was set—till fuckin' Boozanne.

Bob and Melodie got home each night at seven or later—depending if they ate out—so I'd drop down the hole around 6:30, crawl out at dark, and head to a cheap local bar, or out on a scrounge, then later to my chair on the beach to doze until it was getting toward dawn, time to head home. I'd picked 'em good—upper-middle-class workaholics, too distracted about their jobs to notice the house much, lotsa loose change and doggie-bag leftovers that they usually tossed into the bin within two days. Somebody might as well enjoy it all. Once in a while, I stuck a pepperoni down my pants at the grocery for extra meat. I didn't take big chances, didn't need much. Any violation would send me back to a cell.

I didn't have to be too careful at the home, as long as I remembered to pick my long black hairs off the pillowcase, go easy on the tidbits and liquor, and wash my lunch dishes. Sometimes, I got sick of looking at Bob's coffee cup that he'd leave on the bathroom sink, and I'd wash that, too. I was kind of a dark male Goldilocks, only nicer. I felt friendly toward the Lamberts, seeing that I knew so much about their food tastes, possessions, and living habits. Melodie was like the sister I never had, little and dark haired, big eyed and innocent in her pictures. I felt protective toward her. Bob was like an older brother I could live without.

One day, she came home early—I was lucky the lunch dishes were done—and I was in the living room to see the car pull in. I barely made it out the hole. She ran in and tossed herself on the bed and wailed. Her sobs broke my heart while I lay under there listening. I had to stuff my face into my pillow not to make a whimper. I thought maybe her ma had died. After that, all signs of Melly disappeared for most of a week. Her black dresses were gone, and there were tons of used Kleenex in the wastebasket in her bathroom. She had her period on top of it all, so I hoped no cramps. Eventually, from the sympathy cards, I figured out it was her pop that died.

Trying to be of some help, I dusted, wiped out the refrigerator, vacuumed, and cleaned the toilets for her while she was gone. Bob didn't go to the funeral, and I knew he wouldn't take over the cleaning neither. I couldn't do anything obvious, but I just thought she'd feel better if the place somehow didn't seem to get dirty—and the refrigerator needed cleaning bad. Bob was your regular slob and never noticed nothin'.

Melly brought home some mementos from her father, his fishing license and a pin from the Marines, so I knew they were close. I admired the old fella, seeing he probably enjoyed life and had guts. I found these heavy dark blue folders right after that, sitting in plain view on the desk. I thought they were books at first, but when I opened 'em up, they smelled musty and were filled with U.S. silver dollars in little slots marked with the years—the real silver dollars that this country don't make anymore. I could tell by looking at the edges. I didn't know what they were worth, but there were close to four hundred of 'em, and a few from way back in the 30s. I wondered if Melodie knew the value. I wished I could warn her to put 'em in a safety deposit box, in case of burglars, like the Weasel.

I buddied up with their cat, too. He liked his water freshened a couple times a day, and he would have starved while Melodie was gone if I wasn't there to refill his dry food. I really performed a service. He was smart, and I taught him to give paw and roll over for Whisker Lickin's tuna-flavored treats. I hid the packet in the empty cabinet above the refrigerator, and I had to laugh every time I pictured the Lamberts finding it and being downright stumped. I expect Bones thought I was his owner, considering all the quality time we spent. I wished I knew his real name. I listened sometimes, waiting under the house, but the words were usually too muffled to make out anything, unless Bob and Melodie were having a fight. Bob could get pretty loud. I went through their address book, hoping for something like TIGER'S VET, but no clues. He answered to Lazybones— or Bones—as much as any cat answers.

I generally took a long nap each day with Bones on my chest. It was like working the night shift, except no work! I sold off a lawn mower and weed eater—garage items from down the block— and got myself a gym membership so I could shower, swim, hot tub, and work out with the hardcore sissy fellas every day if I wanted, and especially on weekends when I was stuck out of the house all day.

Things were going good. That night I was still holding some cash, and I thought I'd slug down a few shots at one of them outdoor South Beach bars, take in the fancy scenery, meaning women. It was just then, when I'd got my life all in order, I run into Boozanne. I come up to the bar and there she was, her back to me, lapping a little over the stool in the thigh area, a big girl with lots of curly orange hair and freckled white skin on her upper arms. She had on a thin nylon shirt that clung to every ripple of her, the handles of love, and the lush flesh above the back of her brassiere. When she turned my way, there were those double Ds, staring at me, talcum still dry between 'em, and the smell of a baby, despite eighty-five degrees and heavy humidity. Stars were winking in the black sky over her head, so I shoulda known the joke was on me.

A flamenco guitar strummed away in my left ear, traffic and ocean crashed together in the right. "Hi, there," I yelled. I pointed at the only empty seat, the one next to her, where she had parked her pocketbook.

"I'm Junior," I said. I was more often called Mouse, but I didn't like it.

"Name's Susanne," I thought she said.

I nodded. "Pleased to meet you, Susanne."

She scrunched up her little pig nose with the freckles on it, but I didn't know what the problem was. She had a puckered set of red lips to go with that nose. "Boooz-anne," she drawled.

That there was the killer. Her voice flowed out like syrup and I damned near choked. I wondered if she could be a Kentucky girl, hot and smooth as the bourbon I'd left behind those two years ago. I musta stared at her—I wasn't sure what was polite to say.

She picked up her beer can. "Booooz-anne!" she hollered. "Buy me one."

The bartender looked at me, and I put up two fingers.

Boozanne stared at my legs. "You need a hoist onto that stool, pal?"

I ignored her and used the step under the bar to give me the extra lift. Boozanne lit a cigarette. Her cheeks sucked in and her lashes kinda flickered in pleasure as she drew the smoke. When her chin tipped back on the exhale, I remembered how Ma used to aim her smoke at the ceiling by protruding her bottom lip like a funnel. Boozanne's white neck and the pattern of freckles spilling down resembled one of the girls' chests in Bob's porno video. The smoke hung in the air and the flamenco ripped to a finale as she focused on me. When she finally talked, she didn't slur.

"You're pretty cute for a shortie. Been working out?"

"Some," I said. It came to me that she might want to get naked, and I wasn't against it.

"You know how long a man's legs are supposed to be, don't you?"

I shook my head, getting ready for a joke about my height, figuring it was worth the ridicule to get laid.

"Long enough to reach the ground," she said. "Abraham Lincoln."

"Abraham Lincoln said that?" I scratched my head. "He had real long legs, didn't he?"

"Yeah, but that's not the point. Yours are long enough."

"It all evens out horizontal, don't it?"

She laughed, and after that my memories are spotty. Sometime, Boozanne and me staggered across the street, holding hands and bumping together, and we stumbled over the sand toward the water, to my favorite wooden lounge chair, chained behind a small dune of shore grass, far enough from the street to be dark. My mind wasn't working too good, but I recall taking off my pants, falling over once.

Next thing, there was Boozanne, buck naked and white as whipped cream, like an art model with all the rich layers of her unfolding, as she lay down on the lounge and opened her arms to me. I stopped trying to brush off sand and leaned over her and straddled one of her thighs. We did some tonguing, I think, but mostly I remember the feel of her, meaty and cool, as I pawed over her big tits and nuzzled her neck. When I scooted on down, that baby powder drowned out the fishy smell of the beach. I suckled her nipples and crawled onto her lap. She weren't my first woman, but there hadn't been many, and none of this size. I poked into her soft gut and jelly thighs a few times, and then I located that sweet spot you don't never forget.

Over the next week, besides picking most of the quarters out of the change jar, I had some easy pickings from a tree service trailer, and took a chain saw to the South Dixie Pawn Shop. Boozanne—surprise, surprise—could put away the liquor, and I didn't want to seem poor. I knew I amused her, but it could all end fast if I stopped giving her what she needed. I figured I was some kind of rebound catch anyway, since otherwise she was out of my league. I convinced her to go to my favorite local bar, where it was homey. Quantity was more important to her than scenery, and she didn't complain much.

Besides liking sex, she was a woman who could tell a joke. I enjoyed her stories about idiots at the office, and the quick way she saw through her boss with his snooty manners. She had some schemes for easy money, and she promised to let me in. I'd started talking to Bones about her, and when I pictured her pretty face I felt something way stronger than the tightness in my balls.

One night when we were sitting on the lounge chair smoking some weed, I dropped the roach into my shirt pocket and the damn fabric flared right up. Boozanne was fast with her hand to pat it out. "Your heart's on fire for me," she said. She was laughing, but I couldn't deny it. I took that as a sign.

Course the subject came up of going to my place instead of the sticky, sandy lounge chair, and I couldn't fend her off for long. She had an efficiency and a roommate, so it was up to me to make arrangements if I wanted to "continue enjoying her womanhood." Now, I was really working her pussy hard, and I had a suspicion that she liked the fucking as much as me, but I knew there were plenty more men where I come from—taller ones, with better incomes—whereas she was the only woman ever come on to me that didn't ask for money up front. The wood chair hurt her back, and she wouldn't get on top 'cause she was embarrassed about how she outweighed me. She kept harping on it until I let loose of the truth. I thought it would be the end of us, but it turned out my living conditions were a real amusement. I'd lied that I was on disability, but now I gave out all my secrets, including my nickname Mouse—that she promised never to use—and my recent incarceration.

Before I had time to think, she'd took the day off work, and I was sneaking her in between the air conditioner and Bob's garden hose. I had to bend some bushes to get her through, and they took some damage, but probably only Bones would notice.

I had a long sheet of plastic stretching to the edge under the house, so I could crawl on my stomach without getting dirty, and Boozanne surprised me with the ease that she wormed on through. She weren't afraid of the spiders or nothing. I went first and moved the bed aside, and she stood and took my hand, and stepped up into the room like a lady. It was a big hole, but she pretty much filled it. I'd told her I could go inside and unlock the back door for her, but she said the porch was too visible, and that was true. She wandered around the house, while I slid the wood to cover the hole, enough so Bones couldn't get out, and scooted the bed back in place so the bedroom looked nice.

Boozanne came floating my way in the living room, with a cigarette, sipping from one of Melodie's good glasses filled with a clear gold liquid. I only hoped it wasn't the scotch Bob was saving from his birthday. She'd stripped off her clothes and put on a see-through robe that left a gap in front, with pink nipples and red muff peeking out.

I grabbed her cigarette and flung it into the sink.

She clucked her tongue at me. "Such a worrier. They've got all kinds of booze in the cabinet, Junior. I'm surprised you haven't polished it off."

"Now I shoulda told you—you got to be careful. They notice things missing, and I'm out. I hope that's the Cutty's."

She tossed her curls. "Why drink Cutty's when there's Glenfiddich?"

"Okay, just take it easy. We'll add a little water. Don't open new bottles, and don't drink more than a couple shots of any one thing."

"No problem. There's lots to try. I haven't had this much fun since I was twelve and broke into the neighbors'."

"Oh, yeah? What'd you do?"

"Not much. Three of us girls—we just put a little hole in the screen door and got excited sneaking around, looking in the bedrooms. Adrenaline rush."

"There is something to that," I said.

"I don't know why we didn't check for money or take anything."

"Maybe you didn't need anything."

"Oh, Junior, you always need money," she said. She cuffed me on the chest.

"I don't. Not always."

"That's why you're special—besides this."

She bent down and undid my belt and zipper, dropping my pants, and pulled me against her big powdered tits for a long sloppy kiss. I was useless, barely able to waddle over to the bed and kick my pants off my knees so I could climb on top of her. I got her breathing hard, grunting and cooing, and we were both sweating rivers. I thought for a second about messing the sheets, but I had plenty of time to run laundry.

After that Boozanne got the fancy platter out of the china cabinet, and the cloth napkins, and we ate a snack—olives and imported cheeses and crackers, a small chunk of goat cheese, Parmesan, some Stilton. I wouldn't've touched the moldy stuff on my own, but the Lamberts had introduced me to lots of new food, and most of it was pretty damn tasty. Boozanne was still hungry so I made her a peanut butter and jelly, which was always safe, but she didn't much like it.

She left around three, and I was exhausted, but there was plenty of cleanup to do. I panicked when I picked up a juice glass and saw a white ring on the coffee table. I found some furniture spray that didn't work, but as I stood there pulling out my hair, the ring started to lighten up, until it finally disappeared. I did the dishes and threw the napkins into the washer with the sheets. I hoped there was no ironing required.

Bones came out from somewhere to lie on me while I waited for the fabric softener cycle. He was purring and it felt good relaxing with him on my chest after the wild afternoon. "Bones," I said, holding his head to look into his eyes. "Here's a woman who knows all about me and still likes me." I massaged behind his ears and his jaw went slack because it felt so good. "I'm pretty damned fond of her, too." I couldn't say the word *love* out loud, not even to Bones.

He stared me in the face with his big gold eyes, and I thought I saw sadness. 'Course he always looked like that, and just because Boozanne came around, I wasn't gonna ditch him.

Soon Boozanne quit her job. It was understandable—all the typing they piled on her. She was consulting with a lawyer on some female issues. I was glad to see more of her, but it was worrisome, her not having any money coming in. We went on like that for a couple weeks, wild sex and a snack several afternoons. She passed some time looking through the Lamberts' closets and drawers. I'd seen it all already, so I sipped whiskey and watched her flesh move around in that skimpy robe. Lucky I had the place memorized, 'cause caution was not her strong feature, and I had to make sure everything got put back. As it was, a wine glass got broke. She scared me sometimes, but I couldn't think of what I used to do without her.

I picked up bottles and cans for extra money, so I could pay for drinks at night. A couple times I did dishes for cash. I wasn't really allowed out of Kentucky, so I couldn't take a job that checked records. I got into a neighbor's storage shed and found an old waffle iron and ice skates to pawn, and let my gym membership go. There was a workout course on the beach, and I could shower there and let my clothes dry on me Saturday and Sunday. I didn't have much time to work out anyways with all the hours it took to scrounge. Boozanne got some kind of weekend job, just enough to keep up her rent, until she could find something good. She wouldn't take no cash from me.

In early July the Lamberts went to California for a week. It was blocked out on their calendar for a month, and Boozanne and me couldn't wait. Boozanne moved right in and we took over the place. The first morning she cooked me biscuits and fluffy eggs like her grandma taught her, and we took our time eating, and left the dishes all day, and smoked some of the weed that Boozanne found in Bob's chest of drawers. The only problem was that Bones was shipped off somewhere so we didn't have our pet. I wished I could have told Melly that I'd take care of him.

One day we were lazing around in the bedroom, and I showed Boozanne Melodie's "secret" drawer. That was a mistake. My plan was to slip one of the old rings onto her finger to see what she'd say, but she spotted Melodie's gold heart right in front. It was a real delicate necklace that was usually missing, so I knew Melodie normally wore it a lot and must have left it home for safekeeping. Boozanne became instantly attached, and I didn't want to let her take it. Necklaces can get misplaced easy, so it wasn't so much that I thought we'd get caught, but it was probably a present from Bob, or maybe even an heirloom.

Boozanne put it around her neck and asked me to fasten it. "Please, baby?" She was stroking my bicep and I liked that.

"Can you just wear it while you're here and put it back?"

"My birthday's coming up, and I know you don't have money to buy me a gift."

"When's your birthday?"

"November, but you won't have any money then either."

It was true, and I had never bought her a present.

"It'll be a nice memento of our vacation," she said. "Please, baby, please?"

I suggested a small silver heart that was far back in the drawer, but she said she was allergic to any metals except gold. I felt terrible about Melodie, but seeing how pretty the gold looked in Boozanne's freckled cleavage, and how much she wanted it, I let her take it. I checked for extra Kleenexes in Melodie's bathroom trash when the Lamberts got home, and there weren't none, but deadlocks appeared on the doorjambs after the weekend, and that creeped me out. I tried to get the heart back to plant it, but Boozanne wouldn't give it up. She didn't understand my feelings about the place.

Things went good for a few more weeks, and then Boozanne got tired of the job hunt and lack of money. Safe pickings for the pawn shop were running slim in the neighborhood. Boozanne said she had a plan to make some real money, live high on the hog for a while, do some traveling, then get an apartment of our own. Sneaking around was exciting at first, but she was tired of it. I didn't want to leave the Lamberts after only two months, but my odds for getting caught were climbing, and if I wanted Boozanne, I had to go.

We were sitting on the couch, me petting Bones, when she gave me the specifics.

"I'll handle it," she said. "We've got credit cards, social security numbers, birth certificates, checkbooks, bank statements, passports, and salable goods. You've heard of identity theft."

"But they're nice people. Melodie is. I don't want to steal from them."

"What are you talking about? You've been stealing from them for months."

"Not enough to matter."

"That's what I'm saying. It's time to do something that matters. They've got almost ten thousand in their checking account."

"I can't," I said. "They're like relatives."

"And I'm not?"

When she put it like that, I had no argument. I'd only seen them at a distance and in pictures, but it still didn't feel right.

"You don't have to do anything," she said. She went to the desk and brought back some insurance papers. "Look, they're well insured for their possessions—and the credit cards pay for fraudulent charges. I won't write checks if you don't want me to. It seems tricky anyway."

"I can cut a hole somewhere else for the burglaring."

"Too much trouble and you might not be as lucky. Besides, I already started." She pulled two credit cards out of her pocketbook and held them in front of my face. There was one card for Melodie and one for Robert.

It was all real then, and my guts were shot out. "Jesus," I said.

"We've got their other cards, plus these new ones I applied for, five thousand limit on each."

She dug back into her pocketbook and pulled out a small satin pouch. I looked inside and saw the glitter of gold and cut stones. "Necklace and earring set—off the Internet. I've got more stuff coming. I bet you can find somebody to buy the passports."

It was too late to stop her without calling in the law.

She patted my head. "I'll get us flights to anywhere you want. You deserve it, baby."

I let her kiss me then, and my mind went into a haze, a kind of protective vision of us sipping bourbon on the porch swing of some cozy cottage in the mountains of Kentucky, Boozanne exhaling smoke into a cool summer breeze.

Three weeks later was moving day. Boozanne had bought two suitcases on wheels, filled them with our new clothes and more high-end jewelry pieces she'd ordered. She was busy wrapping up old silver trays she'd found in a chest. I'd liquidated the necklace and earrings and some nice watches, and we had $6,000 cash, airline tickets, and room reservations for someplace exotic—a surprise—and the new credit cards to charge whatever we needed when we got there. Visa and MasterCard had called about unusual activity, but Boozanne answered all their questions. We took the bills for those old cards out of the mailbox, so we had plenty of leeway. She figured we could vacation for two weeks and still have resources to rent a place when we got back. When we ran low on money, we'd start over again. I was excited about traveling with Boozanne, but I hated ripping off the Lamberts. They'd been good to me, in their way.

I'd finished wiping all the furniture and appliances for fingerprints and closed the suitcases, and Boozanne was wearing rubber gloves, still poking around. Bones was sleeping on the couch, and I gave him a good-bye pet, feeling real sad.

I went into the kitchen and looked at the clock. I couldn't believe it. "Damn!" I yelled. "It's a quarter to seven!"

I went back into the living room. She was searching the bottom drawers of the desk.

"Boozanne! We gotta go. It's not like we're headed to a movie."

"Five minutes. I don't want to miss anything. Money goes fast on vacation."

"We're cutting it too close. I never stay this late."

"No worries." Just then she opened the drawer with the folders of silver dollars. I held my breath, hoping she'd pass them by again, thinking they were books.

She flipped open the first cover. "Oh, wow!" She lifted them out and carried them to the coffee table. She opened another and another.

"We don't have room for those old coins. They're too heavy," I told her.

She pulled out a dollar and studied it. "Mouse, these could be worth a fortune! They're antique silver dollars."

"Naw, put 'em down. You're allergic to silver. We gotta get out of here."

"No way. Open the suitcase."

"Boozanne, I won't take 'em. They're Melodie's inheritance. It's all she got."

"You're insane. You with your freaky crush. Now open that suitcase, or I will. I'll leave you here with your fucking Melodie."

I didn't have time to let that sink in. There was the sound of a car pulling into the carport. "Jesus Christ," I whispered. I ducked and took a glance out the corner of the window. "It's her." I grabbed Boozanne's hand, but she didn't budge. "Come on!" I hollered. We can make it out the hole."

"I'm not leaving without the coins."

I just stood there, unable to gather a thought. She was digging into her pocketbook.

"Stand next to the door," she said. "Grab her mouth from behind and hold her."

I did what I was told, and Boozanne ducked around the corner. In seconds, the key turned and poor Melly stepped inside. I yanked her from behind, clamping a hand over her mouth and kicking the door shut before she could scream. I pulled her against me and fell half on top of her. She was more delicate than I thought, and her face had wrinkles I couldn't see in the pictures. My eyes filled because I knew I hurt her. She whimpered and my heart broke. When I looked up, Boozanne was bent over, those double Ds loose near my head, her shirt pulled up covering her face and hair. It was nylon, and she was stretching it so she could see through the thin mesh. A .25 in her other hand pointed straight into Melodie's ear.

"What the fuck?" I was so stunned I let go of Melodie's mouth and she screamed and yanked her face sideways. I cut her off fast and pushed her head under my armpit, but she'd already seen my face. Bones was there staring at me, his eyes huge.

"Move away!" yelled Boozanne.

I grabbed the barrel of the gun and tilted it toward the ceiling. "Go!" I yelled. "You go! I'll hold her while you get away."

"You sure?" she said. She didn't sound too disappointed.

"Hurry up."

She blew me a kiss, opened a suitcase, threw out my clothes, and dropped in the books of coins. I stayed on top of Melodie, my head sagging onto her neck. I could smell her hair, clean and flowery. I tried to soothe her by stroking it. Bones gave paw onto my cheek, but seeing no treats, climbed up and lay on my back. I watched the squeaky wheels of the suitcases roll past my nose.

"We could've been great together," Boozanne said, "if one of us was a different person."

I looked up and thought I saw a glint of tears in her eye, as she shut the door. Boozanne was gone, taking my dreams with her.

It all hit me then. Melodie had no idea I'd saved her life, and she was never gonna think of me like a brother. She'd freak when she found out how long I'd been living there, even if I did keep the house nice and feed Bones. Some of her ribs were likely broken. I'd never be able to explain. I was headed back to the slammer for a long, long time.

I thought about Boozanne. I didn't even know her real name and hadn't never seen those airplane tickets to ponder where she was headed. It could've been so perfect, if she hadn't got greedy. Our plan was to walk down to the bar, have a beer, call a taxi to the airport . . . She wouldn't do that now.

Bob's car pulled in, and I was still lying there, half on Melodie. My arm went limp, and Bones jumped off my back as I sat up. Melly rolled to her side wailing, her eyes flat as those silver dollars. I said, "Sorry, so sorry, Mel," but she didn't hear.

I leaned against the wall and pictured Boozanne, down the block, big and bold as she was, sticking out her thumb—and a gold Cadillac stopping, its doors opening up like wings, to fly her away.

ERASURE

Christine Lee Zilka

Myung-Ja came home from her overtime shift at the hospital before dawn, her tired steps crunching gravel in the courtyard with an unfamiliar tempo that awakened Yong, who then lay tensed on the heated ondol floor waiting for either a key in the door or the brutal sounds of someone breaking in, his morning erection fading with an alacrity that rivaled that of his heartbeat. He wondered if a day would come when he wouldn't react to sudden noise like this, when he might even sleep through any shift in environment. In the darkness, he vowed to protect any future children from this ever-vigilant state, one that made him aware of survival on a minute-to-minute basis. He vowed to spoil them rotten, coddle them, never let them heave into consciousness with great fear. He pondered how he had gotten to this point in the night. He thought of flexed muscles, a bead of sweat swimming in his brow. He thought of violence he thought of the news of his brother's death, his mother calling for Dae-Sang, and he thought of disbelief he thought of the long walk to Seoul from Pyongyang he thought of soldiers whose uniforms could not define whether or not they had good intentions or if they were con-men and rapists, he thought of looking at the face of every soldier his brother's age was his brother still alive he thought of con-men who traded bags of pebbles they pawned as rice in exchange for sex he thought of rapists who took sex without prelude he thought of covering his ears he thought of blood he thought of closing his eyes he thought of seeing daylight red through his eyelids he thought of screaming he thought of silence he thought of cold mornings he thought of fresh water he thought of relief. And then she called out in a voice that shredded the morning. Open the door. She knocked. Open the door.

Myung-Ja was not smiling but not crying either, because she had the disciplined heart of all doctors and nurses. She looked bedraggled under the doorway light, just as one might expect someone who'd lost a night of sleep to appear. Her skin was dull, cheeks flushed pink from exhaustion or perhaps the chilly morning air, and though her usually crisp nurse's uniform was wrinkled, creased with dirt and splattered with blood despite her pride in a pristine outfit, her hair was neatly pinned back and her face clean as if she had tidied herself in the last hour. Yong smiled at the thought.

Yong ushered her in. "You look like war."

"I feel really sorry for them, really sorry for them. Those commandos were so thin, they were suffering." She first took off her shoes at the steps and then put her purse down on the heated floor that would soften the lonely lipstick tube at the bottom beneath her wallet, before she folded her legs onto the floor beside Yong, disregarding the silk sitting cushions they had received as wedding gifts from her aunt, and began kneading her feet.

Blinded with grogginess in the silent night, Yong could smell the faint smell of her unwashed body like wet pavement next to him and could hear her nails scratching nylon stockings. If he had ears that moved like a dog, he thought, they would be turning to that sound and then she would know what it was he was thinking. He thought of sauntering through the whispering grass in the sticky summertime of Korea with his sibling. He thought of singing cicadas. He thought of watermelon and its rind splitting open with the satisfying smack of a scythe. He thought of the buzzing and sizzling in his ears after an arms explosion. He thought about an itch. Yong sat so still he felt a violent need and reached out to her, taking her foot with an atypical roughness, his fingers on polyester scissoring through the silence. Still sleepy but with a growing alertness, he felt her cramped muscles underneath the cold foot encased inside the nylon.

"Harder."

He took the foot in both hands, clasped the arch in his fingers. He felt the taut muscles and tendons beneath, stroked them with the intention of breaking them down.

"Harder."

Her foot was small, an American size six, tiny in his hands, and as he worked her foot, the foot would appear and reappear, and he recalled the first time Myung-Ja had ever given him a hand job, her hand doing the work he was doing now, the appendage appearing fragile, but firm and unbending upon touch. He pressed the ball of her foot, then worked the pressure up to the arch, feeling the bones crack with release. Myung-Ja lay with her eyes closed, a smile beginning to show on her face, a shy grin that Yong wanted to spill into laughter, a sound that he realized he hadn't heard in weeks, maybe months. It was when he got to the heel of her foot, roughly massaging the blood back into that numbed area, that her eyes flashed open.

She let out a deep cleansing sigh, the kind that felt like a release of worry and strain, twisting her body around so that her head was now in Yong's lap.

Yong's hands, still remembering the curves of her foot, burned.

Myung-Ja untied her hair, allowing it to cascade over his lap. Her cheek brushed against his erection.

Yong felt a hunger for that laughter again, and to break the miserable spell that had fallen over him. Fallen over them, actually. He wanted his wife to suck his cock, and then he wanted to fuck his wife. He wanted to fuck the panic out of his head. He wanted to erase his memories and replace them with a pleasure that Yong could only describe as heat and light and flight and rushing warm water. He took his wife in his arms.

He thought of Myung-Ja, of her sparrow-like body. He thought of eating sparrows and breaking their tiny necks in his hands their hearts' fluttering beats the nervous wings and he thought of stillness and he thought of hunger and sustenance he thought of picking through edible weeds in the mountainside (her breasts) and he thought of wild radishes and watercress and fern bracken and he thought of the pleasure of first bites of food like apples (her lips) and the flavor of rice sweet and starchy and hot and steamy (her tongue) on his taste buds ever more pronounced in the first spoonful he thought of mountainsides picked clean he thought of eating trash he thought of a can of tuna found after days of hunger he thought of salt he thought of thirst he thought of clean water. He thought of war, no his erection was going down, he thought of peace he thought of unencumbered sleep (thrust) he thought of conflict no he thought of peace he thought of guilt no of his brother Dae-Sang no he thought of escape (thrust) he thought of running (thrust) he thought of wind in his face (thrust) he thought of leash-less pleasure (thrust) he thought of whores (thrust-thrust) he thought of breasts and supple skin he thought of perfume he thought of hair he thought of round buttocks he thought of cunts he thought of seas he thought of warm oceans he thought of cackling seagulls he thought of sunlight he thought of slippery wet heat he thought of salty warm breezes he thought of chili spice he thought of ice he thought of beer he thought of drunkenness he thought of his throbbing cock he thought of virgins he thought of his wife, he thought of Myung-Ja tiny and feverish and gasping in his arms like a shivering bird.

It was not until after Yong could feel her body tense up in climax that she returned from a birdlike state to her true human nature. Her body relaxed, her breath rhythmic and noiseless, and her eyes, open like a deep winter lake in the snow of her skin, stared right into him. His terror had been erased, would dwell in the unseen recesses of memory for a few minutes longer, only staggering back into focus after the calm.

PRIVATE LIVES

Jonis Agee

It was only a matter of time. At least that's what Albert told Frederick. It was okay for Albert to hire the boys and insist that they dress in their cotton, church-blue pants and long-sleeved white shirts. White set off the innocent glow of their faces and the small dirty moons of nails on their delicate twelve-year-old hands. That was okay. Teach them to move softly between the chairs and tables, to inquire discreetly over the customer's left shoulder for coffee, tea, water.

Albert liked to watch them straining with the plastic pitcher he insisted they keep filled to the brim with almost cool tap water. Handling it as if it were heirloom crystal, they paused, sliding the left hand under the bottom as if it were a small animal slipping from their grasp, then remembering his instructions, withdrawing and placing the hand behind the back again. Then they would right themselves, and straining to lift and angle the pitcher exactly, they would pour the water expertly into the glass.

Albert liked to watch the down at the back of their necks prickle with the strain and the small unlined faces wrinkle like a bedsheet suddenly grabbed in a fist and then let go again. There was nothing like that. When he looked at his own face in the mirror, he knew what was wrong with it. When he pulled at the skin pooling under his eyes, it took too long to return and sometimes stood up like an ocean wave until he patted it back in place.

"There's nothing you can do about it now," Albert told Frederick later as they lay in bed, stiff and familiar as man and wife after years of struggle. They had not caved in to the desire to sleep separately but had bought a huge, king-size bed instead. Now each lay marooned on his side, avoiding the imaginary line that bisected their nights, like the sword of Damocles, Albert thought. Frederick worried that somehow the box springs, which were two separate twin beds, would part like the *Titanic* one night and strand them permanently or toss them into the smothering ocean of covers on the floor. When Frederick told him about it, Albert tapped the ashes off his cigarette, put his book down with a sigh, and stood up on the bed.

"What're you doing?" Frederick demanded, as he pulled away from the chasm that at any moment could erupt in the middle. But Albert just marched around, sending Frederick out of bed in a scramble that pulled most of the covers off with him. "Watch what you're doing there."

Albert grinned meanly and bounced his six-foot-one height close to the ceiling.

"Hey," Frederick cried out. "Stop it! Do you want to go through the floor or something?" He tried to pull around him some of the blankets they had piled on for the bitter January cold of Minnesota, but Albert's face was turning red in the effort of his gymnastics, and Frederick knew he'd better do something before he hurt himself. Really, he had almost no sense at all.

"All right, you made your point." Frederick made himself smile and grabbed Albert's legs.

When they'd met in Chicago so many years ago, Frederick couldn't get enough of those beautiful long legs. He made Albert take off everything but his boxers in the apartment and strut around, even though the windows were open and his neighbors across the courtyard were peering around the corners of their curtains at the "two fags" across the way. Frederick smarted under their disapproval and held on tightly to Albert despite the early troubles.

It was like "Jack and the Beanstalk" in the late afternoon when Albert would come back to clean up and rest before the evening rush at the hotel. Frederick felt like Jack wanting to and then doing it—climbing those legs like a stairway to the sky. Then Albert's beautiful white length would be stretched across the double bed that seemed too big to them. They could hardly get close enough, as Frederick ran his tongue up and around the calves, licking the salty smooth down and the milky skin his Czech parents had given Albert. "Why don't you ever tan?" Frederick asked him once, but Albert looked at him as if he were crazy. Later Frederick would come to realize that in the Old World a man with a tan worked outside, was a peasant, and that Albert's family had always struggled to keep their boys inside, in trades, away from peasant life. Twenty years later, when Albert discovered he was going to get old, he spent months in a tanning parlor, basting and turning like a Thanksgiving turkey, but he got old anyway. That's when he started dating.

"What do you mean, you're going out?" Frederick demanded.

"There's this boy who works for me—well, for the hotel. A busboy." Albert buttered his English muffin carefully, trimming the sides with the knife as if he were decorating one of his petits fours.

"A boy? A busboy?"

When Albert nodded and took his first bite, tentatively, the way he tasted all food, checking for flavor and texture even of the items he wasn't involved in preparing, Frederick slammed his fork down on the white Formica in the breakfast nook.

"Now, Frederick, blood pressure, right?" Albert reminded him and took a larger second bite of the muffin. It was perfect. Just the way the busboy was. Puerto Rican, tan, muscular. He noticed the way Frederick, older by three years, was beginning to lose muscle tone, or maybe his skin was getting gray with his hair. Something. Frederick was trying to stare down Albert's inspecting gaze. Pushed back against the wood of the booth, he looked as if he might hurt himself, bruise something, if he didn't relax.

"How can you? Just tell me that we've . . . well, we've . . . What about last night? This morning in the shower? 'I love you forever?' What does that mean?"

Albert put down the muffin and took a sip of Frederick's coffee, made the way Albert had taught him. In fact, Albert had taught him everything about cooking, and more, a lot more. He put that knowledge in his eyes and stared hard at Frederick. "It means I have a date. I'm going out tonight after work. The kid gets off at eleven. We're just going for a couple of drinks. He's been trying to come out for a month now. I just want to talk to him. Guys at work give him the cold shoulder or a load of shit. They don't trust him. He's a good kid, though. Really. Takes care of his mother and sister. Puerto Ricans have strong family ties, like the Ukrainians do." He added the last part for Frederick, who couldn't stand being hugged by the fat Ukrainian aunts smelling of sweat and yeast from their hours of baking in the kitchen, with their hair like flat helmet from the scarves they wore. The women in Frederick's family were beautiful, educated. They never touched you with more than a fingertip, and they kissed the air on either side of your face whenever they met you.

The business of their families was always a problem, well, after the first few months, when they were so dizzy in love they barely had time to work and sleep. Each day a new surprise. Special dishes Albert would prepare at the Drake Hotel's expense and bring home at one in the morning for their feasts. The tiny gifts Frederick would buy to quietly please Albert, who neither shopped nor could afford to shop on his beginning salary as under-under-under chef. Long hours and short pay—but none of that mattered. They would barely have time to eat the glorious dishes—slices of beef Wellington, little pastry birds stuffed with crab—before they would be in the bedroom, then later on the sofa in the living room, on the rug in front of the fireplace, and later on the kitchen table, on the floor of the bathroom, sick with desire, sick with love. Although they ate wonderfully, they lost weight with love—the shudder of a hand sliding up an arm, the careful strokes sponging the kitchen smells from Albert's limbs, the slow massage of shampoo, Albert leaning tiredly and happily back into the bowl of Frederick's arms as they waited out the night in the soothing water of the huge tub.

Now he has a date, Frederick thought. Now. The wink of the ruby ring he'd given Albert seemed like a lewd gesture after all those years. Now?

When the first tears appeared, Frederick fought them. He wasn't going to give in to Albert this time. He was going to fight him as though the playground bully was sitting on his chest yelling, "Give, give."

Then he felt tired suddenly, the way he always felt with the bully. He'd finally say uncle, aunt, whatever they wanted, and feel the sudden relief of their weight lifted from his chest. Looking toward home, he'd pick up his things, clutch them tightly to cover the hole in his chest, and trudge across the playground to the corner exit space torn in the fence. By the time he reached home, he'd be too exhausted to do anything but go quietly to his room and collapse on the bed.

Though he'd just gotten up and showered on the morning Albert made his announcement and thought he had a class to teach at the university, Frederick knew he'd have to go back to bed. He couldn't even think.

"God, I knew you'd do this." Albert banged his mug on the table.

"I can't . . ." Frederick found he couldn't talk. His feelings landed in his throat like a fist. He got up carefully, in slow motion like the old people in his family, put the napkin carefully by the plate with the D for the Drake Hotel in a scrolled monogram at the edge. Albert had insisted that they use the plates and silverware he took from the job. It became a curiosity among their friends, who knew that by now the couple could afford better.

"He's over eighteen, Frederick. He's not jailbait." Albert rose and threw his napkin across the table at the space Frederick had just vacated. "I'm probably not going to do anything, anyway. Really." He followed Frederick out of the kitchen and down the hallway to their bedroom. "I just need a couple of drinks to unwind after cooking. You know how it is."

Frederick stopped and turned. "Of course." And they both saw those long-ago nights when Albert would come rushing home to Frederick's champagne and nakedness.

Frederick could feel the weight of exhaustion settle over him like a collapsing tent. He wasn't a good camper. "Have to call school, can't go." He could feel his language, his sentences slipping away from him as he reached for the phone.

By the time he got the history-department secretary, he sounded as sick as he claimed he was. "Hope you feel better soon," she was saying as he hung up the receiver. Albert knelt down at the foot of the bed and slid off Frederick's loafers and socks. He worked gently and efficiently, undressing Frederick as if he were a tired child carried in from the car after a big day.

As Frederick drifted off that morning, to blanket-warm brown sleep and safety, Albert kissed him on the top of his head and whispered, "I'm sorry." Sometime in his sleep Frederick heard a door slam, and then it was dark and he was awake. Nine o'clock. Albert was at the hotel. Or Frederick supposed he was. As head chef, he had to be. There with another man.

Frederick felt as if he'd slept himself out of time. Now he couldn't go back to the morning. He couldn't explain or ask questions. Albert had launched himself to another planet and Frederick could only stand and watch mutely when Albert didn't come home that night, when he didn't come home for several nights in a row. Frederick felt like an astronomer scanning deep space for something unknown, something unnamed he knew he'd recognize.

Then there were periods of relative calm, and Albert and Frederick slipped back into their old patterns as if nothing had changed. But when Frederick held Albert's cock in his hand, it felt foreign now, not an instrument of love, just an instrument, a specialty tool on the operating table, sterilized, used by others. It had entered the mouths, other . . . It took all of Frederick's concentration not to imagine what Albert did out there at night. It took all of the discipline that had driven him through graduate school, through the books and articles he had to publish to survive at the University of Chicago, through his stint as chairman of the department when it was filled with eccentrics who warred like tribes over food in a drought.

When he kissed Albert, his tongue tracing the polish of each tooth, he sometimes felt like a Marine recruit, given a job to do that was totally without meaning, fruitless, like digging a hole just to fill it up again. He found other tastes in his mouth, or he imagined he did. Where had they come from? New toothpaste? What he drank or ate in love late at night?

There had been little acts of retaliation: the amnesia that took over when he made coffee for Albert and the refusal to make the pilgrimage home for the holidays to St. Paul and to rest uneasily in the dark overstuffed comforter of the living room sofa while Albert slept upstairs in his boyhood bed in the room saved for him from high school, full of the trophies electroplated with gold finish for every kind of sport.

Albert called him at Christmas. "They miss you," he breathed into the distance, while Frederick blinked the lights of Chicago's celebration into single huge bulbs of red and green tears. "They keep asking why you didn't come."

"What did you tell them?"

"I don't know. I made something up."

"What about the truth? You know—you're fucking around."

Albert sighed, as good a sigh as Frederick might have given. "Don't start now. Please?"

For once Albert sounded as though he meant it, so Frederick nodded at the wind-blown lights in the street below, then said,

"Okay. Merry Christmas." What followed sounded like an explosion of laughter, until Frederick realized it was sobbing, sobbing loud enough to wake the parents and aunts.

"Shhh, hush, Albert. God, be quiet, hon. They'll hear you. Albert? Albert?" Suddenly none of the past months mattered, nor the year before. Frederick only wanted to be there, to hold his lover, to kiss the teared eyes before he had a chance to change again.

"I'm so, so, so sorry . . . sorry. God, I can't believe . . . God, Freddy, please don't—"

"No, no, it's okay. I'm not going to leave. Really. Hang on, Ally. Please, don't cry so loudly. They'll hear you and come down." Frederick was fighting the weight of tiredness himself, but he figured he had to pay attention.

"No, you have to forgive me. I fucked up, and I do love you. None of the others count. How could they? I don't know what's the matter. I just get crazy and have to have it. I can't stop myself now. I try, I try, and then something happens, and I . . . God, I'm sorry, Freddy. I don't see how you can stand me."

Frederick would always remember the three-hour session of self-loathing and apology. It saved them in one way. Later, while Albert was in therapy but still having affairs, Frederick would use that moment to keep himself from packing the suitcases he had gathered from the closets around their apartment. Actually, he .was so stubborn that he wasn't going to leave. He was going to make Albert leave. But then he knew that that wouldn't, couldn't happen. Albert could never live alone. He'd always need someone to be there when he got home. That thought once made Frederick so angry that he went to the kitchen and smashed all the Drake Hotel plates, cups, saucers, and bowls. As if that wasn't enough, he got out a chisel and started gouging out the script *D* engraved in the handles of the silverware. While he worked, he played Frank Sinatra records real loud. "Did it my way," he sang along as he tried to avoid the sharp edge of the chisel with his fingers.

When Albert came home the next morning to find Frederick slumped over asleep at the breakfast nook, in a sea of smashed dishes and with the silver curls of metal scattered about him like rain, he realized something had to give. So Albert packed himself and was gone before Frederick woke up and found his note and saw that the toothpaste was missing from the medicine cabinet.

"Jesus Christ," he swore as he mixed the baking soda and salt in the plastic mug he found in the corner of the top cabinet. "Now what? I've got this meeting with the provost, no goddamn toothpaste, and my hands look like I've been doing heavy leather all night."

A month later Albert started dropping by at breakfast. Usually he didn't even appear to have stayed up all night. Frederick didn't put himself out, just gestured toward the coffeepot and smiled when Albert discovered how Frederick liked his coffee now.

There were no more tears, just the hidden misty eyes a few months later as they said good-bye to Chicago and the Drake and their apartment. Both men were silent as they drove their new car north to Wisconsin and into Minnesota.

Putting the bed back together was the kind of domestic ritual that usually annoyed Albert. He refused to change sheets weekly, sometimes even monthly, so Frederick had to struggle with it alone most of the time. In fact, only a real tantrum convinced Albert of the need for the Sears washer and dryer Frederick bought and had delivered. Jesus, what will the Sears guy think? Frederick wondered when Albert ran out in his socks to the wet street, waving his arms and hollering, "Stop, stop it's not ours! Stop!"

"Of course it is," Frederick told him. "Stop being an ass. I ordered them. Cheap, Sears, see? We need to do the laundry, for Christ's sake." The two delivery men stood in the back of the truck, hands on their hips, snickering at the two nannies in their soaked socks, now glued with fallen leaves.

When Albert noticed the two guys laughing, he wanted a fight, but he shrugged and turned away. It was his old family neighborhood in St. Paul. He couldn't shame them here. "I just thought you could walk across the street to the Laundromat. For god's sake, it's just across the street." Then he clumped back into the building and up the stairs, leaving a trail of sticky orange leaves from the maples the city had planted out front when the elms had started dying ten years before. Frederick remembered the worn black linoleum of each step marked by an orange blob.

As they tucked in the blankets now, each man at the corner of the king-sized mattress, Albert stopped and rubbed the small of his back. A spasm of pain crossed his face.

"I knew it," Frederick said.

"Oh, be quiet. You always say that. 'I knew it.'" Albert bent slowly back, then rotated clockwise from his hips to loosen the muscles that were grabbing. "What haven't you known? You're such a predictor, aren't you? Such a know-it-all." Though it sounded mean, Albert grinned and smacked his lips into a kiss that might even have been a come-on.

Frederick smiled and wondered if Albert wanted to snuggle a bit. Later they'd lain in bed like Albert's two ancient aunts, side by side, framed by pillows and covers, looking out with the expression of two survivors in a rowboat at sea, expecting the worst. "I guess there's some things I wasn't too good at," Frederick said.

Albert gave the top down comforter a hard jerk, pulling it momentarily from Frederick's grip. "Hey."

"Sorry." Albert stopped and watched Frederick resettle the pale blue comforter back squarely on the bed. He hated that damn thing, thought it unnecessary, like the washer and dryer. But Frederick had to have a lot of covers. He'd live there with Albert but only on certain conditions: they had to keep warm, and they had to get to know some other couples—no more single men who kept Frederick bird-nervous through dinner. Albert laughed to himself. Maybe he should have listened to Frederick sooner.

Positioned back in bed, Albert picked up his book, then set it down again. "Are you hungry?"

"Well, maybe just a bite of something. What's in there?" Frederick always left the food business to Albert, and he never complained at the extravagance he noticed in the kitchens, either their small one or the restaurant-size one on the main floor below, where Albert ran his Continental-style café.

Albert smiled and put the book back on the antique sewing table that served as a nightstand beside the bed. Then impulsively he leaned over and kissed Frederick's surprised lips softly, not exactly with passion but much more tenderly than their usual pecks hello and good-bye. "Be back in a minute."

Frederick leaned back, watching Albert climb carefully out of bed, straighten stiffly, and walk with a slight limp out of the room. Albert's years of cooking long hours at the Drake had damaged the disks in his back. Frederick glanced down at the book he had been about to open. Those damn French. Just when he'd thought there weren't that many surprises left in his field, the French set off this time bomb. Now they'd have to figure things out all over again. His department at the college wanted to ignore the French. "Just forget it," they advised him. "Who gives a shit. No one ever takes the French seriously, anyway, a bunch of drunks."

Frederick hadn't even considered their comments. He'd come from the University of Chicago, where a scholar didn't ignore breakthrough work, whether by the French or not. For a few years he'd felt, in fact, that something was happening. Philippe Ariès was not a fly-by-night, although it irritated him that Ariès got big play in the bookstores. Frederick's books sat in libraries and on his own shelves, unnoticed after the initial response from the scholarly community. Now he was just a footnote in graduate student papers.

The French based their work on ordinary people, not on highly visible events and powerful figures. Frederick could see the merit. He was picking up a lot by reading *The History of Private Lives, Volume I: Roman to Byzantine*. These guys had really done their homework, and they wrote in a conversational style, and he couldn't begin to write that way.

What was keeping Albert? He must have decided to whip up something special. Frederick hoped he hadn't gone downstairs and started mucking around in the restaurant, because he'd be up all night rearranging the menu again, adding and deleting items he'd be testing on the big stoves and ovens. When he cooked, Albert became as absorbed as an artist or a scholar. The only difference was that he usually needed an assistant. Maybe he was more like a chemist, like that guy from 3M they'd met a few weeks ago. The problem was that Frederick couldn't stand to help him, and the helpers Albert hired never lasted very long. Trained by his twenty-five years in hotel kitchens, Albert was demanding, autocratic, bad-tempered. There was no other way to say it: he was Rudolph Hess in the kitchen. To work with him was excruciating. You never made the right move. You always got berated for the slightest mistake, and the whole thing usually escalated until the assistant left.

They'd had to close the restaurant early some nights because Albert had driven off the help. Some days they couldn't open until Frederick phoned from his office and negotiated with the help, while Albert sulked in the corner under the plastic grapes and vinery his mother and aunts kept trailing in from their days of shopping discount stores and closeouts.

Frederick couldn't imagine how the customers stood it, either. Albert insulted them, kept them waiting to be seated even when the restaurant was empty, and warned them that it would be hours before the food would appear. Some people were frightened off, but those who had been there before just smiled, nodded, and sat down, knowing that the food would appear, heaped generously on the Drake Hotel plates and tasting wonderful. Although he claimed to serve Continental cuisine, it was always the hearty

Czech, German, and Polish dishes of his family's tradition that Albert prepared for the specials.

Albert was kind only to the old men of the neighborhood. They were mostly widowers, although some were bachelors who had spent their lives with their families and eventually lived alone in the little frame workers' houses that lined the streets fanning out from the brewery, whose huge smokestack and neon sign glowed over the lives on the river flats like a benediction. Most of the immigrants had given their lives to the long lines of bottles rolling train-smooth to machines that cleaned and filled and capped and loaded them into cases. Now the men walked slowly with bent backs and hearts of retirement. Or they visited one another at their porches or garages all summer. The women walked about the neighborhood in their housedresses, thick-heeled shoes, and babushkas and gathered under the awnings of the restaurant on the first floor of the three-story brick building, which housed Frederick and Albert on the second floor and the Ukrainian Hall on the third floor.

When the mornings were mild and pleasant, Frederick slept in and dreamed, through their murmurings, of spending childhood vacations in the country, where the constant hum of insects, the call of birds, and the swish of trees had made him sleepy all the time. He'd felt his heart slow and pump with satisfaction then.

Sometimes Frederick wondered what the neighborhood thought of them, living together at their age, men in their late fifties without women. But there was the tradition of bachelors. Albert's kindness to these men seemed to testify to an instinct of upbringing more than anything else. Each man had his particular table and timing. They never had to wait to be seated or to receive food. Often they never even had to order. Albert locked them into the grid of a memory that had kept the massive kitchens of the Drake running smoothly through thousands of recipes and eccentric demands. Taking care of a few old men in worn brown and olive clothes was simple. Other customers waited while

Albert poured second and third cups of strong coffee, brought their familiar plates of food, and added a free cookie or cake. Albert never flirted with these men. He was a man among men, his voice deep and regular, his gestures economical.

With others it was different. Frederick had to watch himself when he was down there, because seeing Albert's fingers brush the shoulder of another man or seeing him cock his head and say something caustic, full of double entendres as thick as the raisins in his rice pudding, made Frederick crazy. He wanted to hit him, throw the dishes on the floor again. It wouldn't do any good with the silverware. Albert had decided that it was a fine idea to gouge the *D* out. Frederick had spent nightmare hours after that, cutting his fingers as he chipped silver tears out of the handles of everything Albert brought home. After twenty-five years they could stock a restaurant.

Thank god, at least that part was over. Frederick put the book on the floor beside him and scooted down in the covers, pulling them up to his chin. His foot touched the side of the bed, and he decided to move over, spread out, luxuriate as long as Albert was gone for a few moments. From the middle he could spread-eagle, and even though he was on the fault line of the twin boxes below, he felt safe there.

When the thought of the French came back, he shrugged. So what. There was always going to be something new. That's what attracted him to history to begin with, right? Old and new. His work in the classics was pure pleasure because of that paradox. Maybe the French had an angle he could use. A full professor, turning sixty next summer, he knew his colleagues were waiting for him to hit retirement and leave. But he had some news for them: Not at sixty-five, which they figured he could afford. Not at seventy, which up until last year had been mandatory. And if he worked the French angle somehow, not until he dropped dead in the classroom, a piece of chalk in one hand, the slide-projector remote in the other. By god, he'd outlive and outteach all of them. He just needed to get going on this French thing.

Frederick was dozing off when the clank of dishes announced Albert's arrival back from the kitchen. "Still hungry?" Albert smiled and stood beside the bed, his arms full of things: a huge tray he must have gone downstairs to get, five covered plates, wineglasses, a loaf of French bread teetering across the top, a sherbet glass of chocolate mousse, another of something pink that wobbled, and a bottle of wine under each arm, champagne and French red. "Don't just stand there," Albert said, and Frederick crawled out of the covers to help him.

Later, with the remnants of the food and dishes spread around them, Albert reached down to the bottle of champagne chilling beside the bed on the floor. He slid the wine smoothly into the crystal champagne flutes Frederick had bought because he'd wanted one thing that hadn't been used by a thousand lips before his. Handing a glass to Frederick, Albert sat a bit straighter, cleared his throat, and said, "It hasn't been that bad, has it? I mean, regardless of what is going to . . . Well you know, I've always loved just you, Freddy." Frederick smiled, and they nudged their glasses and drank.

Later still, after their lovemaking, which took some time because it had been such a long time, the shower had felt good. Rubbing their tired muscles for each other, ignoring the bellies and buttocks that sagged now and the way the skin behind their ears had gotten old while they weren't looking, they had felt something different come over them.

"Maybe I shouldn't hire another kid," Albert said softly into the darkness of their room, lit now only by the slice of moon that hung outside their windows like a rind in a glass of night sky. He sighed and rolled closer to Frederick. "Nothing's safe anymore, I mean. What if—"

"Don't worry so much," Frederick said, stretching his legs wide again, then rubbing his toes up the length of Albert's long calf.

"Don't." Albert shifted irritably. "No, this way. Roll over. Yeah, like that. Let me hug you, yeah, there." And Albert pulled Frederick's smaller, rounder body into the lean cup of his own. "Anyway, I'm not just worrying." Albert wrapped his arms more tightly around Frederick's body and grabbed his own wrists in front, as if he were going to perform a rescue in deep water. "Face it, our friends, people we used to know in Chicago, are dying, Freddy." Albert felt Frederick's body stiffen and he held on even harder.

"No." Frederick groaned and pushed against the embrace of Albert's arms and the grip of Albert's leg thrown over him.

"Yes," Albert whispered, as he kissed the gray hair of Frederick's head softly. "Yes." He kissed the curious loose skin at the jawline and rested his mouth where the pulse pushed lightly against the rough hide of Frederick's throat.

PATIENT

———————•———————

Kristin Thiel

Super Bowl Weekend, 2005

. . . pushing my hand away. My thumb rubs the knuckle of hers
and she's still kissing me and my hand moves back. My tongue
finds her farthest molar, her fingers find my penis—it meets her
halfway, really—my finger slides farther. I think of slick broad
river boulders, soft as mattresses on warm days; when *there* is
exactly where I'm supposed to be, her hand is on mine again. She's
still kissing me, still working her other hand, but the one on mine
is clearly on a different mission. Her fingers pucker around each
of mine one at a time, delicate but persistent as a fish's mouth
investigating toes dangling off the pier.

What's up? I ask, pulling my lips away from hers just
enough. She reaches my middle finger, which is wet with her,
and strangely, *I* blush.

Do you have a hangnail? Or are your nails long? she's asking.

Umm. I shift back, look at my hands. My left hand has a
bruised thumbnail and the edges of the pads of those fingers are a
little rougher, but I wasn't touching her with that hand. Suddenly
we're both sitting up, cross-legged; she's slouched so her breasts
tap against her stomach, and her arms are folded on top of her
thighs. She reminds me of those coil pots my son makes in art
class. I look back at my fingers. Out of my body, from afar, I see
us, and we look like a still life. Two Friends on a Picnic, Without

Food. A Game of Hearts, Before It Starts. Business Meeting. She's swung her legs out of bed and is plucking her clothes from mine.

I'm sorry. I guess I'm not . . .

Sweetie, I say.

And we're both smiling, but like you do at a cat you come across in the dark, or at an exotic bird, and she's got a couple tears on her cheeks.

Sweetie, I say. And we're pulling on our clothes and she kisses me, and I remind her that the six-pack is still in the snowdrift outside and it's almost time for the game if we want to turn the TV on. I linger just a minute more to take a photo of the bed's topography. The blankets look like a sprawled gorge, and I'd like to try to recreate the look in felt and wood.

Singing Ice, 2005

I'm spending more time in the workshop, rising earlier to drink my coffee on the deck overlooking the lake, getting to the office later, letting e-mails from my son, typed by my ex, wait two or three days for my response. Coryl is a marker on my life's timeline. Time moves differently since I met you, I told her once, over one of those early dinners before she started joining me for nights at my apartment.

Coryl joins me outside, one of those first early mornings—I was wondering where you went—reaches her arms around me, slides her hands, still warm from sleeping, under the elastic of my pajamas. One set of slender fingers cups my balls, gives a gentle squeeze while the other hand traces the head of my penis. It stirs, of course. I set my mug down on the railing and reach my arms back around her and forcefully, with two hands, grab her bottom.

It's cold out here, you freak! She moves her hands up and forces me around to face her. That grin—Jesus, I'm fully hard now and all I want is to be inside her, goddamnit, I won't even try because we'll just end up feeling like shit and then I am inside her, her tongue circles the head, traces long, slow paths down.

The snow's melted under my grip on the railing, I think I feel my hand knock over the coffee mug, she presses her mouth and nose into my hairs, god, don't stop there, get back to—oh the tongue, her lips close, squeeze, she moves her head back and forth maybe twice before I come. Her mouth is almost like being inside her. Almost, not enough.

She stands up, grinning under heavy-lidded eyes, jauntily, jokingly swiping the back of her hand across her lips. Look at my knees, you ass! She likes to pretend to be in the stereotypical man-drags-woman-back-to-cave relationship, god knows why, like I made her suck me off. I'm going to make breakfast—I better see you inside soon.

But she doesn't—I move through the kitchen with a wave and not even a new cup of coffee on the way to my workshop. I do join her for dinner, but drive Coryl a little batty, she says, with my head so full after a day in the basement it's all I talk about. Paper, plastic, glass, I've used everything to make puppets, I say, tearing and folding her napkin.

Yeah, I wake up to the sound of you sanding fingers, curling eyelashes, painting liver spots and moles.

No liver spots on this one, but there is one distinguishing mole, I say pointedly, but I don't think she understands that I'm referring to one inspired by hers. Chairs, hubcaps, lint, money, mugs, silverware . . . But this one I'm just using basics, keeping it simple, wood where you'd expect wood, yarn where there should be yarn.

I stick the napkin wings to one side of the salt shaker with a bit of mashed potato and fly the fairy over the table, sprinkling crystals that wink in the light as it goes. She leaves the table, and her dishes. I pour myself another cup of coffee.

I count the ideas we've tried the way I count sheep, or in this case, while I'm spooning sugar into my cup.

Before our ideas, there were hers. She went to her first gynecology appointment for a pap—this didn't even have to do directly with sex, yet. And the doctor and the nurse assisting both laughed at her. I couldn't even keep my ass on the table, Coryl told me. It was like this nervous reaction I couldn't control. A squirm to get away, but up into the air because I was lying down, my feet were hooked, what other direction could I go?

There are very few things that my brain decides it's best to immediately physically fight, but every time I remember this story, I want to punch that doctor—hell, even the 1-800-DOCTORS operator who took Coryl's call and the doctor's receptionist— right in the neck and just keep moving.

She stayed away from doctors, and men, then. For a while.

Then her ideas became ours. She made an appointment with a different doctor, and I sat in the waiting room for her. Set to repeat.

No one laughed, but no one knew what to do with Coryl either.

The first one said, Look, this seems to be traumatizing you. And you clearly can't be sexually active anyway, so just give it time.

Vaginitis.

Vaginismus.

The second said, Wow, yeah, that opening is small, isn't it? Well, you know, I don't want to traumatize you . . .

No cervical problems.

Not endometriosis.

Not the ovaries.

The third said, I'm trying the tiniest instruments I have. They won't even fit. Work on stretching yourself yourself, because you'll be more comfortable then.

Probably not pelvic inflammatory disease.

Definitely not menopause.

Or ectopic pregnancy, or an injury during labor.

Or STDs, ha ha!

Of course at first we joked. I called her the Wild Thing Academic. I majored in anthropology and biology, is Coryl's pickup line, with a minor in philosophy. She gets the logic and the logical illogic behind sex. But in personal practice, Coryl was never a masturbator, and she'd never used tampons. She bought a box of tampons. Six months later, she donated the unopened box to a women's shelter.

The fourth gynecologist said, Okay, if doctors aren't working, and you're not working, you may need to consider surgery.

Hymenectomy. Hymenotomy. Outpatient, but you have to stay until you pee, so we make sure we didn't bother the bladder. But then, back to work.

I stack the dinner plates and take a sip of my coffee. Gagging, I dump it and the dishes into the sink as I pass—way too sweet.

Winter, 2008

The physical therapist has a young face but old knuckles. I think about them even when she steps out of the room to let Coryl change into the medical gown. Coryl gives a little shimmy in my direction as she slips her skirt and panties off together. I wolf whistle low, but I'm thinking about those soft knuckles. Wrinkled, loose skin. I imagine the knuckles rattling around within their roomy skin sacks. I imagine that the PT actually excused herself to jiggle them back into place after my handshake loosened them. I imagine using those bones like dice, shaking them vigorously and casting them out.

Halloween, 2005

I read through the folder of materials Coryl has left on the hall table—bulleted lists on lavender paper that somehow retains the scent of the hospital and the perfume of middle-aged women, who Coryl says were the others in her class. Stretched vaginas from pregnancies and 1950s-era low self-esteem—no one else like Coryl at all. We're going to try the surgery, she's going to have the surgery, but it's a month away and one of the stores on one of the bulleted lists is on my way home from work, if I take the alternate route.

When I pull the polka-dotted dildo from the paper sack, Coryl giggles. It looks like a Twister mat!

It comes with Hershey's Kisses, a handful from a jar next to the register that the clerk added. Though it seems a little superfluous, right? she said with a wink at me. This big fella *and* chocolate?

I dump what's left of the bag onto the kitchen counter and while Coryl's looking—Halloween wrappers, orange and black—I come at her, my tongue up her neck, bite that chin. The neck gets her every time. She shudders and kisses back, our teeth bang together and I can tell that she almost stops to laugh and ask if I'm okay but both my arms are around her and I've lifted her onto the counter. I flick the switch to its first speed and pull her robe open—she smells like soap and bourbon after a long day in court—and I press that plastic cock against the outside, just in that nest of curls. Her back arches immediately and she catches her breath. I press more, the dildo's just barely inside her. She's laughing this maniacal, ecstatic laugh. I have to undo my pants and grab my own cock, hold everything in, oh god, just a little longer. I've never heard her laugh like this, seen her flush like this, the external vibration is enough to quiver the internal, oh god, I laugh and pinch the end of my penis. I've come just watching her, but I stand there longer, kissing her face and holding two cocks, one in each hand, the plastic the more easygoing one that finally dissolves her into hiccups.

Valentine's Day, 2008

The PT calls me a good guy. A really good, amazing guy. If this doesn't say love . . . she trails off at the latest appointment, while I sit in the examining room's one metal chair and she perches on Coryl's bare feet, warming them and holding them down. I'm used to these appointments by now, this wobbling chair, by now, but there will never be anything for me to do about that comment. The first time the therapist said it—I'm a good guy because I have stayed faithful to my girlfriend for years even though we can't seem to have normal, regular old sex, even though a Man should have taken off after the fifth date, maybe at the most after one year—I dropped my gaze and kept my eyes on her hands when we shook till-next-time forty-five minutes later. What's the answer to that? Not, Thanks. Not, Aww shucks, ma'am, it ain't nothin'. Well, you know my—or is it "our," now—Coryl; she's a keeper. Or, I'm really sorry you've had such poor experiences with Men that I shock and delight you.

Coryl develops this superhuman leg strength, and I can see she's working hard to relax and control those almost uncontrollable muscles. The PT looks and sounds completely calm, but she's working hard, leaning all her weight against Coryl's far leg, keeping it pressed against the wall so her hand can slowly circle— I'm going to touch your inner left thigh, now your right. I'm going to start feeling the outside, now I'm going to part the outer lips, just a little, I'm not going inside yet, it's okay.

The puppet I'm crafting is in every way a version of Coryl, but its knuckles are just as assuredly this PT's—I shift in the chair, tug the flap of my long woolen coat over my leg, and visualize that first knuckle sinking into my girlfriend.

Home with the Flu, August 2009

Okay, so you looked on the S-drive? I switch the phone to my other hand and reach for the blanket that's fallen on the floor. The AC is on super-blast, but that's preferable to the alternative.

Coryl clicks the television from *Jeopardy!* to *Oprah*. She took the day off to keep me company.

No, Pete, no.

Coryl takes a gigantic inhale and aims a tiny smile at me. I would smile back, big, huge, encouraging, but I really need to get that quilt off me. And. Pete. Is. Still. Talking.

"Pete, I'm still sick, man. I'm not at the office doing this myself because I've got the flu, and no, I'm not coming in tomorrow either, so—"

Coryl pushes the blanket covering her lap to the side. She's cross-legged, those beautiful, tight golden curls, and then she's pushing the applicator inside herself—So, ah, Pete . . . Right, exactly—That damn applicator, skinny as a piece of chalk, and her body can barely manage that, and she's sitting there frozen, working just to relax and breathe again after inserting that thing— Exactly right. Okay, good. Yeah, that's really good, that'll work. Okay, call me tomorrow, if you need to.

I throw the phone on the pile of blankets and stand up. Wobble a little, grab the pen from my work pad, and the plastic barf bag—I'd better—and walk over to Coryl.

When appointments with doctors just scheduled to do a pap didn't work and then the surgery didn't work, there were therapists, plural.

No, a conservative religious upbringing doesn't count as abuse, no, but really, there's nothing else from your past?

And your current relationship is going well . . . ? And your records show the doctors haven't found anything physically abnormal . . .

Vaginismus!

Breathe deeply.

Think positive thoughts.

Have you tried a glass of wine or two? (Whispered—I'm a doctor, I shouldn't be telling you this, but . . .)

How do you feel about anxiety medication?

Take more baths.

Massage yourself with lotions.

Read Anaïs Nin.

When Coryl went in for her first post-surgery pap, which the doctor finally did manage to do, Coryl asked her about the remaining sex problems.

So then there was the sexuality class, free at the hospital, which led to a recommendation for physical therapy. All these people Coryl has had to tell her story to—"our" story now—

including an insurance agent in her cubicle (Ummm, a hymen-what? I don't know that term . . . let me look it up here on WebMD . . .). For all these people she's told, it's remarkably easy to be referred around and around the medical system.

About once a month, the PT works on Coryl internally—The pelvic floor is amazing! So few PTs specialize in this area, but the pelvis connects to, and can affect, so many parts of the body. She describes Coryl's insides like a clock—I'm pressing on three o'clock, does that hurt?—and she says some women feel hard as a rock inside. Coryl's actually not too bad. Maybe an extra-firm pillow at nine o'clock . . .

The PT gives Coryl homework assignments. What she's doing now, lounging with me with what amounts to a long and nonabsorbent tampon sticking out of her, is that homework. She looks up at me, and I kneel down by her, and we kiss, even though I probably have puke breath. I uncap the pen and draw a smiley face on the applicator's protruding end.

Almost Done, 2008

Petite Petunia's head is beautiful—glowing oak sanded and polished into soft curves—but her eyes are drained, like a vampire victim's. I know I did everything right—used silicone molds to form the eyeballs and the leftover urethane to cast clear irises—but I am still failing her. I gently set her on the table and move to the bookshelves—taxidermy catalogs among anatomy books from the premed days I didn't finish out. I turn a couple of glossy pages, looking for realistic irises, and then return the catalog to its shelf.

Petunia's jaw, yes, her jaw, is another problem, its movement inexact. I rub my eyes and my jaw, rummage through a box, and find a small coil of piano wire. Stretching it out, I know it will be enough to fit along the inside of the jaw and to feed through the two jaw hinge holes. While measuring confirms the length is right, it also says the wire is too thick to fit through the holes.

A drill or saw is too cumbersome for this work, so I reach for a utility knife to carefully shave the hinge holes wider.

After widening the holes and feeding the piano wire through, I test her jaw. It falls low, hitting her collarbone. I add metal washers, one by one, to the doll's neck to lift the skull. Three washers are not quite enough but, when I add a fourth, I find the neck does not stick into the skull enough. It's not working. Not even the jaw works. I sit down and close my eyes.

After the Surgery, 2006

We try again, but it's all just the same.

    Isn't it in?

    No.

    Even a little?

    Sweetie . . .

    Fuck it! She pushes up on her elbows, and her eyes look like they do in court, when she thinks she should be winning her case and she's just not. Just rape me. Come on, you're a man, just force yourself in me.

    Okay, I say, that is enough. My penis has deflated anyway. Immediately. I pull on my sweatpants, squeeze her toes, and leave the room.

My One Time Dancing, 2005

At work, Pete says I'm too young to commute out of the city every night at six. He acts like I shake my fist at the neighbor kids on my lawn and drink warm milk and fall asleep in front of FOX News, too. I say I'm a divorced dad, I'm old enough for Chrissake. After work I just want to get pizza and feed my fish and watch TV on my couch. No, I'm not *old*, Pete, but I'm probably older than your newbie eyes can imagine.

    But one night, this night—*that* night, I will consider it happily, later—I agree to join him and his friends for happy hour. Which becomes dinner. And then drinks. And then a club. No,

I'm *not* old, but I also admit I'm not sure they call this kind of place a "club" anymore. For one, everyone here is legal—I assume, because the atmosphere is classy and clean and there is a top shelf offering top-shelf bourbon. For another, everyone also seems to be gainfully employed.

Yeah, it's a *lounge*, Pete says. Now who's the frat boy? You need another drink.

And Coryl and I meet. On the dance floor—the lounge does have a dance floor, like a club, loud, the bass turned up. She's dressed like a lawyer or a fine art dealer, but she moves down and up and against me, closer and closer, somehow closer still. All I know at that moment, besides Coryl's mouth, and the top of her breasts, which I touch while we dance because she's unbuttoned her shirt three buttons, is that she is the one.

Your face is smooth like the finest wood! I breathe in her ear, lick the lobe. The twinkle in your eye, like a dot of high-gloss paint.

You bet you can have my number.

I'll be good for you, I tell her without any doubt. I'll be better for you.

The Physical Therapist's is Lovely in September, 2009

For once, I run back. I touch Coryl's shoulder and tell her, I forgot something in the examination room, I'll be right back. I jog down the hallway and catch the PT leaving the room.

I don't understand, I tell her.

She reopens the door and we step back into the room.

No one does. We know a little, and we keep learning more. People talk about it now, at least. Coryl is not alone. She's not crazy, you two aren't doing anything wrong—something can just still be wrong, even when what we know about isn't.

I'm about to sit on that metal chair again. If we know we don't know, we can talk this out, figure this out. But she opens the door again and smiles that it's time for me to leave, until October.

FROM *IN THE DARK OF THE MOON*

Suzanne Hudson

Royce Fitzhugh was feeling pretty good for a change, knowing there would be a way out soon, away from Sumner, Georgia, away from his slut of a mother, and out into the world, a world that was lining up for war, he hoped. The only sad thing about leaving was that he wouldn't see Elizabeth Lacey, who was finally, at twelve, coming into her own, in exactly the way he predicted to her at a political rally, a little over two years earlier.

Royce had always been curious about Elizabeth, ever since the days when she visited Chen Ling and the three of them would toss horseshoes in the Chinaman's backyard or play dominoes on the porch. But now Royce was seventeen years old, a frustrated pursuer of girls, still watching Elizabeth, ever and always miles ahead of the other girls her own age, but never more than now. What he saw in Elizabeth these days promised to overtake even the girls *his* age, girls already three, four, five years older than she, girls who criticized her while they vied for her attention, hoping some of the mystique might rub off on them. These days, when Elizabeth visited the Chinaman, Chen Ling blushed and looked down with increasing frequency. These days, Royce felt a shift in the repartee—both spoken and unspoken—between himself and Elizabeth. These days, boys in the upper grades were mentioning her name, looking at Royce with a new respect, keenly aware of his access to her. Royce knew what she promised to represent for the boys in town: the magnetic force in their tiny universe, the sun at the center of their solar system, already exemplified by their willingness to take up one, just one, of Lizzie's dares, win her delight when, the task complete, she charged over to offer a hug, a kiss, or, for himself, Royce hoped, someday, that confection of a galaxy between her legs.

At only twelve years of age Elizabeth was getting noticed.

But Royce also knew that Elizabeth had something much more than extraordinary good looks, something not as obvious as overly developed curves and thick, wavy hair and sapphire blue eyes; but something subtle and stinging and sensual, some kind of musky certainty that promised to intimidate as it beckoned, overlaid with the ripening glaze of potential, just on the verge, poised there, on the sweet verge of something he sensed in the most primal way. Hell, she was just a kid, on paper; but he could always see that those blue eyes knew things, that she was watching far into some peripheral kind of anticipation and had the carnal capacity to wash over men with the pull of a rip current, carrying them out to sea on a sweet, rough-and-tumble tide. It was the precursor of swollen flesh and hidden renderings of sexuality, the burst of an egg through a Fallopian bloom, the sigh of a scent of that first heat, folds of skin pushed out, making ready, waiting for the lunar signal to set it all in motion.

"You've been bruised, on the inside, like me," Elizabeth said to him from time to time.

"Why do you think that?"

"I've seen it in your mama's eyes," she'd say, and her own eyes would fill with tears, but only for a second.

Bruised on the inside? It seemed to make her feel tender and kindly toward him, so he let her believe it was true. Hell, he would let her believe anything as long as it gave him an edge, a shot at being the one who would get close, who would conquer that sweet, rich part of her. If she wanted him to be bruised, by god, she could have him that way, though he was anything but bruised.

Royce had, in fact, calloused over so many times he was hard as stone by the time he was twelve. His daddy was long gone, had spent only five years as a fixture in Royce's life, a presence that reminded him daily how worthless and stupid he was, welting Royce's back with a razor strap or a buggy whip, wrenching his little arm in its socket in order to lay into his bare buttocks with one of his brogans, snatched in anger from beneath the sofa. Royce hated him, resented his mother's silence, her tacit approval of Lucas Fitzhugh's brand of discipline. The only days his daddy missed out on administering a beating were those welcome periods when he disappeared for weeks at a time, on a drinking and cheating tear, his mama said, seeming relieved that her husband was at the moment not a presence in her life, a relief that gave way to fear and fretting over money, which gave way to nights out, away from Royce, when she stayed out late, sometimes overnight. Royce had vague memories of playing in his crib in the dark, in the silence, having cried himself spent, and without anyone coming to see to him.

The Chinaman came, though, from next door, every so often, when he heard Royce screaming for a mama who was not there. On those nights Chen Ling would sit by his crib and tell stories half in English, half in Chinese, until Royce fell asleep. By the time he was three, Royce knew not to mention Chen Ling's presence in their home—she had gone next door one Sunday and railed at Ling for meddling, screaming and cussing so loud the law had to come—and by the time Royce was four, he began to notice that his mama had grocery money on those mornings after she had stayed out all night.

His daddy would finally come home and there would be cursing accusations and arguments and his mother thrown into walls or slapped around or punched. "You need to sport a shiner for a while behind that shit," Lucas sometimes said. Then he proceeded to give her one while Royce looked on, at once both afraid for her and glad she was getting what she allowed Royce to get with brutal regularity.

Finally, one day when Royce was five years old, perhaps after weighing the solitary freedom Lucas's absences afforded her against the misery and cruelty he brought, his mama finally stood up for her son. His daddy had just cussed him and slid the belt out of his pants, whipping through the loops, a quick leather snake to accompany the venom of his words: "You goddamn idiot. Why you want to be such a goddamn idiot, boy?"

But on this day his mama stepped forward with a Colt .45, a gift from one of her man friends, leveled at Lucas Fitzhugh, a gesture that said, without hesitation, *Stop*. It was the first time Royce had ever seen that side of his mother, the reservoir of determination, the certainty that acted in this brief battle as the element of surprise.

Lucas let go of his arm as an expression of shock took his face. "Woman, have you gone around the bend?"

"You ain't going to do him that way," she said. "It will come to your fists by the time he's eight, and then what? Either you'll kill him or he'll get growed up and kill you. Best for you to get on gone, right now, before I kill you instead."

Royce always thought it strange how quickly his daddy left, and how permanently, too. Royce never laid eyes on him again, and if his mama did, well, she never let on. His daddy didn't even pack up his clothes. Lucas Fitzhugh offered up no argument, no inclination to compromise, just a sneer of a snarl at Royce's mama, with the words, "He ain't none of mine noway."

The boy watched him walk away, the back of his neck wearing the V of dark hair that curled all the way down his back, beneath the work shirt, arms bowed out at his sides, fists balled up, itching for a fight. It was only a few months later that the implications of his daddy's last words began to sink in, when his ears picked up on the whispers of the decent folks of the town, how Mona Anne Fitzhugh was a two-dollar whore for sale down by the tracks, down near nigger town. And, even though Royce could not fully comprehend—not yet—what a "two-dollar whore" was, he could not help but notice that, once Lucas was gone for good, the men began to trickle in to the little shack, for drinks and laughter, until his mother's bedroom door swung shut and the bedsprings squawked out a rhythm picking up faster and faster. Sometimes the boy heard mumbled curses or loud moans, even shouts that startled him out of his slumber and into those provinces of the man-woman world he was only beginning to fathom, and much too early.

When he was six, seven, eight, he wandered out on the back porch when the bedsprings started screeching. He lay on the glider and waited for trains to roar past and drown out the sounds. Sometimes the Chinaman stepped out on his own porch, saw the boy lying there, and whispered, "Come here, Roy Fitz. Come play domino Chen." And they would steal into the Chinaman's little shotgun house and play rounds of dominoes until Royce was sleepy enough to go home and crawl into bed.

"You stay night if want," the Chinaman always said.

But Royce never stayed. He asked his mother, once, if he could stay overnight with the Chinaman, but she squashed the idea fast. "Hell no, you can't sleep over there with that slanty-eyed devil. He ain't like us," she said. "He's a foreigner. They got strange ways that you ain't liable to know what he might be up to. Worser than a nigger. Now go on and don't ask me about that Chinaman again."

So Royce continued, when he was eight, nine, to sleep on the glider some nights, play dominoes at the Chinaman's house other nights, and feel relief on the nights when his mama did not have company. It was the late nights that got him, though, when he heard a knock at the door around midnight, the swish of his mama's bare feet against linoleum, a hushed, murmured conversation ending with his mama's "Okay. Come on in." Then muted words from the front room, the room next to his, followed by his mother's moans and the uneven squeak of the bedsprings, the sound that drove into him like a jackhammer, stirred in him the suspicion that his mama could not be okay, not with that racket going on, yet the human sounds he heard seemed to be expressions of pleasure. It did not make sense, and so finally, at ten, Royce slipped to her cracked bedroom door one late night, just past midnight, just as the mattress began to squawk. He put his face to the doorway's opening and let his eyes adjust to the dark, making out a man's bare backside, that bare backside moving toward and away from the bed. And then he realized it was his mama the man was moving onto, and her knees were drawn up, and he heard her say, "That's good, Daddy. Do it like that. Show me." Then the man moved faster, and Royce was afraid to stay there, afraid of what he would see next that he did not understand.

He tried, in his child's way, to get the Chinaman to explain it over dominoes one night.

"Ah, no," Chen said. He seemed embarrassed and just as awkward as Royce had felt in asking, the Chinaman's English breaking up even more from the awkwardness. "No say much. Maybe say too much. Mama no make fuck. Now you play domino."

By the time he was eleven, Royce had figured out what the man was doing to his mother, there on the bed with her knees drawn up, and he had figured out some of the other things she probably did, things he heard older boys bragging about. And it was around the same time that some of the boys at school began to taunt him once in a while on the playground, where they played baseball to the peripheral squeals of the smaller children, and thick ropes dangling tire swings groaned their deep-toned rhythms.

"Know where we can get a piece of tail, Fitzhugh?"

"A piece of tail for sale?"

"Who can pleasure many a man?" one rhyme went. "Go see moaning Mona Anne."

Royce knew he was fated to be either a sissy or a scrapper, with no in-between. He chose to be a scrapper, to be Lucas Fitzhugh's son, whether or not he was claimed as a son, and beat the shit out of anybody who teased him, and then some, serving up preemptive beatings before the other boys had the chance to think. Sometimes he lost the fight, but most times he won, getting a meaner and meaner reputation that eventually silenced those inclined to say anything about Mona Anne—to his face, anyway.

So it was that, as Royce entered adolescence, his already muted love for his mother had grown tainted with disgust, and he spent more and more time away from the shack and the men and the woman who spread her legs to keep him in milk and eggs and cornmeal and shame. He never mentioned her to his friends in high school, and they were by then mature enough and kind enough not to mention her, either, even though there was the occasional rumor that some of the athletes were going to go visit Mona Anne this night or that one. The bitter taste of her name in its carnal contexts slid down his throat and deep into his gut, eating away any kind of respect or caring he might have been able to conjure up for her. Finally, in the months leading up to his seventeenth year, he began to see a way out.

The Germans were all over Europe and folks claimed it wouldn't be long before Roosevelt went on and committed to helping out, running the Krauts back to Berlin, and Royce aimed to be signed up and in on that detail if it happened. He even began to hope for it, in spite of the fact that the popular sentiment in Blackshear County was that Roosevelt had no business even thinking about sending troops. Royce didn't care whose opinion was right; he only wanted to get the hell away from his whore of a mama, away from the stares of the church folks, and maybe even come back a hero in the process. He already had a career for himself in mind. He had taken to killing time around the sheriff's office, talking tough with the High Sheriff, sometimes cleaning up or running errands for him and Elizabeth's father, Deputy Jack, for a tip or two. Old Man Lacey seemed to like him, telling him more than a few times, "You got a hard edge to you, Royce, and I guess you come by it honest. You ought to get into law enforcement."

"Would you take me on?"

"You just a pup. I need me a full-growed feist. Get out in the world and get some experience. Then we'll take another look."

It was during his days as a hanger-on at the sheriff's office that he began to plot and attempt to worm his way into Elizabeth's heart in earnest. She was young, certainly, but it was not uncommon for girls of twelve, thirteen, fourteen to be married, here in the rural part of the state. Maybe he could rescue her from her burgeoning reputation as a flirt—she was, after all, coming out of her social seclusion, and dramatically, to amuse herself with the antics of a few of the boys around town—and make a war bride of her, or at least make an engagement come about.

He knew it was a long shot, though, knew she had a flip attitude about having and keeping a boyfriend, pronounced it "a bore." Moreover, she did not even seem to care that there were social codes demanding adherence or that folks looked to judge the missteps of others on an hourly basis. The gossip about Mona Anne and his low-level social status always ate at him; Elizabeth cared not one whit about the talk she generated with her wild actions as well as her simple ones, such as strolling through town with Hotshot trailing after. Hotshot had been orphaned over to the jailhouse, certainly—and as a young boy— becoming Elizabeth's childhood playmate, but she took no note of his skillet-black skin or his simple-minded demeanor. She cast thoughts of propriety to the side, in most matters, like the day she confirmed her sexual confidence, just strolled right into the sheriff's office, where Royce sat alone doing some filing for Mr. Jack.

"Where's Josephine?" she asked, referring to one of a couple of courthouse cats that roamed in and out of the sheriff's office, the office of the judge of probate, the county clerk's office, animals who served as pets for those county employees who took the time to feed them. Long blond braids hung down her back, brushing at her tiny waist.

"I don't know," he said, rolling his eyes as Hotshot followed her into the room. He couldn't for the life of him understand Elizabeth's willingness to put up with Hotshot's idiot ways.

"Oh, but I want to pet her," Elizabeth said.

"She's probably off somewhere getting knocked up again. I think she's about ready to be. Again. Why don't you send the nigger to find her?"

"Shut up, Royce," she said. "Hey," she said, sitting on the sill of the open window, turning sideward, propping her feet on the sill as well, "you think you'll ever get sent to go fight those Germans?"

It was an autumn afternoon. She wore a light green shirtwaist dress, patterned with cherries, apples, and grapes across thin cotton, thin enough for Royce to know the new secrets her body was keeping, the fresh, rounded rises at her chest, unencumbered by a second dressing of an undershirt or even, he suspected, step-ins; and the juncture of her thighs, the slope of those very thighs set off by the sun spilling its light through the open window. Hell, she was just twelve years old, but she did something to him.

"If I do, you're going to see some flat-out dead Germans," Royce said, thinking how that would sure as hell give him some experience in the world to put before Campbell Lacey.

"My grandmother says they're running crazy all over Europe."

"Well, that's a fact. Crazy as hell. Done took Poland, France, coming right at England."

"My daddy said I was crazy as a one-eyed dog." This came from Hotshot, who was standing at the bulletin board, staring at WANTED posters.

Royce could hardly abide Hotshot, with his stupid sayings and his gappy-toothed grin. He was close to Royce in age but acted like a little kid, had been a fixture at the jailhouse for years, had become a source of amusement for the townspeople who threw him change when he sang and danced on the street.

"You aren't crazy, Hotshot," Elizabeth said. "You're original."

"Why you got to carry him around everywhere you go?" Royce chewed on a toothpick he took from Jack Lacey's desk drawer.

"I don't 'carry' him anywhere. He's my shadow. That's what my daddy says."

Royce rolled his eyes again, not believing Mr. Jack condoned his daughter running all over creation with a nigger that was probably up to no good, putting on an act for the white folks. "Well, you ought to be careful. Do you even know what people think about it and what they say?"

"Why would I care?"

"Well, because of your reputation, I reckon."

"Who am I trying to impress? The people who think they are so good and then talk bad about other people? I don't care about any of what anybody says."

"Not even about what they say he done to you when y'all hopped that train that time?"

"Shh!"

Hotshot whirled around. "I didn't, I didn't, I didn't," he said.

Elizabeth got up and took Hotshot by the arm. "It's okay, now. Stop that." She led him to a chair by the door.

"He ain't going to get that gun. Is he? I didn't," Hotshot said, eyes large and fearful, looking for the weapon associated with that specific time and place and incident.

"No gun," Elizabeth said. "Don't worry, Hotshot."

"I can get you a gun," Royce grinned. "Does your shadow want a gun?"

"Shut up, Royce," she said, and he kind of liked the way she said it, so he did.

"I didn't, I didn't, I didn't," Hotshot whimpered.

"Wait here," she said, stepping out into the hallway, turning back to Royce. "Don't get him scared any more than he is," she said, "or I'll . . ."

"Or you'll what?"

"Just don't!"

"Yes, sir!" he said, saluting her, playing at being a soldier.

Royce glared at the boy sitting opposite him. Hotshot did not look up, only rubbed his palms back and forth across his thighs, staring down at the backs of his black hands.

Goddamn retard, Royce thought. One day he's going to do something crazy, hurt somebody, and then what? Those Laceys were loony as hell, letting a girl like Elizabeth—just now coming into a more inviting kind of womanhood than most, a rare kind, even—take up with a nigger who was bound to step over the line, would have to step over it, being grown, if he—and here was a thought that made the blood burn through Royce's veins: if he hadn't already.

When Elizabeth returned she was carrying Josephine, a gray and orange tabby with honey-colored eyes. "Here, Hotshot," she said, laying the cat in his lap.

Hotshot rubbed the cat's back. "Josephine's a crazy cat," he said. The animal mewed a guttural sound and writhed against Hotshot's palm.

"You really don't care what folks think about you?" Royce asked.

"No, I don't," Elizabeth said. "The Bible's full of warnings about gossip and judgment."

"Still and all, you ought to know folks don't think a girl your age should be roaming the streets with a grown nigger."

"He's not grown," Elizabeth said. "My Aunt Frances says he'll never be grown in his mind. And even if he was, I would still take up time with him, even more, because he would be more like a friend and not a shadow."

"A friend?"

"Yes."

"Well you better be goddamn glad he ain't grown in the head, then, 'cause you ain't got no business, at your age, taking up with a nigger friend."

"That's all you know," Elizabeth said, as Josephine mewed in agreement, wallowing against Hotshot's thighs.

"Yeah, I do know," he said. "You need yourself a big brother kind of guy, to look out for you." He grinned, letting his gaze glide down her body.

"I'll never need a boy to look out for me," Elizabeth said.

The cat mewed another deep-noted sound.

"Oh, yes, you will," Royce said. "Believe me. I know. You're turning into something that's going to need a lot of looking out for."

"Says who?"

"Says me. I hear things."

"Like what?"

"Like how you smoke cigarettes on the street."

"So?"

"I bet you already been into the brandy, just like your mama."

Elizabeth shrugged.

"Well, have you?" It was appealing, Royce thought, the picture of a liquored-up Elizabeth with her braids down, lying on top of him, loose hair hanging down across her face and into his.

She smiled. "Maybe."

Royce laughed. "I heard how you dared Bobby Dees to steal a pack of his daddy's Picayunes, how the preacher caught y'all smoking on the front steps of the church."

"I'll say it again." She flipped one braid back. "So?"

"And I heard you got Stew Weatherall to steal all the ladies' corsets from the Empire department store round the corner."

Elizabeth broke into laughter herself then. "We had the best time lacing them onto the pine trees by the picnic grounds!"

"Yeah, I heard old Stew got a whipping from his daddy behind that."

Elizabeth rolled her eyes. "I'm afraid so," she sighed with exaggerated drama.

"I don't reckon anybody whipped you?"

She laughed again, and the sound melted over him.

"You didn't get in no kind of trouble?"

"Well, my mama got drunk and my grandmamma fussed, but my daddy just had to laugh. It was a funny prank, that's all."

"What about your granddaddy?"

She bit her lip and her eyes shadowed over with a kind of angry sadness. "He did *his* usual prank with his pistol and—"

A sudden screech and the pop of a hiss came from the cat.

"Josephine, what?" Hotshot shouted.

The cat had leapt from his lap and lay writhing and growl-mewing on the floor. Then she rolled over, the front half of her body in a crouch, her hind end raised, twisting at her rib cage, making more feral sounds, long, drawn-out groans.

Hotshot stood, agitated. "What you doing, crazy cat?"

"It's all right," Elizabeth said, and Royce winced at the calming effect her words had on the solidly muscled, solidly black teenager. She got up and squatted down next to the cat, her dress sliding up over her knees. Royce wanted to be in front of her, getting a look up that thin dress.

"She's in heat again," Elizabeth said. "Remember the last batch of kittens, Hotshot? Remember I told you she had a litter once or twice a year, spring and fall?"

"She ain't hot," he said, kneeling, putting his hand on the cat's haunches. Josephine wriggled against his touch.

Royce stood, thinking how Elizabeth had not one whit of shame in her, to be squatting down watching a needing-to-be-fucked cat with a horny nigger.

"She wants a boy cat," Elizabeth said, pointing to a place beneath the cat's tail, where its fur made a deep black Y shape, "to put it in her."

"Like them dogs at Miss Martha and them's house," Hotshot said.

"Yes, like that. But cats have really vicious fights, the boys against the boys, and even the girl fights it. And when the boy cat finally gets on her, she makes all kinds of racket, like she is now."

Royce had maneuvered around to the chair in front of Elizabeth, who had dropped back on her rear, sitting with her knees drawn up now, ankles crossed, not caring, enthralled as she was with watching the cat, that her dress crept farther up her thighs. Royce glanced at Hotshot, to see if he was looking up that dress, but the ungrown boy was only studying the cat's rolling, writhing motions along with Elizabeth.

"Poor thing," Elizabeth said. "She wants a boy cat really bad."

"Just what we need around here," Royce said. "Another mess of kittens for me to have to carry off and drown." He let his eyes take in the flesh of her thighs, already promising himself he would touch them one day.

"No! Don't talk about things like that! And don't you dare hurt her babies," Elizabeth said. "Ever." She scratched Josephine's head.

Royce did not tell her that it was her own grandfather who routinely gave him the order to execute the kittens no one cared to adopt from the courthouse grounds. Usually he carried them in a croaker sack to Cane Creek on the edge of town, weighted the sack down and chucked it under the bridge. Sometimes, though, he would wring their necks or pound their skulls with a heavy rock before throwing them in the water, but that was only if there weren't too many of them and he didn't need a sack to carry them all.

"Do you see how puffy it gets?" she said. "And sometimes the way they carry on is like they're really hurting."

As if in response, Josephine let howl an even longer cat moan, flipping to her back, twisting back and forth sideways against the floor. Royce let his eyes find the place, the white cotton of her step-ins, and stay there a while, wondering what she looked like, right—*there*, thinking it would maybe be smooth and pink and sweet, not like the overused, worn-out one that certainly resided between his mother's routinely pounded thighs. He conjured up the image of Elizabeth's flesh, where his gaze rested, shucking the undergarment from his vision, seeing it there, waiting for him. Then he noticed the silence in the room, save for the cat's fevered growls, and he glanced up. Elizabeth was watching him, a knowing smirk on her face.

Royce looked at Hotshot but the boy was focused on the cat's contortions. "You ought not to go letting your skirt up," he said.

"Do you think I give a care if you look at my underdrawers?"

"Well, you should," he said. "Look at you. You ain't even trying to cover up."

"You're pretty stupid," she said, scratching Josephine's head. "You really think I care if you see."

"You know what the Bible says about modesty, don't you?"

"How do you know what it says?" she countered.

"Because the Primitive Baptists are all the time hauling me to Sunday school, trying to make me out a lost lamb."

"Are you a lost lamb?"

He liked the way she looked at him in that moment, all concern and tenderness, so he replied, "Maybe I am," before adding, "but hadn't you better cover up your drawers?"

She smiled. "Maybe you better read more Bible verses if you're so concerned about my drawers."

"What the hell more I got to learn from the Bible?" She still had not moved, and his eyes kept making fleeting returns to the white cotton underwear.

"Well, for one thing, the Bible says, 'Flee also youthful lusts.' That's Second Timothy." And she giggled as Royce's face went red. "Let's go, Hotshot. We'll go find Josephine a boyfriend. Pull me up."

Royce watched Hotshot take her hand and bring her to her feet, hating the boy's familiarity with her, the ease with which she cared for the jailhouse orphan. He sat for a long time after they left, watching goddamned Josephine carrying on like a cathouse whore, growling and gyrating. He thought of the untouched place between Elizabeth's legs. He hoped like hell it was soft as a hen's feather, pristine, that the whispers of speculation about Hotshot and the long-ago train ride were just rumors. Was that place she had just shown him really untouched, unlike the one used so regularly by Moaning Mona Anne? Elizabeth sure acted like she knew more than other girls her age. He stared at the cat, struck again by how Elizabeth had described Josephine's estrus with such utter unselfconsciousness, just as she refused to feel embarrassed to have him studying her underwear, imagining her flesh. Shit, she would probably describe the fine details of her own body with an equal absence of shame, a thought that teased excitement into him. He put his hand to his crotch. Maybe she would do that sometime, tell him what she saw when she looked at herself.

Josephine let out a piercing wail that droned into a groan and lifted her haunches again, curving her backbone downward, amber eyes pupil-dilated with a primal, wild look, and his mind took a turn. Maybe she would tell him what she really saw when she looked at that ungrown nigger. He imagined Elizabeth and Hotshot sitting side by side on the floor of a boxcar. They were watching a coupling of cats, to a quickening rattle of the rails and blows of a train whistle. Swallowed up by the motion and the rhythm, they were fascinated by the orgasmic tenor of it all, maybe even aroused by it. Maybe they had felt it before. Josephine rolled over again on the office floor, pawing her feet at the air, then over again, to raise the vulval offering high as she mewed, deep and long. He stood, leaned over her, reaching with both hands, getting both hands around her neck, squeezing tight and lifting fast. And just as fast, before the animal could get the first claw in him, Royce flip-flopped her body over with a circular swing of his arms, feeling the snap of the spine's crack from the cat's skull, Josephine limp and heavy in his grasp, dead weight hitting the floor. He walked into the bathroom and opened a cabinet beneath the sink. He found a croaker sack there and raked the lifeless feline into it, unapologetic, unsympathetic, and unaware of the lifelessness within himself.

He wasn't sorry for his mama, Moaning Mona Anne, never for one second bought her story that she had to get money to support him, that there was no other way when times were so bad for everybody. He wasn't sorry for Hotshot. Lost from his daddy? It was probably more like his daddy lost him on purpose, saw through that retard act and knew he was a lunatic likely to do somebody in one day. And Josephine? He wasn't one bit sorry that goddamn cat was dead. Elizabeth would sure as hell never have to know, and if the sheriff ever figured out what he did, well, Old Man Lacey would probably thank him for solving the population problem. Royce smiled and reached down to grasp the rough weave of the fabric into a tight bunch, bringing it up off the deep brown hardwood floor, straightening his body and his sense of purpose. He slung the sack over his shoulder and headed for the bridge over Cane Creek.

IN THE FIRST PLACE

Vanessa Carlisle

At forty-four years old, I was still managing a bar on the eastern end of the Sunset Strip. My staff at the bar was at least fifteen years younger than me, crazy with ambition and hormones, alternately drunk and hungover. On the nights when I filled in pouring drinks, I made twice what they made—because I had so much more experience, is what I told them. The truth was that I just didn't care about any of it: money, customers, bottle counts. My wife and I were separated, had been for years, but we hadn't gotten around to finalizing the divorce. Her boyfriend didn't seem to care. They lived down in Long Beach, so I wasn't forced to interact with them. I thought about them, though, every day.

I had a closet of black clothes, a stubbly goatee, and long days in which I'd walk the Venice boardwalk or sit on my porch, smoking Swisher Sweets and drinking Argentinean reds from Trader Joe's. One night when I came out of the bar manager's office, where I'd been drawing my name in 3-D letters on the desk calendar, I saw this unbelievably cute young woman sitting by herself, drinking a martini with three olives. She had short, jet black hair cut like a flapper's, red lipstick, and blue eyes. The girls weren't wearing red lipstick much then. I immediately wanted to take her neck in my mouth, wanted to lift her arms up and feel her fingers in my hair. She had small breasts, but they were round and spaced wide on her body, so she had a perfect hourglass from the front. She left before I talked to her.

She came in every Thursday for two months. I started filling in at the bar those nights. Her name was Sandi. She was twenty-six, an actress. I had the banter down pat, of course, but when she gave me her number I was shocked and couldn't call for days. I didn't understand what she could possibly see in me except that I always made sure her martinis were strong and free. I knew better than to theorize why she came in alone.

We set up a date over a series of voicemails. In her last message before we were to meet she said, "I've never seen you without a bar between us, and I've never talked to you live on the phone. I hope you're not a robot."

I felt like a teenager on our first date because I didn't know where to put my hands, and she seemed so much older than she was, sitting next to me at the sushi counter in a black skirt. When I went to the bathroom and tried to get my straw hair to settle over the thin spots on my forehead, she ordered herself a drink. I came back to find her joking with a cocktail waitress about how annoying first dates always were. I didn't know what to talk about, and I was desperately afraid that I would say something painfully inappropriate like, "You know, I remember when Kennedy was killed," so I tried to ask her questions, but every time she told a story about her lovely family, I ruined it with a story about my alcoholic, divorced, neglectful parents. Every time she talked about becoming an actress, I reminded her, somehow, that the odds were against her.

I said, "I was surprised that you gave me your number," and she smiled. I said, "You seem much more mature than twenty-six," and "I've had a pretty difficult life," and various other ridiculous things. At the end of dinner I noticed that she had twisted her paper napkin into a knot, ripped the ends and tied those in knots, too, and I wanted to keep it, take it home and hang it on my door, it was so beautiful and tortured, a wrinkled and sweaty star. I was too nervous to get a hard-on, even with her black lashes and dimples flashing me all night.

In the car, she leaned in and looked at me sidelong. "When was the last time you got laid?" she said, and I stuttered, because it had been almost two years, and she patted my hand and said, "Don't worry, sweetie, this is what I do."

I didn't understand, and told her so. She said she was a sex therapist. She said men like me were her specialty. She would "do a session" with me for five hundred dollars.

I felt like we'd stumbled onto some indie film set. Any moment now her director would come swooping in and tell me I needed to stop tapping the steering wheel. He'd tell me to act more natural. The future audience would be laughing. "What does that mean, 'men like me'?" I said.

"There are a lot of older guys in this city who—for a reason that isn't their level of physical attractiveness—don't have regular sex."

"I'm not really older," I said, automatically. "I'm just older than you." She waved it off. We didn't talk for a few seconds. She was calm, looking forward as we drove. "Even if I had five hundred to spare," I said, "what's in a session?"

"Depends on you," she said, shrugging, "and what your issues are."

"Is it like going to therapy?" I said.

"It is therapy," she said, "but I don't stay on the other side of the room."

I thought about her sitting in my lap, while I talked about my wife. I imagined her stripping while she told me I needed to keep a journal.

"Most people ignore their sexual problems," she said knowingly. She put a hand on my thigh, which felt more like a test than a come-on, and stayed quiet until I pulled up to her place. When she asked me to come up to her apartment I almost said "What for?" before I realized that that sounded idiotic, juvenile, and rude. So I went upstairs and tried not to seem astounded when she kissed me. Her place was in the north end of Korea Town. She'd taken a frowsy tenement box and strung it with Christmas lights and tapestries.

Later, I asked her why she'd kissed me, and she told me that she wasn't exactly sure, only that she wanted to try and calm me down some way. I wanted her so bad I was afraid. She backed away from the kiss and said, "Wow. Hey. You're a great kisser. Do you like eating pussy?" And while I nodded dumbly, she said, "Listen, I'll make you a deal. Go down on me, and if you can make me come, I'd like you to talk me through it so I can help other guys get better at it. We'll barter."

I wanted to say no, aware that there was something emasculating in this proposal. But I couldn't quite put my finger on it. Normally she'd charge someone five hundred dollars to touch her, and I'd get to do it for free. It was the weirdest thing to happen to me for years.

"Well?" she said, eyebrows raised. "Yes or no?"

"Okay, yeah," I said, reaching for her. She snaked into my arms, made little cooing noises, and then after two minutes of kissing, she pulled off her skirt and lay back on her bed. She nodded at me. She was wearing red lace panties, which I guessed I was supposed to take off her. She kept her black top on.

I knelt down and kissed her belly. She smelled sweet, like one of those cookie-flavored lotions, and her body was covered in a very fine layer of blonde hair. I hooked my arms under her legs, pulled her panties off, and kissed her softly on her pubic bone. She was totally clean-shaven, or waxed, no stubble, like a little girl, which made my whole body throb a time or two, made me hard, then I felt guilty, got soft—all of this happening while I started to kiss and suck her inner lips, her clit, and she closed her eyes and breathed calmly, normally. She had almost no taste, which surprised me. The vague musky salt of her, when I could catch it, was like her secret, real self, the one she kept safe from clients, maybe from all men. She wanted my fingers in her, she moved her hips in rhythm with me; she reached down and pulled on the back of my head. She never got that wet. Eventually she came, but the orgasm seemed short and light, to me.

"That was nice," she said. "You can sleep here, it's late. We'll talk about your technique tomorrow." So I curled against her perfect body, her skin like heated porcelain, her back muscles taut. I stroked her black hair when she slept. In the middle of the night she woke up gasping.

"You okay?" I whispered. I touched her face.

She moved her cheek away and said, "I have these drowning dreams." Then she snuggled closer and closed her eyes. "It's no big deal."

The next morning, I tried to describe what I'd done. I was miserable at it. "I sucked first, then licked, then sucked again?" I couldn't figure out what she wanted from me.

"You've got to be more precise!" she said. "Sucked what? How hard?" Eventually she gave up. "Forget it," she said, "I'll just figure it out by feel. You do what you do, and I'll put the words to it."

I agreed. I asked her if there was one guy in particular this was for. She nodded. "He's my only reliable client right now," she said.

We became friends, sort of. Sandi would make me see romantic movies with her, the kind her other client never wanted to see. She had perfect, tall posture, and spoke with the cynical wit of a Stanford grad to the snotty-scene people we met at West Hollywood dinners. I knew she wanted to conquer the Hollywood scene more than anything, but she was never intimidated, and I admired her for that.

I met her father completely by accident on a morning when he came to town unexpectedly. His face was calm with that same assured confidence Sandi always had. He'd come to surprise her for brunch, and he invited me, but I declined, knowing that she never would have invited me herself. She hugged me lightly in her father's presence and offered a breezy "Talk to you later," before they drove away. I thought he looked like me, and wanted to tease her about needing a sex therapist herself. I didn't, though, afraid she'd stop calling. We'd been seeing each other for about a month then.

Later that day, she called me on her way to see a new client. She complained about being broke, teased me about how wimpy I was for not fucking any of the girls who worked at my bar, and then slipped into a wistful discussion of her aspirations to become an actress, a great actress, one of the great actresses of our age. I said almost nothing. She said, "Come over after work. I'll be tired, but come over anyway."

The bar was a madhouse that night—some Barbie had a birthday party, and I was muddling mint for a glittery knot of mojito drinkers for hours. My wrists killed by 3:00 AM. I went to Sandi's anyway.

It always smelled vaguely like pot there, as if the party had just barely broken up. She pulled two microbrews from her fridge and said she was worried I was falling in love with her.

"I think you should get an older, more interested girlfriend," she said. "Like, get a real girlfriend." We sat in Ikea armchairs, facing each other. She was sniffling, like she had allergies or a cold, and running her hands up and down her calves occasionally as she talked. I tried to hold her gaze while I explained that I didn't want a girlfriend right now anyway. I told her that I wasn't even emotionally capable of falling in love.

"Sandi, you're an incredible person," I said. "But I just don't have that kind of depth of feeling for anything at all right now, much less another person."

"What a relief," she said. "I'm so glad we can talk like this."

She relaxed back into her chair, and the mischievous smile, the one that made it okay for me to touch her, appeared slowly. I put my beer on the floor. I knelt in front of her chair. She smelled like chocolate and cigarettes. I whispered that I didn't expect to stay the night, which she always wanted to hear, and I slid my hands under her shirt, trying not to scratch her perfect, soft skin with my calloused thumbs.

Every time I saw her, I thought she might change her mind and want to make love. She would pull me on top of her and I'd worry I was crushing her. A few minutes later she would rock her hips and moan like a Siren while I sucked her clit. I'd push her up to the head of the bed so I could rub my hard-on into the mattress. So I could feel something, too. Sometimes I'd balance on one arm and masturbate while I drew circles just inside her vagina with my tongue, but then I'd feel guilty for not keeping focus. She would touch my back with palms so urgent I would feel them burning my skin throughout the next day. I started noticing that when she was about to come, she'd clench her toes. She had these long, perfectly manicured toes, and her feet were so powerful they looked like angry fists for a few seconds, and then she'd shudder two or three times, her toes would uncurl, and one leg would float over my head so that she was whole, intact again. Every time I saw her, I would realize in that last moment that we were not going to have sex.

Afterward, I would listen to her worry that she was sending me mixed messages.

My desire for her would make it seem worth it—her flighty, infrequent phone calls, the way she refused to fall asleep anywhere but her own tiny apartment, her demand for witty banter, and the way she justified her not wanting to have sex with me. When I brought it up one night, the possibility of having sex, she quickly started discussing how sex would add a level of commitment to the arrangement that she just wasn't prepared to handle. She told me that oral sex was different; it was tougher to help other people with, so this was good research, she enjoyed it of course, but.

"But what?"

Then she reminded me, again, of how I still had a wife down in Long Beach, and she teased me about being too lazy to sign divorce papers even though we hadn't been together for three years, or in love for five. When I offered to get the divorce she looked offended and told me that unless I was prepared to start paying her she wanted nothing to do with it. "We have a good thing here," she said. "If you want help with your issues it's no longer a barter."

She told me, without saying it directly, that I was too old, had too much emotional baggage, and posed too much of a social imposition to her sharp-tongued, tight-abbed, up-and-coming self for her to really care for me. She would remind me, without ever saying it, that she could date whomever she wanted.

"But you can sleep here tonight, if you want," she would say, which was an invitation to cuddling and cunnilingus. I would agree, because she was so fascinating and young, like a wild kitten. I would summon up nearly twenty-five years of experience being an attentive lover to make her orgasm, sometimes two or three times in a row, and then she'd sleep, sweaty and twitching, with her leg between mine and her arm pressing my chest. I would feel some deep sense of accomplishment at this, because she was such a little nymph, a professional, and the fact that I could make her come meant she did feel some desire for me, at some level.

When I was honest, I could admit that she made me feel less lonely because of the way she nuzzled me in her sleep. It was her soft, sleeping self that would finally lure me, because asleep she was such a young girl, so tiny, and she wanted to be held tighter than anyone I'd ever been with before. When I masturbated at home, after seeing her, I'd picture her asleep.

I told people I was dating a twenty-six-year-old actress. I told them that story even though I barely ever saw her, because her scent on my clothes would jolt my insides like the psychic who one time sent an electric current through my whole body simply by touching my hand. I was forty-four, and I was starting to think about death and what it all meant and why the hell I didn't have any kids yet. I was tiring of the bar business but caught in the inertia of only working three nights a week, and I was finally seeing the languid promise of Los Angeles as some kind of big community delusion, like God or the free market.

Months after Sandi stopped returning my calls, when I realized that I would work for someone else all of my life, and when my not-quite-ex wife returned to me in a silent, private exhaustion of her own, I began to remember Sandi the "sex therapist" like a fairy tale or a waking dream. I told my wife about her years later, and she accused me of having drunk fantasies during the "dark years."

On our first date, Sandi had rolled her eyes when I listened to Elton John in the car because he was such a geezer.

"Not 'Tiny Dancer'!" she had said.

"It's a great song," I said.

"Not only is it drama, it's nostalgic drama," she said.

"It's a beautiful story."

"Oh, please. Are you kidding me? It's just an acid trip he never got over."

She did not allow me any romantic gestures outside of paying for dinner, but she kissed me on the beach in Venice once, because the beauty of the sunset took over. Her eyes went sparkly, her hair wild, and I could see that she was searching for the same thing I was: the Beautiful Moment, the Ultimate Moment with the Right Person, where the questions are answered and the future is clear. And although she seemed to always be disappointed, always protected, always ironic, at that time in my life I would call and call and call because I was forty-four years old and she was twenty-six, and it was unbelievable that I got to touch her at all.

THE GARDEN OF EARTHLY DELIGHTS

Lidia Yuknavitch

Bosch centers his vision on the forehead of the clock and says *seven, eight, nine.* On at six, off at twelve, on again at six, off again on again. Salmon and sea bass slide beneath his hands, his hands palming and fingering the scales and the touch of slime, his breath sucking in the sea and the guts of thousands and thousands of slit-open bellies.

Pimply boy next to him, bleached blond hair, fingers like an artist; *he won't last a month, or else he will he'll be reborn and vex his family.* His thoughts curl around the boy like water. Bosch already wants to take the pimply boy home. He can't help it. In the small gray-green of things the boy sticks out like delight. He can smell his hair. His mind's eye is visioning the boy's head resting on his chest, he's thinking of showing him the ropes, how to take care of his hands, how to sleep awake, how to turn the boy to cruise control and let the limbs, hands, move themselves. Thoughtlessly. Something about his face. How young in the eyes. How little membranes stretch over the blueness—like the film of a fish eye, lensing-over sight.

The boy is smoking in the alley after the shift, his left foot up against the side of the building, the cigarette drooping from his lip and his hands shoved down so hard in his pockets he looks armless. What else to think of an image like that except this is what a boy looks like, hunched and smoking in the night, his whole life ahead

of him but his body resisting itself. Wanting but not. It is too easy
to offer him scotch from an inside pocket all warm and surrender.
It is easier yet to take him home after maybe ten minutes of not
saying anything, just passing the bottle back and forth, just their
breath hanging suspended in the white cold night air there before
them. Home to a one-room house packed to wood walls with one
small black stove, one square white icebox, one makeshift bed, one
toilet behind a curtain, one window, asking night.

"Nice place," know-nothing says.

"Works for me."

"Bet you never expected this, huh?" He turns to look at Bosch.

"What?" Bosch begins the slow undoing of layers of clothing,
his skin hot and cold at the same time.

"*This.*" The boy's clothes shed themselves, his collarbone
and shoulders dipping and curving, his hands hanging down the
length of his arms.

Bosch thinks and thinks what *this* means. Is it the boy before
him, his crotch bulging up like prayer between them, the gap of
not knowing each other at all luscious and ripe and making him
salivate? How long the wait, or was *this* his whole life, the long wait
waiting again and again until new seasons and tides and moons
turned the world back over? The boy's lips puff out; *mama's boy,*
Bosch thinks, only it's nothing but a mouthful of bliss.

The room heats up in nothing flat, stars illuminating their
nakedness. Bosch can't see his own hands, but his hands find the
form, working and reaching and sliding their way along. The boy
is no longer a boy, he is swimming beneath Bosch, he is licking
and teasing, he is moving in the underwater of night. Breathing
forgets itself back to its blue past. Their mouths gape and suck.

Two faces pointing up toward the surface of the night. He tells
him about the last boy his age to come through. People saw him
out there in the nothingness making a goddamn snowman with
his bare hands, frostbite, but the dumb motherfucker didn't know
it, pumped himself up so full of meth he had two numb clubs for

hands, came to work, worked the row without the massive yellow rubber gloves, until someone finally looked over and said *Jesus God—look at that, he's got meat for hands.* And they took him away with those red and useless weights of flesh hanging from the ends of his arms, and he lost one of them; boy couldn't have been more than twenty-two years old.

"That's the trouble. You're all fucked up on dope and shit half the time. A guy could get himself into a lot of shit out here that way. There's no room for error. You have to find the rhythm of the place, being here. It's a whole different existence, see? Don't come to work fucked up. I'm telling you right now. Guys'll take advantage of you, try to mess you up, because if you are out then their pay goes up. All you young guys come out here, college boys, trying to score the big bucks over the puny summer so you can quit waiting tables during the year, or buy some shitty-ass car, or more dope, or whatever it is you do. Just—all I'm saying is, watch yourself. Pay attention. Get into the rhythm of it. You'll be jake."

The boy runs his fingers over Bosch's stomach, light as feathers, flesh whispers. Everything inside of him, intestines, muscles, squirms and lifts in the direction of touch.

He is in the bed of his childhood, in his mother's house. His father has been gone for two years now. His father a no-good, his father a cook at a crappy diner, his father a clerk at a 7-Eleven, his mother needing to feed her baby. It is night in this memory. The front door is rattling and cracking and splitting open with his mother and a man. Laughter brings the bodies into the house; he holds his breath, his boy heart dull thudding in his ears. He is sweating under covers from not moving. Not breathing. They careen off edges, furniture, cacophonous, they nearly crash through the wall of his room; no. They are going to her room to his parents' room, blue walls, blue bed, perfume and a mirror.

In the morning a man driving away in a Pinto wagon. Bosch eating cereal, his hair arguing with itself, his hands little fists around spoon and bowl. He stares at the milk. The flakes floating there, bobbing up and down, he stares and stares at anything but the tired woman entering the kitchen smelling old and distilled and too sweet. Something—breathing?—something gives him away.

"What are you looking at you little shit? You ain't gonna find any answer in your Wheaties, that's for goddamn sure!" She snort-laughs. "Hey. I'm talking to you. Hey Mr. Man of the House. When are you going to get a fucking job and start earning your keep? I can't keep stuffing your little fat face with food, you know. You're old enough to take care of yourself. Goddamn little suckerfish, that's what you are, a bottom-dweller. Suck suck suck. You make me sick."

Bosch looks up for a slow second before she leaves the room with a bottle of Jack Daniels. He sees her eyes magnified and blurry, he sees bubbles escaping from her mouth instead of words, his mind drifts away from her without sound, water filling his ears, his nose, his mouth. Only his heart beats out a rhythm. She is dissolving from sight, she is nearly invisible, wait, she has disappeared in a wave of stained faux silk.

The boy's name is Aram, and he is out of vision, down and down the line from Bosch. Now and again he can see a patch of bleached blond out of the corner of his eye, and he is glad. His own flesh seems warmer than before, warm-blooded, he can feel his own pulse and his hands glide and cup and dive between fish bodies as never before. His neck does not ache in a knot at the base of his head after three hours, his vertebrae do not feel leaded and distorted when he has an hour left, his feet do not throb and spike with the day coming down on them. It is as if his mind is coming back to him in small increments.

He sees an image of Aram gently turning in the night, his torso white and the muscles of his back barely emerged, the fin of his rib guiding his sleep. The odor of blood and waste mingles with the image of the boy, and the image overtakes the present moment, he breaths in the sight, he lets go the work, his body moves without thought, his mind's eye deep in the dark memory, or is it the future, coming to him like a pool of water?

Aram puts his mouth over Bosch's cock. He can see the woodstove and its little light just behind the boy's head appearing and then not, like that, in the dark. His own member sucks thought from his brain, as if the body could will the mind into instinct and primal drive. He closes his eyes and when he cums it is into the mouth of the young and beautiful world. He is lost there. A boy's mouth takes him out of himself. He places his hands on Aram's head, he can see the brightness of his hair, halo-like, and for a moment, stunning. He is caught there. Dazed and electrified all in the same second.

In Seattle there were jobs, but the boys emerging from Issaquah and Chehalis and Sequim were malformed somehow, their bodies too white, or twisted away from offices and college degrees. A high school diploma was simply a ticker tape running across his forehead for anyone to see, saying *I do not speak your language, you must speak more slowly, what are the directions, where are we going?* They had a different smell and habitat, even their hair and shoulders looked different. Contained and quick smart like the click of heels on pavement. When he'd landed a job at the corner bar as a busboy his mother had said, "That fucking figures. You're just like your father, aren't you, pretty boy? I just hope you can do something for a lady with those hands, that's all he had going for him, I can't tell you mister. You sure got shorted on the brains, and come to think of it, the brawn, too. Ain't nothing in this life gonna come easy to you. You got big lips like a mama's boy, too. I bet you get your nose busted before you're eighteen." And she laughed with the open mouth of a bass, huge and obscene and devouring.

Nights he'd come home and she wouldn't be there, and then she would, him in his room of a world with earphones closed so tight around his skull his lips puckered, music pounding so hard it outdid his heart. She'd bang on the door or even open it, swagger there, framed by the disconnected air around them, foreign and malevolent but without origins. Then she'd cry, or shout obscenities at him.

Other nights men would come, men with hair greased black slick as a record album and with teeth missing, or with the leathery skin of alcohol and marbled eyes swimming in their little sockets. Once he saw her walking naked to the bathroom in the earliest hours of morning. Her breasts dropped down like dangling glass globes. Her face appeared to wear a map of things. Her shoulders sank, as if her spine had given over years ago, her ass dipped in instead of out, and her belly, rotund and hard as a melon, balled out from her spine, almost as a child's. She'd fallen to the floor just in front of the bathroom that morning, and in the bruised light and half-consciousness of the vision he'd watched her wriggle there on the floor before turning her head back, contorted and begging, in the direction of his room. Her mouth slit down in a terrible arc. He simply closed the door, not listening, not thinking, not being anything at all. In his bed his mind made waves, *I am weightless, I am as if adrift.*

The boy lasts, Aram takes time from one month to two and to three, from three to four, and in the space of a half year the young man and Bosch swim through labor into deep undulations of form and heat. Fatigue takes on new definitions as their desire wets itself. Physical pain multiplies and deforms into ecstasy like hours on a clock, endlessly repeating, until there is no telling night from day, pleasure from torture, a single room from the cavities of the body.

Hot coffee between palms; dusk.

"Did you think it would be like this?"

"No. Yes. I mean the work. Yes."

"And this?"

"You?"

"Me?"

Who is speaking, Bosch thinks, and who are we that we lose ourselves?

Bosch neither nods nor signals his hands nor reflects any answer in his eyes. He just sits there looking at the beautiful boy in his one-room world, the blond fire-headed boy who gives light to dark making.

"No. I didn't figure there would be anyone like you out here. And I wasn't thinking about anything . . . well, happening." Aram slides from his chair over the edge of the bed where Bosch is sitting like an old beast of some sort. Hunched over and quizzical in the face. He entwines himself—arms, legs, torso—in between the lines of Bosch's body, in between the spaces where flesh meets flesh, where limbs move away like fins, everywhere of him. He makes cooing noises.

Bosch closes his eyes and tries to remember this feeling for when it is gone. For it will be gone, will it not, that is the way of things, this time, and time is a fucker, and except for this one time in all of his life he didn't care about the boot-sludge drone of time at all, and suddenly it is everything, isn't it. It is the whole of life and death stuffed into a tiny room with not enough oxygen to breathe or keep a fire going. It is strange to be remembering before the thing itself is gone from you, strange to have that pressure; memorize, fold the images and the impressions of skin into the gray labyrinth of the brain. Picture them over and over again in the mind's eye, day and night, like repeating words.

"I don't want to know you, I just want to know the idea of you," Bosch says, almost begging.

"But we do know each other," the boy grins, he is too blond, "we keep knowing each other more and more." He traces lines on Bosch's back, up and over his shoulder to his chest and heart, as if he knows the way, knows it by heart, every vein every scar every road of skin or thought since before he was born. Bosch's heart beats too heavy in the chest and tightens and squeezes into a hard ball. His face twists as if he might cry, then releases itself. What is a boy what is a boy what is a boy.

He has a black eye, a shiner from a man he's never met except in the hallway of his mother's home. A black eye as black as the night he got it, and for no reason that he could tell, just there at the wrong time wrong place wrong world, sledgehammer hand big man drunk coming down the hall at him saying "What the fuck are you grinning at? I'm gonna slap that goddamn grin right off your face." Alone in his room with his stinging face pressed against the wood grain of the door he hears them arguing, the rise and fall of voices, the rise and fall of fists or the sound of something breaking, a lamp, a glass, a rib. She is all mouth. His mother, she can rage on with the best of them, she doesn't flinch. She's gutsy that way.

But then he hears her incomprehensibly small and quiet. His whole head against the door he hears her not at all. He hears the lumbering dull and swollen thick man banging his way out of the house, wall to wall to floor and up and out, slamming out, wheels peeling. Nothing nothing nothing from the other side.

Sweat forms on his upper lip and it is cold. His face is swollen and wet and white. His knuckles, white. He bangs his head gently against the door once.

"Mother."

Nothing.

He opens the door to his room and crosses the stream of the hallway to her room. He opens her door. There she is as he pictured she would be, stretched out on the floor in a kind of S shape, her mouth bloody, her eyes puffy, her peach satin negligee twisted up her torso, the blue of the shag carpet floating her still body.

"Mother."

He helps her get up and into bed. She is not dead. Just submerged and bleary. She is mumbling and slurring and her mouth slides around. "I've got to get it out of here," she is saying and saying. He tells her he's gone now, he'll lock and bolt the door. He's gone. He puts ice in a dish towel and soap on another. He washes her face and holds the cold to her eyes and mouth. Her lips bulge and the words keep spilling out; she shakes her head no and no. "Out of me." He thinks, *What is it like for a woman to get fucked like that?* It's foreign to him. Like another species. Nothing about her seems like him.

After she swims toward sleep in her slurry speech he goes back to his room. Just before dawn he thinks of ice caps and the white expanse of Alaska. He thinks of an ocean bearing us away into an Arctic otherworld.

He takes off his hood, unzips his gigantic red parka. The down shape of him shrinks, like he is removing layers of himself, like a Russian doll within a doll within a doll. He pulls his wool sweater over his head by reaching at it from the back. His hair ruffles. He unbuttons the silver tabs on his Levi's. Not one at a time but in a swift pull from the top, so that they all pop in a single motion. He then stretches his torso down and up to take off his T-shirt; his nipples harden. His lip quivers for a moment. He inches his long johns down goose-pimpled legs, over muscle and knee and bone to ankle, twists each foot out. Down his boxers. He is a naked boy. He is beautiful and almost absolutely still. His breathing is the only thing that moves. Bosch feels as if he might weep. Bosch can smell the sex of him. Sweet sweat and soap and skin. His cock grows, pulses up red between them. Bosch's mouth is watering and his hands ache at the ends of his arms.

He wants to hold him like an infant, he wants him to suck at his tit while he rocks him and squeezes his cock. He pictures an almost perfect medieval painting of Madonna and child. He nearly vomits from desire before he reaches out to touch him.

They wrestle-fuck on the floor. As Bosch is driving into him he is also handling the boy's cock in front. The boy is arching hard back so that his head is in the place between Bosch's shoulder and neck; he can see the boy's face, contorted angel. The boy cums first all over himself and all over Bosch's hand and Bosch can see the milk-white spray and his own release pulses out of him up and inside. The boy says he can feel it in his spine and lets out a kind of laugh, glorious. The boy says, "I want to stay like this forever, I never want anything to change, it's this that I waited for my whole life, this feeling." Bosch thinks sentences give us hope in all the wrong ways, language tortures us into faith. What's true is that they can only stay like that on the floor until the heat begins to die in the room. Eventually Bosch has to get dressed, go out to the woodshed, and refill the woodstove. He leaves the boy thinking, he'll get into the bed, and then we can sleep for a few hours. He leaves the boy but keeps the smell of him sucked nearly all the way into his heart as he enters the outside white.

When he awakens Bosch hears birds. He thinks of a boat taking him to Alaska, of seagulls. But then it is not birds. It is fainter. It is human. He comes conscious and understands it is the little whimper of a boy; no. It is his mother whimpering. He goes to her room. She is not there. He goes to the sound. She is in the bathroom. It is barely light. Something smells wrong. He does not want to open the door, and then he does, and there they are on the white floor, mother and child, a little red and blue lump of fetus curled near her. Five months, six? His mother is so pale she looks dead. As if she ran out of oxygen hours ago. Her mouth opens and closes. Her hand twitches for an instant. He bends down and looks at things. It is a boy. It was.

At the woodshed it is clear that more wood needs splitting. Bosch considers not taking the time, then remembers how much the boy likes to sleep, how his sleep swells the room with the smell of a world starting over. He decides that an hour will have no meaning to a beautiful, sleeping boy. Let the boy dream. Let sleep take him away and underneath the surface of things. Let the image of death be reborn in a boy, every single night. With each heave he lets loose a terrible and mindless sobbing. He fills his arms with wood; there is no weight heavy enough to release him.

Later, maybe two hours later, with arms full of wood he has trouble opening the door, but then it gives and a great whoosh of warm air hits the incoming cold. It's a wonder lightning doesn't form from their meeting like that, man and boy, or some electrical charge, some white spark cracking between inside and outside. There he is, unmoved on the floor where he left him, a beautiful pale smile on his face, his eyes closed, lashes painted down onto cheeks. His arms are stretched out on either side, his blue veins making rivers across his infant thin skin at the wrists. *There is no other heaven than this*, Bosch thinks, *this is a heaven on earth*, and he closes the door and builds the fire like a new faith for all of the white against them.

CHICKS WITH TWO FIRST NAMES

Susan Solomon

Not far from the video store Vince goes to sometimes is a matchbox-size women's boutique with scrolls of wrought iron on its doors and a window display of pink scarves and dark purple shoes. In front of it is where Vince found the little silver purse last night. It was sitting in a puddle of rain and beer, reflecting the dull light of a nearby streetlamp. This part of Belmont gets a little gritty at night, with drug dealers loitering on the stoop of the nearby transient hotel, and gang members smoking unfiltered cigarettes by the cluster of newspaper caddies up at the corner, drawing attention to the graffiti on the caddies' smooth steel sides. It's not the kind of street you'd want your girlfriend walking alone on late at night.

Amanda Kim. That was the name on the license inside the bag. An attractive, twenty-eight-year-old brunette with big lips. Vince stuffed the purse into his coat pocket and walked into to the small, accordion-gated video store to rent some more DVDs.

On the way home, he called Amanda. The voice on her machine sounded breathless, but enthusiastic. Like someone jogging. Or maybe fucking. Vince had once left a message like that for his old girlfriend, sort of. They were doing it against the dresser in his bedroom, and she was making this involuntary tweeting sound that he knew meant she would be coming soon. So he speed-dialed her mobile and held his cell near the back of her shoulder as she came. She later told him it weirded her out, but that's not why she broke up with him. She broke up with him because she wanted to take a three-month camel expedition across the Sahara Desert from Mali to Algeria with a band of Tuaregs, and he couldn't leave his job or his sister for that long.

On Saturday mornings, Vince picks up his sister Melissa and takes her to a local café for jumbo donuts and coffee. He's late this morning, because he can't stop watching this Swedish chick getting fisted by a bald Bavarian fireman. The fireman has his sleeve rolled up to his bicep and is grunting with each thrust like a wildebeest. She's panting and biting her fingertips on each upward stroke, and her breasts are firm and heaving. Vince is fucking turned on and trying not to touch his dick, because as soon as he does, it's all over.

Melissa's clutching her fuzzy yellow pillow when Vince pulls up. Unlike most of her housemates at the living center, Melissa's not pudgy. She's tall and taut and takes pride in being able to do ten pull-ups without any help. She's wearing her black skullcap today, which means she wore her blue one the day before. Her shoes are scuffed, and tufts of her reddish brown hair fan downward from the bottom of her cap like the copper fibers on a drum brush. Coarse and straight.

Vince apologizes for being late, and she shrugs.

"Just a shrug?"

"I don't care." She shrugs again and dips her chin into the pillow.

"Damnit, Melissa. You should care."

She taps the manila folder wedged between the pillow and her underarm, then smiles. "Okay, then. You should be more responsible!" she says, mimicking the words he's used with her a thousand times. She wags her finger at him: "Life is all about being on time!"

Vince laughs. "That's better."

The living center is a coed home for developmentally disabled adults. It looks like a big, red brick fraternity house with lots of windows and has a large, latticed-wood gazebo in the back where the house counselors go on their breaks. Today, Melissa and Vince are going to talk about her big move. She and her boyfriend, Gordon, are renting a place together. Gordon's developmentally disabled, too. He and Melissa met at the center a couple of years ago. On the way to the café, Melissa fidgets and tugs at her seat belt. Vince knows that this means she has something on her mind.

"What's up, Mel?" he asks.

"We got a new counselor."

"Oh yeah?"

"Vicky Diane is her name."

"Diane?"

"No! *Vicky* Diane. Diane is her last name."

"Ah. Is that good? You like her?"

"Yeah." She sits up and bends forward. "Definitely. Her teeth are big and super white and she has awesome earrings—like forks, falling." She points some fingers down and plunges them into her lap.

"Wow. Great. But she's nice, too, I hope?"

"Yeah. Super nice. And she's really pretty," Melissa says, jabbing Vince's arm as he parallel parks into a tiny spot in front the café. Vince guesses it's in the genes. Their dad used to do that, too. He'd throw punches like most people give winks—to let you know he means more than what he is saying. He'd tap their mom in the arm all the time after saying something suggestive, and the two would laugh like a couple of school kids.

Vince smiles and opens the car door. "The pillow stays in the car today."

Melissa's had the yellow pillow since she was a little girl. Its fuzz is mangled on the edges, and there is a small knot near the tufting.

"I hate that knot," Melissa once told Vince.

"Why don't you cut it off, then?" he had asked.

"Because it'd leave a hole."

The line inside the café is moving slowly, and Melissa feels boxed-in. When this happens, she crouches for a minute to hold her world together, and then she's okay. She's crouching now, and a short man behind them smirks at Melissa when the line moves, then looks at Vince. "Can you move the girl, please?" Vince thinks he looks like the limp-dicked voyeur in the fisting video Vince was watching this morning, wearing suspenders and square, wire-rimmed glasses. Vince leans in close to him, intentionally invading his personal space. "She's a woman. And moving up eleven inches right now isn't going to get you to the counter any faster."

After they sit, Melissa takes a huge bite out of her donut and starts fishing through her folder. She points at a picture of her standing in front of her new apartment. "That's me," she mutters through her stuffed mouth.

Vince had seen the apartment, along with about six others, last weekend when he was helping her with her search. "And here's the lease. The landlord told me to sign it right here," she taps the signature line, "and I told him no way; my brother is a lawyer and no way was I signing anything unless my lawyer brother looked at it first."

Vince couldn't help but smile. Melissa's IQ is 75, but she's not stupid. "You did exactly the right thing. Glad one of us got some sense in this family."

"What?"

"You—you're smart, Mel, you know?" She sits back, arches her left eyebrow, and nods in obvious agreement. Vince leans in. "Speaking of which," he sweeps away the crumbs in front of him, "you're still using protection, right? You know, with Gordon."

She rolls her eyes. "Yes."

He lowers his head. "And, you're not gonna forget your old bro when you move, are ya? I mean, you're still gonna call me if you have any problems with the apartment or, you know, with Gordon or anything, right?"

She looks at him as if he's just eaten a worm or something.

"I mean I know Gordon's nice, but, you know, he's a big guy and he has a bit of a temper. I'm just saying."

"Gordon loves me! God!"

Gordon does seem like a nice guy to Vince. But Melissa hasn't ever lived with anyone before, and she's only twenty-four and, well, sometimes still acts like an eight-year-old. Someone's gotta keep her grounded.

Vicky's back is to Vince when he and Melissa return from the café. She's leaning over the counter to help one of the residents roll out some dough, and Vince is impressed even before he sees her front side.

"Vince!" Mark yells, then grabs Vince's arm and pulls him over to the counter. "Do it how you did it last time!"

Vince chuckles and glances over at Vicky. "I'm Melissa's brother, Vince," he says, extending his hand. In addition to a nice ass, she's got a big rack and a cute face—the trifecta, as Vince and his buddies used to say in college. Vicky smiles, raises her dough-filled hand, and nods as if to explain why she can't shake.

"The lawyer, I know. Melissa's mentioned you once or twice." She winks as if to suggest that the "once or twice" is a gross understatement.

The residents tell Vince that the dough isn't rolling out the way it did last time, and Vince shows them the one thing he knows about baking: how to add a little flour to make it less sticky. They make gingerbread people, and Melissa puts pink frosting boobs on hers with white frosting nipples. Then Mark grabs the green frosting tube and squeezes a giant mound onto the crotch area of his cookie. Melissa laughs and lowers her cookie on top of Mark's for a pretend kiss. That prompts Mark to pick up his cookie and gyrate it around Melissa's. And before you know it, everyone in the kitchen is watching a couple of gingerbread puppets humping.

Vince excuses himself from the decorating, asks Melissa and Mark to grab their anatomically correct cookies, and takes them aside to have a little discussion about appropriate behavior. He speaks with them using deep tones and a flattened inflection to convey his seriousness. They're adults, so he tries not to be condescending. That's the trick, he believes. To teach, but in a way that nurtures and doesn't alienate.

"Guys, I think this is funny, too, but not in front of other people, right? It might make some of the other residents feel uncomfortable. Do you know what I mean?"

He sees Vicky watching, probably wondering why the hell he is trying to do her job, so he later takes her aside to apologize and explain that he's known Mark and the other residents a long time.

"No need to apologize." She wipes her hands on her apron. Vince smiles, taking a step backward, and trips over a grocery bag. "That's why I always walk forward. Call me crazy," she says and grins. She's got a light-hearted, fun side that Vince finds attractive.

He wipes his backside as he stands up. "Still working on my walker's license, heh."

She pulls off her apron. "Seems like you come here a lot; is it a far drive?"

"Nah. From Lakeview. Not too bad."

"That's where I live, too. What street?"

"Near Eddy's on Belmont."

"Really? Eddy's? I hear they've got great burgers."

"They do," Vince confirms. Then he nods and looks proud: "The Vincent is the best."

She smiles and acts impressed. "The Vincent, huh? And what exactly is in The Vincent?"

"A hot dog," Vince says, totally deadpan, "sliced up and put on a hamburger bun with some mustard and a couple of pickles."

She laughs. "So, you must go to Eddy's a lot to have a hot dog—I mean, a hamburger—named after you."

"I go every now and then," Vince says, looking at his fingernails as if he'd just had a manicure. "Usually on Sundays. Play your cards right, and I'll take you there sometime—introduce you to the big guy himself. Doesn't get much better than that."

She nods and laughs. "Ooh. A big lawyer hanging with the local boys." She folds her apron. "I may have to see that."

"Going tomorrow night if you're up for it."

She pauses. "Maybe, but only if it's okay if I ask for a burger on my, you know, burger."

"No problem. I'll even let you have ketchup."

They chat a bit more, and Vince can tell she's interested. Maybe it's his hair, he guesses. Unlike Melissa's, Vince's hair is thick and black and curly, and female friends have told him it's the kind of hair women like to run their hands through.

On Sunday mornings, Vince likes to do what all city folk do: read the paper and drink strong coffee. Amanda still hasn't called him back, so he leaves another message. Her purse has about twenty in cash, some men's business cards, a couple of condoms, and a small, plastic troll on a keychain. He pops in a DVD, jacks off while holding the troll, and then laughs about what a pathetic perv he is as he plunks the troll back into Amanda's purse. But hey, he figures, these have been dry times.

Sunday night. Vince meets Vicky at Eddy's. She shows up wearing a tight shirt and black boots.

"You're lucky," she says, as she sips her beer. "I normally have a policy of never dating a guy with an ass smaller than mine."

Vince laughs. "I don't think you'll ever have to worry about that, but if it'll make you feel better, I'll have an extra chocolate-covered cruller tomorrow morning."

And that's how the evening goes: She jabs him with her sarcasm, and he absorbs it like a ball-less, self-effacing twit. But he likes it. He likes how she makes him laugh. He likes how she is bright and seems relatively free of drama.

Toward the end of the evening, they talk shop a bit. She really wants to make a difference at the living center and seems interested in hearing everything he knows about the place and the residents. He tells her about Mark; how Mark used to hit himself in the morning, not understanding his hard-on, and how the counselors brought in a sex therapist to help Mark learn how to make it go away. She nods and seems perfectly relaxed talking about something so sensitive.

"So, he's now an expert at making it go away?" she asks, smiling.

"Well, I haven't actually seen his technique, but I'm told he's developed a certain aptitude."

She laughs. Definitely not an uptight personality. He visualizes what her face will look like the first time they do it.

They chat outside the bar at the end of the evening. When the conversation falls silent, he moves closer.

"I had a lot of fun tonight."

"Me, too."

He touches her face. "You're beautiful, you know?"

She blushes, but holds his gaze. So, he moves in for a kiss, hoping to God that she doesn't turn away. She emits a little sigh when their lips meet, and he feels like he is going to explode.

"I wish I didn't have to go," she says, "but I've got to get up early tomorrow."

"I understand," he says, burrowing his head into her chin and trying to stop thinking about letting his hands slip across her chest. "What are you doing Tuesday night?"

They make a date and she kisses him before hailing a cab, letting her mouth linger a bit on his and moving her lips in a way that tells him she really does wish she did not have to go.

Vince works in one of the city's now aging Mies Van der Rohe skyscrapers. A tall, glass and steel box. His office is on the twentieth floor, and he has a view of the Chicago River—the same view he's had for five years now, and he still loves it. This morning, the city officials are dyeing the river green for Saint Patty's Day, and Vince is trying not to peer out and watch the spectacle of the dye as it slowly infuses the waterways, like Midori spilling into a swirling glass of vodka. He's meeting with clients soon and needs to review some documents first.

His phone rings. It's Melissa. She's sobbing something about Gordon. Something about him being an asshole. "Asshole!" she repeats several times before Vince can get her to listen.

"Mel, tell me what happened."

"Fucker!" she says.

"What'd he do?"

"Uh!"

"Mel . . ."

"I saw him kissing Patty this morning in the gazebo."

"What? Who?"

"Gordon! He was kissing freakin' Patty!"

"Oh, Mel—" Patty's another resident at the center, friendly with, but not friends with, Melissa.

"Fucker!"

"So sorry—" He hears a muffled boom from the other end of the phone, like someone punching drywall.

"Mel?"

"Ow. Shit," Melissa says.

Vince waits, picturing Melissa rubbing her fist.

"What are you doing now?" she finally asks.

"I'm at work."

"Oh."

There is a long silence. Vince looks down. He knows her silence means that she wants him to come over, maybe take her on a drive to help her get some distance—both physically and emotionally—from what happened this morning. These are the times, these times of crisis, when it's hardest for Vince to look after Melissa. When he has to rearrange his schedule to meet her needs.

"Is Vicky there?" he asks.

"Uh huh."

He immediately relaxes. Vicky's the perfect person to help Melissa out on this one. She's female and nurturing, yet irreverent and funny. He suggests that Melissa talk with Vicky and that he'll swing by for lunch. Melissa seems to like this plan.

"Can we go to that new hot dog place?" she asks.

"Absolutely."

He leaves Vicky a voicemail and then glances up at his clock. His meeting is in ten minutes. He takes a deep breath and stares out at the river, thinking about how glad he is that Vicky has come into his life. And then he realizes his less than ideal fate: he's falling for Vicky and hasn't even slept with her yet.

On the way to the living center, he hears a report on the radio about a string of rapes on Chicago's North Side, near Belmont. He thinks about Amanda and decides to drop the purse off at the local precinct on his way home tonight. Then he thinks about Gordon kissing Patty when Gordon's about to move in with his sister. Some men are such fuck-ups, he thinks, ruining it for the rest of us guys who are actually nice.

Melissa is calmer when he sees her at lunch, but distant. She doesn't touch the Chicago Red Hot he has bought for her, but twiddles occasionally with a French fry, running its ridged edges along the underside of her nose.

"So, did it go okay with Vicky this morning?"

"Yeah."

"And . . . how are you doing?"

"Fine." She starts drawing loops on the table with one of the longer fries.

Vince traps the fry. "Mel. Seriously. You okay?"

She looks annoyed. "Me and Vicky already talked. I don't

want to talk anymore, all right?"

He decides not to push it. So they sit without speaking, while Melissa draws invisible mandalas on the table. Even though Vince has got to get back to work, he knows the silence between them is productive. Melissa regenerates when quiet, and over the years Vince has noticed that his hushed presence seems to help her in the way certain kinds of drugs potentiate the effects of others: it helps Melissa regroup a little faster, a little better, even if not completely.

Unfortunately, he decides to break his silence just before they leave: "Well, luckily you haven't signed the lease. You don't have to move now."

Melissa starts to cry.

Vince hugs her. "Oh, don't feel bad, Mel. Not all men are pigs."

She pushes him away. "Gordon's not a pig!" she yells. "He still loves me, and he's not gonna do it again."

"How do you know that?"

"He told me."

"You talked to him? When?"

"After Vicky. Just before you came."

Vince wants to tell Melissa that Gordon *will* do it again, but he decides not to—not now anyway. Wait, he tells himself. Until she is ready. This much he has learned. So he settles with, "Okay, okay," and strokes her back.

He walks Melissa into the center when they return. Vicky greets them and tells Melissa that she just made popcorn and some of the residents are watching a movie. Melissa trounces off, seemingly over this morning's ordeal.

Vince turns to Vicky. "Thanks for fielding that one."

"Everything okay?" she asks.

"Time will tell, I guess."

He decides to leave it at that, wary that everything may soon again change.

"Got a minute?"

"Sure," he lies.

She leads him into the office. After he steps in, she locks the door and sucks his face off for five minutes, then pushes him out.

"See ya tomorrow night," she says, smiling.

He is totally whipped.

En route back to the office, Vince's phone rings. The voice at the other end sounds rusty and spent.

"Is this the guy that has my purse?"

"Amanda?"

He somehow feels like he knows her.

"Yes."

"You okay?"

"What?"

"I mean—yeah, I'm the guy that has your purse."

"Great. Where d'you live?"

He gives her his address and tells her he won't be home from work until after seven o'clock.

When he arrives at his condo, Amanda is leaning against the door frame. She's wearing some kind of chain-link belt made out of little abalone medallions. It's the third thing he notices after looking at her heavily made-up eyes and taking a quick peek at her breasts, which command his attention because they are large and appear to be free-ranging under her thin, deep V-necked top. He asks her in and slips into his bedroom to grab the purse on his dresser. "I was worried when you didn't call me back right away," he says from his bedroom.

"Well, it's a long story," she says.

She's near the coffee table, holding one of his DVDs when he returns. Her profile reminds him of a darker-skinned version of his mother's favorite actress, Grace Kelly—another hottie with two first names. She's really fucking gorgeous, he thinks, except for the heavy make-up.

"So, uh, you like this shit?" she asks, holding up the DVD and smiling.

"What's the long story?" he says, trying to change the subject and hoping it is the more innocuously titled *Firemen of Bavaria* and not *Gang Bang Bungalow*.

He hands her the purse and holds his hand out for the DVD. She takes the purse, but lifts the DVD over her head and laughs like a French schoolgirl. Then she extends it toward him, slowly, and he takes it.

"Thank you for my purse," she says. "I don't have much to give you as a reward," she says, perusing the contents of her purse (as if she doesn't trust me—*me!*—he thinks). "I don't even have my apartment anymore."

"What do you mean?"

"I got kicked out—landlord didn't like my lifestyle, I guess." Then she turns her attention to the DVD he is holding. "I don't normally give out freebies, but maybe we could just watch that a bit and see what happens."

He must look confused, he thinks, because she frowns.

"I've got friends, okay?" she says. "It's not your issue." Then she nods at the DVD. "Those girls are amateurs, you know."

He smirks and looks down.

She approaches and stands in front of him, her breasts about half an inch away. Then she leans in slowly and kisses him on the cheek. She keeps her face close to his and whispers, "You're nice."

He feels her hand touch his thigh and begin to work its way upward. And fuck if he doesn't get a hard-on. Goddamnit, he thinks, and steps back. She is smiling.

"Please don't tell me you're that nice," she says.

He thinks about Vicky's power suck, and Gordon's clandestine kiss in the gazebo. "You're welcome for your purse," he says, and he moves toward the door, motioning her with his hand.

She looks at the couch and wraps herself in her arms. "It's chilly out there, you know."

"I thought you had friends?"

She walks toward the door and pauses to look at him before leaving. "I do."

After she leaves, he pops in the DVD and rocks his world. Fuck yeah, he thinks. I'm a nice motherfucker. Kaboom!

He's on the phone with Melissa when Vicky knocks. On Tuesday nights, Melissa and Gordon usually go to the community center to play Texas Hold'em poker with plastic chips. Not tonight, though, because Melissa's just been dumped. During the course of their conversation, Melissa's gone from disbelief, spewing expletives and wondering how she might get Gordon back, to crying, and now, finally, defiance:

"I don't want him anyway. Fucker," she says. "I'm still moving into that apartment. Fuck him."

"But Mel—why would you do that? You'll be all alone."

"Well," she pauses, "yeah. So? I'm way more responsible than Gordon anyway. He doesn't even make his bed in the morning—asshole."

That's my sister, Vince thinks, rapid-firing through the stages of loss like a Browning M2 because she doesn't want to waste any more time on this shit. He chuckles to himself. Buck up, Elisabeth Kübler-Ross, acceptance is really defiance uncorked and exposed to the air a little. Then he looks up to think. "Well . . ." He doesn't want to tell her his real concern—that he'd feel better for her safety if she had someone else there to help her with things like remembering to lock the front door. "What about the rent?" he suggests, mentally patting himself on the back—excellent point. "It's too expensive if you're not splitting it."

Melissa doesn't respond, so Vince continues, "What about maybe finding a roommate?"

"A roommate? I don't know anyone, and it sure isn't gonna be Patty!"

"Okay, well, maybe Vicky has some ideas. Can we at least talk to her?"

"Uh!" Vince hears some tapping. "Fine."

They're laughing by the time they hang up, and Vince sees Vicky smiling at him.

"She okay?" asks Vicky.

"She'll always be okay," he says, glad that he remembered to put the DVD covers in the back of the shelf. Then he winks at her: "But you're gonna have to help her find a roommate."

She shrugs. "Gordon's not a bad guy," she says, pulling a Thai take-out menu from the pile on Vince's counter. "He just needs to mature a little bit more."

"I probably should've talked her out of moving in with him in the first place."

"No." She frowns and puts down the menu. "Don't take that on, Vince. You do enough. You teach her how not to spend all of her money; you make sure she's going to the dentist every year. You're there for her." She touches Vince's arm. "Melissa's an adult—you know that. Adults have relationships, and we sometimes miss little signals telling us that maybe a relationship isn't what we think. You can't possibly shield her from making those kinds of mistakes, you know?"

Vince nods, then grins and lifts up his chin. "*I* don't make those kind of mistakes."

Vicky laughs. "Well, that's true. You did ask *me* out, after all."

They order Thai food, and Vince is impressed that Vicky not only orders beef but asks them to make it spicy. She lets him taste it, and he has to swish some cold beer around in his mouth to stop the burn.

"Milk works better," she says, laughing. She's wearing a tight, pink top and form-fitting black leggings.

"I thought I could take it hot, but damn!"

He pours her a glass of wine, and they sit on the couch. She leans toward him with one arm on the back of the couch and the other resting on her thigh. They talk about working out and tell each other Saint Patty's Day stories. (She threw up green beer on her friend's boat; he got jumped by a six-foot-two Leprechaun on the El.) He asks her if she has to get up early, and she says no. All the signs are there, so he kisses her.

She immediately emits that little sigh again and starts tugging at his shirt. He starts kissing her neck and lets both of his hands cup her breasts, rubbing them and squeezing them and wanting to go under and feel them for real. She bites his shoulder and pulls up the back of his shirt. He can feel her warm hand on his back. He pulls up her top, then off. She starts unbuttoning his shirt. He unclips her bra. Oh fuck me, he thinks. Look at those. He picks her up and carries her into his bedroom.

This girl is real, he thinks. She's sweating and tense as she moves up and down and around on his pelvis, until finally she collapses onto his chest, holds her breath, and begins to tremble quietly, like an underwater surge.

They joke about all of that spicy food afterward until she grows quiet.

"It's been a while for me, you know," she says, looking away. A scintilla of vulnerability that makes Vince want to kiss her and tell her that he thinks he's falling in love. But he quickly dismisses the idea. I'm a lot of things, he thinks, but not a complete dolt.

In the morning, he smells coffee and the leftover scent of Vicky in the crumpled sheets. The lights in the bathroom are on, and the walls of the glass shower are dribbling water. A towel is flung over the bathroom door.

He walks into the living room, still naked and yawning, and hears the sounds of a grunt and a whimper coming from the TV.

Vicky's standing there, fully clothed, holding onto a coffee mug and staring at the screen.

Oh shit, he thinks. He looks at the TV.

One Bavarian fireman has his fist in the Swedish woman's cunt and a second one is jamming his hand up the woman's ass.

He leaps in front of the screen, just as he hears the Swedish chick start to moan.

Vicky twitches when she sees him and snaps off the TV.

They look at each other for a long second or two, and then she picks up her coat. "Hey, I gotta get to work."

He holds out his hand. "Vicky." She frowns and looks down. "It's just a movie," he says, not really knowing what else to say.

"Yeah, movie." She puts on her coat and pauses. Then she turns toward him. "Snuff films are just movies, too."

My God, he wonders, did she just say what I think she said? "Ouch." He moves closer. "You can't be serious, Vic. This is nothing like that. It's just porn—I mean—I don't watch it all the time. It's not like I'm some weird addict or anything."

She stares at him for a second as if she is waiting for him to say something else. Then she starts buttoning her coat. "A waitress fucking her well-hung customer in a restaurant booth is just porn, Vince. Or a scrub nurse banging an orderly in a hospital linen closet. But that?" She points. "That is not just porn." She starts walking toward the door.

"Wait. I'm not following."

She turns. "Do you really think the female in that scene was enjoying that?"

Ah. He gets it now. "I hadn't thought about it on such a deep level. I just liked the title, so I rented it." He tries to smile to lighten the tension. It is a pretty rough scene, he admits to himself, but she can't possibly think I'm some kind of sadist or misogynist pig based on a five-minute clip of a movie I rented. "It's not real, Vicky. I know."

She's by the door now. "I have to go." She sighs and looks at him for a second and he can see disappointment behind the faint smile that she is holding steady on her face. "Bye Vince."

Vince and Melissa are splitting a jumbo donut this morning, because neither of them is very hungry. It's been a few days since Vince last saw Vicky, and she hasn't returned any of his calls.

"Vicky wants me to meet some girl named Daria who wants to move into her own place."

"You mean as a possible roommate for you?"

"Yeah. Vicky says she's nice."

"Well, hopefully you'll like her."

Melissa purses her lips and shrugs, then looks over at the counter, deliberately avoiding Vince's face. "You should call her again."

They are sitting in the back of the café near the kitchen, and there is a fetid smell coming from one of the bathrooms.

"Yeah. Maybe." Vince sees a party near a window table get up to leave and suggests he and Melissa move. Melissa gathers up her coffee and fuzzy yellow pillow. They find a table in the sun, and Vince looks for something to wipe up the crumbs and coffee dribbles left by the previous customers.

Melissa sits and starts stroking the knot near the tufting of her pillow.

Vince nods and looks at it. "I thought you hated that knot."

She eyes it. "I do," she says, and pulls the pillow in close to protect it from getting soiled.

THE WHIZ KIDS

A.M. Homes

In the big bathtub in my parents' bedroom, he ran his tongue along my side, up into my armpits, tugging the hair with his teeth. "We're like married," he said, licking my nipples.

I spit at him. A foamy blob landed on his bare chest. He smiled, grabbed both my arms, and held them down.

He slid his face down my stomach, dipped it under the water, and put his mouth over my cock.

My mother knocked on the bathroom door. "I have to get ready. Your father and I are leaving in twenty minutes."

Air bubbles crept up to the surface.

"Can you hear me?" she said, fiddling with knob. "Why is this door locked? You know we don't lock doors in this house."

"It was an accident," I said through the door.

"Well, hurry," my mother said.

And we did.

Later, in the den, picking his nose, examining the results on his finger, slipping his finger into his mouth with a smack and a pop, he explained that as long as we never slept with anyone else, we could do whatever we wanted. "Sex kills," he said, "but this," he said, "this is the one time, the only time, the chance of a lifetime." He ground his front teeth on the booger.

We met in science class. "Cocksucker," he hissed. My fingers were in my ears. I didn't hear the word so much as saw it escape his mouth. The fire alarm was going off. Everyone was grabbing their coats and hurrying for the door. He held me back, pressed his lips close to my ear, and said it again, "Cocksucker," his tongue touching my neck. Back and forth, he shook a beaker of strange potion and threatened to make me drink it. He raised the glass to my mouth. My jaws clamped shut. With his free hand, he pinched my nostrils shut and laughed like a maniac. My mouth fell open. He tilted the beaker toward my throat. The teacher stopped him just in time. "Enough horsing around," she said. "This is a fire drill. Behave accordingly."

"Got ya," he said, pushing me into the hall and toward the steps, his hard-on rubbing against me the whole way down.

My mother came in, stood in front of the television set, her ass in Peter Jennings's face, and asked, "How do I look?"

He curled his lip and spit a pistachio shell onto the coffee table.

"Remember to clean up," my mother said.

"I want you to fuck me," he said while my father was in the next room, looking for his keys.

"Have you seen them?" my father asked.

"No," I said.

"I want your Oscar Mayer in my bun," he said.

He lived miles away, had gone to a different elementary school, was a different religion, wasn't circumcised.

My father poked his head into the room, jiggled his keys in the air, and said, "Got 'em."

"Great tie," I said.

My father tweaked his bow tie. "Bye, guys."

The front door closed. My father's white Chrysler slid into the street.

"I want you to give it to me good."

"I want to watch *Jeopardy*," I said, going for the remote control.

"Ever tasted a dick infusion?" he asked, sipping from my glass of Dr. Pepper.

He unzipped his fly, fished out his dick, and dropped it into the glass. The ice cubes melted, cracking the way they do when you pour in something hot. A minute later, he put his dick away, swirled the soda around, and offered me a sip.

"Maybe later," I said, focusing on the audio daily double. "'Tie a Yellow Ribbon.'"

"I'm bored," he said.

"Play along," I said. "I've already got nine thousand dollars."

He went to the bookcase and started handling the family photos. "Wonder if he ever sucked a cock," he said, picking up a portrait of my father.

"Don't be a butt plug."

He smiled. "I love you," he said, raising his T-shirt, pulling it off over his head.

Dark hair rose in a fishbone up and out of his jeans.

I turned off the television.

"We need something," he said as I led him down the hall toward my room.

"Something what?"

"Slippery."

I ducked into the bathroom, opened the cabinet, and grabbed a tube of Neosporin.

"Brilliant," he said. "An antibiotic lube job, fights infection while you're having fun."

Piece by piece I undressed with him, after him. He peeled off his socks; I peeled off mine. He unzipped his jeans; I undid mine. He slipped his fingers into the band of his underwear, snapped the elastic, and grinned. I pulled mine down. He slipped the tube of ointment into my ass, pinched my nipples, and sank his teeth deep into the muscle above my collarbone.

My parents got back just after midnight. "It was so nice of you to spend the evening," my mother said. "I just hate to leave you-know-who home alone. I think he gets depressed."

"Whatever," he said, shrugging. He left with my father, who

was giving him a ride home.

"You don't have to come with us," my father said to me. "It's late. Go to bed."

"See you in school tomorrow," I said.

"Whatever."

A week later he sat in my room at home, jerking off, with the door open.

"Stop," I said. "Or close the door."

"Danger excites me."

"My mother isn't dangerous," I said, getting up and closing the door myself.

"What we've got here," he said, still jerking, "is virgin sperm. People will pay a load for this shit." He laughed at himself. "Get it—pay a load?" Come shot into the air and landed on the glass of my fish tank.

"Very funny," I said. I was working out an algebra problem on my bed. He came over to me, dropped his pants, and put his butt in my face. "Your luck, I haven't used it for anything except a couple of farts all day. Lick it," he said, bending over, holding his cheeks apart. It was smelly and permanently stained. His testicles hung loose and low, and I took them in my hand, rolling them like Bogart's *Caine Mutiny* balls. "Get in," he said. I buried my face there, tickled his asshole with the tip of my tongue, and made him laugh.

Saturday, on her way to the grocery store, my mother dropped us off at the park. "Shall I come back for you when I'm finished?" she asked.

"No," he said flatly.

"No, thanks," I said. "We'll find our way."

"Ever fuck a girl?" he asked as we cut across the grass, past the playground, past the baseball fields and toward the woods.

"No."

"Ever want to?"

"No."

"Wanna watch?" he said, taking me to a picnic table where a girl I recognized from school was standing, arms crossed in front of her chest. "It's twelve thirty. You're late," she said. The girl looked at me and blinked. "Oh, hi. We're in history together, right?"

I nodded and looked at my shoes.

"Miss me?" he asked, kissing the girl's neck, hard.

My eyes hyperfocused and zeroed in on his lips, on her skin, on the feathery blond hair at the base of her skull. When he pulled away, the hair was wet, the skin was purple and red. There were teeth marks.

She stood in the clearing, eyes closed. He reached for her hand and led her into the woods. I followed, keeping a certain distance between them and me.

In the trees, he pulled his T-shirt off over his head. She ran her fingernails slowly up and down the fishbone of fur sticking out of his Levi's. He tugged at the top of her jeans.

"Take 'em off," he said in a familiar and desperate voice.

"Who do you think you're kidding?" she said.

"Show me yours," he said, rubbing the front of his Levi's with an open palm, "and I'll show you mine."

"That's okay, thanks," she said, backing away.

He went toward her; she stepped back again. He stuck his leg behind her, tripping her. She fell to the ground. He stepped on her open palms, holding her down with his Nikes.

"This isn't funny," she said.

He laughed.

He unzipped his pants and peed on her. She screamed, and he aimed the river at her mouth. Her lips sealed and her head turned away. Torrent released, he shook it off on her, put it away, and stepped from her hands.

She raised herself. Urine ran down her cheeks, onto her blouse, and into her jeans. Arms spread, faces twisted, together she and I ran out of the woods, screaming as though doused in gasoline, as though afire.

THE FAMILY BED

Cris Mazza

Afterward, he left the house and walked down the street. He'd tried explaining to the kid: why continue playing the game when it's a lost cause for your own opponent—that's like torture. Finally he'd had to slap the kid and send him to bed.

They hadn't lived here long and so far he'd only walked around the block. This time he turned left then right then left again. The road lost its sidewalk and he was walking through tumbleweeds. It was summer and his legs were bare, so he stepped into the street and walked in the gutter. The road was on the rim of a canyon, which was why the only houses were on the other side of the street. The houses were small and the yards weedy. Not that his house was spacious and grand. He'd lost another job and this was all he could do until he could find something better than delivery boy for a print shop. "Don't worry, Dale," Muriel had said, "Barney's so smart—when he grows up he'll finish high school and go to college and have a lot of money!" Dale scooped up a handful of pebbles and started throwing them one by one into the canyon. "Look at him," Muriel kept saying. "Look at him count the money and make change; he does all the figuring in his head. If he doesn't become a movie star, he'll be a big businessman." Dale had to put his hands over his ears or go deaf. Muriel had found the faded, tattered Monopoly game on a shelf in one of the closets of their rental house. "Throw it out," Dale had said, hardly glancing at it. He was busy putting the bed frame together. "Barney loves it," she said. "Look, he already has all the squares memorized—he knows how much rent you owe without having to look on the card!"

"Okay, okay, Jesus Christ!" Dale shouted.

They'd sold everything before moving here, but Muriel wouldn't part with her bed—a queen-size with a sagging mattress and a walnut headboard that needed refinishing. They'd bought the bed in the first place at the Salvation Army. He woke up stiff every morning. The kid slept in the living room on a loveseat they'd found in the backyard. He kept the Monopoly game beside him on the floor at night, or sometimes he pushed the box under the couch if it was one of the days Dale threatened to get rid of it. Like tonight.

Muriel had sobbed, "You're teaching him to be a quitter."

"Hey—everyone needs to know when to duck out." He might've hit her, too, if she hadn't flung herself onto the bed, or if he'd ever hit her even once before.

Dale scooped up another bunch of pebbles and threw the whole handful. The rocks spattered into the leaves of a pepper tree growing down the side of the canyon.

"Hey you!" someone called from one of the houses across the street.

Dale turned. "Can't a man take a walk without being yelled at," he shouted back.

"Come over here—we're having a party!"

She wasn't exactly pretty. Red hair like her head was on fire. That's all he could see from across the street. She was standing on the porch barefooted. When he started crossing the lawn he saw her huge nose and mouth. She laughed. "Come on, come on, the more the merrier!"

"Who is it," said someone inside the house.

"Someone else to help us celebrate."

"What could you possibly have to celebrate," Dale said. He looked past them into the dim living room.

The redheaded woman danced in a circle around him on the porch, then took his arm and led him inside. At first the room appeared to be furnished, but as his eyes adjusted he saw there were only old wooden crates used for tables and shelves, posters taped to the walls, flowers that grew as weeds in the canyon arranged in jars. For a sofa there were two or three large, faded, lumpy pillows propped against a wall, and two or three more pillows on the floor in front.

"I don't have furniture, but at least I don't have junk," Dale said.

"Huh?" said the redhead. "Come on . . . come on and meet everyone."

The other two women in the room weren't any better. One had sooty black hair about a half inch long except on her brow where it was slightly longer, greasy, and combed into a point between her eyes. She also had a million freckles that didn't seem to match the color of her hair. The other was very short and very fat, wearing white shorts that cut into her pink thighs, making a bulging V between her legs. She had a husky low voice.

"I'm the talented one in the act," the fatty said. She handed him a drink, which tasted like tap water.

"That's what we let her believe," said the redhead, still holding Dale's arm.

"Don't tell me *you're* actors," Dale said.

"Comics," said the freckly one. "We work little nightclubs and vegetarian restaurants."

"Haven't you ever heard of us?" the fatty said. "The Hot Flashes. Gosh, we plaster our posters all over town."

"Thank god I haven't lived here long."

"Huh? Well, come on girls—let's give him a free introductory show!" They lined up, the fat one in the middle, arms across each other's shoulders and began doing a can-can dance while the fat one sang a wild melody and the other two provided percussion sound effects.

"Hi, what's going on out here?" A tall, sweaty young man was coming out of a dark hall. He was gaunt and looked like he hadn't shaved in three or four days, and there were purplish lines beneath his eyes. The sweat circles under his arms extended all the way down both sides, and he had a red rag tied around his head, which was also soaked.

"Don't tell me you raise pigs back there in your bedroom," Dale said.

The sweaty man stared. The three girls broke up their act. "He's joining the party," the redhead said, "helping us celebrate—but we haven't told him yet!"

"Oh!" The sweaty man smiled. "Glad to meetcha. My name's Danson. Come on back and meet Rhonda."

Dale followed the sweaty man down the dark hall. The three comics fell in behind, single file. "Who's goosin' me?" the freckly one said.

"Pass it on."

Someone pinched Dale's behind. "Knock it off!" Dale turned and the fatty smiled at him.

Then they were at the doorway of the bedroom. All the windows were open but it was much hotter than the rest of the house. It smelled of heavy sweat and dirty clothes, and a hugely pregnant girl was on the bed, naked from the waist down, her legs spread. Her pubic hair was soaked, as was the dingy towel she was lying on. There was a plastic bowl with some cloudy water steaming near her feet. "Hi," she gasped, then smiled. She leaned to her side so she could raise one arm and wave. Before anyone could say anything else, the girl's smile rippled and her eyes almost disappeared as she squeezed them shut. Her whole face strained. When her eyes appeared again, she began panting, and she repeated the smile. "Thanks for coming, all of you."

Dale held his nose. "Wouldn't you rather be in a clean hospital?"

"Nope." She continued smiling, then grimaced and shut her eyes. Dale shrugged.

"We've performed at grand openings before," the redhead said, "but this is the best."

"Can you see his head yet?" the girl gasped.

"Not quite." The sweaty man poked between her legs with his finger while he bent down and squinted.

"Get your glasses, Danny," the girl said. She groaned and smiled.

"You have any air freshener around here?" Dale asked. No one seemed to hear him. "Hey, if this is a party, how about something to eat?"

"Do we have any peanut butter left?" the girl asked, laughing.

"I don't think so." Everyone laughed, except Dale. He turned to go back down the hall and the three comics also trouped back into the living room, singing a Scotch army song through their noses. Muriel said the kid had a singing voice and wanted to buy him lessons—she said she'd get a job to pay for them. "I'm already going deaf as it is," Dale had to tell her again. He picked up his drink from one of the tables made of wooden crates. "Do you have something I could add to this?" he asked. "It tastes like water."

"It *is* water," the freckly one said. "Anything wrong with *that*?" She was glaring at him, so he glared back.

"Yes—it tastes like shit, just like all the water in this lousy city."

"You think booze is going to be any gentler on your guts?"

"Yeah, that's right, immediately assume I'm a boozer just because I got laid off and—Maybe I wanted milk, didja ever consider that?"

"Milk is for cows. Maybe I *should've* considered that!" From the bedroom came a shriek, then laughter.

"Look, weirdo, I didn't invite myself here. I thought if we were going to be neighbors—but I can see you don't have a hospitable bone in your body . . . or should I say freckle on your face—"

"Who invited this racist sexist bastard in here—".

"Hey!" The sweaty man ran halfway down the hall. "Knock off the shouting, Rhonda can't concentrate." He didn't wait for an answer. The freckly comic turned her back and began staring at a wall.

"Jeez." Dale shook his head.

"I've just got to go out," the redhead said. "I've got to keep telling people. If I can't find any people, I'll tell the canyon, the rocks and trees. Everything has to know and share what's happening here."

"Why don't you go tell those two what's happening here," Dale said. "*They're* responsible."

The redhead stopped humming and said, "What's that supposed to mean?"

"Look," Dale said, approaching her, "you invited me here— how about taking care of me before you go out looking for someone else already."

"Huh?" She scratched her leg. Her skin was chalky and flaked off. "You're here to share with Rhonda."

"Rhonda has nothing I want."

The redhead slapped his face then went out, slamming the door. Dale jerked the door open and shouted, "Can't have a guy come to a party and at least expect a handful of peanuts for his trouble?" She was singing, and her voice grew louder as she crossed the street and stood on the edge of the canyon. She was singing "Waltzing Matilda."

Dale came back into the room and flopped onto the big pillows. Just once he and Muriel and the kid had started a pillow fight, and he'd knocked the kid clear off his feet, but then Muriel and the kid had ganged up on him from two sides, so he went out and watched TV. That was when they had a TV. The fatty sat beside Dale and touched his arm. "You know, this is the best thing that ever happened to Rhonda. She couldn't get a job so she slept around. If she didn't get picked up, she had nowhere to go, then when she was sixteen she met Danson."

"You mean *he* has a job?"

The freckly girl turned and sat abruptly on the floor in a lotus position with her eyes shut, and she began to hum. The fatty picked up Dale's glass. "I'll go look for a slice of lemon for you."

Dale glanced about. There wasn't much light in the room. In fact, the only light came from an aquarium that was bubbling on a rickety table in the corner. The whole table vibrated because of the noisy motor that ran the air pump. Next to the pillows was a bookcase made of bricks and boards. Most of the books were paperbacks that had been opened so many times the titles could no longer be read on the spines. Muriel kept getting books at yard sales for the kid. "He reads like he's in high school and he's only ten! He reads better'n us!" How many times had he told her to stop squealing in his ear before he went deaf. He pulled the books out one by one to see the titles. *Health for the Millions*, *Diet for a Small Planet*, *The Making of King Kong*, *The Family Bed*, *Fasting Can Save Your Life*. There was one hardback, a coffee-table book with a padded cover, *The History of Southern California*. Someone had penciled 50¢ on the inside cover. Dale leaned back and opened that book on his knees. The fatty came back into the room. "Oh, let me show you something in that book." She handed him the water, which now had a slice of lemon attached to the rim. "Look," she started fluttering pages with her thumb. "Here it is, look at this, isn't this incredible? For entertainment the early settlers used to capture a bear and chain it to a post then make it defend itself against a long-horned bull."

Dale looked into the fatty's eyes for a moment.

"Isn't that terrible?" she said.

"Come on, let's dance."

"What do you think of this idea," the fatty said. "We're going to ask Rhonda to join The Hot Flashes for our next gig."

"You think you can get people to *pay* to see her do this?"

The fatty was sitting cross-legged on the floor near Dale's feet. "I'm going to ignore that," she said. She turned a few more pages of the book. "There used to be herds of deer around here," she said softly. When she closed the book it sounded as though the covers creaked, but it was only another moan from the bedroom.

"Come on," Dale said.

"I heard that sparring deer can get their antlers caught together and then starve," the freckly one said, opening her eyes.

"Ugh." The fatty shivered. "But when you think about it, that's okay because it's natural. The other is . . . well, naturally, horrifying."

"It's also natural for a guy to want to have a little fun at a party," Dale said.

"Aren't you having fun?"

The girl in the bedroom screamed, a scream that seemed to go on for hours. Then Dale could hear her panting and she said, "That was a *good* one, Danny."

"Come on, come on!" Dale said. He stood and pulled the fatty to her feet. Her head only came to his chest. Her stomach was touching his groin. "How about putting on some music we can dance to, Janey," Dale said to the freckly one. She shut her eyes again. Dale shrugged. He put both his hands between the fatty's shoulder blades and pulled her as close as possible. The fatty began to hum "The Tennessee Waltz" and Dale swayed with the music, rocking from one foot to the other. "Can't you follow me?" he said.

"You're not with the rhythm."

"Hell with the rhythm." He let his hands move down her back and slip under her T-shirt. He kneaded the rolls of flesh just above her buttock. She didn't yelp even when he pinched her a few times. But the girl in the bedroom began screaming again, and this time didn't stop. Her voice rose and fell like a siren, grunting like a hungry sow when it dipped too low to actually be a scream, then rising again, shriller and higher.

"Goddamn that hurts my ears," Dale muttered. He pushed his hands down under the waistband of the fatty's shorts and grabbed two handfuls of her butt, squeezing and releasing like bread dough. The fatty continued to hum "The Tennessee Waltz." The freckly one kept her eyes shut. If the redhead was still singing outside, she was being drowned out by the screams in the bedroom. The sweaty man was shouting, too. Sometimes the kid knocked on their door at night and Muriel always wanted to let him in. "Everyone's trying to make me deaf!" He pushed the fatty's shorts and underwear down to her knees. She seemed to lose her balance and sat down on her butt, knees apart, looking up at him. But because of the size of her thighs, he could barely see her crack. "Get ready!" he said, shouting above the screams.

"What?"

"Lose the shirt." Dale dropped to his knees between her legs. He started pulling her shirt over her head and at the same time tried to get her legs farther apart by spreading his own knees. It wasn't easy. Her arms were tangled in her sleeves, so Dale left the shirt over the fatty's head and grabbed her giant breasts with both hands. The fatty had to struggle the rest of the way out of her shirt by herself.

"Hey, listen!" she said. The screams went on and on. Then grunting, moaning, and a sound like gargling, and more screams. "Hey—we're missing it!"

"Wait a sec—you've started something here, you can't just leave." Dale unzipped his pants and pulled himself out. "Come on, come on, we'll hurry." He pushed her to her back.

"Let me help you," the fatty whined.

"I know where it goes." He mounted her and began pumping. She stared up at him, then reached up and cupped his face with both hands and began singing the words to "The Tennessee Waltz." Suddenly the sweaty man started shouting "Here it is, here it is," and the screaming subsided before Dale had come. The fatty kept singing and looking at him, but he went soft, so he abruptly lay down on top of her and made guttural sounds, straining and twitching. Then he sighed, got up, turned around, and quickly put himself away. The fatty also jumped to her feet, pulled her pants up, grabbed her shirt and ran down the hall. Dale looked at the freckly one, but she closed her eyes again as soon as he turned toward her. She was swaying slightly from side to side.

"Some party," Dale said.

The sweaty man came out of the hall, drying his face on a towel. "It's all over!"

"You can say that again." Dale checked to make sure his fly was zipped.

"I'm going to ask you nicely to leave," the sweaty man said. He put the towel across the back of his neck and walked once around the room, kicking the pillows back into place, picking up the coffee-table book. He fed the goldfish, glanced once more at Dale, then went back down the hall toward the bedroom. The freckly girl leaped up and ran after him. A baby was crying. Someone was laughing weakly. Dale started following them down the hall but stopped for a second outside the bathroom. He saw the bucket of slimy blood steaming in the sink.

There was no light in the bedroom. The freckly one and the fatty were kneeling on the bed on either side of the girl, hovering over the plastic bowl and helping to tip it gently, sloshing the water around a baby who was in the bowl.

"What the hell are you doing?" Dale asked.

"I don't want birth to be too traumatic for her," the girl said, "so we're simulating the womb environment and will take her out of it gradually." Her lips looked dark and puffy as though someone had slugged her. But she was smiling. "That's why she's always going to sleep in our bed, too," the girl added. The fatty looked up at Dale, wet-eyed and tear-streaked.

"Oh brother," Dale groaned, "don't give me that bullshit." He said it to the fatty, but everyone stared.

"Get the fuck out of here!" the young man shouted.

"Danny, the baby—we're supposed to keep our voices smooth and soft for the first several hours."

"Get out, get out!" the young man continued yelling.

"Danny, stop it, please."

"Get out!"

"Danny!" the girl shouted. She picked up her pillow, damp with her sweat, and threw it at Dale. "Get out of here!" Dale swatted the pillow away, then turned and went back into the hall. "Some party," he shouted, but he kept going, out the front door and back down the street toward his own house. By the time he got back to where the sidewalk started, he realized he was humming "The Tennessee Waltz." A coolness had come into the air and splashed over his sweaty face. He entered his front door softly and went over to the couch where the kid slept. The Monopoly game was halfway under the couch and the kid was on his stomach drooling all over his pillow. Dale picked up the game and went back outside. He tried to remember the words to "The Tennessee Waltz" as he walked back to the party. Their door wasn't locked so he went straight in and straight to the bedroom. The baby was nursing on one of the girl's small, pointed breasts. They were *all* on the bed. The redhead had returned and she was on the bed, too. Even the man was on the bed, but he jumped off when he saw Dale, and he came toward the door with his fists clenched. When the young man got near enough, Dale thrust the game into his hands.

The young man stared at it.

"What fun!" the girl cried.

Dale watched them make room on the bed and spread the board out, deal the money around, sort through the properties. They covered up a blood spot on the sheet with a dingy white towel. The fatty came around the bed and kneeled with her back to Dale, her heels pushing into her big ass. They were choosing tokens. "I'll take the cannon," the fatty said, then she turned and pointed it at Dale. "Pow pow."

Dale went into the hall and straight to the bathroom. He took the bucket of afterbirth into the backyard and buried it. He didn't want to go home.

FROM *BACK ROADS*

Tawni O'Dell

I gave up and walked back to the abandoned mining office. I was thinking about leaving even though I knew I wouldn't, when I heard gravel crunching. I went to the door and she was coming up the tracks carrying a backpack and a Little Playmate cooler. She unpacked a blanket, a couple roast beef sandwiches, four beers, a flashlight, mosquito repellent, matches to start a fire, and stuff to make s'mores. There were some definite advantages to screwing a mom.

She asked me how my week went and I told her fine. I apologized for the condition of the place since I was the guy and I had asked her to meet me here. She said she didn't mind. She said she loved the calm of decay and desertion that reigned there, and I told her she sounded like Shakespeare. She smiled and asked me what I had read of his and I said nothing but I knew how he talked.

"Stand over there," she told me.

I could hardly see her in the dark, but I saw the blanket being snapped and floating down to the floor.

"Don't you want me to sweep out the place?" I asked her. "There's all kinds of shit on the floor. Even glass."

"I don't mind," she said.

She didn't waste any time. She came right at me and pushed Dad's coat off my shoulders and down my arms. When she touched the coat, my instinct was to grab a handful of her hair and smash her head into a wall so hard, it would break her neck and crack open her skull. I could cover her shattered face with the blanket, and if I fucked her fast enough, she would still be warm. But warm wasn't good enough. I wanted to make her come again. Feeling her do that was almost as good as the rest of it.

I took a deep breath and let the coat fall off my arms onto the floor with a dead thud. She pulled my T-shirt out of my jeans and over my head and kissed me on my mouth and my neck. Then she stepped back and stripped.

I still could hardly see her. She was just a pale form without details like someone had cut the shape of a perfect woman out of a piece of black fabric. I went for her and knocked her down.

We hit the floor kind of hard. I should have asked her if she was okay, but I already had my hands on her ass and a nipple in my mouth. She made a groan that could have meant she was hurt, but then I felt her hands in my jeans and knew she was functioning.

"Lie on your back," she told me.

"Huh?"

"Roll over."

I did and she straddled my chest.

"I want to ask you something and I want you to be honest with me. I don't care what you say. There's no right or wrong answer."

Jesus Christ, I thought to myself. She was talking in complete sentences.

"Sure," I panted.

"Was I your first?"

"Huh?"

"Was I your first?"

"First what?"

"Woman."

"Huh?"

She slid a little lower and leaned over until her breasts were in my face. She stuck her tongue in my ear then whispered, "Was I the first woman you ever had sex with?"

I wasn't in any condition to try and figure out what I should have told her. All I heard was a question and I answered it.

She sat up on my chest again. I couldn't see her face in the dark. I ran my hands all over her body while she talked some more.

"I wasn't sure. I thought maybe I was, but you are nineteen. I didn't think about it until after it happened. I'm sorry your first time was in the mud. I hope it was still memorable. Was it?"

"I remember it," I said.

I felt her get off me. She kissed my mouth and neck again and my chest and stomach. Each time she kissed my stomach, I felt her breath near my dick. I dug my fingers into the rotting floorboards and prayed to God to let it happen. I didn't even care that I was praying for something perverted, that I was breaking Commandments, that He was probably pissed at me because I never prayed for Daddy's SOWL or Mommy's SOWL or any of our SOWLS anymore but now I was praying for this. I prayed harder than I did to shut up Brandy Crowe. I prayed harder than I used to pray every night for my dad to love me.

She stopped kissing.

"Harley," I heard her voice come from the darkness. "Has anyone ever given you head?"

The question alone almost made me lose it. I tried thinking about disgusting things to help me hang on. Rich's fat ass waddling out of Shop Rite. Mike Jr. running for a touchdown. Betty's thighs in a short skirt.

"No," I answered.

"Would you like me to?"

"Sure."

She took me in her mouth, and at that instant I believed in God again. I had been doubting His existence ever since my mom killed my dad, not because of what it did to me but what it did to the girls. I couldn't believe He would hurt innocents. I knew God wasn't merciful. I knew He wasn't reasonable or farsighted. But I never thought He was a bully. I decided I'd rather not believe in Him at all than believe in that.

But now I knew He was out there and He was good and kind. He had given me her and she was the answer. If every man had her, there would be no wars, no crime, no contact sports.

I was still in her mouth when I fell asleep.

She was gone when I woke up. I probably should have expected it. She left me a note this time, two beers and a sandwich. She said I was sleeping so soundly she didn't want to wake me, but she had to get home and it was a long walk. She'd meet me here next Wednesday.

Every bone in my body ached from lying on the wood floor, and my hands were on fire from digging them into the splintered boards. Everything bothered me all of a sudden. The night was too cool. The night was too dark. I had a three-mile walk ahead of me, a lot of it through the woods. But she bothered me most of all. I wanted her to suck me again. I wanted to make s'mores.

CRADLED

Aimee Parkison

My good friend Richard, a genius with olive green eyes, masturbates constantly in his mirrored bedroom, walls painted a peaceful sage green. Glossy pornographic images scattered, his glazed eyes stare at gleaming cocks. Pierced tongues explore luminous asses, shaved pussies, oiled titties, and painted lips. Richard writhes. Beneath the reflective ceiling, he carefully avoids paper cuts while moving from photo to photo.

It's a lonely life for a man who once used to be a world traveler. For decades, Richard flew across oceans in search of exotic lovers—girls with strong bodies, slender necks, impossibly beautiful manes, and brilliant dark eyes.

Some of the girls stayed with Richard long enough to become mail-order brides—for other men. Richard discovered the girls of Juarez, the Czech Republic, Colombia, the Netherlands, Macedonia, South Korea, Israel, China, Russia, Pakistan, Vietnam, Kazakhstan, Uzbekistan, and Turkey. Even before our domestic-trafficking days, I stayed in the U.S. to manage Richard's women and girls. Dealing with complex documentation, I negotiated the paperwork of sexual tourists through complex money laundering schemes at our immigration "law firm."

Friends since boyhood, Richard and I moved into linked Los Angeles penthouse apartments, decades ago, after finishing law school and opening a firm in our late twenties. Now, Richard's orgy room is the only space in the penthouse that remains un-renovated, retaining retro charm.

Imagine me as a young man in the orgy room. Pretending to watch naked women dance, I see only Richard.

Richard's enormous cock is so long and so hard that it chooses women for him, selecting new lovers by pointing across the mirrored room. I dream about that cock. I masturbate to it in secret, hoping that Richard won't know his cock controls the lives of everyone it touches. He strokes his enormous erection. When he smiles at women, the light of God shines on their faces. The cock points at them, and they swoon.

If the massive cock points at me, I run out of the orgy room, fearing what cameras might capture. As a young man, I pretend to fuck women. As the years go by, I eventually stop pretending, although the tameness of finger-fucking remains acceptable to me. I allow Richard to finger-fuck me as I do the women, but for the longest time I avoid full intercourse with Richard.

Every time Richard slips his fingers inside me, I recall us working together.

Women and girls who survive the orgy room become mail-order brides. They gradually bend away from Richard's light while agreeing to help others bend toward his light. Cameras capture a frenzy of money shots. Amateur pornography reflects in mirrors feeding triolists' intoxicated eyes. Above giant waterbeds, girls become women. Women become objects as timeless, ritualistic, and perverted as history itself. Secretly, I long to become an object, rather than a man who controls objects.

On rare occasions, real women still enter and depart the orgy room like souls leaving bodies. Lipstick stains are love notes left on faces, cocks, and wine bottles. A tortuously talented lover, Richard can find the man inside the woman and the woman inside the man. He can do what most men can't. He can make love to a woman like a woman. Then, he can turn around and make love to a man like a man. He can also make love to a woman like a man and make love to a man like a woman. In the bedroom, he humbles me, yet he tells me not to worry about the women, my lack of technique, or the impatience of sexual tourists.

Richard's negotiations create profitable, long-standing business relations with wealthy visitors from all over the world. There are surprisingly few negative consequences for candor with upscale society women, whose ages range from eighteen to seventy-one. However, the socialites' husbands desire discretion and prefer to deal with me, rather than with Richard, because I don't refer to certain acts by their rightful names.

"Leonard," Richard says. "Leonard, come here. I have something to tell you."

"What?" I call out, not wanting to return to the orgy room, now uncomfortably warm, foggy, and reeking of sex.

"Penis worship is a symptom of sanity, yet a mere side effect of madness," Richard calls out, as if reciting his manifesto. "Insane women are the ones who don't love penises enough. Sane women are the ones who can't love penises enough. Modern psychology has taught us this crucial difference between *don't* and *can't* when it comes to penis worship."

Richard uses sex to separate sane females from insane. I am neither sane nor insane, but it doesn't matter because I'm not a woman.

Through Richard, I've learned there are only four types of females: real, imaginary, sane, and insane. They are desirable in the following order: imaginary insane, real sane, imaginary sane, and real insane.

It takes a long time to understand. Richard teaches me the categories, which become his new religion. Imaginary insanes are not submissive and not real. Therefore, they are impossibly ideal whores, goddesses available only in men's dreams. By contrast, real sanes are submissive and real, the perfect category for actual sex workers. Imaginary sanes are a fantasy of a reality. An example of an imaginary sane is any real sane Richard wants to possess but can only know in dreams, perhaps because she's not available, or no longer among the living. For most men, famous women fit into the category of imaginary sanes or imaginary insanes. Richard sometimes calls unattainable, desirable, or iconic women "imaginary reals." However, real insanes are the least desirable category, because real insanes aren't submissive. As a result, they're too unpredictable to become reliable sex workers. Even Richard can't consistently control real insanes. In the best-case scenario, he converts real insanes into imaginary reals, through fantasy.

Ever the dutiful friend and lawyer, I spend my days competing with Richard's fantasy of the imaginary insanes while attempting to find real sanes willing to visit Richard in his home.

Pornography is as necessary as food or shelter to men like us. Voices and visions of real women awaken dream women who cradle us. Imaginary insanes are a constant source of comfort. Childlike and mothering, they are never submissives. Yet, Richard orders me to obtain whores and alcoholics—the only real sanes now brave enough to stumble to his mirrored doors.

In his best years, now gone, cameras capture Richard's brilliance. At the height of manhood, Richard buys and sells the finest women while drinking the finest wines throughout the world. Negotiating his way between the minimum amount due and the unpaid balance, he isn't just a trafficker—he's a god among men—a talent scout, an acting coach, a modeling agent, an entertainment lawyer, and a connoisseur of intricate sex acts devoid of intimacy. In cities that never sleep and in little towns that never wake, he buys daughters from their fathers and then purchases ladies of the night from ladies of the day. He negotiates film rights, travel reimbursements, and complicated credit schemes while bidding and bartering for bodies. Bodies without green cards become women without souls. The women and girls exist as real sanes, even though most of them change their names, never go home, and forget who they are. Richard redefines women's culture from one of kitchens, nurseries, and churches to one of the orgy room.

Every time Richard masturbates, he tells stories about imaginary insanes. He says things like, "I talk to her like this, like, *Hello, Ruby. Thanks for coming in. Just remove your clothes, sit on the bed, and make yourself at home. I'll be with you in a minute.*"

When the next woman comes into the orgy room, Richard gives her precise orders, and she obeys. He calls her Ruby, even though she's not Ruby.

He says, "Now, lie back. Keep your wrists stable at the elbows, shoulders down.

"Lift your knee so your leg is just floating. Good! It's hard work, but it's a really deep position. That's nice.

"So, ass up at this end? Pretty far back. You were much tighter when you came in, when you first started.

"Breathe deeply. Bring the leg farther, and make sure you only go as far as you can keep the pelvis stable. So, right, thrust a lot stronger, though. Can you feel that? I want you to flutter inside. I want to feel you flutter."

She looks confused, but does it anyway.

Later that same night, beating off with cocoa butter while gazing into a mirror, he says, "I'll bet with mermaids it's all the same hole. You just have to find the right place to fuck the tail, in between the scales, after she sucks you off underwater."

With a friend like Richard, it's easy to become a trafficker—all one has to do is to have the right connections and to find the appropriate words for certain women and girls. One has to find a way to see women as if they aren't human and to find a way to hear girls' voices without understanding their words. Through the laws of supply and demand, women and girls are labeled, evaluated, priced, classified, ordered, shipped, transported, stored, sold, and resold from sea to shining sea. Like most eye-catching and irresistible goods available in this country, the best sex workers are manufactured overseas. As Richard often says, so few real sanes are MADE IN AMERICA these days. I try to ignore Richard when he says these things. I laugh, even though I don't think it's funny. I can never compete with his women—real or imaginary. Cheap or expensive, bought or sold, I am nothing compared to them, and yet I pretend I amuse him.

Skirting boundaries between disgust and desire, Richard fantasizes about being a warlord. Real sanes become damsels in distress, falling naked before his giant sword. As he slays the dragon, women are his personal property. I can never be as wild or as voluptuous, nor can I keep up with the rhythmic, musical motion of the dying dragon. Nude women float on a raging sea of waterbeds. Richard's sword falls as he ages.

Another thing that relaxes Richard is that black ball on the other side of the big-screen television. "I wish there were more ways to extend women," Richard says while doing his exercises. "Gyrotonics—it's not good to totally expand without having that contraction. Let me show you the swan on the barrel."

Even when on a diet, Richard eats pussy like pasta. To him, pussy is a health food. Having the woman fully splayed on the dining table, he sits down and pulls her open legs closer to him as if she's a big bowl of buttered spaghetti he could eat without his hands. He eats her out while drinking a glass of good white wine. When she starts screaming, he asks me to bring in the other girl so he can properly finish the bottle.

Richard hates screamers and moaners. He has no patience for slutty gestures that hint of desperation, filth, or rudeness of any sort.

He longs for graceful long-haired women—sultry, not smutty—elegant females. Closing my eyes and clinching my jaw, I see full high breasts gently swaying, touching at tightening nipples. Ripe for suckling, they should be perfumed, pinkish, glistening, and should taste faintly of sweat.

Three can be charmed by candlelight at his well-stocked bar.

Always, it's necessary for naked strangers to remain dignified. The statuesque, moving like dancers, are transformed into living symbols of sexual angels—comfortable, comforted, and eventually comforting.

Gracefulness should match gratefulness. It's the only way.

Naked bodies and long hair and laughter and drunken eyes, the alcoholic angels are a rather old-fashioned and picturesque dream, "painterly" in imagistic inspiration. Women's mouths and legs open like doors onto invitingly warm rooms.

Money holds the key to the room of angels. Long ago, Richard and I learned it's polite and wise to allow the truth to remain unspoken.

Richard likes finger-fucking me, almost as much as he likes finger-fucking real sanes. Perhaps this is why he has gone so long between lovers and yet has such short stints between whores, whom he calls "wives."

Orgies vanish like memories, fog on a sunny morning.

Now, in order to fulfill his current fantasy, I must pretend to find a way to convert three real sanes into imaginary insanes, much in the same way that dollars can be converted into pesos.

I show him photos of three sex workers from Madrid. "The beauty of it all is that they know and like each other. They actually enjoy each other's company, so they won't be fucking for you or for me. They'll be fucking for themselves."

On the back of one of the photos, I read the inscription: *Take me . . . by surprise.*

"This one is Chameleon. This is Phoenix, and this is Lynx," I say, holding up the three images of women in compromising positions.

Chameleon, the brunette with green-brown eyes, lies spread-eagle over scratched hardwoods, her eyes staring into the camera. She has lovely eyes, dramatically arched brows, and pretty pale smooth feet with pointed toes like a dancer. In fact, she's smooth and toned all over, her long dark hair like silk.

Phoenix, the redhead, is captured in a sunlit pool of brilliant blue water, her bright hair floating weightlessly around her arms and breasts and belly. Her nipples are perfectly pink, luminously sparkling in the sun. Richard's too old for this one, who has surely lied about her age. He knows it, and doesn't seem to care. She's pouting at the camera like the child she is, her brilliant eyes matching the blue water, her slender fingers splayed beneath her tiny breasts, as if in an offering.

The blonde Lynx is the final image, an exquisite woman on all fours, her rump high in the air and pointed at the camera so that anyone can stare into her asshole and her eyes at the same time. It's an image Richard finds unbearable.

"Get out of here," he suddenly says. "You're disturbing my privacy."

In this fantasy of imaginary reals, the brunette—her long dark hair soft, fine, weightless like feathers or a long shadow—cradles him. The silken refinement, waves of glistening strands flow across face and body as she turns, sweeping from feet to legs to chest to groin to belly to chest, and then to what he fears is the true nakedness of his expression. Masturbating constantly, he comes beneath the shadow of her hair and she mops up the semen with her luxurious strands. The blonde and the redhead watch—waiting, approving—no words, no sound but breath.

More than anything, Richard wants to maintain the illusion of class, taste, elegance, even refinement and gentility, if possible.

The performance, carefully orchestrated, yet with no true rehearsals, has to be perfect the first time—all evidence of lust or crudeness camouflaged by beauty.

The women should be taken care of in a luminous fashion. Young, pretty, and slender, all three must have very long legs and extremely long soft straight hair.

"Sisters?" I ask.

"No!" Richard says, filing his nails.

"Should the carpet match the drapes?"

"No carpet. Just drapes."

"Of course."

"And I don't want them wearing a lot of garish makeup. Keep it soft, only translucent pink lip gloss, none of that harsh red and black and blue paint."

"What else?"

"I need them all to be alcoholics—polite alcoholics with excellent manners and good dancers and perfectly shaped breasts."

"What else?"

"They need to do everything I say, without question, and be completely naked when I enter the room."

"Does that cover it?" I ask, knowing real sanes will never do. "I intend to follow your instructions to the letter and to get the best available, considering the circumstances."

"The circumstances need not be apparent to the women."

"But at thirty thousand each, they should be happy. That leaves ten thousand for you to buy flowers and party favors."

I lie to him. I tell him that the three will arrive just before midnight and remain until dawn. I tell him that with the kind of money he's shelling out, it should be simple.

Even though it pains me, I've told lies about women lately, and he seems to understand. Tonight, he suffers humiliation. I lie to save his pride, to protect him from reality. I can't bring real sanes to his penthouse, as promised. He wouldn't want me to.

Even though he's now obviously suffering from erectile dysfunction, I am not allowed to admit he suffers. I could never trust real sanes to do the same. That's why I bring Richard photographs of reals. He uses pornography to construct intricate fantasies in the orgy room, where he converts images of real sanes to fantasies of imaginary insanes. It's easier than actually bringing real women to his mirrored home so that they can see he has the unpredictable, rare, and fragile erection of a man in his eighties. This is what he gets for taking so many illegal recreational drugs along with prescription medication, including designer antidepressants, in dangerous combinations with hard liquor for so many years.

Neither of us will ever admit it—at least not to each other.

We both pretend his dick is as hard as a rock.

Even while he's obsessively masturbating like a patient in a mental hospital, his limp dick resembles a dead shell-less turtle with a broken neck. He asks me to lick his asshole while attempting to bring the dead turtle back to life. I spend night after night pretending the turtle isn't dead, that the turtle hasn't been dead for days. That's how I know I still love Richard, even when he whispers the name *Rebecca* in sleep and for a moment the turtle looks like it might revive itself.

All my life, ever since boyhood, I've been trying to *flip* Richard, even though I didn't know the word for it then. I hated my sister Rebecca because she had what I wanted. Ever since childhood, Richard has been torturing me by trying to turn me into what I say I'm not. He knows me too well. When we were teenagers, he began teaching me.

To me, this is what *love* is—the pain of becoming what I fear the most.

To Richard, love is *the other*. Richard's true other is my sister Rebecca.

My sister Rebecca is the one type of woman that Richard could never stand after she left him—*a real insane, a woman who does not love penises enough to become what men want her to be.*

Even though Richard still secretly loves her, he now dreads meeting her in person. He doesn't know how to deal with women who can't be controlled in his intricate living fantasy. Rebecca isn't talking to me anymore—because of what Richard and I have done to women she calls our "victims."

"But she doesn't know," Richard says, whenever we argue about Rebecca.

"What?" I ask.

"I've traveled all over the world—several times—and learned different languages," Richard says. "In your entire life, where have you and she gone? Who have you two spoken to, but me? You've been nowhere. Meanwhile, I've fucked women from every continent. Women from every civilized nation in the world!"

"So?"

"Why not go somewhere? Travel—fall in love."

"Love?" I ask.

"See the world. Learn a new language. We can travel together, just like we said we would when we were kids."

"That was a long time ago," I say. Even though I know better, I feel myself getting increasingly depressed and confused and philosophical with Richard. I say too much, yet I say nothing at all. "Some people learn to speak many languages, but say nothing. Some people travel all over the world, but end up going nowhere. Others stay in one place their entire lives, and yet have traveled to places you couldn't even imagine."

"How? By fucking?"

"No. Just by staying still."

"And where have you gone, Leonard?" Richard asks, rolling his eyes before rolling a joint.

"Nowhere you would dare to go. And you wouldn't care to speak the language."

The language is silence. Rebecca's language, like mine, comes from the eyes of women and girls, as they stare at themselves in Richard's mirrors, long after he has given up trying to translate what their words might really mean. The language flows into the eyes of a man like me who sees himself in Richard's mirrors and does not recognize himself as a man, because he does not long to possess women but to become them.

Don't hate him, I tell myself. *Love him.*

He has made me a very rich man, yet nowhere near as rich as himself.

Richard isn't going to leave my office anytime soon. For the next three hours, he masturbates intermittently, an interior-design magazine and trench coat on his lap while he tells me exactly how he will conduct his business with Chameleon, Phoenix, and Lynx. The magazine keeps falling off the trench coat, which moves crazily like a cat trapped beneath fabric. Richard keeps running out of breath. I just sit at my desk, hands folded, listening in a quiet yet professional manner.

Staring at the three photos, he says, "The lesbians will obey my every command."

"Thank you," Richard finally says, cutting me a nice fat check.

"Anything else?" I ask, shocked as I notice Richard has an egregious hard-on as he stands up to leave my office. This hasn't happened for years. Years ago, the last time I saw him like this, I had tried to avoid him and cursed myself ever since.

"Can I see that ass, again?" he asks. Adjusting himself, he suddenly stops trying to cover his erection with the trench coat.

"Sure," I say.

"It helps if you tuck a little bit, rather than arch."

I take off my pants and bend over my desk. The next thing I know, he's right behind me, on his knees.

"What the hell?" I ask.

"Stay still," he whispers, his voice hoarse.

He crawls closer and then he grabs me and pulls my ass cheeks apart. He licks me, and I start to laugh. His tongue tickles. He's not joking, and it's starting to feel good. It feels great! The next thing I know, his tongue is actually inside me, and I have a hard-on and feel like crying. His tongue's exploring is so intimate, it surprises me. I don't even know why I let him do it, except that it feels better than I could have imagined and is like an unexpected gift.

"Don't stop," I say. "Please."

When he finally takes his tongue out, I'm close to coming. He kisses my ass cheeks and the backs of my legs. The next thing I know, he's slowly working his fingers inside me. Because I wasn't brave enough to allow it, until now, he has never fucked me with his dick, but he has finger-fucked me numerous times. His fingers—long and smooth and thick and patiently moving—gently yet firmly explore as I open for him with discrete and hidden movements.

With his free hand, he reaches around and grabs my cock, masturbating me with quick, light, expert motions, tugging and gliding while he works his fingers farther and farther inside me.

Both of us are silent so as not to disturb the other lawyers and clients and secretaries in the nearby offices. Wanting him, I grab onto the desk, and he removes his fingers and thrusts his dick deep inside me. Now I'm moving back and forth, back and forth, and he's moving in and out, in and out, both of us perfectly coordinated. He glides inside me, and I pull him in deeper. I'm in another world, and he's making love to me like I'm a woman, telling me more of the things that he has done to the imaginary insanes, and I know I'm one of them.

"I love you," he says.

Then, I whisper of his first Rebecca, the woman who taught him what love was.

Your face, Rebecca said to Richard. *I want to fuck your face.*

All right, he said. *I want you to fuck my face. I want you to ride my face. But first, I'm going to fuck you with my dick.*

This isn't going to work, she whispered before leaving him for a woman. *I don't want your dick in my pussy any more than I want it in my mouth.*

Maybe I'm not as good as Rebecca. She never knew what submission was. That's why he wanted her.

After getting dressed, we go back to Richard's apartment, again, where he shows me how he wants the dream women arranged in his bedroom, how he wants the imaginary insanes positioned before his giant mirrors.

Removing my clothes, he turns me upside down and into an imaginary real by bending me so that my ass is high in the air like Lynx in the photo.

"Lynx," Richard says. "Oh, my sweet Lynx."

He rides me like a demon on a bike.

Afterwards, I'm so tired I sleep without dreaming, waking when he takes my face in his hands, smears transparent pink gloss on my lips, and kisses me like a lover would.

IN RITA'S LAIR

———————•———————

Wanda Coleman

He knew all her death scenes by heart.

The beauteous banshee in gold lamé screamed at him, pulled and tore at herself, ripped away strips of cloth, bared delicately veined alabaster mounds with golden nipples. Her not-so-old face was a bitch-queen's painted mask of seduction.

"Fuck me, nigger!" she shrieked. "Do as I say. Bring that big black cock here immediately!"

"First things first, Rita!" Jimbo leaped at her, pushed her into the couch and wedged her against the pillows as he wielded the nail clippers. She squirmed and cursed to no avail. "I'll be damned and go to hell before I let you claw me to pieces!"

Her lips had a natural redness, quick to become a slur, quick to become a heart, quicker a rose.

He found he could quell her by replaying videos of her old movies. Sometimes she watched in silence, seeing them for the first time, completely unaware that she, herself, was the "sassy vixen" cast in the female lead. At other times she mouthed the dialogue in robot-like synchronization. Once she yelled at her former self, scene to scene, spitting at the screen.

"Don't listen to the sweet-talkin' bastard! All he wants to do is screw you and brag about it all over bloody creation.

"Hours of ungodly heartbreaking work! Baked under those scrims! They won't pay you shit, Rita baby! Not a tenth of what that fuckin' peacock kissin' ya makes!

"Vamos . . . vamos. Mi Rita, mi Rita puta loca! Fuck Hollywood, fuck 'em all!"

She screamed for hours afterward, until hoarse. He held her against the mattress until his nearness stilled her. It was days before her voice returned. But her senses remained wildly skewed.

Legs still to be envied by the lesser-gifted, hair the color of the western sky ablaze.

The times when she was gentle, occasional at first, became steadily rarer. Patient hands that groped to find and stir him became persistently frantic, grasping and impatient, demanding service until exhausted and swimming deliciously in his sweat.

He had nightmares about taking that rickety old gated elevator to the third floor. "The penthouse," they called it. Her lair, was more like it. Expensive digs to maintain, situated in an old Venice Beach storefront. The second floor was used for storage of the things Rita had accumulated over her stellar career: art objects, furniture, canisters of film projects, letters and memorabilia, gifts from fans and lovers. Every crack and cranny seemed to smell of the fragrances she favored. The first floor housed one of the few art galleries on the boardwalk. The wealthy tenant, part friend and part cover, dealt chiefly in landscapes and pastorals, the gallery opened to the public a few hours on Sundays, its exclusive clientele seen largely by appointment. Her mother's apartment was in the rear of the gallery. The old woman had entombed herself, seldom went out, quietly received visitors, medical doctors, the agent, and those spiritual guides in whom she sought hope for her daughter.

Jimbo and Rita were introduced. She always seemed capable of control as long as a third party was present. She was cold yet intense. He brought enough of his belongings to make himself comfortable. He had made up his mind to let things move at her pace.

Those first nights passed with an awkward and deceptive sweetness. He would wake to find himself in her caress, long limber arms with only the trace of flabbiness appropriate to her age. He had seen younger women in worse physical shape. At those moments, he had to agree with the agent that "sex was the best sedative." But unnervingly quick, the peaceful moments passed. He learned as quickly. It was the mornings and afternoons that came with teeth.

It was hard to believe the devil inside of that.

"The woman's insatiable," Jimbo complained to his cousin and confidant. "It's like she's a vampire, tryin' to suck me bone dry."

"Rich and hot! I've heard of women like that." Larry shook his head and laughed. "I've been lookin' everywhere for one. Leave it to you to be the lucky chump."

"I don't know about that. Care to stand in for me? I could use a break."

"We all have our crosses to bear, Jimbo," Larry sniggered.

"The lady really lets it all hang out."

"I see she's about worn you down to a nubbin."

"The sex? I can deal with that. But the profanity is hard to take. You should hear her when she gets a hold of her mother. That poor old woman, now there's a great lady, lookin' after her daughter like that." Jimbo shook his head. "It's a sad situation. I don't know how much more I can take."

What was once a spirited beauty has become a hellion.

"She becomes violent beyond belief at the slightest dissatisfaction. One never knows what to expect."

"A man has to be a physical marvel to take care of her. When the mind goes, God is not always kind. Such behavior by a man would be accepted as the basest part of his nature brought to the fore. But it causes shock and disgust when a woman behaves in such a manner. Believe me when I tell you she was nothing like that, not as a child and certainly not growing up."

"Our family knows no end of grief. We've been blessed in our choice of caretakers, so far. But none of them have been able to stay with her for very long. She burns them out."

The tall pale-skinned man, breathing heavily with a permanent congestion, discreetly slid the envelope across the counter with puffy glove-white hands.

"You will take care of her, won't you?"

Marked by her trials, the diminutive old woman watched quietly at the agent's side, a half-hidden step behind him. Worried occult beads bounced anxiously in their assessment of Jimbo's dark manly attributes: bullish neck, broad thick-muscled shoulders and arms, cask of a chest, hard stomach, thick waist, heavy hips, legs like redwoods—fine hands, yet strong, with a workman's split nails. He wore a belt to protect his back. His head was square, its features handsomely symmetrical, waxed black mustache curled at each end, thick rivulets of hair parted center scalp and combed neatly to each side, features unlike the usual Bantu—perhaps he was descended from one of the more northerly African tribal lines, or a Caucasian in the plantation woodpile.

"Please," she begged, "your absolute silence is vital."

The pale man nodded. "We've spent weeks investigating you, as we have all the others. You're well liked along the beachfront. Everyone swears by you."

Jimbo nodded, picked up the envelope and riffled the large bills. If he were able to collect enough of those envelopes, he'd have funds to either relocate or underwrite his fight against the racists pressuring the business commission to close his boardwalk cafe. He looked at the pair and grimaced.

"I'll take care of the lady for you."

She was vanishing before everyone's eyes, and her own.

He made a breakfast of soft-scrambled eggs, sliced fresh pear, lightly buttered toast, prepared the tray and carried it to her. She lay corpselike, nude under a silk robe, a waning beauty enhanced by the early morning shadows. He hesitated, watched a moment. When she didn't stir, he stepped into the lounge and set the tray on its stand.

"Rita, time to eat."

"Good morning, Jimbo. I didn't sleep very well."

"Yes. I know."

"I feel half drunk almost all the time. Was I naughty last night?"
He smiled wanly. "No more than usual."

"You're a decent soul, Jimbo. Not like the others. You like me in spite of yourself, don't you?" She asked it as a matter of fact, her hands dropping to the tray, teasing a wedge of toast, a slice of pear. He was caught off guard.

"Yes, ma'am."

"Rita. Call me Rita. That's not my real name. But I like it. It's so Hollywood. Don't you think?"

"Very."

"Some of the others, the violence, the sex, it excited the bastards. Made them want me more. And want my money more. But I fixed them. I got rid of them. One by one."

"Ahhem."

"I like you, too, Jimbo. You're the best yet. Mother has good taste in men. Always has. My father was a fine specimen, tall and straight, with eyes like a bull in heat. She actually used to say that about him. Your big brown eyes are soft, loyal, and intelligent. Like a Saint Bernard."

Something caught in his throat. He turned to leave. His hands trembled and she noticed.

"Breakfast is lovely, Jimbo. See you later."

"Yes, Rita. Later."

Our tragedy . . . our misfortune . . . our curse . . .

Simple domestic chores were done during his hours alone, usually when Rita slept or was simply lost somewhere in her head although she stared at a magazine page or the television screen. One could never be certain when she was there.

A housekeeper came by twice a week to tend Rita's wardrobe, change the sheets and the like, brought groceries in on Saturday afternoons, anything he wanted he ordered—his stomach's desire. He did the heavy stuff; emptied the trash, ran the vacuum cleaner, took care of the plumbing and miscellaneous needs.

He worried about being away from the cafe, about Larry's ability to keep things going. His hard-earned success had been half business acumen and all charm. People liked feeling valued even when they were worthless. It was his ability to imbue them with value, despite his obvious minority status, that drew a largely white clientele and which made the other merchants on the boardwalk envious.

Jimbo's Place had been the realization of a longtime dream. He had lucked into the lease through an old tennis partner. But dreaming came at a price. Repeatedly he had painted out the racial slurs scrawled on his restroom walls. Repeatedly, he ignored the vitriol screamed into his ear when he picked up the receiver. The death threats had been the most difficult to ignore. Reporting them to the constabulary proved an embarrassing act of futility. The heavy menace had promised to stuff his balls down his throat and leave his bleeding carcass to the sharks.

"We'd like to see 'em try, Jimbo. You look like the type who can take care of himself. You won't be needing our help anytime soon." They held their laughter to his face and released it behind his back.

He missed life beachside: the old Jews taking early morning and late afternoon strolls, extolling life in one old country or another; the muscle men lifting weights before tittering girls and jealous boyfriends; the handball and paddle tennis jocks; the skaters, bikers, and skateboard riders; the arts and crafts vendors; the chess players, the drummers, the Hare Krishnas, the sideshow performers. It was carnival all summer long, and summer, of course, was endless.

Whenever he found himself in the caretaker's room, he spent those rare moments alone worrying the circumstance. Just how crazy was crazy? Her rational moments were daunting in contrast to the hysterics. The frequent erotic interludes were beyond definition. There were days when they were never out of her bed and in her greed she refused to eat. He didn't know what to call it, but she had his nose open, as the saying went. While he told himself that he had no aversion to playing the stud whore to save himself from bankruptcy, this was a first. The manner in which it had come about somehow placed it in a special realm. Above all, it was a challenge.

The rest of his time he spent brushing up on his acoustical guitar. One time he looked up and saw Rita watching, amused. She came over and stopped his playing by clutching the neck. He released it. She looked at it, grunted, gave him a few pointers then serenaded him in Portuguese, fado style. He could not understand a word, but the music spoke to his blood. She laid the guitar aside and voiced her command with a toss of that silvering lusty flaming mane. He yielded and performed dutifully.

Once she interrupted him while he mopped the kitchen floor. He was sweaty, bare-chested, and barefooted in an old pair of dungarees. She got down on all fours and snaked toward him through the soapy skim. A water moccasin.

"Take me. Take me, now." She hissed and slithered along his arms, pulling at his fly. In the heat, he slipped and knocked over the bucket. They twisted together in the filth and foam, locked in namelessness.

His acceptance of her was wrongly interpreted.

"Damn, man. You're startin' to look like a haint."

Jimbo's eyes burned in his skull. "The receipts are down."

"I know, Cuz. Sorry about that. I've done my best. But you know how it is. I ain't you. Customers ask for you all the time."

"Well, tell 'em I'll be back soon."

"I keep tellin' them exactly that."

"How's the stock?"

"Holdin' up. New orders in on time. No complaints there."

"But there are complaints?"

"Look, Jimbo—I'll hold out as long as I can, but some of these muthafuckas 'round here are pure-dee crazy. They jes might do somethin'. Ya know? And I was kinda plannin' on someday collectin' my social security."

"I hear you."

"The sooner you get unbollixed from that Rita chick—"

"I said I hear you!"

Romance was a myth. The void, a void. There was no prelude to the day that would sour him forever on surprises of any kind.

Jimbo had exited the old gated elevator and was digging in his pocket for the keys to the apartment when Rita jumped out at him from the alcove, half naked, swinging a piece of pipe. Shrieking full volume, she launched a series of swings that sent him reeling backward. He didn't want to hurt the woman, afraid he might accidently kill her. Then where would he be? On death row. He stumbled for the elevator, whammed on the button, wrestled to pull the gate open with one arm, fended off blows with the other. He jumped. No car. It had gone down to the first floor, leaving the shaft empty. Instant reflex and a weightlifter's grip came between Jimbo and his maker.

He dangled there, furiously, gripping the ridge with the flats of his fingers, waiting for Rita to slam them with the pipe, anticipating the fall, thoughts angling in a bid to save his life. He was willing to accept a certain amount of injury, but . . . he could hear her sweeping steps along the entranceway followed by the opening and banging of the door. He was able to summon enough force to pull then drag himself out of the shaft where he lay staring into visions of dying until they passed and his heartbeat returned to an approximation of normal.

He went in, headed for the bathroom, cleaned and treated his cuts. Then he stumbled around the kitchen and prepared tea and sandwiches. He grabbed a beer for himself.

He found her in the lounge, freshened up and dressed, humming happily over one of those thumb-worn movie magazines.

He set up the tray, seemingly unnoticed, and looked around for the pipe. She had it hidden.

He took the chair from the writing table and sat it squarely by the tray. He helped himself to the lion's share of the sandwiches and washed them down with the beer, unable to satisfy the deep and strange hunger that had suddenly beset him. Rita nibbled indifferently on one wedge and savored the tea.

"Why'd you do that, Rita?"

"You know what's so wonderful about movies, Jimbo?" She had a faint smile and a faraway look.

"Rita, I want to talk about it. Now."

"Movies capture one at one's finest. How one works as much as how one looks. There you are, the sweat of your brow captured forever, for all to enjoy and appreciate. Like a poem or a pyramid."

"You tried to kill me, Rita."

"I don't regret having made them, Jimbo. Not a one. Even though I didn't make the kind of money a star of my caliber deserved. Even if I was a slave to the studio system, I wasn't the only slave, you know." She took a napkin, wiped her mouth daintily, and returned her attention to the magazine.

She was thrilling in the cold light.

What was she trying to say? If she could say anything meaningful at this juncture. He huffed at her, eyes narrowed, fists clinched. Violence and arousal had become a habit. He shook it off. She had nearly put him in a humbug, whether she knew the ghetto expression or not. It was time for him to take his bow and make his exit.

As he left to pack his things, she called after him in tones that rang like crystal.

"Drama makes it all worthwhile. Do remember that, dildo."

Broken things wash in on the tide and settle in the sand.

The sounds of early morning were pierced by the dull thumps of a medicine ball pushed against the beachside boardwalk by a tough-muscled septuagenarian in his gray sweat suit. Two preteens, twin girls, still rubbing the sleep from their green eyes, skipped along in the custodial spume of their swift-walking divorced father. One of the girls stopped before the boarded-up cafe and peered through a dirty pane of glass. There was nothing detectable in the dimness but emptied crates on a tiled floor, a couple of empty beer bottles gathering dust on a wide counter with dusty red vinyl stools, an old wall clock, hands frozen at nine forty-five. There was an announcement posted two panes down, pasted over the remnants of a sign on which ghostly block letters spelling JIMBO's bled through. The girl scanned it, smiled then ran to catch up with her sister.

"So what's the news?" Her likeness smiled.

"A yummy new pizza place!"

Slowly, the community was awakening. Two lovers, university students on vacation, glided their ten-speeds leisurely north along the bike path toward the stretches of Santa Monica, noting the distant thunderhead gathering offshore above Malibu and rolling inland. A black-and-white patrol car was parked helter-skelter where one side street kissed the sand. One officer held two large steaming Styrofoam cups of coffee, while the other frisked a rag-cloaked derelict so filthy the only clue to his race was the texture of his stringy hair. A sailboat skittered the choppy horizon out beyond the pier where the closed amusement park Ferris wheel stood frozen against the overcast sky.

BLOOD

———————•———————

Gina Frangello

Saturday, 10 July, 2:13 PM

"Let's play the memory game."

Michael didn't look, but out of the corner of his eye he could see Rachel turning toward him, white Keds still propped up on the dashboard, legs extended straight. "What game?" he said.

"You *know*, the one me and Mom play. Like I say A is for ant and then you say A is for ant and B is for bug, and then I do A, B, and C. Remember we used to play it on the way to Michigan?"

He didn't. They had always been doing something in the car, Rachel and Leigh. Singing usually, and then afterward Leigh would start an argument over the fact that he had not joined in. He said, "Mom and I. It's not Mom and me, it's Mom and I."

"God, Dad, I know that. But I'm not in school right now. I don't have to think."

He said, "If we play that game, you'd better think enough to come up with more interesting words than ant and bug or I'll fall asleep at the wheel with boredom and get us both killed."

She started laughing. "Yeah, then Mom would really be mad."

"Okay," he said. "A." Thought, *Anus, aberrations*. Said, "A is for Attila."

"You mean like Attila the Hun?"

354

"Mmm. So all that money I pay to send you to Latin School actually has some purpose. Or does your mother give you history lessons on the side to fool me?"

"Yeah, she keeps me up studying for hours every night." He thought there was a note of smugness in her voice, due either to her recognition of barbaric dictators or to her newfound ability to (sometimes) enter into the sparring he invited. But then she paused.

"Come on, no stalling." *B is for beatings, bulimia, bingeing, bruises.* "Your turn."

"Okay, okay. Um. Okay, I've got one. A is for Attila, and B is for Barishnikov."

"A is for Attila, B is for Barishnikov, and C is for (*cunt, cuts, crying*) calligraphy."

"What's calligraphy?"

"It's that fancy writing your mother does on invitations."

"Oh."

"Do you want me to pick one you've heard of?"

She put her feet down on the floor of the jeep, straightened her back. "No, that's okay, I can remember it." Looked out the window and repeated the list. "D is for . . ."

Death wish, defecation, degradation, destructive relationship.

She indicated a passing truck. "Diesel."

"Those damned things should be outlawed," he said.

Her lipstick had been the exact same color as her blood. Really it was so uncanny that at first he thought she must have planned it that way, had somehow managed to take in a sample when buying her makeup and matched the shades directly. But of course that was absurd; something he *might do. Most likely she didn't even know the name of her own lipstick shade, had bought it randomly at Walgreens for three dollars so she could get change for the bus or something. Still he felt a subtle disappointment on the evenings when she wore a different color: the one that was more purplish-black than red, or the pale pink she sometimes wore with her retro sixties clothes. That one made her look like a ghost.*

The first time he'd made her bleed, she was wearing the blood lipstick, though. The matching of the colors was so striking that he'd wanted to reach his fingers into the tracks running down her neck and smear it right next to her lips to show her. But they had only been sleeping together a few weeks, and she might have thought that strange. When he thought of it later, by the time she would have expected something like that from him, he preferred to keep it a secret, something she didn't know he had observed in her. She watched him to see what he was watching, to know how to play him. And after a certain point, he didn't want her to know.

Saturday, 10 July, 9:08 PM

Rachel wanted to put the tent up herself. She claimed to have learned to do this at camp and shooed Michael away, leaving him to sit on the hood of the jeep watching while she struggled with poles that were taller than she was. It impressed him that she got anywhere at all, but when she failed to get the whole thing assembled, she grew upset and wouldn't help him finish the job because she "didn't know how."

He had to undo some of her damage, which took awhile. When she had put on half a container of Cutters, and they were both inside the tent, she said, "Mom said when you used to go camping, you always brought a flashlight so you could stay up all night reading and that she could never sleep with the light in her face. I'm supposed to tell you, you aren't allowed to do that."

"I guess she'd rather me wander around in the woods and get eaten by something or fall down a steep hill in the dark."

"She would not!"

"Rachel, I was only kidding." He looked at her: a skinny fetus, knees drawn to her chest, arms wrapped around them tight. "You can put the airplane eye mask on, you won't see a thing."

"You *brought* it?" She widened her already-big, brown eyes. "Why don't you just try to sleep like a normal person, Dad?"

"You sound more like your mother everyday."

She scowled and didn't say anything else.

It was already dark, and Rachel was exhausted from the ride. Neither of them was hungry either. They'd stopped at a diner on the way up since Rachel had acquired her mother's fascination with all things "quaint" and wanted to eat in the middle of nowhere and get stared at by the locals. Michael had no appetite, though, hadn't for weeks, and was vaguely worried that he was losing weight. He suspected that he couldn't afford to get any thinner without looking like one of those ex-hippies who dropped so much acid in the sixties that they lost the brain cells required to remember to eat. But his appreciation of food was sporadic; in times of stress he always lost weight. Only during his marriage had his body ever really filled out, looked *solid*. When he'd gone out to dinner with Leigh, he finished his food. With Kendra he picked at her dinners and ignored his. Since she had gone, it was worse.

Now he wished they hadn't stopped, that they could make a fire and cook something, anything to postpone having to go to bed. Rachel was rummaging through his brown leather overnight bag looking for the mask and finally produced it and stuck it over her face. It was black and said *Virgin* across the front in white letters. He'd picked it up on an international flight on Virgin Airlines six or seven years ago, because the idea of blindfolding his wife with a mask that said *Virgin* struck him as amusing. Although Rachel had been wearing the mask for years at his apartment, the sight of her there now, blindfolded on the ground bearing a label that proclaimed her untapped sexuality, was suddenly disturbing.

As if she'd read his mind, she removed the mask and sat up. "Mom said to ask if you ever take those pills she gave you?"

"Her voodoo pills? No, I certainly do not."

"Melatonin, Dad." Slow and pseudo-annoyed, a higher pitched version of Leigh. "They're hom-e-o-path-ic."

"They're synthetic hormones. Don't worry about me, okay?"

She pulled the Virgin eye shield back down and settled into her bag. He felt like telling her to take it off, didn't think he could stand to look at her all night wearing it, some joke waiting to be told. Like when he was standing on a platform waiting for the El and could envision jumping—one sudden movement—onto the tracks and to his death. The impulse was so powerful that he had to touch a pole or a sign, anything to steady himself, though in truth he knew he would never do such a thing. That *had* to be the way it was with this, too: her stalk-thin arms, no definition to her waist under three layers of sweats, breasts mere timid, half-inverted buds. Nothing but the power of suggestion: meaningless, harmless. Anything but erotic.

What possible reason to run and jump before the oncoming train?

No, that wasn't the first time at all. Not the night he finally got the nerve to bite her hard enough to break the skin. The first time was earlier, accidental almost. Back when the windows of his apartment were covered with frost. Inside he was naked, his heart racing from having fucked her so hard, from the fear of having done some permanent damage. By then he had untied her, and she lay in a ball on his bed, long, pale hair spilling over her face, knees pressed flat against her chest. She looked like she was trying not to cry.

He said, Get up and walk.

She glanced up at him. Go to hell.

He backed away, moved to the other side of the room, surveying her there alone. Get up and walk to me, *he repeated.*

A curious look came across her face, like she wanted to know what he thought would happen if she did. He could see the process behind her eyes, the wondering. Then she unwound her body and slid to the edge of the bed. But the minute she stood her legs buckled. Air came rustling out of her asshole with a crude sound, and she sank to the floor. He watched her, refused to smile or do anything, just waited for the humiliation to register on her face, for the tears. A tightening in his stomach. Not even breathing.

But she started to laugh. Started and couldn't stop. Choked, Okay, Michael, did you know that was going to happen? Is this some test you put all your new lovers through? *and fell onto the rug. He smiled, felt it on his lips before he could stop it. Lied,* I guessed. *She said,* So how about "guessing" how many times it will take before I can walk after? *He tried to keep the surprise off his face.* Only once more. *She stared at him.* Come inside me *there* again and it'll be the last time you see me. *He said immediately,* I won't do it again.

He had to press the backs of his legs into the wall to keep from moving. The urge to go across the room and take her in his arms was that strong.

Sunday, 11 July, 3:49 AM

He felt trapped while Rachel slept. Even with his Discman spinning the usual dark refuge of Mahler, the tent was like being stuck in a cubicle for observation. Outside, too, there would be nothing but blackness all around—he wouldn't even be able to see the stars for all the trees. He wanted to get in the jeep and drive, wanted it so badly he could feel it in his skin, the longing to get up and leave. To go to an open meadow and look up, feel something big, bigger than him. The sky held a promise of something else, not the punitive God of his childhood who, if He existed, could not forgive what was unrepented. The ambiguity, the uncertainty of nature. Something huge.

Rachel breathed evenly only feet away. Maddening, yet he dared not move too far beyond the sound for fear he would snap and not come back. He tried to stay with this image, his daughter's air-flow an invisible cord securing him to reason, to life. Too soon, though, she turned, the mask falling askew, slipping over her nose so that the "Virgin" was off to one side. He could see only "Virg." Michael switched off the flashlight. Stood up fast, the unexpectedness of the motion rendering his legs momentarily unsteady. By the time he got outside the tent, he felt himself breathing in gulps. Breath like fire now, begging him to enter, to burn. To accept that which he clearly could not—did not want to—change.

Kendra choking from trying to swallow her own tears, gasping for air. Marks from his belt rising upon already-layered welts on her ass.

What would it take to embrace this perversion, the broken part of his soul? His hands moving over himself, slow at first, automatic. *Their* hands were the same size, he had noticed earlier, watching Rachel grasp the poles of the tent, knuckles whitening as she shoved the sharp end into the dirt. Kendra's were paler, of course, blue-tinged fingernails as opposed to his daughter's healthy tan. White, the flutter of her pulse weak beneath the skin. Growing faster under his touch.

She'd have woken with a start, no need of a mask or label to prove her innocence. A whisper in the dark, Daddy, what are you doing here? *Henry's voice:* Don't worry, princess, don't be afraid. *Hissing,* Don't tell your mother, *before he tore her apart.*

The orgasm left him drained but not calm. Wiping himself off with his T-shirt, his back itching as if from a healing burn, eaten alive by mosquitoes he hadn't noticed until now. He moved back toward the tent, but even this, the gnawing of his skin, could not make him step inside once he heard the sound. The sound of Rachel's breathing, needing. Closer. Mixing with the half-stifled sobs still ringing in his ears.

Monday, 13 July, 12:16 PM

It was easier when they *did* things. Sunday had been lazy hours just sitting in a canoe with fishing poles, Rachel reading one of her damned romance novels and sunning herself while he thought, pretended to read, too. Time consuming to let her try and build a fire like she'd learned in Brownies and at camp, though he'd let his mind wander and hadn't jumped in to help her until she was already in tears. He worried at how easily frustrated she was, how quick to scream or cry like a much younger child—different than she was at home, where she usually seemed calm, more even-keeled than he. Made him wonder if she sensed something and felt ill at ease being alone with him. But that night she'd eaten two hamburgers and a hot dog, wanted to make s'mores, rattled on about her best friend having invited some other girl to sleep over and asked what he thought she should do to win her back. He had discarded the damned airline mask. Let her think she'd misplaced it, and then he finally slept some, too. Hard. Close to four hours.

But today there was no sun. So instead they hiked, not wanting to be out on the water in case a storm hit. Rachel was full of camp stories; Michael was sure she embellished most of them to make them more exciting. Being lost in the woods overnight, an encounter with a black bear, falling down a mud hill and needing stitches. He was pretty close to positive that if any of these things had been as catastrophic as she made them sound, Leigh would never have let her leave the house, much less go camping again. It was reassuring though, her wanting to impress and entertain him. At first he found it hard to concentrate, kept drifting off and heading in some opposite direction than the way she was walking, didn't answer questions when she asked. But they picnicked for lunch, and he felt more alert after actually eating something. Let himself believe her, get drawn into her tales.

"I never set foot in a woods when I was your age," he said, so she'd feel more capable, not dwell on her failed tent construction and fire starting. "We had no money for camp. My brother and I used to play in the alleys. I didn't even know how to swim until college."

She fell into silence, as if waiting for him to say more. He knew she was fascinated by his side of the family, an inaccessible web of estranged men, perpetually cloaked in the gauzy strands of anger that followed his mother's slowly deteriorating, cancerous death. But Michael didn't feel like weaving soap operas out of his past, letting her construct Harlequin fantasies about things that had been only unfortunate at the time, rather dull in their aftermath. So he, too, did not speak, and they walked on awhile oblivious to each other. Almost, for a moment, happy.

"Mom said you must've had a fight with your girlfriend," Rachel said, and it was a sudden weakness in his knees, the rocks beneath his feet markedly larger. Then breathing. Then nothing.

"Why would she say that?"

A shrug. Poking the ground with a long stick she fancied glamorous to walk with. "Cause you wanted to go away for a week with me, I guess."

Stupid, vengeful . . . "I'm sure your mother didn't mean that."

"Mom said that's why I haven't seen you for three weeks. Because you were in a love bubble and not thinking with your head. But that now you probably dumped her 'cause you always get sick of people after a while and then you felt guilty for not calling me. That's what she said."

He felt his teeth clench. "Rachel, I don't think your mother intends for you to repeat things like that to me. And frankly, I'd rather not know. She is wrong, though. I didn't see you for a few weeks because Ke—because my girlfriend has been sick. I was worried about her."

"What's the matter with her?"

He touched her shoulder, but she kept walking, didn't look back at him. "Sweetie, I'm sorry I haven't been around much. I wasn't in much shape to go out, even with you. You could have called me, though. Sometimes I get distracted, but that doesn't mean I wouldn't want to hear from you."

"Mom says *you'll* call people if you want to talk to them."

"For Chrissake, can you please stop quoting your mother before I lose my mind? You know she and I had a disagreement recently. She's just very angry at me right now."

"After you slept over."

Heat in his legs at the thought that she might, that she *must*, know full well what that meant. "Yes. Since then."

"How come? What did you do bad?"

"Not 'bad,'" he said. "Wrong."

"*Whatever.* Can you stop correcting everything I say? I thought since you stayed over, you and Mom might be making up. I thought you'd get back together, not be more mad."

"Sometimes it doesn't work like that."

"So is that why you broke up with your girlfriend? Because you slept with Mom?"

Slept with. Leigh drunkenly, obliviously running her fingers over the deep scratches on his back while he pushed into her in some half-formed hope that he could disappear into the familiar safety of her body. Then staring at him in shock the next morning once the alcohol wore off. *For god's sake, you look like you've been sliced open with a serrated knife. Who the hell did this?* Him, *Look, one fuck does not mean I suddenly owe you explanations.* Her, so loud he envisioned Rachel bolting up in her canopy bed, *You manipulative bastard. Get out!*

"I told you, Rachel, the woman I've been seeing is just sick. We did *not* break up." His hand reaching out to flip her dark hair, get rid of a bee circling her head. She jumped. He dropped his hand, kept walking on ahead. It was not until he heard her footsteps following him that he called over his shoulder, "Now let's just drop it, okay?"

Summer in Chicago, the heat oppressive and heavy. After five years as an attorney, it still did not seem right to him, wearing a suit in such weather. He could not help but feel foolish in his stiffness, especially there in Henry's car, driving with the windows rolled up as if the air-conditioning was necessary to keep them both from touching anything real, from breathing in the living world. She was there on the sidewalk, head bent down like a heavy flower on a broken stalk, tracing some imaginary vision with her fingers. She wore a skirt the color of dead grass. It extended to her ankles, but she had pulled it up to sun her calves, each of which displayed the taut, ball-like muscles of a dancer when she arched her feet. Henry said, Good Lord, would you look at her, she acts like she was raised in the gutter. *Michael smiled. He was fully erect before he even realized it, stared at her harder and longer than he'd have dared if he thought anyone would ever guess what was on his mind. She didn't even see them pull up. Henry had to honk twice before she rose, scooping up her shoes and running barefoot to the car.*

Inside Henry's BMW, Kendra reclined on the backseat and rested her feet out the open window. Henry told her to put them back in, but she ignored him. Michael asked her a question, anything to turn around and see her there, on her back on the leather seat. Her hair was much too long and hung in her face. He had never thought her as classically pretty as her mother; both she and her twin sister had inherited some of Henry's less-chiseled features, rougher angles. But looking at her now . . .

She bolted upright when he spoke. Almost as if she had only just realized that he was in the car (which was impossible). She pushed her hair from her face, and he caught sight of a small, blue vein pulsing in her neck. The movement was slight, but enough for him to see. She answered him, something about her dance school, and it did it again, twice. He wanted to reach out and wrap his fingers around her throat, to feel the steady throbbing of the blood-flow that kept her alive. The scent of her—dust from the dance studio, mint, and carefully masked cigarettes—made him dizzy. Henry started talking, and Michael felt as though there were some understanding between them, like she knew what he was thinking and had somehow orchestrated it. Absurd, like the numb pain making rounds through his body: his cock, his stomach, mostly his head. More likely she thought he was old as the hills, asexual, couldn't keep it up for more than three minutes (if she even thought about such things). For god's sake, she was only fifteen.

Wednesday, 14 July, 3:47 PM

The water was flat. Flat and disappointing as the option of running away from the firm he'd been at for ten years, of alternately remaining a silent co-conspirator with his partner and mentor, the man whose daughter he'd fucked, whose trust he'd betrayed. Yet even his betrayal was flimsy, incomplete: he'd still avoided confronting Henry with the truth. For what in the end? There *was* no going back—to either of them. He would tell no one his plans or why he was leaving, though in all likelihood they would not find that strange coming from him. His resignation would be unexpected, of course, and hard for the firm. But they had always thought him unpredictable. It could never occur to them that the reason for his departure was Kendra.

The canoe swayed lightly, jarring him, though Rachel didn't even open her eyes. She reclined, stretched out before him like another possibility. Another reality just on the edge of the knife he felt there in his stomach, twisting every time he looked at his daughter, every time he let himself think. A reality in which he could go into the office and beat Henry to a pulp, maybe kill him, and it would have been the thing to do. If this were a movie after all, that would be the only resolution any director worth his weight would choose. Then the actor playing him would sit a vigil outside Kendra's hospital room until she talked to him, would buy her flowers and promise never to hurt her again. She would make him sweat but then accept, and they would join some therapy group . . . but no, that would be another movie. In the film where he would kill Henry, he never would have done those things to Kendra in the first place. The men who avenge women are never the same ones who abuse them in the movies.

The boat was rocking before he saw her. Rachel suddenly standing, her arms spread out as she gaped down. The stain on her peach-colored shorts looked to Michael like a lethal wound between her legs. He leaned forward to steady her, then recoiled in a split second, could not touch her. The canoe tipped, water rushing fast into his ears. The sound of his daughter yelling, "Dad." Then no noise but a slow throbbing. A cold, soothing numbness. Something like, *Stay*.

But he did not. At the surface of the lake, Rachel was flailing her arms frantically. Crying, not so much with fear as with frustration, trying to grab their cooler and her book, which were floating out of reach. She struggled in vain to catch them, her lifejacket keeping her afloat despite her random movements. Michael made himself touch her arm. It was slippery and cold. "Sweetie, let them go." Her movements ceased. She clung to his shoulder. It was all he could do not to pry her off. Even in the chill of the water, her touch burned.

For the moment, though, it was safer there, like that. The red of her invisible beneath the rippled surface of the water. He closed his eyes against the image of a lake filled with her untouched blood. A sacrificial virgin, her dark hair stuck to her face in strands. Someone in the woods that lined the lake was calling to them, "Hey, do you need any help?" A strong impulse to do nothing, just drift. But Rachel was sniffing, "Dad, make him go away. I'm bleeding all over the place." Michael called back, "It's okay, we're fine," but the man didn't listen. He was already wading into the water to give assistance, a woman in the background on the shore. Rachel began to bawl, uncontrollably, the closer the man came. The woman on dry ground was shouting to her, "Honey, it's okay, you'll be all right," like Rachel was afraid of drowning with a life jacket on and three adults around. Michael tried to concentrate on how to avoid hitting the unwanted do-gooder once he reached them, from yelling back at his (wife? girlfriend?), *Shut up, you stupid bitch.* He took hold of the canoe, hissed at Rachel, "For god's sake, stop crying." She grabbed onto the edge of the boat as he moved with it toward the shore.

Once on land, they had no choice but to get back in the boat and paddle to the dock where they'd rented it. Rachel sat with her arms wrapped around her torso, pressing her legs together

like a child who had to pee. The water had calmed the angry
bloodstain between her legs, and amid their heroism, neither the
man nor woman seemed to notice her plight. They were gone
now, but Rachel's face was still pink. From the sun, her tears, or
embarrassment Michael couldn't tell. He was trying to think of
what Leigh would do if she were here. Hug Rachel, pet her hair.
But Michael couldn't. Hard to believe she was the same daughter
he'd mock-wrestled with just weeks ago, had boosted into trees,
had sat on his lap and smelled her hair. Her body, her blood
seemed poisonous. He sat in his corner of the boat. Could not
move, could not speak. If the sound, the muffled sniffling, did
not stop soon, he was going to scream.

When they finally reached the dock and climbed out of
the boat, Rachel immediately bolted up the hill that led to the
parking lot. The two frat-types who ran the canoe rental turned
their eyes curiously toward her as she ran. Michael stayed to get
his deposit back, did not see her until he was halfway up the
hill. She was standing by a tree, not crying as hard but looking
accusatory, as though what had just transpired was all his fault.
He did not meet her eyes as they got in the jeep and drove to a
gas station with a minimart.

"*You* go in and get them," she pleaded, when he reached for
his wallet.

He said, "I'm not exactly a connoisseur of these things. Should
I just get the same tampons I used to buy for your mother?"

"No way!" she just about shouted. "I'm not using a tampon.
Gross."

He imagined himself saying that he failed to see how a tampon
could be grosser than sitting in a quasi-diaper of your own blood.
He kept quiet.

"Just get *anything*," she mumbled. "Please, Dad, hurry."

He got her curved Kotex regulars. He remembered having
seen them in the bathroom of a woman judge at a party, and
they'd stuck in his mind because the idea of a judge getting

her period seemed funny. When he gave them to Rachel, she scurried to the restroom around back. He sat in the jeep waiting. After she came out, he felt strange, like he had walked into somebody's house while they were having sex, then had to wait in the living room while they got dressed. She had combed her hair and looked more together, but he was painfully aware of the fact that he knew what she'd been doing. She kept looking down. Finally, halfway back to the campsite, she said, "I guess we have to go home now, huh?"

The impulse rose up in his throat to say, *Yes, immediately.* Instead he said, "Why?"

She stared at him with something close to hatred. "I can't believe you'd even ask that! Like I'm going to stay here when I'm all bloody and disgusting."

Something in her tone made him react, the way a girl who does not want to be seen naked brings out a man's impulse to compliment her body more than it deserves. "What's so disgusting about it?"

"Stop it! I don't want to talk about it!"

He glanced at her to see if she was hamming it up, just saying what she thought was expected. But she was curled up in the passenger's seat looking beaten and ashamed. "Listen," he said evenly, "every woman in the world gets her period. You should be excited to be entering a whole new phase in your life. A lot of cultures view a girl's first menstruation as her transition into womanhood."

She looked at him in surprise, then something closer to disgust spread across her face. "It's not my *first.* That was right after Christmas."

His voice moving around the lump in his throat, the horrible need to say, *Why didn't anyone tell me?* Instead he managed, "So what's the big deal then?" But he already knew, didn't have to hear the rest—*Only happened once . . . didn't think it was coming back . . . so embarrassed . . . the whole world saw!* He sat looking at the steering wheel, then up, straight ahead at a thin blonde girl of eighteen or so sitting on the hood of a beat-up car, shoeless, smiling at a long-haired man who handed her a bottle of water. He moved his eyes away. "It's nothing to be embarrassed of, it's perfectly natural for women to—"

She whined, "I don't want to be a woman. Boys don't have anything awful like this happen to them."

He had to bite down on his tongue to keep himself from arguing with her further. Felt like calling Leigh and saying, *I hope you know that you've taught our daughter to be ashamed of her own body.* Except that she would probably laugh in his face. Would tell all her friends how her asshole ex-husband, the one who'd screwed around throughout their marriage, was now upset that his daughter had negative ideas about being a woman. And what else might they have hidden from him, Rachel and Leigh, long before this, before he'd even suspected anything was off? He felt like hitting something, like punching holes through a wall the way he'd done after his father remarried—some terrible release. But now before he could even relish the feeling, it was gone, the familiar check of his impulse kicking in. The uncontrollable (if artificial) calm.

"We can leave in the morning if you still want to," he said.

"I want to go right now! Why are you making me stay? Please, don't make me sleep here like this, please."

"All right, fine, stop whining, we will leave tonight. Can you tolerate at least going back to the campsite first, or do you expect us to abandon all of our belongings because you can't stand being out in public with your period for one second longer?"

She burst into tears. "Why are you being so mean to me? You hate me!"

A cold jolt to his spine, sharper than the water an hour before. "Rachel, please. Of course I don't hate you. Calm down."

"I want to see Mom! I don't want to be here anymore!"

He forced himself to pat her hand. But the minute his flesh made contact with hers, she pulled away. He moved his hand slowly back to the steering wheel. Tighter, his lower back beginning to ache from the tension. She was still sobbing. Christ, how long could she keep this up? Didn't she ever get tired, just have to relax? He pulled into the campsite, and she bolted out of the jeep. It was a long time, though, before he could move. Before he could get out and gather up his things, admitting with every motion that this whole damned trip had been a failure. That from here on out, he could only do everything wrong.

There was something suddenly old in the way he stood. Michael moved aside to let him in, but Henry immediately took hold of his arm as though he might collapse. Started talking, words that bounced around and made no sense: binge, ruptured stomach, hospital, sepsis. And her name, over and over again, like some point of common reference. Kendra. Kendra. Necessary in order for either of them to believe that it was real.

Henry said, I thought it would be better if I came in to work. She won't see her mother and me; they say she's in shock. But I can't stay here. I have to leave. *Michael did not react. Had to force himself to nod, heard his voice saying,* That's understandable, *as if through a tunnel. Held on to her father's arm, the father he already suspected had molested her, and said something like,* If there's anything I can do. *It just hadn't seemed the time to say,* By the way, we're lovers. I've been screwing her three times a night for the past two and half months. *Henry was chalk white, a nightmare vision of what lay ahead, only eight years separating them. Eight years between now and gray, now and losing his hair, now and a soft paunch, a defeated slouch in his walk. Horrifying, her lying in a hospital bed and him standing there with another man who'd fucked her, maybe beaten her, too. Standing there thinking,* Eight years before I start to die.

But after Henry left, he went into the bathroom and threw up. It struck him as funny, even, as a kind of sympathetic barfing. The thought of her there, too weak to resist anything, rendered mute, unnatural. And if he saw her now, all the nights he'd watched her not finish dinners, joked about her excessive thinness, would instantly be revealed as obscene. Moments she'd dared lay her head on his chest, when he hadn't wanted to ruin the mood or act like her father— hadn't said, Why are you disappearing before my eyes? *The thought that there might have been some other course of action, another possibility, made his chest feel like he was going to cry. Except that he had not cried since he was seventeen, since the day his mother died. Rather, leaning there against the cold, white dampness of the toilet, he couldn't stop himself from laughing at the irony of it. At the irony of his own puke.*

Wednesday, 16 July, 7:21 PM

Rachel stirred next to him. Michael checked his speed and slowed down a bit, afraid that the rough motion of the jeep would wake her. It had been a long time since he'd driven outside the city, driven anything but the Porsche he'd bought after his first year at the firm. It wasn't in the best shape anymore, but was still too small, too close to the ground to rattle this way, no matter how fast he drove. He hated to have to compromise on speed for smoothness, thought that the jeep was as incongruous to him as Rachel herself, one intertwined with the other. The kind of automobile to take your kid out in. The kind of man to have a kid at all. Rachel scratched her leg in her sleep, her cheek pressed up against the windowpane. Michael's bladder was full, but he didn't want to stop the car and risk waking her. He needed the silence, the respite from her tears and hostility, more than he could need anything concerning the body. Or at least more than to piss.

She was awake now, though. Staring at him from under sleepy eyelids, the sun an orangish blur, the kind of light that makes everything seem out of a road flick, hazy and cast in a cheap-looking but oddly beautiful glow. She glanced between her legs, and he felt himself look, too, automatic. But nothing. She cleared her throat, and he knew he should speak first, let her know he wasn't mad, but he couldn't. The awkwardness in her voice hurt, filled him with disbelief that he hadn't managed to make some joke, tell her some story that would have made everything normal again. Now it was only this, her body, a traitor in every way, undignified, unladylike. Like it was enough to make her cry, just saying, "I . . . I have to pee."

"We can stop at the next rest stop."

"How close is it?"

He had not been paying attention, could only assume he hadn't taken some wrong turn so that they'd end up in fucking Iowa or something. "I'm not sure."

She checked between her legs again. "You don't think it's far, do you? I have to make sure everything is . . . you know. Okay."

Something stirring in him. Sad and compelling, her desperation, and even more the shame that accompanied it. It made him want to pull over to the side of the road right then and send her off behind a tree—whether to get it over with or to heighten the baseness of the situation he couldn't be sure. But he imagined her there, squatting behind a tree changing her pad, pissing into the dirt. The image came before any recognition of it, overlapping with the memory of Kendra the last night he'd seen her, the string of her tampon hanging between her legs when he bent her over his desk and fastened his belt tight around her thighs. Her first period in the months they'd been fucking. Too thin, she was too damned thin to menstruate. Though eleven years older than Rachel, her body was less of a woman's than his own daughter's.

"Aren't there any signs, Dad? I *really* have to go."

Pain in his groin. The pressure in his own stomach was mounting, but overtaken now. Growing, pushing against the denim of his jeans, and he needed to adjust himself but didn't dare. She was crossing her legs, face contorted in a complete surrender to body, agony mixed with the anticipation of relief. Harder, rubbing. She said, "Dad." He pulled over to the shoulder.

"Why are you stopping?"

Opening the driver's side door. Stepping out and leaning against the hot metal of the hood. He breathed in, then out. Felt his fingers run through his hair. Could see her, plain as day. Kendra, on the camping trip *they* should have taken. Pissing in a hole dug in the dirt while he watched, lying across his lap while he bathed her welts with Vitamin E. Then on her knees in the leaves and twigs, the sound of approaching hikers growing closer. Whispering, *Hurry*, though of course he'd have taken his time, let them get caught at least once. Only his zipper would be undone but she'd be fully naked, ass in the air. Exposed.

"Where are you going?"

Unrepentant, in thought and deed. A small, frail body in a hospital bed. Then Rachel, thin, tanned legs pressing against each other to hold back her womanhood, to keep the dawn of her sexuality at bay. He felt his legs moving from the car and into the tall grass. Bile rising in his throat, throbbing between his legs. The sound of his daughter beginning to cry, and he wondered for a moment if she'd wet herself before she'd get out of the jeep to run to the ditch just beyond the shoulder of the highway. Sank down into the grass, the smell of warm earth, still musky from a storm. Crying for him, crippled with indecision, Rachel alone outside the jeep wailing. Not a survivor, not tough like Kendra, who'd have tossed her head and pulled down her jeans right behind the parked jeep, who'd laugh herself sick if she could see him now. Who'd eaten so much food after spending a night with him, getting fucked and beat by him, that she'd split her stomach in two.

Footsteps approaching in the grass. Crying, her hand grasping his shoulder. "Daddy, please. What's wrong? Aren't you coming back?"

He stared up at her. Grabbed her arm and pulled her down to him, against his chest, held on to her so tight he felt the fine bones of her ribs pressed right up flat against him, grating against his flesh. She clung to him, silent now, her face buried in his chest. She was trembling, or maybe it was him, and her thighs were wet from when she must have squatted and leaked on herself. Darkness taking over the orange film-set sun, her arms weak, the smell of her sweaty and dirty from water, heat, and blood. The sound of nothing, of loss, pounding in his ears, and he couldn't let go, even when she started to squirm, to say, "Ow." Something like relief and something like the fever of illness, of drug. He whispered, "I'm sorry, baby," and she murmured, "It's okay." A woman already, comforting him for his own inadequacy. Itching grass, the buzz of crickets. A faint trace of much-needed wind.

THE GIFT

Kim Addonizio

I find a dildo on the street: thick and slightly curved, flesh-colored, dark fluff around the balls. It looks so convincing that for a second I think it is a real penis, and I feel a sense of vertigo. It's brand new, wrapped in white tissue that has ripped open. There's a thin blue-and-white-striped ribbon tied around it, and red Scotch tape with little Christmas tree designs holding the corners.

I look around to see if there is someone nearby who might have dropped it. The street is full of people entering and leaving stores, carrying oddly shaped packages or dragging enormous bags full of gifts, no doubt intended for loved ones, yes, it is clear that everyone but me has loved ones to buy for. The dildo could belong to anyone. It looks elegant and expensive and forlorn, lying there so vulnerably, perhaps about to be stepped on, trampled underfoot, a smudged heel mark left on the still-pristine tissue; perhaps it will be kicked aside, to lie all night beside a garbage can, or even placed inside it with the reek of old hamburger wrappers to which well-chewed gray gum clings.

I can't bear these thoughts. I bend down to cradle the object in my hand. I think for a minute of its rightful owner—perhaps some woman like me, a woman who is lonely, isolated in fact, a woman who has no one to be with at Christmas. Maybe she bought herself a present, a present she would wait until Christmas morning to open; maybe she would take it to bed and close her eyes and moan and rock back and forth on it, saying "John, John" (for that is his name, the man who walked out on me at the start of the holiday shopping season, leaving me devastated, perhaps even suicidal, who knows what I may do next), and then she would come, her legs stiffening, her juices flowing, and she would begin to cry afterward and perhaps fling it across the room with a curse; but now I have deprived her of all that. I have picked it up and put it into the pocket of my long black coat and hurried home with it.

Now it sits—or stands, rather—on the dresser, freed of its wrappings. It glows in the light of the lamp, its veins seem to pulse, a rosy aura suffuses it. I take off my clothes and approach it. Something seems to radiate from it—a sense of ease and power, a kind of self-satisfaction, a kind of . . . lust—yes, it is clearly lust I feel. I seize it in my hand, I fall to the floor with it and writhe around, it throbs under my palm, swells and hardens as I pump it faster and faster. My orgasm builds until I explode all over the rug; come spurts from me, one spurt, another, I lie exhausted holding it in my hand. I pass out from the sheer pleasure of it.

I wake up, not knowing how long I have been unconscious. Maybe minutes, but maybe years. I could be an old woman, finished with sex forever, content to sit on a sagging plaid couch and stare at the television in an ugly room with no visitors day after day; I eat candy bars from the vending machine, at night I take pills and lie awake listening to the radiator and the nurses' shoes going by my door and the person in the next room trying to breathe with his weak collapsed lungs. I stagger to my feet, feeling strange and dizzy. I look in the full-length mirror and see that I am not an old woman at all; I am a young man.

I have a large penis, thick and slightly curved, dark hair around my balls. I yank at it and feel it at the base of my belly. I look at myself in horror. I would gladly turn into something else—a werewolf, a vampire—I would happily be like Gregor

Samsa and live out the rest of my life as a dung beetle. But I am a man. And already, as I look at myself, the horror begins to fade; I can no longer think or feel anything but—yes, again it is lust I feel. I touch the head of my penis and it quivers, it longs to dive into the bed sheets and thrust, over and over, it takes me with it, I come all over the sheets yelling and thrashing about.

Afterward, I sleep deeply. I wake the next morning and think it has been a dream, perhaps I am delusional, perhaps the doctor was right after all and I should begin taking Prozac; but truthfully I feel better than I have in weeks, and besides, I have a hard-on; I lie there dreamily pulling on my penis and come again in the sheets, which are already a little stiff and sticky. I think of doing the laundry, it has been so long since I have washed the sheets, or my clothes, or cleaned the apartment; I have been so depressed over John's leaving. But I do not want to clean today. No, I want to take a shower and eat a large breakfast and take my penis out into the world.

Now the streets look different, the shoppers so hurried, so pathetic in their desperate efforts to find just the right gift. I walk confidently, feeling my penis bulge against the zipper of my jeans; it is my companion, I will never feel lonely again, it will accompany me everywhere. I thank god for this gift of a penis, my beautiful wonderful penis, tucked so cozily inside my silk underwear, nestled like a little wren; I see an attractive man and the wren begins to grow talons; it lifts its great wings and follows the man with its fierce eagle eyes, it wants to swoop down and carry him off to my apartment and feast on him for hours.

I follow the man down the street, into a store where he fingers scarves, looks at expensive earrings, takes down pretty kimonos from a rack. I remember that I am a man, too, and suddenly a wave of revulsion rises in me, the thought of dragging him home with me is crushed and drowned by the wave crashing over it. I am normal, I say to myself, normal; there is nothing wrong with me. I have never been a woman or wanted to make love to a man, I must wipe all that from my mind—especially the image of sucking on a penis, the joy of taking it into my mouth, licking the clear liquid that forms a bright drop at the tip, swallowing the slightly bitter fluid as I kneel before John, as he strokes my hair and says Baby, oh baby—I must erase all that.

I hurry from the store, and now I see the women, their breasts bulging inside sweaters or hidden under coats, their asses moving just ahead of me like beacons to guide me, I think of their cunts and their smells, their soft inviting mouths. The eagle circles and circles, hunger gnaws at its belly, and now a kind of terror: I must find a woman, a woman who will have me, suddenly my penis is profoundly lonely and cold and sad.

I go into a bar and the terror is greater; there are women here, all around me in twos and threes, my penis is about to leap from my pants. I want to go up to one of them, to lean her back over a table and plunge into her, but I must stop myself; I drink beer after beer to quell my anxiety, to try and think of a way to do this politely. I stumble to the back of the bar, into the men's room, stand at the urinal and watch the arc of piss, golden and fragrant, and I am so fascinated by it I forget about the women. I go into a stall and jerk off, sitting on the toilet, and then emerge calm and in control once more. I return to the bar and continue to drink. I talk to no one. I think bitterly about my life, my past lovers, I resolve not to ever love anyone again; somewhere in the deepest recesses of my brain I remember who I am, I know that something is wrong, but it no longer matters. I get gloriously drunk, so drunk that everything goes black and disappears . . .

I wake up in a strange but prettily decorated room. I am lying in a canopy bed, tiny lights strung around it, blinking on and off; Bing Crosby is singing "White Christmas," and I can smell sugar cookies baking somewhere. I want to reach between my legs to see if I still have my penis, but I can't move my arm very far. Perhaps I have had a stroke, and there is no hope I will regain my bodily functions; I am in a hospice, no one will visit me but volunteers doing their Zen practice, who will sit beside me to experience dying close up and tell me I must learn to let go. Forget John, they will say; life is but a dream, they are saying, or someone is singing; yes, a little girl is singing "Row, Row, Row Your Boat," in a high, pleasant voice. Now she is standing over my bed, but her face is huge, impossibly huge; surely I am dying, and this is the angel of death, wearing enormous wings and a white gown and holding a plain wooden wand in one hand, a glittery silver star stuck to the end of it. She reaches down for me and lifts me, naked, into the air. She sets me on the dresser, and I see in the mirror that I am supposed to be female, I have long slim legs, a tiny waist, but I have no nipples on my otherwise perfect breasts and nothing between my legs but a sort of hinge, no sex at all anymore. I try to open my rosebud mouth to scream, but it is painted shut and smiles happily back at me. "Merrily, merrily, merrily," the little girl sings, and begins to brush my hair.

CONTRIBUTORS' NOTES

Kim Addonizio is the author of five poetry collections, most recently *Lucifer at the Starlight;* two novels, *Little Beauties* and *My Dreams Out in the Street*; and two books on writing poetry. Her story collection *In the Box Called Pleasure* was published by FC2. She can be found online at www.kimaddonizio.com.

Jonis Agee is the author of twelve books, including five novels—*Sweet Eyes, Strange Angels, South of Resurrection, The Weight of Dreams*, and *The River Wife*—and five collections of short fiction—*Pretend We've Never Met, Bend This Heart, A .38 Special and a Broken Heart, Taking the Wall*, and *Acts of Love on Indigo Road*. She has also published two books of poetry: *Houses* and *Mercury*. Agee is the Adele Hall Professor of English at The University of Nebraska, Lincoln, where she teaches creative writing and twentieth-century fiction.

Steve Almond is the author of a bunch of books, most recently *Rock and Roll Will Save Your Life*. His new story collection, *God Bless America*, will come out in October 2011. He is also, somewhat crazily, self-publishing books, which can be purchased at readings. He can be found online at www.stevenalmond.com.

Allison Amend was born in Chicago on a day when the Cubs beat the Mets 2–0. She attended Stanford University and holds an MFA from the University of Iowa Writers' Workshop. Her work has received awards from and appeared in many publications, including *One Story, Black Warrior Review, StoryQuarterly, Bellevue Literary Review*, the *Atlantic Monthly, Prairie Schooner*, and *Other Voices*. Her IPPY Award-winning debut short story collection, *Things That*

Pass for Love, was published in 2008 by Other Voices Books, and a novel, *Stations West*, was published in 2010 as part of Louisiana State University Press's Yellow Shoe Fiction Series. She can be found online at www.allisonamend.com.

Su Avasthi writes both fiction and articles for a range of publications. She received her MA in Fiction Writing from New York University and has worked as a staff writer at the *New York Daily News* and the *New York Post*. She currently lives in New Mexico.

Aimee Bender is the author of four books; the most recent is a novel, *The Particular Sadness of Lemon Cake*. Her short fiction has been published in *Granta*, *GQ*, *Harpers*, *The Paris Review*, *Tin House*, and more, and heard on NPR's *This American Life*. She lives in Los Angeles and teaches creative writing at USC.

Elizabeth Benedict is the author of the novels *The Beginner's Book of Dreams*, *Safe Conduct*, *Slow Dancing*, *Almost*, and *The Practice of Deceit*, as well as the classic fiction writer's guide, *The Joy of Writing Sex*. She is the editor of *Mentors, Muses & Monsters: 30 Writers on the People Who Changed Their Lives* (Free Press/Simon & Schuster, 2009). Her essays and articles appear in the *New York Times*, *Esquire*, *Tin House*, and elsewhere. She can be found online at www.elizabethbenedict.com.

Rosebud Ben-Oni is a writer for New Perspectives Theater, which produced her play *Quimera on the Storm* in 2010, and she has been the recipient of a Horace Goldsmith Grant, given so she could complete her first novel, which deals with her experiences as a Jew of mixed race. She has upcoming and recent work in *Pear Noir!*, *Camera Obscura*, *Slice Magazine*, *J Journal*, *Wreckage of Reason: An Anthology of Contemporary XXperimental Prose by Women Writers*, *Arts & Letters*, *Identity Envy—Wanting to be Who*

We Are Not, and *The Texas Poetry Review*. Recently produced plays include *Don't Call it Returning* (Thespian Production, Joria Production Studios, 2010); *Owless of Santa Clara* (Snorks and Pins, Roy Arias Studios, 2010), *Nikita* (Shotgun Theater Festival, Gene Frankel Theatre and Thespian Productions, Producer's Club, 2009); *Nary a Bodega* (Leah Ryan Benefit, Producer's Club, 2009); *The Amaranthine Thread* (Leah Ryan Benefit, Producer's Club, 2009), and *Where Eagles Dare* (Producer's Club, 2010). She is currently finishing her first novel, *The Imitation of Crying*, and has recently joined *Vida: Women in Literary Arts* as a co-editor for "Her Kind" at www.vidaweb.org.

Stacy Bierlein is an author, editor, and independent publisher. Her award-winning anthology, *A Stranger Among Us: Stories of Cross Cultural Collision and Connection*, is used in university classrooms across the country. She is a founding editor of Other Voices Books as well as the Morgan Street International Novel Series. She serves as editorial director for Emerald Bay Books. Her articles about writing, publishing, and the arts appear on various websites, including *The Nervous Breakdown*. Her story collection, *A Vacation on the Island of Ex-Boyfriends*, is forthcoming from Elephant Rock Books in 2012. She lives in Southern California.

Vanessa Carlisle recently completed her MFA in Creative Writing at Emerson College and is a PhD candidate in Comparative Literature at UC Riverside. Her writing has appeared in various magazines and anthologies including *NinthLetter*, *Boink: The Book*, and *WordRiot*. Her first novel, *A Crack in Everything*, was released in 2010. She blogs at www.gorgeouscuriosity.com and can be found also at www.vanessacarlisle.com.

Wanda Coleman has been a Guggenheim fellow, Emmy-winning scriptwriter, and columnist for the *Los Angeles Times* ("Native in a Strange Land"). Her recent books include *Ostinato Vamps* (Pitt

Poetry Series), *The Riot Inside Me: Trials & Tremors* (Godine/Black Sparrow Books), and *Wanda Coleman: Poems Seismic in Scene* (de la chienne). Her double-genre collections are *Heavy Daughter Blues*, *African Sleeping Sickness*, and *Jazz & Twelve O'Clock Tales* (Godine/Black Sparrow Books). Her earlier books include *A War of Eyes and Other Stories*, *Mambo Hips & Make Believe*, and the 2001 National Book Awards finalist, *Mercurochrome: New Poems*. *Bathwater Wine* received the 1999 Lenore Marshall Poetry Prize, making Coleman the first African American woman to win the award. Her work has been featured in various anthologies and reviews, including *Writing Los Angeles*, *Poet's Market*, and *A Stranger Among Us: Stories of Cross Cultural Collision and Connection*. She was C.O.L.A.'s first literary fellow (Los Angeles Department of Cultural Affairs 2003–04) and a 2005 nominee for California's poet laureate.

Jennifer Egan is the author of *A Visit From the Goon Squad*, winner of the 2011 Pulitzer Prize for fiction and the National Book Critics Circle 2011 Fiction Award. Her previous books are *The Invisible Circus*, which was released as a feature film by Fine Line in 2001, *Emerald City and Other Stories*, *Look at Me*, and the bestselling *The Keep*. Also a journalist, Egan writes frequently for the *New York Times Magazine*. She can be found online at www.jenniferegan.com.

Alicia Erian is the author of a book of short stories, *The Brutal Language of Love*, and a novel, *Towelhead*, which was made into a film by Alan Ball in 2008. Her memoir, *The Dragon Lies Down*, is forthcoming from Crown in 2012.

Gina Frangello is the author of two books of fiction, *Slut Lullabies* (Emergency Press, 2010) and *My Sister's Continent* (Chiasmus, 2006). The long-time editor of the literary magazine *Other Voices*, she co-founded Other Voices Books in 2005 and currently serves as Executive Editor of the press. She is also Fiction Editor of the popular online literary collective, *The Nervous Breakdown*. Her recent short fiction has appeared in *Fence*, *Five Chapters*, *Fifth Wednesday*, *MAKE magazine*, *ACM*, and *F Magazine*. Her nonfiction and journalism have also been published widely in venues such as *The Huffington Post*, the *Chicago Tribune*, *The Nervous Breakdown*, the *Chicago Reader* and *The Rumpus*. She teaches at Columbia College Chicago and can be found online at www.ginafrangello.com.

Vicki Hendricks is the author of noir novels *Miami Purity*, *Iguana Love*, *Voluntary Madness*, *Sky Blues*, and *Cruel Poetry*, which was nominated for an Edgar Award in 2008. Her collection *Florida Gothic Stories* was published in 2010. Hendricks lives in Hollywood, Florida, and teaches writing at Broward College. Her plots and settings reflect participation in adventure sports, such as skydiving and scuba, and knowledge of the Florida environment.

A. M. Homes is the author of the novels *This Book Will Save Your Life*, *Music For Torching*, *The End of Alice*, *In a Country of Mothers*, and *Jack*; the short-story collections *Things You Should Know* and *The Safety of Objects*; the travel memoir *Los Angeles: People, Places and The Castle on the Hill*; the artist's book *Appendix A:*; and the memoir *The Mistress's Daughter*. Her work has been translated into twenty-two languages and appears frequently in *Art Forum*, *Harpers*, *Granta*, *McSweeney's*, the *New Yorker*, the *New York Times*, and *Zoetrope*. She is a contributing editor to *Vanity Fair*, *Bomb*, and *Blind Spot*.

Suzanne Hudson is the author of two literary novels, *In a Temple of Trees* and *In the Dark of the Moon*. Her work has been included in anthologies such as *Stories from the Blue Moon Café*, volumes I, II, and IV; *The Alumni Grill*; *Climbing Mt. Cheaha*; *A Kudzu Christmas*; *A State of Laughter*; *Christmas Stories from the*

South's Best Writers; and *Delta Blues*. Her short-story collection, *Opposable Thumbs*, was a finalist for a John Gardner Fiction Book Award. Her latest work is a "fictional nonfiction" book of humor, social commentary, and self-help, with a few poems and country lyrics thrown in. It is titled *Second Sluthood: A Manifesto for the Postmenopausal, Pre-Senilic Matriarch*, and was written under the pseudonym Ruby Pearl Saffire. She lives outside Fairhope, Alabama, on the Waterhole Branch Arts Compound with the author Joe Formichella.

Sheri Joseph's books are the novel *Stray* (MacAdam/Cage, 2007), winner of the Grub Street Book Prize, and a cycle of stories, *Bear Me Safely Over* (Grove/Atlantic, 2002). Her novel manuscript, "The Cloud Forest," was awarded a 2010 National Endowment for the Arts fellowship. She teaches in the creative writing program at Georgia State University in Atlanta, where she also serves as the fiction editor of *Five Points* literary magazine.

Cris Mazza has authored sixteen books, most recently *Various Men Who Knew Us as Girls*, a novel. Her other fiction titles include *Waterbaby*, *Trickle-Down Timeline*, and *Is It Sexual Harassment Yet?* In 1995 and 1996, Mazza was co-editor for the original Chick-Lit anthologies: *Chick-Lit: Postfeminist Fiction*, and *Chick-Lit 2: No Chick Vics*. In 2006, her essay "Who's Laughing Now: Chick Lit and the Perversion of a Genre," explaining the co-opting and corrosion of the title, appeared in *Poets & Writers Magazine*. In addition to fiction, Mazza also has published a memoir, *Indigenous: Growing Up Californian*, and has another hybrid memoir, *Leave Her Alone*, forthcoming from Jadid Ibis Press. A native of Southern California, Mazza grew up in San Diego County. She currently lives fifty miles west of Chicago and is a professor in the Program for Writers at the University of Illinois at Chicago. She can be found online at www.cris-mazza.com.

Kat Meads is the author of *Little Pockets of Alarm*, *The Invented Life of Kitty Duncan*, *Sleep*, *Born Southern and Restless*, *Not Waving*, and other books of fiction, nonfiction, and poetry. She has received an NEA grant, a California Artist Fellowship, and artist residencies at the Fine Arts Work Center in Provincetown, Yaddo, Millay Colony, Blue Mountain Center, Dorland Mountain Colony, and the Montalvo Center for the Arts. She has also received fiction awards from *Chelsea* and *Inkwell Magazine*, the *New Letters* award for essay, and the Editors' Choice Award from *Drunken Boat*. Her short plays have been produced in New York and Los Angeles. Her novel *Sleep* was long-listed for the James Tiptree award, and *Little Pockets of Alarm,* a short fiction collection, was runner-up for the University of Massachusetts Press Juniper Prize. Her short-fiction chapbook, *Wayward Women*, won the Illinois Writers Inc. competition. She teaches in Oklahoma City University's low-residency MFA program.

Susan Minot is an award-winning novelist and short-story writer whose books include *Monkeys*, *Folly*, *Lust & Other Stories*, *Evening*, and *Rapture*. She has also co-authored screenplays, including *Stealing Beauty* with Bernardo Bertolucci, and *Evening*, based on her novel, with Michael Cunningham. Minot was born in Boston and raised in Manchester-by-the-Sea, Massachusetts, attended Brown University, and received her MFA in creative writing from Columbia University. She currently lives with her daughter in both New York City and an island off the coast of Maine.

Tawni O'Dell is a *New York Times* bestselling author of four novels including *Fragile Beasts* and *Back Roads*, which was an Oprah's Book Club pick and a Book-of-the-Month Club Main Selection. *Back Roads* is currently in development to be made into a film by Michael Ohoven, producer of the Academy Award-winning *Capote*. O'Dell is also a contributor to several anthologies, including *Becoming Myself: Reflections on Growing Up Female*. Her work has been translated into ten languages and published in more than twenty countries. She lives in Pennsylvania and can be found online at www.tawniodell.com.

Aimee Parkison is a graduate of the MFA creative writing program of Cornell University and the author of *Woman with Dark Horses*. Her short stories have won several awards: the Jack Dyer Prize from *Crab Orchard Review*, an emerging writer prize from *Fiction International,* a Writers at Work Fellowship from *Quarterly West*, and the Kurt Vonnegut Prize from *North American Review*. Her work has also appeared in *Other Voices, American Literary Review*, *River City*, and *Denver Quarterly*. She is an Assistant Professor of Creative Writing at University of North Carolina, Charlotte.

Nava Renek is a writer, publisher, and educator. Her short stories and nonfiction have appeared in a number of literary magazines, newspapers, and websites. Her first novel, *Spiritland,* was published in 2002. In 2008, she edited *Wreckage of Reason: An Anthology of XXperimental Women Writers Writing in the 21st Century.* Her second novel, *No Perfect Words,* was published in 2009. She lives in Brooklyn.

Rachel Resnick is the author of the memoir *Love Junkie* and the novel *Go West Young F*cked-Up Chick.* Her articles, essays, and celebrity profiles have appeared in the *Los Angeles Times, Marie Claire, Women's Health, BlackBook*, and other publications. She is a contributing editor at *Tin House,* and the founder and CEO of Writers on Fire. She is currently at work on a new book about her adventures as a culinary virgin and blogging at *The Art of Boiling Water.* She can be found online also at www.rachelresnick.com.

Elizabeth Searle is the author of *My Body to You, A Four-sided Bed* and *Celebrities in Disgrace*, as well as the new novel, *Girl Held* *in Home* (New Rivers Press 2011). Her musical, *Tonya & Nancy: the Rock Opera*, has a new production beginning in 2011. Searle's theater works have been featured on *Good Morning America*, CBS, CNN, NPR, and elsewhere. Her novella, *Celebrities in Disgrace*, was produced as a film that premiered in 2010, for which she co-wrote the screenplay. Searle has published more than thirty stories in magazines. She teaches at the Stonecoast MFA Program in Creative Writing.

Susan Solomon is a lawyer and writer. Her fiction has appeared in a number of online and print publications, including *Moondance Magazine, Polluto, Wilderness House Literary Review, Pebble Lake Review, 42Opus, The Chick Lit Review, Gator Springs Gazette, Salome Magazine, Long Story Short, Pulse Magazine*, and *Writelink*. Her story "Smile Catchers" placed in the top ten in *Writelink*'s 2004 Weekender Challenge (United Kingdom), and her story "Medici, For Beginners" was selected as an Editor's Choice story for 2005 by *Pulse Magazine*. She lives in Chicago.

Kristin Thiel is a writer, book reviewer, and editor. With the technological age aiding her wanderlust, she lives at www. kristinthiel.com and www.indigoediting.com as well as on various social media sites.

Diane Williams is the author of six books of fiction. Her most recent book is *It Was Like My Trying to Have a Tender-Hearted Nature*. Her stories appear frequently in a variety of magazines including *Harper's Magazine, Bomb, Conjunctions, McSweeney's*, and *The Brooklyn Rail*. She is the editor of the literary annual *NOON*.

Lidia Yuknavitch is the author of the memoir *The Chronology of Water*, three works of short fiction, *Her Other Mouths, Liberty's Excess*, and *Real to Reel*, as well as a book of literary criticism, *Allegories of Violence*. Her work has appeared in *Ms., Iowa Review*,

Exquisite Corpse, Another Chicago Magazine, Fiction International, ZYZZYVA, and elsewhere. Her collection *Real to Reel* was a finalist for the Oregon Book Award, and she is the recipient of awards and fellowships from Poets & Writers and Literary Arts, Inc. Her work appears in the anthologies *Life As We Show It* (City Lights), *Forms At War* (FC2), and *Wreckage of Reason* (Spuytin Duyvil). She teaches writing, literature, film, and gender studies in Oregon.

Christine Lee Zilka is the fiction editor at *Kartika Review*. Her work has appeared or is forthcoming in journals such as *ZYZZYVA*, *Verbsap*, and *Yomimono*. She received an Ardella Mills Fiction Prize from Mills College in 2005, placed as a finalist in *Poets & Writers Magazine's* Writers Exchange Contest in 2007, and received an honorable mention in *Glimmer Train's* Fiction Open in 2009. Zilka earned her undergraduate degree from UC Berkeley and her MFA in Creative Writing from Mills College. She and lives in Berkeley, California, with her husband and two wiener dogs.

CREDITS

"Why We Undress," by Steve Almond. Copyright © 2011 Steve Almond. Published by permission of the author.

"A Blow for the Picaro?" by Cris Mazza. Copyright © 2011 Cris Mazza. Published by permission of the author.

"Claiming the Penis: A Celebration of Narrative Cross-Dressing," by Stacy Bierlein, Gina Frangello, and Kat Meads. Copyright © 2011 Other Voices Books. Published by permission of the authors.

"The Gold Cure," by Jennifer Egan. From *A Visit From the Goon Squad* by Jennifer Egan. Copyright © 2010 Jennifer Egan. Reprinted by permission of Alfred A. Knopf, a division of Random House, Inc.

"From *The Practice of Deceit*," by Elizabeth Benedict. Excerpted from *The Practice of Deceit: A Novel* by Elizabeth Benedict. Copyright © 2005 Elizabeth Benedict. Used by permission of Houghton Mifflin Harcourt Publishing Company. All rights reserved.

"And a Dead American," by Elizabeth Searle. Published in *Roger: The Literary Magazine of Roger Williams University*, Summer 2010. Copyright © 2010 Elizabeth Searle. Reprinted by permission of the author.

"Evening at the Cryo-Crystal Circus Hotel," by Rachel Resnick. Published in *Black Clock #7*, Spring/Summer 2007. Copyright © 2007 Rachel Resnick. Reprinted by permission of the author.

ACKNOWLEDGMENTS

Anthologies require teamwork, and certainly ours benefited from the hard work and creative energies of many people. With this in mind, the editors of *Men Undressed* have several to thank for their support and inspiration.

A sharp team of associate editors added vigor and verve to the discussion. It was a pleasure to work with Wendy Duren, Keala Francis, Tracy Miller Geary, Laura Taylor Kung, Barbara Shoup, Iliana Regan, and Rob Roberge, whose queries and considerations made this collection of fiction stronger. We are indebted as well to the steadfast dedication of Other Voices Books staff editors, Allison C. Parker, Kathy Kosmeja, and Leah Tallon.

We are grateful to Steve Almond for his vibrant foreword; for joining our endeavor the very moment we asked. He said we had him at undressed. In truth, his work has inspired us for years. Steve Almond had us at heavy metal.

Book designer Steven Seighman and cover photographer Margo Berdeshevsky provided a stunning home for our work—one that continues to hold us in awe.

We feel humbled by and grateful for the booksellers and literary event coordinators who expressed interest in this book long before it went to press. We look forward to seeing *Men Undressed* in your venues and on your bookshelves.

Finally, we thank Dan Wickett and Steve Gillis of Dzanc Books, champions of independent publishing, for their trust in our vision; for their generous support of this project and many others.